A SINISTER VISION: KNOW THIS MUCH IS TRUE

The Sinister Series Book 2

A. NICKY HJORT

Lavish Publishing LLC

First Edition

The Sinister Series Book 2

All Rights Reserved

Published in the United States by Lavish Publishing, LLC, Midland, Texas

Paperback edition

ISBN: 9781944985264

Cover Design by: Wycked Ink

Cover Images: Adobe Stock

www.LavishPublishing.com

Contents

For my sister Angel
Who I love with all my bonfire heart…
This much I know is true.

Acknowledgments

Writing this book has been an incredible journey from impossible to possible, and I will forever be changed by writing it. Specifically, I would like to thank Lavish for believing in me and my work; my CMO who reminded me to remember my truth; my amazing editor, Kathy Moczerniak, who finds everything I miss and then some; Lark Adams and her brilliance in design; Robin and my family for their support on every level; and Paula Munier who taught me how to stop overwriting and murder my darlings.

But there are three people without whom this book simply could not have existed. The first is Tim who taught me a lot about seeing masks, finding authenticity, and being brave enough to love myself first. The next two adorable people are my children, Emma and Jakethe two cheeks I love more than all the rest.

Thank you, life, and thank you, love… I am honored to have written this story. This much I know is true…

Prologue

A MANUSCRIPT IS DISCOVERED on a curious grave in Glenwood Springs, Colorado. The headstone has no name, no date. The only thing written there is, *Know this much is true.*

The first two pages of the mysterious text are missing, but the rest are mostly intact. The pages feel satiny and light, almost magical to the touch. Once you hold the book, you can't tolerate putting it down.

It calls you. It owns you. It welcomes you back from the darkness.

Quiet now, my Livie. Hush...
Can you feel me reaching out for you?
Hush now. Be quiet. Listen, my love!
Wake up. Open your eyes. Accept your assignment.
The problem is not to find the answer,
But to face it.
Know this much is true.
For you, for me.
-A Voice From Within.

And in my heart I've felt you too often to deny.
I sometimes meet you inside my dreams.
My love!
How I'm reaching out for you.

"My Love!" by Dimitri Arion

ONE

Dreamcatcher

ELISE PHILLIPS HAD BEEN HERE BEFORE.

She looked first to the right and then to the left. Anywhere but straight ahead. Yet there was no way to avoid the inevitable storm of terror.

The odor of adrenaline enveloped her. Disgusted her. Saturated her.

Her hands shook. Her stomach flipped. Her knees buckled.

She reached down to check her pulse. One hundred and twenty.

Too fast, Elise. Slow it down now. You know what will happen.

She was an expert at biofeedback. She had to be, or there was no way she could survive. In fact, she would have died years ago. Five years ago, to be exact. A heart like hers just couldn't take what a normal heart could. It would fail. Again.

Breathing slowly in and out, she imagined herself somewhere else. Anywhere but here…in front of the house that had tortured her.

Why the hell am I here of all places? What's the lesson now?

One hundred and fifteen. *Too high.*

She imagined rolling hills. She imagined the sound, the smell of the ocean spraying the beach. She imagined the first sip of an ice-cold Chai. She imagined dancing slowly to a Dimitri Arion song.

I don't care who you are; you have to love Dimitri. He's just that good. My love! Yes, Dimitri. How I'm reaching out for you. Take me away.

She checked her heart rate again. One hundred and ten. One hundred and four. Ninety-eight. Eighty-five.

Better, baby. You got it now, Elise. Just a little slower, my love. Tell me where to seek your heart, for I cannot find the way.

Seventy-six.

Good, baby. You did it. Thanks, Dimitri. Let me start a lifetime loving you.

She looked back up. Really, she had no other choice. Eventually, she would have to face this house. Eventually, she would have to really face…him. The monster that had…

Like the smell of her morning breath, his stink was all over her.

Why now, Elise? What the hell does it want this time?

She stared calmly at the front of the three-story house. She couldn't risk fearing the structure…nothing more than a vision created by her tripped-up neurons, a projected image formed in her traumatized brain.

Seventy-four. *Good girl.*

The physical strain of an activated sympathetic nervous system threatened her broken heart. She refused to go under the knife again for some experimental cardiac surgery that would probably fail and finally kill her…for real, while simultaneously making her surgeon famous for attempting such a novel approach. She could think of a few more interesting ways to die than on a page in some no-name surgical journal.

A snow-covered but empty grave in Glenwood Springs flashed in her mind. *Jill Vickerey.*

Besides, these days, she held the scalpel, not the other way around. Supposedly.

Even asleep, she still blamed her mom for ruining her heart.

Why didn't you give me the damn medicine like the doctor had prescribed, Mom? Why? This is entirely your fault. If I had been stronger…

The front of the house looked more like a face than a house. The creepy windows stared with eyes full of evil wonder. The wooden planks bore deep crevices, deep wrinkles made from hate. The chimney exhaled rotten, smoky breath. The front door begged she enter its grinning mouth.

"University of Death opens wide. So, what? You can eat me? I don't think so. Piss off. Not this time. What if I don't go in? You can't make me. I have to be willing, right? I have to walk down those horrible stairs. I have to want to remember what you did to me. Aren't those the rules?"

Her argument was futile.

She looked down at her feet moving her body forward. *Shit, here we go.*

She was already in the house, heading for the stairs. Thankfully, the stairs up…not the stairs down. Her mind screamed for her to stop. Her gut begged she go back. But her heart, that same broken and bleeding heart of hers, pulled her forward. The pain might have pushed her back hard, but her heart pulled forward even harder.

Screw this crap!

Then she saw the numbers. Six, sixteen, thirty-six.

Six days. Sixteen hours. Thirty-six minutes.

There was no turning back now.

The timer flashed on the dirty wall at the top of those same awful, creaking stairs. The metallic scent of blood filled the air and started dripping down the wall. She heard the drip, drip, drip of thick crimson heme stain the musty, old floorboards. Bleach followed. Then she heard the clock tick.

Tick tock, tick tock, tick tock.

The lesson had begun.

That was all the time she had…until someone died.

Unless she found them. Unless she changed their fate. Unless she faced her deepest demons. Unless she learned the lesson, accepted the assignment…for them both.

No. I won't. You can't make me. Not again. Not fair. This is my life. My choice. My decision. I don't want to remember what happened.

It would be five years ago next month that they had found her mostly dead body on Strawberry Lake. No one knew how she had gotten there. Not even her. Then the surgeons saved her, sort of anyway. She thought she was done having visions, but here she stood smack dab in the middle of one. *Damn it!*

She had no memories of her kidnapping, of this house, of him...to speak of. Yet here she was. Again.

The frost-coated headstone popped back into her mind.

Jill Vickerey
Survived by her loving mother.
May her heart rest in peace.

In peace? "Whatever, Mom."

She glanced at the blood running down the wall. Too much, yet also too little, red goo. *May my heart finally rest in peace, not.*

The same evil place. The top of those stairs. Back at that horrid wall.

What happened to us, Jill?

The last vision had occurred...one year ago? Elise had effectively ignored it the last time by covering her eyes, sticking her fingers in her ears, and screaming as she ran back down the stairs.

Not this time. It wasn't working. *Shit!*

She awoke, panting in her on-call room still holding onto one word:

"Levi."

It was just a dream, Elise. Just a dream about blue jeans or something. Calm down.

Even then, though, she already knew better. The space between her eyes felt hot, tingled. *Not a dream. A vision.* She rubbed her forehead and sighed.

Maybe she could pretend she didn't remember. *What vision? What house? Me? Who?*

Looking for relief for her parched throat, she grabbed the water bottle and downed it. It wasn't enough.

Not better. Crap, crap, crap. I'm screwed.

She looked at the nightstand table. The pen on the floor had been knocked off the side table. *Oh no!*

She glanced at her notepad and shook her head violently side to side in disbelief. *Please be empty. Please. Nothing. It's blank. Please.*

She had to know for sure. Unable to stop herself, she looked back.

Her wish went unanswered. On her morning patient census, the figures taunted her. The ink, still wet, was scratched across the notepad in her own handwriting:

6 16 36 Jill + Levi

. . .

That was all the time she had to save them.

TWO

Blank Space

WELL, she had better write the time down then. Otherwise, how would she know when it had expired?

It was Tuesday, 5:00 a.m., so she had until Monday at 9:36 p.m. to figure it out. To hunt the intended victim down first…before he did. To dissect the clues. To save her… the intended victim. To save herself and the victim both, actually. Whatever that meant.

Well, who's going to freaking save me?

She looked at her rounding list. As the on-call Intern, it was her job to see every stinking patient before her Chief Resident showed up. She usually started before 5:00 a.m. so that she could do everything for everybody before anybody else had to get his or her lazy butt out of bed.

Residency sucks like the Grim Reaper's vacuum.

Eleven patients, morning report, one more unnecessary surgery, and then the glory of her own bed. Her own sheets. Her own small joke of an apartment as far away as possible from this bacteria-free death factory.

As a first year Obstetrics and Gynecology resident at Saint Lutheran's Hospital of Grace, Elise Phillips' job never ended. Yet, somehow, she remained the boss of no one and nothing. There were the nameless patients to round on, the daily progress notes to write, the orders to march out by hand, and the dressings to change. In surgery, she had the honor of wheeling the surgical patients to the OR, placing the Foley catheter, prepping the abdomen, and then trying to remain still while holding retractors for cases that lasted an eternity. All the while, she did nothing more educational than answer stupid pimp questions so the attending could prove how brilliant he was.

Attendings̶what a bunch of pricks.

She hadn't delivered a single baby yet.

For what? The honor of working eighty, maybe ninety hours a week and taking home a sliver of a doctor's paycheck?

Screw this. I came here to deliver babies. Where are the sweet, little babies?

She imagined wrapping the sweet, little creature in a warm blanket and smiled. Then she looked back at her rounding sheet and grimaced.

She accepted the fact that she had to pay her dues. She just couldn't figure out why. *The grand prize of becoming a future slave to insurance companies and call schedules? What was I thinking? I must be a masochist.*

As she turned the corner, breakfast tray in hand, she decided she better develop a new attitudefast. She was almost off call anyway. Really this place could only smother her for a few hours longer. Then she could rest and breathe something other than bleach-soaked disease.

Besides, the grits looked good this morning. The coffee smelled delicious. The fruit looked fresh. Most importantly, there was a seat open way in the back of the conference room where they held their daily morning report meetings.

Yes. No one will see me in the back. No more stupid pimp questions for me today. If they ask me to draw out the course of the ureter one more time, I'm going to toss my grits.

Her brief moment of peace ended.

"Doctor Phillips? Is that you all the way in the back? Yes, Elise, I'm talking to you. Can you come up to the front and draw out the anatomy of the ureter?" the attending said.

Elise cleared her throat, turned around, and rolled her eyes.

"You guys have it so easy these days. When I was an intern, I was too busy for morning report. I had to work and figure it all out myself."

That explains it, you creep. Doctor Wilson, my least favorite prick of them all, why I'd be delighted to be made an example of.

"We were up by three a.m. In fact, I don't think we even went to bed."

"And you walked both ways up hill in the snow with one good shoe too."

Elise grinned. The image of Doctor Wilson shoeless, trembling in the snow felt lovely. Showing him up sounded even better.

It was almost worth the trek to the front.

As she marched past, she felt thirty pairs of eyes burning holes in her back. All of them thrilled it was Elise instead of them at the board.

She imagined the words seared across the whiteboard: The Board of Shame.

Grow up, you fools. Get a life, you bottom feeders.

But who cared? She was way too tired to give a flip. She traced out the anatomy on the dry erase board.

She explained and simultaneously drew the figures perfectly.

"After passing over the bifurcation of the iliac arteries, just medial to the ovarian vessels, the ureter descends into the pelvis. Here, the tube of the kidney is attached to the medial leaf of the broad ligament. Then it crosses down like water under the bridge of the uterine artery in the cardinal ligament about one centimeter from the cervix. Then onto the anterior vaginal wall it travels where it finally enters the bladder."

The attending's smile slithered down his face, stained his coat, and oozed onto the floor. He nodded, still scrambling for a way to pick it back up.

Silence.

Twenty-nine pairs of eyes scanned the floor.

Intern Wendi Patterson, front row to the right, covered her mouth, the corners of her smile visible to the intelligent observer, but looked straight ahead.

No intern ever answered this question correctly post-call. But Elise was no ordinary intern. She was good, damn good. And they all knew it. Some of the senior residents hated her for her natural talent, which they had worked so hard to acquire. If she read it once, it stuck. If she did it twice, it was like she had done it a thousand times.

Elise stared back the attending. He cleared his throat, straightened his jacket, and fired more questions back at her, several of them well above her years of training or appropriate intern knowledge base.

Elise wondered when she would finally submit to the game.

Wendi dug her reflex hammer into her thigh. The pain kept her laughter at bay, but just barely. The remaining twenty-nine pairs of eyes explored the glorious patterns in the carpet accentuated by an odd crumb of food here and there.

Unable to tolerate this torture another minute, Elise sighed in pretend defeat and tapped her nose like she just didn't know. "After you repair the hole in the bladder, you take the catheter out the next day. Then you see the patient back at six weeks as usual." She smiled, quite pleased with her answer.

Twenty-nine confused gasps. One understanding giggle.

The attending picked his grin back up and plastered it back on his previously sullen face while Elise suppressed her own giggle by pinching her right leg.

"No. Wrong. Obviously, you aren't paying close enough attention in the OR. The Foley stays in for a week. Duh, Elise. You may sit down now. You must be so tired, being post-call and all. Poor little, sleepy intern. Do better next time."

She would have smiled at the others when she sat down, knowing it was someone else's turn to be tortured next, but she was just too tired. She could join in the fun of laughing at the next idiot at the Board of Shame tomorrow.

Then she remembered six days and fourteen hours was all the time she had left. She pinched herself again, only this time, hard enough she left a bruise.

THREE

Butterfly, How Long It Takes to Die

ELISE PARKED in the only spot available on the block—the one behind the alleyway of her four hundred and fifty square foot apartment. Up the ten rickety-rackety white metal stairs she climbed. She looked over her right shoulder and then the left. She checked her pulse. Ninety-five.

She took a deep breath and unlocked the one-hundred-year-old door with what strength she had left. While the hinge complained with a slow and painful creak from being painted one too many times, she hummed.

Let me start a life of loving you. Eighty-eight.

The homeless people were already up and about rummaging through the trash bin in the alley. What they searched for was beyond her. Was it food, half-finished booze, or some forgotten childhood treasure to fill their King Sooper's shopping cart? Seventy-four.

I'm home late today if the boozers are already up. Damn Denver traffic! Screw you and your snow-covered roads, Colorado. As if the clock didn't count down fast enough.

She looked at her watch and frowned. Ninety.

She started the song again.

Six days. Twelve hours. Thirteen minutes.

Her shoulders felt heavy, burdened yet again with the task at hand.

She had always been special. That's the word her mother used: "Special." Branded was the word she used. Abused was the way she felt. Even as a little girl, she understood things she shouldn't, things she couldn't. A knowing that went beyond normal plagued her as far back as she could remember.

She was born different.

The first time it happened, she was only five. She closed her eyes to blow out the birthday candles on her pink butterfly-shaped cake.

She could still see it clear as day.

Flash! She was back at her party. The same one soon to be ruined. The smell of

15

wasted pink icing wafted up into her nostrils. Tears streamed down her innocent cheeks. The heat of her five useless candles burned her lips while she stood frozen by the images.

She had planned to wish for a new puppy. Instead, a vision filled her mind. Her estranged grandmother screamed as flames engulfed her and her small New York City brownstone.

Elise cried out, impotent to save her granny.

After that, her mother never looked at her the same. Almost blamed her, it seemed. Like she should have been able to stop it somehow.

I'm not a butterfly like the cake; I'm a shrunken caterpillar in a melted cocoon.

Her self-judgment was ridiculous, of course. What could a five-year-old do about a fire two thousand miles away? But she swore next time she would stop it. *Next time I will save you. I'm sorry, Granny. I missed you my whole life. I know I would have loved you.*

Marcus Kincaid woke up feeling fresh today. He tossed the perfectly white Egyptian cotton sheets on the floor. First he sniffed his right armpit and then the left.

Ah, fresh as a spring mountain morning. Just like the commercial.

He slipped on the mahogany floor as he rushed to get ready. Then he slowed down. What did he care if he was late for work?

It had been almost five years since he lost her, his precious prize. The voices, just a whisper...had already started again. This year, they promised to help him find her, the Queen. They assured him he would be rewarded for his service, for his patient restraint. The wait would be well worth the suffering if only he surrendered to the master plan. *Six plans. Six masters.*

Five years ago, he blew it. He lost the best doll of all. She escaped. Well, just barely. She disappeared the morning he planned to give her the precious crown. Then the useless bitch died before he got the chance to kill her first.

The voices said he was still worthy; he would prove his royalty this time. This year, he would finish it properly. The voices pledged to guide him to victory.

Who was his next doll? That was the only question left.

He knew where to go. He knew when. He prepared for the special sign.

He climbed into the front seat of his Range Rover and headed to the grocery store. Aisle six. She would be on aisle six.

Perfect. Six was his favorite number.

He twirled his keys back and forth six times up, six times down.

He calmly glanced from one cereal box to the next. He waited for her, waited for the sign.

Jolene Waters rounded the corner while her two-year-old son went into a full-blown temper tantrum.

"I told you, baby, no more chocolate cereal. It's playing food, my sweet baby. You need growing food, my little man. I love you too much to feed you that junk."

He cried louder, demanded her surrender.

"Kiki-Cho, Kiki-Cho, Kiki-Cho, Mommy. L-yut wants Kiki-Cho."

"Okay, okay, let me see, baby. Let me see," she bargained. "No more tears, baby Elliot, okay? Mommy says okay."

She knew she shouldn't give in so easily, but what was a loving mother supposed to do? People were staring at her now. Who knew what they were thinking. The store closed in all around her like a coffin. She tasted the disrespect of the other shoppers. She was a failure.

She felt their eyes through the aisles. Their glares from the check out stands. *"Time out...for the screaming baby in aisle six with the blond headed idiot of a mom,"* they demanded.

What a joke. She was the one who needed the time out. Really, did holding her ground matter that much? It was just stupid cereal, after all. Besides, last night had been a good one. She had the money this time.

If she were a better mother, then maybe she could control her own baby, her own life. *My two-year-old runs over me like a bulldozer. No wonder Jimmy never loved me. I'm a big, useless wimp. Who could love someone as worthless as me?*

She never noticed the man observing from the other side of the aisle. Why would she? He was just some guy on aisle six looking at cereal boxes.

The man discreetly watched her every move.

She blew Elliot a kiss. She made her cutest face. She did a pretend peek-a-boo behind the cereal box. She had the baby now. She knew it. Game over. Elliotone. Momone. Finally, they were tied again.

She made the sound of a loving mother. "Sh-sh-sh-sh, baby."

"The sign. The sign," the man whispered.

He clenched his fists. His pants tightened.

"I love you, my big boy. Good boy, baby Elliot," Jolene said, forgetting all the glaring eyes and furrowed brows of strangers.

Elliot. The one and only good thing she had left.

The fiend sniffed her tempting scent as she walked happily past, oblivious to his evil plan. She had made the sign. She must be the one he had come here to find.

She was chosen.

As she turned the corner, the man mumbled, "Perfect. She is perfect. The little boya nice bonus. The voices had been right. This doll was definitely worth the wait."

Six days. Eight hours. Twelve minutes.

FOUR

Dead in the Water

ELISE SLOWLY DIPPED her foot in the steaming water. The burn was proof that she was really there, not dead at all like the official documents suggested. As the redness spread from her toes to her knees, she smiled.

She loved her claw-foot tub even though the white plaster looked more grey than white. She lit the four candles on the lip of the bath and sighed.

Dimitri sang softly in the background.

"Oh, Dimitri," she said. "I wondered if you wrote that song for me. Thank you." She laughed and climbed in.

Man, if I had a voice and talent like that, I would leave this stupid place. I would run away and never come back. See you later, Board of Shame. Can't touch me.

The fantasy offered her release while she succumbed to the glorious intensity of the scalding water. She heard the swish-swish of her heart murmur perfectly in her own ears.

Who needs a stupid stethoscope to listen to a pig's heart like mine?

She traced the scar down the middle of her chest.

But it wasn't just an ordinary scar. Maybe it was a fairy brand...like the one her favorite heroine, Lola Littleton, wore. Lola, the half-fairy princess who saved all seven realms of the magical world from her evil uncle, the self-proclaimed wicked Dark Fairy King.

After all, just like Lola in the Newberry Medal winning fable, Elise was short...ish with perfectly curly hair that sprung easily into place. And she wore a mark that looked like a scar. At least, so the oblivious humans claimed. But in the fairy world, it was the proof she was half-human, half-fairy. A Firling. She scoffed at the clueless humans; she was half-fairy.

A smile consumed her lips. One so big she felt the pull of the scars in the corners. The plastic surgeon had done a perfect job. No one could tell but her.

The smile quickly disappeared.

She heard Doctor Izmaiof's voice in the back of her mind, *"No more hot baths, Elise. It is simply too dangerous. What would you say if you were your own patient?"*

A frown. This was one thing her broken heart shouldn't be able to take away from her. Without this release, she would surely die or evaporate into nothingness.

She checked her pulse. One hundred and ten.

Okay, okay, Elise...just a few drops of cold water to cool your pumper down. Just a few degrees cooler. Dimitri, take me down softly, my love.

She flicked the cold faucet.

The candles and Dimitri would have to be enough.

Okay, that's better. Down to ninety-eight. Good girl. And yes...one day, I will take my flawless fairy wings and fly away from this terrible place.

She climbed out of the bath and wrapped herself in the luxury of the one expensive piece of clothing she owned, her fluffy, white robe. The socks Mom sent were cute, but her robe was spectacular. Heavenly even.

Come with me, Dimitri.

As soon as her head hit the pillow, the flashes started.

Give me a break. Screw this.

Six days. Five hours. Fifteen minutes.

Jolene tenderly wrapped Elliot in his favorite blanket, which was covered with balls from every sport. She traced her baby's forehead down to his cheek softly with her index finger. She blew him a kiss and closed the nursery door.

Curtain, more like.

As a mostly uneducated single mother, she didn't have money for luxuries like bedroom doors. A one-bedroom efficiency apartment in this quadraplex would have to do.

Will it ever be good enough for him? Will he ever understand why I left his daddy? Will he ever forgive me for what I am? God, I'm such a failure. Why can't I ever get it right?

Well, back to business. Nap time and at night were the only times she had to make the money they so desperately needed to survive. She picked up the phone and keyed in all the codes. She took a big breath. Some days it was harder than others. But she would do it. She would do anything she had to do to keep him safe, fed, and out of daycare. She knew all about the dangers of daycare. Her mother had told her about closed curtains at daycare.

She put on an imaginary layer of armor and pulled out her notes. By now she had a few regulars, so she had to keep the stories going. They remembered the story even if she didn't. And if she screwed up...even once, then she would lose the client to one of the other more experienced girls.

What did a small-town college dropout know about sex talk anyway? She was no pro. But she could pretend. She was good at pretend. She had to be...to survive her childhood.

Pretend Mom ever loved me. Pretend Mom ever worried about anyone more than herself. Pretend I was ever good enough, ever had a chance to be worthy of anything more than this.

"Yes, baby. I'm here," she said in her sexiest voice.

"Tell me more, Lyla," the client said. "I can call you Lyla, right?"

"You can call me whatever you want. I've been waiting for you. All day, all I could think about was you. You and your love."

Oh, no. Not love.

She felt his discomfort over the phone line all the way from Cleveland.

Never, never say love. They don't want love.

"I mean you and your manhood. It's so big and painful. It hurts me so good, baby. Give me more. Give me all your lo Ummm...pain. Give it to me good. Give me just what I deserve."

"Tell me what a useless piece of shit you are, Lyla. Tell me how I can push you around. Tell me how you will beg for mercy when I slap you silly, you stupid whore."

The client was getting off now. She could hear him. His breathless grunting climaxed with a final gooey gasp.

She had him hooked with her uselessness. Actually, he had done it for her. She was an expert at this kind of garbage talk. At this, she was a pro.

She reminded herself that if she kept him on the line for fifteen more minutes, dinner...at least for another night, was served. If the call lasted for thirty, she might be able to keep the heat on for another week.

Keep the client hot, Jolene. That keeps Elliot warm at night. Whatever it takes to keep that baby safe and sound.

She imagined herself taking another blanket into Elliot. She pretended to play hide-and-seek with him in her mind. She thought about anything but what she said to the client.

Her mouth tasted sick from the disgust of it all. She lit a cigarette and hung it out the window. If she smelled burning tobacco, perhaps she wouldn't notice the smell, the stink of shame that saturated her.

But he's worth it. My baby's worth it. Even this. Even if he is a bastard. 'Cause he's my bastard.

FIVE

Don't Let Me Down

ELISE BREATHED SLOWLY in and out. She could fight the pull inward, or not. What was the point? To attempt to delay the inevitable? *Whatever.*

The clock ticked no matter how hard she resisted.

"What you resist, without fail persists."

"Thank you, Doctor Suzie the Super Shrink, for misquoting Jung's billion-dollar advice. Well, screw your self-help mumbo jumbo bullshit, and try putting someone else on the cover of your magazine for a month or two. Okay?"

The swirling colors in her mind's eye took over. Now she was spinning, not dizzy just spinning, in a swirling bowl of green peas.

Green peas? What the hell? Whatever. Surrender, girl. Good, Elise. Don't fight. It just wastes time. Don't think. Just allow. Breathe into it.

She recited the words of her favorite Mystic. "Spirit didn't give you your breath; Spirit is your breath. It is the grace of what called you into being that fills your lungs. So breathe it in."

"Okay, Spirit, take my breath away."

An old Calgon ad surfaced in her mind, and she chuckled.

The gateway appeared as always, subtly and then more clearly. She followed it willingly. Slowly at first, and then faster and faster it took her where it would.

Flash!

A million glittering lights encircled her as she traveled deep within. An outsider might have said she meditated or prayed or put herself in a self-hypnotic state, but she would have just laughed. All three were exactly the same thing labeled with different names.

Oh the irony of modern religion and modern self-help.

Even from another plane of existence, she gagged.

They are all the same: in to the center of being, in to where the real work needed to be done–the heart space.

23

She told herself she was there. Then she was. The inkling was enough. Her faith made it so.

Her feet were trapped in concrete blocks, but her wasted heart tugged the rest of her forward. She looked up at the three-story house again.

Why here? What the hell happened to me here? I know this place, yet I don't. Why? Why can't I remember?

Even in her deep state of connection, she laughed. She already knew the answer to her own stupid question. Probably, anyway.

Because I don't want to.

She possessed some awareness of what would happen next. As she explored the depths of the demons that waited for her in this house, she would find cluespieces of clues, at least. Visions were always like that, just bits, just fragments that had to be dissected and put back in the right order. Each clue would likely lead to the next. If she missed even one, that might seal the deal. Then she would fail to learn the lesson and fail to save whoever depended on her.

For a moment, she considered turning back, getting back in the hot tub and letting her heart implode.

Why do I have to save some idiot I don't even know? Can't they save themselves and just leave me alone? Didn't I save myself already? Why should that chick's story end any differently?

She knew the answer to this question too, of course. By saving them, she really saved herself. Again.

Because one ride at this circus wasn't enough already? Lifeone cruel bitch coaster.

She went back in time as she surrendered to the swirling peas.

Five years ago, she had woken up in a hospital bed in Utah after being emergently transported out by helicopter from the small hospital on the outskirts of Strawberry Lake.

Who names a lake after a fruit?

Apparently, the cops found her almost-dead body on some random boat at the Strawberry Lake Marina and Yacht Club.

How can they call it a yacht club without a single freaking yacht?

Immediately, she underwent surgery at Salt Lake City Regional Hospital to repair her damaged heart already weakened by a childhood case of rheumatic heart disease. They had to put in a porcine valve and xenograft a new septum, or she would have died.

A pig valve to fix a pig-hearted goddess so they could give her a new life with a new name in a new city.

You mean...half-fairy princess. There is no goddess here.

The peas transformed into hot-n-sour soup.

As of last week, Elise Phillips stood behind seventy-two others on the heart transplant list. She had moved up three spots last month...because three others had died from a terminal case of low man on the totem pole.

No one knew how long she had left before she suffered the same fate of bad timing. The doctors couldn't tell her. Her heart, one of the first to survive such a drastic salvage procedure, beat well into no-man's-land. Each year, her cardio-thoracic surgeon was more thrilled than the last that she was still alive.

"Perhaps you will outlive me, little lady," he answered the last time she asked her one and only question. Always the same question.

If not, the pig valve would have to do as long as it could until her bleeding pig heart finally bled to death like all good pig's hearts should.

We all bleed red when we're dying. Maybe we are all already dead.

Her visions had just stopped after the accident...or her kidnapping, as the cops called it. She missed them, sort of. Sort of didn't.

The afternoon her captor took her, she never came home from the Humane Society where she worked part time. The next two months remained a void, an empty wasteland of nothingness in her mind just like a vault with no keys left to open it.

The cops kept accusing her of holding out on them. Like she suffered that same victim syndrome the rich girl from California did.

Patty Hearst-itis for the pig that used to be named Jill.

After about a thousand attempts, the cops and the head shrinks finally gave in and accepted that she wasn't lying.

But then, wham! Here she was back again in the world of flashing visions and dreams. This time, of her least favorite three-story househis house.

From the street, she stared at the structure. She took mental notes. A clue was here somewhere. She had better figure it out, or he was going to kill someone in exactly...

Six days. Two hours. One minute.

But instead of walking up the stairs, she fell asleep. She was just too tired to go in and face her demons.

◎

Wednesday, 2:37 a.m.

Finally, Jolene's last client was done; his genetic material spilled like pearl jam all over the floor...or the blanket...or whatever.

That thought always felt better left...un-thought.

She walked to her bedroom exhausted and disgusted. Wholly unsure who she hated more, herself or her clients, she suppressed the urge to vomit. The slime of it all threatened to strangle her and crawl right out of her nasty mouth.

But the heat would stay on for the rest of the month. *Thank God. No. Thank the devil.*

She and Elliot lived in Denver, so heat in January was no small thing. It was a matter of life or death.

She examined her silhouette in the glass shower door and frowned. If she had been born prettier. If she had more curves, perhaps. If she had something special about her, then maybe Jimmy would have loved her enough to marry her.

She remembered the awful conversation like it had happened yesterday.

"Mom, I'm having my baby. I am. So just shut the hell up. There is no way I'm going to that clinic where they do that. No way. Not that."

"But you just started at the community college, honey. This will ruin you. This will ruin us. What am I supposed to do now? You know the plan: college, nursing school, and then...then you can start your own family. Marry Jimmy if he will still have you.

Just as long as you have a back-up plan for when he leaves you. Because, baby doll, they always do. Men always leave you for a younger woman."

Jolene's thighs ached to sprint away from her mother's painful words. Instead, she paced up and down, back and forth, trying to find the words to defend herself and her unborn baby.

Her mother shook her head and avoided eye contact as she continued. "And what about me, Jolene? How easily you forget about your mother. About all the things I've done for you. The things I sacrificed. All of it for you. What about me? What about our plan?"

"I should have told Jimmy about the baby first, Mom. This isn't fair. What about what I want? It's my life, too."

"Not anymore, Ms. Slut! Whore! Not if you have his bastard. That's what this is, a godforsaken bastard. Jimmy will leave you, too. I know it. Just like your daddy did. Jimmy doesn't want a baby with you. I know what I'm talking about. How could he love you? Look at you."

Those aching thighs got the best of her. She covered her mouth to stifle the screams while she ran out the back door. Without a dollar or a suitcase, she went to the first big city she could find. Anyplace but home would do. What could be home now? Anywhere far enough away from Cheyenne would have to do.

She still heard her mother's terrible words in her sleep.

Denver seemed right. Big, but not too big.

One and one-half hours later, she pulled off I-70 into Denver proper.

The sign on the street said *Room Vacant*, so she stopped the car and took it. Washington Park sounded full of hope, full of promise.

In history, she had loved the old stories about George Washington and the cherry tree even if they later proved to be a big fat lie. Funny thing…how her teacher taught the class about telling the truth by telling a lie. And good old George owned the dollar bill. Maybe he owned her ticket to the big bank of life, far away from the life she screwed up so badly?

She tried to call back home once, but she hung up as soon as she heard her mother's voice.

"Jolene? Jolene, baby girl, is that you?"

The sting of the blade still cut too deep.

Click. The line went dead.

In that second, she decided to raise Elliot all by herself. She didn't need her pushy mother. She didn't need anyone. She didn't even need God.

She never told Jimmy about the baby. She had started to right before she had left. She rushed over to his place, trying to be as brave as possible.

Maybe he would help her. Maybe he could love her no matter what.

He had been watching a program on the television. A news flash cut in about a doctor murdered at the local woman's clinic. When she saw the expression of horror on his face just hearing about the clinic, she ran, hand over her mouth, to her car. She couldn't risk facing that look, his rejection, and vowed she would never tell him the truth. And if he told her to have...an abort She couldn't even stomach the half-formed word. No way. She loved her baby already. Bastard or not, he was her everything.

While she snuggled tightly in with Elliot, she asked for her baby's forgiveness. She begged that one day she would be worthy of him, her little precious bastard.

"I love you. Forever and always. Always and forever." She put her fingers to her lips softly and pressed them to his cheekthe cheek she loved more than anything.

The words felt truer to her than any words she had ever spoken. He filled a void within her that was so big that it otherwise would have swallowed her completely. She loved him so much that her chest ached from the pressure of it. Her heart threatened to break free from her body just to be one bit closer to him.

A half-formed tear moistened her cheek as sleep fell heavy and hard on her broken heart, her broken life, and her broken self-worth. Then it landed perfectly on the pillow of her beloved bastard's cheekthe cheek she loved more than anything.

The Range Rover waited patiently around the corner in the parking lot at Pete's All-Night Liquor and Snack Shop. The heat of its engine cooled quickly in the freezing drizzle. The tires rolled effortlessly out of the piss-stained ground cover that was nothing compared to the formidable ice in Steamboat Springs.

"Denver babies don't even know what real ice looks like."

The car spit radiator fluid at the boozers that stumbled past.

The curry hook in the front seat just wondered when it would ever get used for anything other than Chinese food. *"Really? Garlic chicken again?"*

The back hood creaked with complaint to open for the bag of trash its master brought back from the alleyway behind the lady's house.

It slammed shut again in disgust.

"Trash? Seriously?" the SUV shrieked.

The odor of baby vomit, maxi pads, old McDonald's french fries, and rotten waste-soaked baby diapers flooded the Range Rover. It was not pleased. Wasn't it supposed to be a luxury vehicle?

"Perhaps the garlic chicken isn't so bad after all."

The back right tire of the SUV snapped a defenseless cockroach's back in two as it rolled away. As the creature seeped his brown, slimy innards on the asphalt, the vermin found a fleeting moment of peace; his struggle for shelter this winter had finally ended.

Once the Rover pulled into the driveway, its master noticed the way it glided to a perfect stop before its four-wheel-traction system kicked in. A sound, somewhat hollow and soft like a cloud of marshmallow, welcomed the SUV home.

Soon, the master wouldn't be alone. Maybe next time he'd have a new doll with him. Another doll to join the others. The master looked up at his three-story house and grinned.

"I'm home, honey." The master winked at the window.

If the lights hadn't already turned off, the SUV would have winked, too. The front of the house had always reminded the Range Rover of a face.

The master walked through the front door.

"Open up and say 'ah'. The Doll Doctor is back," he announced.

The familiar scent of bleach wafted out the door, and the tires sunk into the snow for tonight's rest.

. . .

Five days. Fifteen hours. Seventeen minutes.

SIX

White Flag

"BEEP, BEEP, BEEP," Elise's alarm sounded.

"What? What? What time is it?" she shouted.

Elise urgently wiped the crusty sleep from her eyes.

Crap, I fell asleep.

She looked at the owl-covered journal next to her bed and sighed. The all-seeing eyes of the feathered creatures just stared blankly back at her. The page was empty. Her notesno notes. She remembered nothing.

She glared at her clock in anger.

"Tick, tick, tick," it criticized her.

It shook its little hand at her in harsh reprimand.

She imagined it saying, "*How could you have wasted a night? Don't you know that someone's life depends on you...on this...on your dreams...on the visions?*"

She looked at her watch. If she drifted back off for fifteen minutes, she could still get her rounds done at the hospital in time for morning report. So what if she skipped one shower? She had perfectly bouncy hair whether she washed it or not. An Italian shower would be fine.

She barely had enough time to consider her options when she noticed a CD cover tossed carelessly in the corner. *How to Save a Life* by the Fray demanded her attention. It called her out of the corner. It shoved her to the front of a hero's stage.

This place is a pigsty. Perfect. Perfect conditions for the pig inside a pig-hearted goddess. Are you kidding me? Okay, okay, okay. You win.

She looked intensely at the CD cover.

Guidance coming from a CD cover. Give me a freaking break.

She closed her eyes and welcomed the reprieve of her inner world. Indigo swirled into her mind first, followed shortly by purple and then green. She followed her breath, the gift of grace, until she entered the All's mind.

Good. I am in.

She dove into the open tunnel and followed it. It oscillated back and forth around her in a supportive yet uncompromising way. The harder she tried to follow it, the more it seemed to elude her. If she just held a space of wonder and curiosity, it enveloped her with its motion of in and out, wrapping her in its warmth like the fuzzy softness of a cashmere sweater. Trying not to strain, not to try, not to force it to happen but to make it welcome, she breathed into the center of the sacred chamber of her broken heart.

Flash! Flash! Flash!

Really, I'm a Firling: a half-fairy princess. I've got the mark to prove it. Just like Lola.

The endearing fantasy helped her relax into the strength of her purpose. Someone depended on her success. If she failed, they would die. The same way that she had almost died.

Remember. I want to remember what happened to me. I do. Really, I do. I want to know. I am willing to know. I am determined to know, really.

She gasped. She wasn't standing in front of the menacing house. She looked at her legs, half-collapsed beneath her. A trickle of dried blood stained her leg. The congealed red cells hinted at something critical about her past torture, something unthinkable.

Don't go there, Elise. Your pulse is rising too fast. One hundred.

She inhaled, and then exhaled the image.

Give me my breath. Slow me down. It's just a memory. It can't hurt me anymore. I already survived this; I am still alive.

Or am I?

She surveyed for clues. The stains on her feet were brown, almost black. They were deep, permanent looking. Old mud, maybe? Ink, perhaps? Something was wedged under her toenails. A large splinter? A rock?

The intensity of the pain in her feet overwhelmed her. Her head spun from the heaviness of it. Why did she hurt so badly? She focused on the colors to stay conscious, but the waves of ripping pain kept coming like evil crests from an ocean of torture.

Flash!

She stared at the bright lights and wondered if the brilliance was God.

Where am I? Is this love?

Then she noticed the be-beep, be-beep, be-beep of the cardiac monitor. She heard the sound of the machine lifting and compressing someone's chest. Her chest.

It pushed her lungs full and then empty again.

I'm on bypass. Oh my God. My heart surgery.

Crunch!

She heard the sound of a million dreams shatter while her chest split in two from the prying force of the metal device intent on saving her life.

She heard the voices of several men. Doctors, probably.

"What the hell happened to this poor little girl? She looks like a bear attacked her. For God's sake, what kind of monster did a thing like this to her?"

The surgeon slammed his fist on the OR table. He inhaled deeply, steadied himself, demanded the scalpel, and sliced open Jane Doe from stem to stern.

"I don't know, Doctor Mantle. I don't know. It's so unreal. This is all so unbeliev-able. Is this really happening?"

The OR scrub pinched his right arm.

"No, Don, we are really here. She looks like a nice enough girl to me. Poor child."

"Do you think the police will ever figure out who she is? Maybe she's one of those homeless street kids."

"I don't think so. Did you see her necklace? Street kids don't wear gold and silver butterfly necklaces like that. Bet she's somebody's baby. Man, that would kill me. Poor kid. Her poor mother. Fuck. God, where were you when she needed you?"

"Should we get the on-call gynecologist to check her out?"

"Yes. Rape kit. Come on, Don. Let's fix her heart. Hopefully the Psychiatrists can repair her mind after"

Flash! Flash! Flash!

The sound of her mother's voice filled the room. The moans of pain reverberated off the hospital walls. The ceiling echoed back the suffering of a loss too big to measure or ever mention.

"Oh God. My baby. My little baby. What did he do to you? Your lips. Your fucking lips. That bastard!"

Something smashed on the floor.

Feet rushed in.

"You okay, Ma'am?"

"Yes. I just can't… I'm so sorry. Nurse, help her. My baby. What did he do to my baby? Help us. Help me. Help me."

The wailing lasted for what seemed like hours but was probably only minutes.

The door slammed again.

"Oh, my sweet pea. Baby, come back. Your eyes are so blank. You've been gone so long. Where are you, my baby? My baby. Your sweet lips"

Pressure over her mouth. More wailing.

"Mommy's here. Mommy's here now. Come back to Mommy. I will keep you safe this time. I promise. I'm so sorry. It's all my fault."

"Beep, beep, beep," her pager shrieked. *"Wake up!"*

"Ring, ring, ring." The telephone rudely interrupted the cries of her devastated mother.

"Yes, Doctor Phillips here," Elise said as she struggled to get her bearings. "What day is it? Wendi? Is that you, Wendi?"

"Yes, my friend. Wake up! Where the hell are you? Did you go to Snake Pit without me last night after all, little lady? But darn, girl, you missed morning report. It did not go unnoticed. Chief Buhl wants you in her office now. You are in big crap."

"You mean big shit." Gulp.

"Elise, get here fast. Really fast. I can't cover for long."

"Coming now. Shit. Thanks for calling. And no. I never go there without you. Ever."

She glimpsed at her unmade yet shockingly flawless face in the rearview mirror while she backed out of her tiny parking spot over the crunch of half-melted snow. She wondered how many bugs crunched with it. She wondered even more how long her surgery had taken to replace her lips. They looked so good, so natural.

The flicker of gold from a butterfly-shaped necklace caught her attention.

I haven't worn this necklace since... It's in my jewelry box...under a thousand pairs of earrings.

But it wasn't. It was around her neck.

She stopped the car and took out her journal.

She smiled and wrote:

Clue oneButterfly necklace. Black feet. Rape kit. Ink on the soles of my feet. Something under toenails. My lips.

Five days. Eleven hours. Twenty-two minutes.

SEVEN

Hospital Food

THE WIND BLEW LIGHTLY, east to west, over the front entrance of Saint Lutheran's Hospital of Grace, whistling its tune of life and death. The automatic, spotlessly shimmering glass door opened and shut to accept or deny the nameless visitors bearing flowers, balloons, and, on occasion, tears.

An almost indiscernible waft of bleach-tainted oblivion blessed the air. A fifteen floor lipstick-shaped tower of medical-surgical floors rose with spelling-bee championship posture into the clear and sunny Denver sky. Birds stopped here and there to rest at the sanctuary out back. On the second floor helicopter-pad, the red and white striped chopper waited patiently for the next cardiac transport, the next gynecological catastrophe, or the next critically ill neonate.

A tertiary care center of excellence, this hospital remained a mecca in the world of beautiful, private, top-notch facilities. Its granite countertops and marble floors oozed luxury, perfectly poised to polish over terminal diagnosis. The cafeteria boasted award winning health-conscious gourmet meals to feed visitors too sick or devastated to eat its fabulous meals.

At the top of several categories in the U.S. Healthcare Commission's Top-One Hundred Hospitals, this building tailored to the wealthy, but dying. The rich, but laboring during an imminent birth. The affluent, but ruined. The loaded, but physically flailing.

For twenty years, the Ob-Gyn residency held the honor of recruiting some of the best medical students in the country. Here, they became the best obstetrics and gynecology doctors in the world. Here, these doctors were honored to scrub the toilets or draw blood on HIV-positive patients if their nametag said "Doctor So-and-so, Resident OB."

Here, they faced the Board of Shame. And if they survived...even just barely, these same residents were reverently called "Doctor" and offered a lucrative spot in any practice in the nation.

If they knew the course of the ureter.

If they knew the cranial nerves.

If they knew the branches of the pelvic arteries.

If they knew how to suck up hard enough to Doctor Buhl.

Doctor Elise Phillips talked herself down the whole way over the bridge that ended in the back parking lot. Dimitri Arion played sensuously in the back of her mind while her heart beat steadily at ninety beats a minute.

She locked her car and went in the back entrance to face *the bull*.

Doctor Buhl gave Elise the famous *bull-face*.

Then she said, "One. That's it, Elise. You get one major screw-up."

"But"

"Hush before you even start in."

"I"

"I don't want to lose a second of my morning finding out why or who or where or whatever." She coughed into a tissue and tossed it in the trash without looking away.

"But"

"I really couldn't care less. Your excuses are wasted on me." *The bull* never broke eye contact.

"But my"

"One. After that, you go back to square one." She cleared her throat.

Silence.

"Your one is over now. You have exactly three and one-half years for it to never happen again. Do we understand each other?" A fake smile followed.

"Yes."

"Good. If I'm not mistaken, there is a vaginal hysterectomy still in progress in OR Four." Bigger smile.

"But"

"Yes, actually, you may gladly hold some sticks with enthusiasm. And then you can take the triage calls from home tonight as icing on the cake." Genuine smile.

"But I was just on call night before last."

"And then you can say thank you, and yes, you will be happy to present Fetal Strip Conference tomorrow." A slight giggle.

"I'm an intern. I haven't"

"Yes, I realize that you haven't done your OB rotation yet. That you can't possibly be prepared to present. Here are the tracings. Know them by heart."

"Anything else, Doctor Buhl?"

"Yes. Like I said, I'll remind you once more. You get one screw-up. One."

Piece by rotten and stinky piece, Kincaid searched through Jolene's tossed aside things. He caught the scent of her most private secretions. He inspected the contents of Elliot's stool. He noticed the high-end label of the baby's diapers and the generic brand of her feminine pads.

Like a lover, he read her letters and pressed them close to his chest. He examined the squiggly, black marks. Tear tracks, probably.

Why would you be crying, my love? I'm coming to rescue you.

Most importantly, he observed the absence of the effects of another man.

I knew you were true to us, my love.

His treasure pleased him. It was more than enough information to plan his next move.

Alone and ready for me, my doll. I'm coming. I promise. So soon. No more tears, darling. Together. We will be together. Then we will see if you are the one and can stand by me.

EIGHT

Need You Now

THE PAGER VIBRATED for the third time this hour.

The message *"Nancy Butler. 555-3232. Lost her mucous plug? Call ASAP."*

Ah, to be at the beck and call of the triage clinic. Call ASAP? Are you freaking kidding me? As if interpreting the damn strips that mean nothing to me aren't enough.

Each call more upsetting to her than the last, Elise had completely lost her cool by now. Way past midnight, she still struggled to feel prepared for Fetal Strip Conference. Each ridiculous page from the triage operator took her further away from the goal of getting it done so she could get to work on saving some bimbo she didn't even know.

By now, Elise had a hunch the intended victim would be female. The dried blood on her leg in her vision pushed her into awareness that she had successfully repressed for years. *Against my eternal will.*

Don't go there, Elise. There's no reason. It's over. That's old news. Shove it back down. In. Down. Shove. Shove harder.

As the presenting intern tomorrow, it was her job to question the actions of her senior residents while they managed high-risk patients in labor. The heart tracings would reveal what the senior residents had done right, but more poignantly, it provided irrefutable evidence of what they had done wrong.

All in the name of learning, right? I doubt it, you disgusting bottom feeders. She mimicked Dr. Buhl's giggle perfectly.

Tomorrow, she had the honor of blowing the "you screwed up" whistle. Since she hadn't even done her OB rotation yet, she didn't have much experience to work with. She had better put her ducks in a row. What was left of her ass was on the line.

Marcus Kincaid sat impatiently in his three-thousand-dollar conference chair twirling his feet underneath the fifty-thousand-dollar slate conference table of Board Room Six on the sixth floor of the Mandinka Industries Building located at 626 Sixteenth Street in downtown Denver.

The number six teased him. It begged he pay attention to the wheels in the sky. *Six spokes on an eternal wheel of need.*

Symbolically, the number six was about nurturing, harmony, and caring. Most people thought the number six was about the devil. They were wrong.

He twirled his keys in his pocketsix times forward, six times backward.

He knew better than the others; he knew all about numerology.

Six was the number of *the Mother.*

It…just happened to also be the number of Dark Kings who ruled the Underworldthe only true world. Pure coincidence. Nothing more than that.

What a joke that the common man connected the number six to the antichrist. What a joke that they did their "deals" in room six on the sixth floor, more like the devil than a nurturing mother. The irony rattled him so hard that he almost laughed out loud as he twirled the keys backward for the final round.

His swirling thoughts stole him away on an eternal wheel of need.

Ah, the messages. So many clueless idiots running around who don't even see them. In many ways, women are the antichrist. So perhaps mother and devil are the same thing. The devils and their useless mouths. Stitch them all shut.

His name brought him back to reality.

"Marcus? Marcus, what do you have to say? I think we should move on this one," Robert Stockton shouted from across the room.

Silence.

"I think it's a brilliant strategy. And let's face it; the money looks good. Don't you think?"

"Whatever you say, boss. You're the businessman after all. I'm just the silent guy who signs the paychecks," Kincaid replied almost too quietly to hear.

As Robert continued his quarterly strategy report, Marcus Kincaid drifted off to another dimension. His inner world. His kingdom. His Underworld.

He flashed to an old Charlie Brown comic strip. Robert's voice transformed into Charlie's teacher's distorted and useless words.

"Whaa-whaa-whaa. Whaa-whaa-whaa."

Robert's incomprehensible words fell like pieces of horse dung on the grey slate table with a soft, warm thud. Kincaid looked around the room in amazement as he watched more filth drop from every mouth in the room. The odor enveloped him, and he considered laughing from the absurdity of it.

He decided not to. He gagged instead.

The steam of manure wafted from the pile of feces covering the conference room table and spilled onto the freshly soiled floor.

He picked up his briefcase, wiped it clean, and tucked it under his arm.

As Kincaid stood, Robert called out, "Marcus, you okay? You don't look so good."

Silence.

"Um, aren't you going to stay for the rest of the meeting?"

Shrugged. Turned around.

"I have one more awesome idea to share. Our scouts discovered a whole new line of dirt-cheap African artifacts through my contact in China. We could totally pass them off as originals. No one will know any better. No one even knows what the hell or where Mandinka is. Don't you think?"

The door slammed shut before Robert finished his manure-filled sentence with his poo-covered lips.

Kincaid was done; that was all the shit he could take for one day. He had some needs that mattered so much more.

He had somewhere else to go. His doll waited. He twirled his keys again six times forward and then six times backward.

He had three hours to drive before he got home. He could barely wait for the elevator to open so he could avoid the scent of excrement, which drifted over from the Board Room and down the hall.

As Elise finally settled in for the night, she looked around her apartment. She marveled at the ingenuity of its design, so small yet efficient. She looked at her Lola Littleton books and smiled. Six books just weren't enough to satisfy her.

When will the seventh book finally come out?

She had to know what really happened to the evil Fairy-King. And…who was Sephubel? He had to be important for the author to keep mentioning him in each book. What was she missing? Was the bad guy really dead?

What's wrong with me? I should be busy…flirting with boys...not looking for the next good middle-grade bestseller.

Her eye caught the overflowing trash bin in the corner, filled with TV dinners for one.

She muttered, "My life's a big fat mess. I'm a caterpillar trapped in someone else's cocoon. What butterfly wings? None here."

She traced her finger down the length of her chest scar.

Forty-three sets of staple-track wounds. Forty-three broken promises. Forty-three sports she would never play. Forty-three dance moves she would never perfect. Forty-three classmates she could never see again. Forty-three whispers of death. Forty-three tears of grief.

Forty-three visions.

As the swirling colors welcomed her deep into herself, a peace came over her. Her sense of purpose replaced her sense of loss.

She whispered, "I won't let him turn you into a pig-hearted goddess. I will try to save you even if nobody saved me."

Forty-three reasons to help you. Forty-three ways to save you. Forty-three ways I could end up killing us both if I'm too late.

NINE

Careless Whispers

WHILE JOLENE DIALED in the dirty little codes, a man watched from across the street. With fingers smudged by disgust, she held the phone to her ear. And then she said whatever the client wanted her to say while she shoved her truth, her own words, her own defense, her own worth down further and further.

Across the road, the butt warmer in the man's Range Rover made the man's buttocks sweat slightly. He never perspired. The stink, the nastiness of it was too dirty for him, but he loved to feel his skin grow warm underneath the pulsation of blood.

It proved he wasn't impotent. That he was no failure.

Tchaikovsky played joyfully on the man's CD player, which was cleverly hidden behind the touchscreen navigation system.

The man couldn't help noticing Jolene's street address: 447.

He whispered, "Perfect. Sent straight from my Angels. She will be perfect when I'm done whispering sweet nothings in her ear."

Flash! Flash! Flash!

The dreaming Elise soared deep into her vision tunnel.

"Let there be light."

And then there was, but just barely. It came through in small lines from the metal vent beneath her feet.

She tried to move but couldn't. There wasn't enough room. She smelled the rank yet familiar scent of ketones on her breath stinking like Juicy Fruit gum.

How long had she been here cramped like this? Hours, probably.

She stifled a scream, shocked by the sound of thump, thump, thumping music, which came from above.

Is that techno music playing?
She craned her neck around for a better look.

The odor of old sweat coated her hair. Dry yet sharp and metallic, it reminded her of the smell of the radiator from her childhood home.

She flashed to the memory of being at her mother's feet, ill with strep throat, too sick to stand, the half-used antibiotics left behind on the counter top when the ambulance took her away in heart failurethe first time.

What does that have to do with this? Focus, Elise!
She turned her attention back to the small space that confined herher sarcophagus.

The space only allowed slow, shallow breaths through her nose. She tried to mouth-breathe for better control, but her lips were stuck together.

She reached up slowly, painfully, barely able to move in the space, and touched her face. Her eyes felt puffy, and her lips, dry, matted, lumpy, wouldn't open.

Matted? Why are my lips so deformed? What happened to my face?
She reached down to feel her chest scar. No scar. It didn't exist yet.

I'm not a Firling. No forty-three staples. No pig's heart.
Flash!
Confined, but less so. Clearly in the back of a car.

She heard the engine. She felt the movement, but she couldn't see. The car screeched to a stop. She rolled over and smacked her head on something metal: bars that turned on a ninety-degree angle. More metal all round. A rectangular small box. A metal, moving box.

The fucking trunk, Elise, you idiot. She would have screamed if what was left of her mouth would have opened.

She heard the giggling passengers climb out. Four doors slammed shut. The laughing decreased and faded slightly.

Are they coming back to get me? Am I safe now?
Bu-bump, bu-bump, bu-bump, her heart raced. One hundred and fifty.

Too fast, Elise. Slow your pulse down.
It's a memory. It can't hurt me. It's already over. Slow it down. Come on, baby. For you, for me. Dance with the sexy Latin boy. Such lovely moves.
One hundred and thirty.

His fine fingers. Glorious arms. So soft. So smooth. So feminine, but not.
One hundred and ten beats a minute. *Better.*

Keep going, baby. Ninety-eight, eighty-six.

Good girl. Thank you again, Dimitri. I know I love you. I know that much is true.
The voices trailed away to nothing. For several seconds, she waited, not knowing what to expect next.

Then she remembered!
She rammed her feet hard through the back seat. Nothing.

She foraged for something to help her. A tool. Something. Anything.
A tire iron.

She busted out the taillight. Took kicking force to the back seat again, now with some light coming through the jagged hole to guide her.

Slam, slam, slam. Forty-three slams.

The seat finally gave way.

She climbed through the back seat of the Lexus and sighed. The laughing people had not returned. She was still alone...and alive. She scanned. Spare key on the floorboard.

As the roar of the engine engaged, she knew where she was going: anywhere. Anywhere but here.

Flash!

The sign said "Strawberry Lake Exit 9 miles".

Something told her she had already taken it. Five years ago, to be exact.

Flash!

She climbed into the blue boat slowly, her breath short and gasping.

Drowning. I'm drowning in my own spit.

She coughed up pink, frothy sputum, suffocating in her own secretions.

Heart failure.

Her legs, heavy. So damn heavy.

The pain, like a fire-knife, seared her chest, cooking her from the inside while her heart decompensated.

As she swirled around unconsciousness, the first ray of sunlight pierced the dark night's sky. She had found her way out. Any way out. Like in her nightmares. She tried to pump her arms. Wanted to fly away.

She was gone. Her mind reunited with the All.

They would find her in less than an hour. She would remember nothing except forty-three staples one month later.

Flash! Flash! Flash!

The kitten. So darn cute. How could something be that adorable?

She loved the creature immediately.

"Put her back, Jill, or take her home," a sweet and familiar voice said.

Elise recognized the voice.

Whose?

Mary from the SPCA.

"But she's so stinking cute. I love her so much. I must rescue her."

"Yeah, yeah, Jill. We all know. You freakin' softy. Just sign the papers and she's yours. Maybe she will rescue you in return."

"I know, but it's such a commitment."

"That kitten will be the death of you. Come on, Jill. The party starts in an hour, and we aren't even home yet. Come on!"

"Okay, okay, okay."

Flash!

A chocolate cereal box.

What? Kiki-Chos? What? I hate that rotten kids' cereal. Chocolate little circles from hell. Yuck.

"Beep, beep, beep," the pager shrieked.

Elise sat up panting. She wiped the froth from her mouth. Thankfully, it wasn't there. She traced her finger down her chest and imagined dancing with a sexy boy in pink tights. *So delicious.*

The clock read 4:30 a.m. on Thursday.
Four days. Fifteen hours. Six minutes left.
She grabbed her journal and wrote:

Clue twoJill's Kitten, matted lips, heater vent, trunk, chocolate cereal box.

TEN

Picture to Burn

JILL VICKEREY. The name haunted Elise.

What happened to us, Jill?

Elise stepped out of the steaming bath and inspected her reflection.

She preferred the phrase…vertically challenged to short. The truth was obvious: she was short. Her almost blond, almost brown curly hair fell just below her shoulders, tickling the perfect porcelain skin of her back.

"Dishwater blond, now that's a bullshit term," she muttered.

Elise sighed, not impressed by her fine skin.

"Who thought of such an insulting term?"

She answered herself. "Obviously somebody who doesn't have dishwater blond hair."

She pulled her dishwater locks up in one full swoop and twist, locking the brown clip in place. When her hair was up, she was Doctor Phillips. When it was down, she was Elise.

But where the hell is Jill? How does she wear her hair?

She knew the answer to her own question: *covered in dust.*

Jill has…had…dust-blond hair in a pretend grave in another world in another life. Glenwood Springs.

The image of a grave popped inan empty grave.

Jill died five years ago during a failed post-kidnapping-rescue emergency cardiac surgery while the surgeons attempted to repair her heart valve that supposedly couldn't be fixed even with such a drastic salvage procedure.

The poor girl had apparently survived her kidnapper and escaped to Strawberry Lake in a Lexus. She had not survived her broken heart. Jill Vickery's name flatlined on the OR table along with the possibility of her small-town life.

Beep. Beep. Beep. -------------------

45

"Death. The perfect cover...so he won't come find her. The perfect cover so the world will think she died. We'll say she's already dead," they offered her mother.

They? Who the hell were they? And maybe I already was dead.

Unlike the memory of Jill, though, Elise's body did just fine. In fact, the salvage procedure worked perfectly.

The new and improved version of Jill, Elise Phillips, secretly woke up in a secret recovery room with a pig-goddess heart. Her cardiologist toured the country giving lectures on the novel approach even though he supposedly failed because his patient supposedly died from intraoperative complications.

Only a handful of people were aware of the fact that she was alive and well.

"Bet that pisses you off, Doctor," Jill...or was it Elise...muttered.

Now there's only Elise. Jill really did die. I really did die.

"Bet that pisses you off less than it pisses me off, Doctor."

Every trace of Jill Vickery, dead, gone, and buried in an empty grave.

The whole charade executed without Elise's consenteven the new name picked by her mother. The same mother who hadn't given Jill the antibiotics for strep throat in the first place when she was five and couldn't protect her own heart from rheumatic heart disease. The same mother who now lived in Waco, Texas with a new a life, a new husband, a new name, a new job, a new everything.

The Witness Protection Program took them in as victims and shoved them back out as prisoners in someone else's life with someone else's name.

Is a living Elise better than a dead Jill?

"Fuck if I know," Elise, not Jill, whispered.

At least she has forty-three reasons to stop that wicked son of a bitch.

She told her reflection, "Maybe this bimbo will get to keep her name, her life, her small-town boyfriend, her small-town kitten, her small-town dreams."

If the countdown in her vision proved anything, it was that by now, Jill Vickery would have been dead anyway. So obviously, the Elise name-switch turned out to be a wise move. With or without a pig's heart, she would have been six feet under the ground, the ice, the snow, the whatever.

She imagined Jill frothing up in her toothpaste and gagged. Elise scrubbed hard to clean her mouth of the taste of Jill's death. Elise spit the minty foam out and watched it squirm down the white porcelain bathroom sink.

She touched her almost perfect lips. *One more secret for a secret life.*

Pissed, she rinsed her mouth out and spit again, splattering the mirror with little specks of foam.

"Screw you, Mister Steal My Name, and your three-story face of a fear-filled house. You turned me into a Firling named Elise. We will see who gets the last laugh now."

Forty-three ways to pay you back, you asshole.

By the time she put her white coat on, she felt good. Pissed off was much better than sorry for her dead self.

The clock said 5:12 a.m.

Five years out from surviving her kidnapping, she really was Elise Phillips even in her own mind.

Jill Vickery who? That chick was dead and gone, buried in an empty grave in Glenwood Springs even if the mirror claimed otherwise.

She walked to her car and kicked the front tires clear of snow.

Elise liked the new her better in some ways, to tell the truth. Her new identity allowed her the bare honesty of authenticity in many regards. She had reinvented a barer version of herself. The makeup washed clean.

What was the use of a mask really? Life was short and painful. Why should she waste a minute of it pretending to be someone she wasn't anymore?

She kicked the right front tire again so hard that the ice on her windshield cracked.

So if anyone accepted that her time on planet Earth was marked, it was Elise. She already realized that. No one ever had time to live with falseness. Only, the joke was that most people didn't learn that until they were on their deathbed.

Having faced death once, twice if she counted the heart surgery, what was a third time? *Three strikes and I'm out.*

"I'm a cat with nine lives." She smiled.

Then she frowned.

"What the hell happened to my adorable cat?"

She slammed her fist on the windshield, and the crack spread. Unable to resist, she grinned and put her gloves in her pockets to expose her bare, but most certainly alive-and-well fingers. And as she cleared the rest of the ice away with her bare hands, she laughed.

She wasn't afraid of Fetal Strip Conference, Doctor Buhl, the Board of Shame, or any three-story house in some pathetic nightmare or vision. With a thud, the terror slipped off her shoulder and melted onto the sleet and snow beneath her feet.

She stomped her snow bootsright, then left, then right again to make it official.

Dimitri played subtly in the background with undeniably tantalizing support. Her favorite song called her out to the front of the line. It sang her the tune of a savior. It swayed her out to face her demons.

She made up her mind completely. Her intention shined big and clear in a blurry world of itty-bitty shadows.

"Bring it on, baby. Forty-three reasons you should fear me instead of the other way around, you asshole."

Then she slammed the driver's door shut and started the engine.

Four days. Fourteen hours. Twenty-two minutes.

ELEVEN

All of Me

JOLENE SQUIRMED in an attempt to re-feel her arm which had fallen asleep under the weight of Elliot's gorgeous little head. She moved it right and left to no avail. Then as the blood finally rushed back into her arm, the pins and needles took over. She swung it around in circles to speed up the process.

She tenderly caressed her baby's blond, soft hair that reached just below his ears and laughed about her futile attempts to cut it. Who was she kidding? She didn't have it in her. No scissors were fine enough to cut off a single lock of his precious tufts. She loved those back curls way too much. Of course, she trimmed his bangs here and there so he could see his toys. But that was all. Soon he would have a mullet if things stayed the same.

She smelled the baby lotion on his skin and the fresh cotton fumes of his freshly washed pajamas. This was her favorite smell in the whole wide world...her awesome little treasure. That much she knew was true.

She sang him a modified version of "Brother John":

"I love Elliot. I love Elliot.

Yes, I do. I love you.

I love Elliot very much. I love Elliot very much.

Yes, I do. I love you."

He opened his eyes and stole a glance of the mother he loved so much. A tear rolled down her cheek. She looked away so he wouldn't see her so fragile. She must be strong for him. All of her for all of him seemed a fair trade.

"Mommy. L-yut want hot ba-ba, K?"

"Of course, my little man."

She sniffed. Wiped again.

"Come help Mommy make your hot ba-ba."

She placed him on her hip and sang while they walked the four steps into the corner

49

she called her kitchen. She filled his BPA-free bottle with fresh organic milk and slowly warmed it on the stove. She hummed her tune, and he smiled in delight.

When the bottle was ready, she changed his barely-soiled diaper with another one. After his bottle, she bathed him.

"Mommy go wipe, wipe. Wipe your nose. Wipe your toes. Clean your ears. Don't forget the earlobes."

After Elliot sat happily settled into his morning cartoons, Jolene thought about her own breakfast. She searched the pantry high and low. Only Kiki-Chos remained. It would have to do. She poured her low-fat milk over the brown, little circles, sniffed the slightly spoiled milk, and ate her cereal anyway.

She looked around their apartment and groaned. "One day I will do better by you, my baby Elliot. I will make this all okay. Even if I die trying."

She sat down next to him on the couch, but it wasn't close enough. She lifted him tenderly onto her lap and whispered in his ear. "I love you, baby. Forever and always. Always and forever."

Then she pressed her fingers to her lips, kissed them, and passed the kiss to his cheekthe cheek she loved more than anything.

She had no idea a Range Rover hummed across the street and that the man inside watched her every move. Why would she? She was watching cartoons with Elliot without another care in the world.

Shaking his beady head, the cockroach on Jolene's windowsill slithered away from the disgust of the whole scene. Even he couldn't bring himself to stand the kind of vermin that watched the woman with the platinum hair and her baby. The mice scampered back up the heater vent to another room in the quadraplex, as far away from the parking lot as possible. Terrified by the evil it knew observed this place, it curled into a small ball and trembled. But the snake in the basement slept soundly; he couldn't have cared less. This was not his problem.

Across the street, warmly...almost too warmly, the man waited. The fullness of the villain's groin ached for her...his doll...the one.

Four days. Thirteen hours. Three minutes.

TWELVE

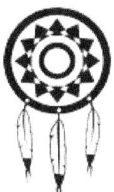

Would You Change?

THE FIEND WATCHED with intensity and frustration. The little boy kept getting in his way. If only the boy would move and get out of her lap, his view would be perfect.

As Jolene leaned in to whisper something in the baby's ear, Kincaid fumed. "What the hell is she possibly saying to that stupid baby?"

He clenched his teeth so hard his jaw clicked.

The engine revved from the pressure of his foot on the gas pedal. He pounded his fist on the black hand-stitched leather dash and looked away. How would he get her alone with that damn parasite in the way?

He gagged and dug his nails into his pant leg, cutting into the firmness of his thick, muscular thigh. Deeper and deeper he clawed into his leg, hoping that an answer surfaced to quench his suffering.

He must have her soon, sooner than originally planned.

Initially, he intended to watch her like this for a while. He wanted to take his time with this one. After all, what if she was the one?

If he rushed, he might make another mistake. Like with that short bitch five years ago. In the beginning, he thought she was worthy to wear his crown, to receive his blade of love, but he had been terribly wrong. She played along perfectly at first...shutting her mouth just like he said. She even seemed to enjoy it when he stitched her lips shut just to be sure she kept his secret like she had promised she would.

She liked it; he was sure. He smiled.

But then she left him. He grunted.

"Bitch."

He remembered where that had landed herdead as a doornail without his precious crown. Dead. Just like all the other falsies, stand-ins, and fakers.

How many times did he have to offer up his gift before someone finally saw his perfection? Before he finally got to share his royal kingdom?

This time would end differently, he promised himself with growing enthusiasm. He had all new tools, all new games to share. He pressed his nail in so hard that a drop of blood stained his pants, and he twirled his foot clockwise.

In perfect timing, he twirled his keys in his pocketsix times forward, six times back.

A boozer rapped on his window, and Kincaid jumped.

"Hey you. Hey, mister. Got any cash? I could use some cash. Throw a little change my way, okay mister?" The boozer spit on the windshield and wiped.

Kincaid rolled the window down and glared at the man.

The boozer stepped back immediately but voicing shaking, asked once more, "D…dollar?"

"If you will just shut up." Kincaid flung George Washington's face on the ground.

The irony forced a smile across his lips.

A little one dollar Washington for the boozer from Washington Park.

The number one played with him. One symbolized the need to stay positive and hand your fears over to a higher power.

"So, one for the boozer and one for the sweet little lady and her baby boy. Oh yes, and one for me. But who's the higher power, me or God?"

He grinned in the rearview mirror, knowing the answer all too well.

I am one of six Kings of the Underworld.

While he pulled away, he made up his mind. Yes. He would listen to the sign. He would stay positive that he was going to get her and that nagging little baby. They had no man to protect them. He was absolutely sure of that. That much he knew was true.

As for the fear, he liked fear. He fed off the smell, the taste of it, so he had no plans to hand that over. Not now. Not ever. He also knew that much was true.

Why would he hand over what he intended to share with all the others? His gift. His secret. His power.

The tires of the Range Rover rolled happily over the few scattered pieces of trash that littered Jolene's block. The half-melted greyish sludge parted easily under the weight of such a powerful machine.

Not a bug remained to be squashed. They were asleep far beneath the ground or had already left, too repulsed to remain here. Even the birds flew away from the park this morning. The scent of madness ruined the freshness of the usually clean Denver air for them. And the trees leaned away from the SUV while the male driver turned right at the corner. The stink of terror made them withdraw as their leaves trembled. But the snake rested peacefully in the basement of the quadraplex; he still couldn't have cared less. This was still not his problem.

Four days. Twelve hours. One minute.

THIRTEEN

Like We Never Had a Broken Heart

ELISE WALKED CALMLY to the front of morning report. Shoulders back and head held high, she set up the fetal tracing strip projector on the screen. She took a full breath and put her notecards in her back pocket.

Involuntarily, she checked her pulse. Seventy-two. *Normal.*

I am so not normal.

For a moment, she regretted that she had taken the time to make them or had wasted even one single precious fiber from some long forgotten tree-turned-parchment that had birthed those paper notecards. They were useless to her. From this place of strength, she didn't need them at all.

Her mind wandered for a moment to the paper makers of the world and pondered if they ever felt a sense of loss for the trees they melted and turned into wasted note-cardspaper tragedies never to be glanced at during presentations like hers.

She thought about the tossed aside colorful boxes from TV-dinner entrees that overflowed in the trashcans of efficiency apartments like hers. She grieved over the endless litany of useless advertisements she regularly tossed out back in the large bin for the boozers to search through.

Perhaps, she supposed, the Christmas roll paper makers felt the saddest of all, knowing their sacrificed trees were so quickly flung aside in lieu of the contents they had so beautifully hidden inside their doomed designs of merry-inspiring beauty. Next Christmas, she promised, her gifts would all be wrapped with a single red ribbon.

Checked again. Eighty-two.

She offered a silent apology to all the trees she had wasted in her life. Then unapologetically, she turned from the Board of Shame to face those thirty pairs of steaming eyes.

Twenty-nine actually. Intern Patterson beamed with anticipation.

Elise waved subtly at Wendi Patterson, her only friend in a room full of sharks.

Wendi cleared her throat and raised her eyebrows in a friendly way. In gratitude, Elise mouthed the words, "Thank you." Wendi just smiled bigger.

The rest of you bottom feeders, prepare yourselves; I am about to serve you and your sarcastic glances of pre-determined lack of approval. As for Wendi, I'll make you proud of our intern class.

The attending, Doctor Wilson, smiled too, but for a very different reason than the kind Dr. Patterson. He walked, skipped actually, to the front of the room. Then he sat down and laughed.

"Are you prepared, Intern Phillips? We surely hope you'll do better today."

"I doubt that you hope so."

Elise said, "Obviously." Pulse check. Sixty-eight.

Wendi giggled softly, and Elise began her presentation.

For the next hour, Elise drilled and was drilled on topics mostly beyond her current level of training. She asked poignant and perfectly timed questions of her superior residents. She provoked intelligent conversation and set the tone of an academic environment. When the ego driven comments of her peers tried to surface and undermine her intentions, either she or Wendi Patterson smoothly redirected the discussion to focus on the best safety-driven practice. Without fail, she honored the patient currently under review by continually moving her audience out of the rational-driven mind to a place of knowing, a place of being.

"Doctor Wilson," the Chief Resident said, stretching out his hand, "thank you. That's the best lecture I've gone to in four years. Man, you prepped that intern well. It's like..."

Elise gathered the cards from her pocket and turned around, suppressing a smile.

Doctor Wilson paused, speechless. He fumbled with fuzz in his pockets and avoided anyone's eyes. "Yes. Yes. She did–"

Wendi piped up. "Yes. Great job, Elise. It's almost like you actually cared about the patients. Dude, that was unexpected. Or not. Not from you. I think I'm a better doctor now. Cool."

After tossing her cards in the trash, Elise smiled, nodded, and walked out the back door and then went directly to Doctor Buhl's office.

"Thank you for such an incredible opportunity to learn," Elise said and meant it.

Doctor Buhl's desk was covered with such interesting papers she couldn't be bothered to look up and respond. But when Elise was half way down the hall, Doctor Buhl stared at the empty seat in front of her and sighed. She leaned back in her chair, lost in the memory of the day she had chosen to become a professor.

As Elise trudged the short walk across the street to her resident clinic, she noticed every person she encountered. *Are you the one he's chosen?*

The victim could be any female on her path.

Are you the one that monster plans to take? Has he already taken you? Are you already dead? "Damn."

If it's not you, do you know who she is? Is she your daughter or friend? Is her name Jill like mine used to be...before he took me? Have you ever met her at the store? Did you speak to her while she pumped her gas across from you yesterday? "Help me, God."

How will I find her? Why did he choose her? Why did he choose me?

Did I meet her once and think she was nice or stupid or fat or ugly? If I could have warned her, would I have? Did I tell her that a speck of broccoli was stuck between her teeth, or did I walk on by pretending not to notice so I could avoid her eye contact? "Tell me what to do, God."

You...lady over there, if her life depended on you, would you remember what terrible, horrible, and unspeakable act of torture happened to you? Or would you let her die so you don't have to remember what he did to you?

"In four days, he..."

She wondered how many times she stood next to a maniac without knowing it. How many times had she met someone who died later that same day and never knew about it. How many friends, family members, teachers, and spouses had been oblivious to the one last opportunity they had to save someone they loved.

"Who might have saved me but didn't?" she whispered.

After she had been kidnapped, the authorities never found so much as one clue to lead to the identity of her captor. For all she knew, he was just some guy who chose her randomly while she shopped down a random aisle at the grocery store.

Maybe even aisle six or seven in some random store on some random street could have been what killed Jill. Could have killed anyone she knew. Evil possibly lurked on any corner on any street and stood silently as it watched with eyes wild with desire to hurt, to punish, to annihilate, to torture, to mangle, to break.

"But why?" she muttered, shaking her head. "Why, God?"

Abusive parents? Abusive siblings? Mental illness? A psychopath?

She attempted to dissect the motivations of such a soulless being but then stopped. The only way to understand madness was from within the world of the mad. Her psychiatry rotation had taught her that much.

And yet sometimes, most terrifyingly of all, the horror itself served as the motivation. Some bad guys were just bad...dark kings, a void of nothingness without any identifiable reason.

But why? How?

Were they born with a circuit loose, a crossed wire, a brain built on evil synapses made by the dirty devil?

Stepping on the elevator, she thought about Lola Littleton, her favorite middle-grade literary heroine, and pressed the button for level three. How had Lola felt when she had realized she was a Firlinghalf-fairy and half-human? How did she come to terms with the fact that her evil uncle had tried to kill her at least a thousand times? How did Lola feel after Lil' Tig brought her back to life in the fifth book? When she finally shattered the villain into a thousand pieces at the climax of the sixth book? And if he was really dead, why did that author, some crazy doctor...supposedly...living in California, write a seventh book? Was Lola the real deal? Was Elise? Was Jill? Was Isla? And who the hell was Jane?

Would things end as well for her as they had for Lola? Would some crazy author write her story one day? Write her memoir? Or would she be the one blasted apart instead? Would her chest crack open again as her bare pig-goddess heart exposed its uselessness to the world?

Forty-three more shattered dreams that I can't bear to lose.

The ding of the elevator redirected her to current time and space. Only difference was that Elise Phillips walked into clinic minus another layer of her innocence painfully wiped away. For the next eight hours, she went numbly about the business of birth control pills and Pap smears for indigent women of Denver County.

As the hours ticked by, so did someone's last chance for survival.

She knew a killer lurked in the shadows, and time was running out. A woman's fate had landed squarely in her tiny, little hands, and no metal, gun-shaped speculum could save her now. Not the woman, nor Elise.

When she walked out of the last exam room, she whispered, "Forty-three reasons to grow up and face him and my memory. Jill, I'm going to save you. Save us both, actually."

A thought popped in: *Finding the answer wasn't really the problem.*

She placed the last chart in the outgoing billing pile and walked out, unconcerned about anything but a total stranger.

The rest of the Pap smears would have to wait a little while longer.

Facing the answer, that's the real problem.

Three days. Eleven hours. Thirty-two minutes.

FOURTEEN

Remember When

JOLENE EXAMINED the church ad closely. *Could I actually do that?*

The flyer from the local Catholic Church had arrived magically on her doorstep yesterday. Twice, she had picked it up and put it down immediately. This time, she looked more closely.

A mother's day out free of charge? Is that really possible? Could these people be serious? Why would they do that...for free?

There must be some kind of hook.

The possibilities flooded her. All the times she had wanted to cut her hair, take a walk by herself, just step away for five minutes, but suppressed the urge on Elliot's behalf.

She tried to think of once that she had chosen herself over Elliot but couldn't. Well, except one time, that was.

She had stepped out for just a minute to calm down. Elliot's incessant colic drove her to the brink of insanity one night. After stepping outside to cool down from shaking him, she came back in exhausted from sleep deprivation and oozing with guilt, and he was quiet. Too quiet. Lethargic. Unresponsive.

His temperatureone hundred and five degrees.

She rushed him to Denver General.

"He almost died, Mother." The pediatrician scowled, clenching his teeth and avoiding eye contact with her. When he stepped out of the examining room, he muttered to his nurse, "Colic. As if! Stupid fucking mothers."

Never she dared make the same mistake twice and, therefore, never left while he napped again. She never stepped away while he cried again. She never left him watching TV alone. She never, never, never...

She couldn't take that kind of chance, not again.

He was her everything. The bastard who gave her life meaning. She knew that much was true.

She read the paper for the fourth time.

Tomorrow morning between eight and noon could work.

She chanced a glance in the mirror. Her split ends formed a rat's nest. Nothing had touched their edges other than her mother's scissors in a decade. Her eyebrows touched in the middle. The circles under her eyes dark and haunting. Her nail beds cracked and inflamed.

I'm a big fat zero. Trailer park material.

She could maximize the time away for both of them, she decided. That way she would feel less crappy for doing something for herself.

Besides, yesterday, she had noticed a cockroach on her window for the thousandth time. Last night, she swore she heard the patter of a mouse scampering up the heater pipes. She could simultaneously fog the apartment for vermin and take a quick trip down the road to the hair salon.

She had noticed the sign in the window just yesterday. Six dollar haircuts...without the shampoo.

Well, surely she knew how to shampoo her own hair. And if she had enough time left over, she might risk a quick but hot, steaming soak in her cracked tub before she picked Elliot back up from the church.

She dialed the number and sighed. Her thoughts wandered from church to God. *What if...? God. Forgiveness.*

She used to love to feel the grace of God in church...before she disgraced herself with premarital sex and Jimmy's bastard, that was. But whores who get caught with their pants down and a penis between their legs deserve to be punished. She knew that.

She almost hung up the phone. Something made her hang on.

What if...? No. I can't. I'm too big a sinner.

She started pacing, first in anger, but then she noticed the cross on the wall.

With a glimmer of hope, she stopped pacing and crossed herself.

Maybe God is so merciful that He...?

She put her arms out wide and imagined nails in her palms.

Could he even forgive...me...broken and useless me...?

She tilted her head and looked up. *If I confessed my sins, said a thousand Hail Mary prayers, and prayed just right. Just right. I'd pray just right if I knew how. Please, God, show me how to win your love back. I'd do anything. I'd suffer anything.*

She saw the roach scuttle across the floor directly toward her and gagged.

"God help me. Help my baby," she begged.

Marcus Kincaid watched with curious delight while his future doll inspected her body. The brat must have fallen asleep because she was finally alone. She played with her hair and toyed with her fingernails.

He twirled his pen six times forward, six times backward.

His pants tightened in delightful anticipation when she placed her arms out to the side like she was offering her body up as a sacrifice.

He tapped the fine leather dash in rhythm to the music and cooed.

She must be getting ready for me. Look at her prancing about like a schoolgirl. She must sense my presence. She wants me too…

His desire to feel the smoothness of her skin multiplied. His mouth watered at the thought of tasting her…just a lick of her fine porcelain skin. A warmth filled his groin. It pulsated with possibility.

Look how wrong they were; look at my manhood now.

He caressed his throbbing spear to flame the fire within.

He must have her, sooner than planned, or he would explode, shriveling back into fearful nothingness. *Kings don't shrivel.*

Up and down, faster and faster, he thrust his favor onto her.

Pictures of delight surged like the ocean tide, each wave more powerful, more fulminant than the last. The vision of his masterpiece, her in perfect form, molded like clay in his glorious hands. He imagined her still, perfectly quiet, frozen forever as his untainted doll of love with lips closed in eternal silence.

With a final surge, his thrusts ended.

The Range Rover, less than pleased, revved in disapproval, but Kincaid didn't notice. He was too busy inspecting the liquid fruits of his labor of love.

Three days. Nine hours. Six minutes.

FIFTEEN

Over My Head

WENDI PATTERSON WALKED into Labor and Delivery for night-shift call totally pumped. After Elise's awesome presentation, she wanted to learn her chosen profession even more while serving the women of Denver County. Her chest puffed out, and she grinned while she picked up her rounding list and joined the others in the L&D Board Room.

One by one, they discussed tonight's cases of significance.

In Room One, a young, wealthy Caucasian woman labored actively, about to deliver. She had a known history of drug abuse and non-compliance with prenatal care. So far, her labor had progressed well without augmentation. Thus, despite a positive cocaine drug screen, things were otherwise uneventful. Child Protective Services representatives had made it very clear that the infant would be a ward of the state upon delivery.

Farther down the hallway, the staff in Room Four awaited the transport of a critically ill patient in severe respiratory distress. She was a nurse from Pueblo who had contracted the flu while working over the Christmas holidays. Colorado Spring's hospital was on divert, so Saint Lutheran's was the closest tertiary care center. The woman's influenza-related pneumonia threatened imminent pulmonary compromise. The head of ICU expected to intubate her immediately upon arrival...and could only hope for the best. Things looked dismal according to the in-flight paramedics. Despite oxygen, her pulse ox readings continued to decline. Her baby, at twenty-three weeks gestation, was too early to survive delivery. If they lost the mother to Influenza, both would surely die.

In Room Three, a recently delivered and previously healthy woman in a hypertensive crisis remained in guarded condition. All attempts to control her blood pressure with intravenous medications had been minimally successful, at best. Her eclamptic convulsions started about four hours after her delivery via an emergency C-section. The last seizure had occurred one hour ago, but her mental status still appeared altered.

The team awaited MRI results, which were expected to confirm she had survived a serious stroke.

"If you can call living with permanent mental dysfunction...survived, that is," the most senior resident who was presenting rounds said. She shrugged her shoulders and moved on to the next patient.

The nurse from Room Seven wheeled her patient, an undocumented immigrant field worker, to the OR for a repeat C-section with an unknown prior surgical history. The woman's broken English afforded an inadequate history. But labor was labor, and the risk of observing her contractions with a prior C-section was just too high. Due to religious preference, she had refused all consents for blood transfusion...no matter the cost. The counseling she received in English for possible complications had been suboptimal due to a lack of in-house translators. The telephone company's translation line was down for repairs and would be unavailable until 0700 in the morning.

In Room Eight, a diabetic woman with extremely brittle glucose readings and a very large baby waited patiently for her induction of labor. Her water bag needed breaking, and her cervix needed stripping.

Most of the post-operative patients on the floor seemed to be doing sort of okay at the moment. Only time would tell if that changed. Two possible, major problems brewed. One patient's urine output had recently dropped below the acceptable range. The other woman in question still oozed a significant amount of blood after her vaginal hysterectomy that had been performed this morning. The possibility that both women would require re-operation tonight could not be excluded at the present moment.

"Good luck, doctors. I'll be sleeping in the call room. Do not page me unless someone is actually dying," the senior resident said and walked away.

The others shook their heads and then walked away, too.

No one asked a single question before splitting off to do his or her assigned tasks. The third year resident left for the OR. The second year trudged over to evaluate the post-op patients.

Wendi sat down and stared at the three charts assigned to her.

She clicked the binder of one chart open and closed over and over again.

After fifty clicks or more, she called over the charge nurse and asked for help. "Melissa," she confessed, shaking her head, "I have no idea what I am supposed to do. Help me. Help me not screw this up."

Silence.

Wendi swallowed hard. "It's my very first shift, and I don't have a freaking clue what I am supposed to be doing."

Melissa sighed. "Just act like you know what to do, and believe it or not, one day you actually will."

"But..."

She grinned. "Go one by one, from room to room, and meet each of your patients. Start at the beginning. Bring the chart and read it while you talk to her. Go on then."

Wendi wiped her sweaty hands on her nonabsorbent scrub pants. *Too wet.*

She lifted her pen to sign her name on the resident on call dry erase board. *Too shaky.*

She stood and caught her balance. *Too light-headed.*

This was no medical school exam. Real people's lives were in her hands. She inspected her hands, trying to find an answer. Were her ten fingers worthy of those two little letters that came after her nameMD? Did she deserve such a title of honor?

She thought of a thousand other ways she could have been an MD: My Daughter, Mighty Dog, Marvelous Dancer, Mystery Detective, Muddy Dodge, Mischievous Deity, Miracle Dieter. The list was endless. Why did she have to become a Medical Doctor of all things?

How could she possibly serve these women? The shaking increased.

How would she ever feel safe making the calls, writing the orders, and catching the babies? She hung her head and sighed. Her palms were still sweating, her fingers still shaking. She tried to steady herself, but the room was spinning.

Her thoughts turned briefly to Elise Phillips, her hero. In this place, anyway. Elise would know what to do. She always did.

I wish I were more like her: so confident, so secure in who and what she isher true self. Just like MDs were supposed to be.

The call rang out. "Doctor to Room One for delivery."

Wendi examined her shaking hands, counting the digits over and over.

About two minutes later, a voice called out again. "Doctor for delivery. Room One, stat!"

"Shit! They mean me," Wendi said and ran across the hall.

On the other side of town, Elise Phillips prepared for her night shift, too. She soaked in a lukewarm bath after eating another frozen entree for one. She lit candles and looked from one item to the next in her small apartment.

She oriented herself to current place and time and then lay down on her bed, wrapped in the comfortable fuzz of her perfect white robe.

She recalled the advice of a brilliant mystical teacher. "*The first step to leading an intuitively guided life is a keen sense of the obvious. Always look closely at where you are before engaging in any internal work. The small details are always the most crucial ones. It makes all the difference. Always.*"

As soon as she closed her eyes, though, her thoughts increased in speed. *Who is she, this girl I need to save? Where will I find her? How will I save her? Will I have to go...there again? Where is there? And who is he? What does he want from her? What did he want from me? How did he choose me? Was it the same for her?*

Her eyes sprung open. This was no use. If she didn't find internal stillness, the visions would never come. Even a beginner at internal work knew that. The harder she tried to push, the further she would be taken from the goal.

She sat up and muttered, "How else can I help her? What else can I do for her now?"

One by one, she traced the line of the staple track scars down her chestforty-three. Each puncture site gave her another measure of strength, another reason to set her intention.

She bothered not to count the scars; she knew their number perfectly by heart. It branded her brain. It coated her soul. It summoned her will. It maximized her fortitude.

Forty-three. My least and most favorite number.

"What?" She swallowed, surprised by the observation.

How could she love and hate those forty-three scars at the same time? She had hidden her pain so well that it now required a map to be found. *I need a treasure map to mark the memory of how I became a pig-hearted goddess.*

A familiar thought popped in: *The problem is not to find the answers.*

Chills.

Brilliant by design, the disconnect of the subconscious from the conscious brain was exactly the connection she must repair.

More chills.

Or someone was going to die.

Another familiar thought followed: *The problem is facing it.*

The exact thing that had served her so well for so long was now her greatest obstacle.

Even more chills.

The fucking problem is facing it.

She stood up, shook her arms, and rubbed her hands to warm them.

She still had three nights left. Surely there was something else she could do. She looked at her bookshelf, and her *US Travels* book caught her attention.

But how do I face it?

She yanked the atlas off the upper shelf and opened it to the chapter for the Rocky Mountain Range. Her finger traced down her scar and then right onto the pages. *Where are you, you piece of shit? You heart stealer. You pig-goddess maker.*

Then she traced her scar again.

Face it.

Chills again.

She whispered, "Forty-three reasons for a Firlinga half-fairy, half-human pig-hearted goddessnamed Elise to find you."

She looked at the clock.

"To face you."

Three days. Five hours. Fifty-five minutes.

.

SIXTEEN

Closer to Love

THEY MIGHT HAVE FOUND Jill Vickery's dying body on Strawberry Lake, but first they had lost her at the Glenwood Springs SPCA. Saving the un-savable animals had nearly killed her.

Her last day at work, she went out to lock up the cages on the outskirts of the property. The next time she was seen, she was mostly dead on the bow of a boat on Strawberry Lake.

No dog's land, on the far eastern border of the forty-acre property was where they kept the possibly dangerous arrivals. It was also where they contained the biters and terminally ill animals before they dragged them down *dead dog's row*.

Pit bulls, chow mixes, neglected or abused dogs required longer observation before they were allowed to join the others in the main adoption-encouraging displays. After passing a personality and general health screen, the newcomers spent a few days with Jilllater destined to be known, even to herself, as Eliseto assist with their acclimation into the general animal population. She had a special way of smoothing the transition for the more nervous animals, especially the mistreated cats and dogs.

One kitten in particular befriended her. Madeline-the-Mangled. The kitten had barely survived the battle between her birth mother and a starving possum over rotten meat in the alley. The possum followed the recently delivered feral tabby back to her den and four yummy defenseless kittens. Maddie, the one-eared kitten, earned the title of sole-survivor of the whole ordeal.

Discovered by a kind woman just a few days after birth, the kitty arrived at the SPCA critically dehydrated and severely infected around the base of what used to be her ear.

Jill, who worked part time while attending the local community college, nursed the critter back to life. After eight weeks of bad luck, the only person Maddie would go near was Jill. So far, all attempts at bringing her into the general population had failed. The director feared the chewed-up kitten would never find a family after her miracle survival story. Doomed to be gassed after such an incredible story, Maddie was scheduled on Wednesday to be executed along with countless other unwanted cats and dogs.

Jill Vickery adopted her on Tuesday instead.

She signed the papers but never made it home. The mangled kitten, much like Jill, was never seen again.

When Elise Phillips woke up in recovery from her heart surgery two months later, only God knew what had happened to the feline.

Elise thought of Maddie and smiled. Sweet, sweet Maddie.

Elise marked the distance from Glenwood Springs to Strawberry Reservation, Utah on her map. Somehow, he abducted her from near Glenwood Springs. That was a no-brainer.

Then he took her to a three-story house. The one from her vision.

Then, he did whatever he did to her.

A memory returned. Cramped in an enclosed space with dirtied feet. Her heart pounded. She considered suppressing it further. Never remembering. Walking away before her feet got even dirtier.

Fingers to her neck—one hundred and twelve. *Face it.*

Immediately into biofeedback mode. *Too fast, girl. Slow it down. You got this. Remember Dimitri, baby. The whole night through, right?*

She glanced in the mirror.

You survived, remember? At least Elise did. There you go.

One hundred and four.

There you go. Better. Ninety-two. *Even better.* Eighty. *Perfect.*

I love you, Dimitri. I know that much is true.

From wherever "there" was, she had escaped, she now knew, in a Lexus SUV to the marina at Strawberry Lake Reservation in Utah. She wondered whatever happened to the Lexus and why the police never questioned her about it. Maybe they didn't know about the SUV?

She marked the locations on her map. She figured she must have made it on one tank of gas in the SUV. So the place she was held must be within three hundred and fifty miles from Strawberry Lake Res. She drew a big circle around the general area and sat back to examine her work.

Glenwood Springs Police Department?

Hands trembling, she picked up the phone.

Can I face this?

Her heart pounded in her ears. Swish, swish, her murmur gathered power, and she almost hung the phone back up. *Must face this.*

What if they harassed her? Didn't even answer her questions?

She dialed the number, taking slow deep breaths that never seemed to be enough.

Left hand on her carotid artery to mark her pulse, she gulped more air.

"Glenwood Springs Police Department. How can I direct your call?" the operator asked.

Elise swallowed. Ninety-nine.

"Agent Blackwater please." She blew the air out and guzzled more.

"He's not in at the moment."

Sigh. Ninety-five. Slower breaths now.

"Would you like to check back tomorrow or leave a voice mail on his machine?"
One hundred and four.

She almost hung up again. Something, or maybe someone, stopped her.

Face this. Face him.

"It's rather urgent, I'm afraid," Elise pushed.

"And?"

"Life or death. Mostly death if you must know." Fingers to her neck.

"I'm listening."

Her pulse increased to one hundred and ten. *I'm okay. I survived this.*

She walked over to her CD player and popped in her favorite greatest hits album. *I love you, Dimitri. Where would I be without you?*

"Mostly dead with Jill," she muttered.

"Excuse me? What?"

"Nothing, sorry. Never mind. I'll leave the message."

"Then I suggest you do," the operator said. "He checks it throughout the night, but I didn't tell you that, okay?"

"Our little secret." Ninety-four. *And by the way, it may just save someone's life.* She looked at the CD cover and smiled.

"I'm connecting you now. Good luck, Ma'am."

Elise left the message, her voice cracking. "Officer Blackwater, I'm not sure you will remember me, but I'm pretty sure you will remember an old friend of mine, Jill Vickery. I think I have some information that might help you find her kidnapper."

She hung up. Eighty-three. *Face this.*

Elise swayed side to side to the soothing music. Her heart rate returned to normal. Seventy-two.

"For you, for me," she sang. All the way to the bathroom, she danced.

No pig-hearted goddess for you, lady. Know it as one. Blessed we'll be.

She twirled and leaned down to shimmy across the edge of the bath.

I had a vision. A perfect vision of light.

"I'm going to save you even if it kills me. Again," she whispered and dropped her clothes to the floor while the lyrics played in her mind. The hot water burned her toe, and a throbbing memory returned.

People on a stage. Loving hearts ablaze.

She checked her pulse. Eight-two. Then she climbed in the tub.

Three days. One hour. Eleven minutes.

SEVENTEEN

Dust in the Wind

KINCAID STARED at the front of his house. He stood silent, hands to his side, glaring at its face. He twirled his keys forward and back six times each way.

He felt better immediately.

For a moment, he expected a tongue to roll out the front door and lick his face. He laughed, curious of how he would respond to such a grand welcome.

He stuck his tongue out and licked the air back. The front door remained closed. His momentary relief disappeared.

He spit on the snow. He couldn't be sure, but he thought the upstairs draperies blinked back in disgust.

Fuck you. I'm moving as fast as I can. If I take the baby, what the hell will I do with him? I guess I will have to kill him before he cries.

He imagined the desperate cries and shuddered.

He twirled the keys again. Six. Six. Six. Six.

That's better. He twirled them six more times...just in case.

He would simply rather die than suffer the sound of a baby crying. He picked up a stray tree branch and snapped it in two. *Better still.*

Then he could take his time with his doll. *As much time as it takes...to do it perfectly...without distraction or noise.*

Slowly, he trudged up the three stairs to the front door. He looked up the main stairwell to the blank, white wall at the top threshold and decided it could use some art. Something symbolic. Something that only he would get. The kind of art he liked best couldn't be hung on proper walls in proper houses in proper neighborhoods like this one. He imagined thick streaks of crimson paint. He could use a little blood and hide it behind a painting. No one but him would know. *Better still.*

A big, black clock would do nicely. I can already sense it ticking.

Then he turned his attention down to his playroom, down to his personal sanctuary, down to the place he reigned King. *Six. I am one of six.*

He smelled the subtle scent of bleach as he descended. It was not his favorite smell, but surely it was better than the alternative.

He knocked on the heavy wooden door six times before he unlocked the bolt. Then he typed the entry code into the keypad. He took out his keys, turning them six times forward, then six times back in the second safety lock.

This apparatus was a new addition ever since that short bitch escaped. That short, curly-haired liar that had died in the hospital three hundred miles away. Thankfully, that traitor never had a chance to tell a soul about him and his little party room.

He visited her grave in Glenwood Springs several times. Stupid fucking cops didn't even notice him at the funeral, blowing her dust in the wind.

How she got out that night was still beyond him. It was almost as if she vanished like a ghost during one of his parties. Without a trace, he lost her in the big wide world of dirty bother.

Since then, he had taken five other dolls. None of them even came close to lasting as long as Jill had. She had almost been the one, but then she wasn't. She was just gone. *Traitor!*

His nostrils flared. Then he spit on the snow again.

He wasn't stupid. He knew the house was ashamed of him. Even the toilet mocked him with its stinky shit-water every time he flushed his feces down. He could hear the pipes roaring at him from behind the walls. The voices in the heater vents laughed at his failure, his uselessness, his impotence, and his dung-coated life.

His power at work meant nothing to him. His disdain and exploitation of the African people and their culture never satisfied him anymore. Once, it had quenched his need to spread pain, to manipulate others, but no longer. The exploitation of the resources and manual skills of these poor people filled his pockets but not the emptiness that haunted him in the middle of the night.

"I can be so much more. I know," he promised the stairwell.

As the largest importer of African goods in the US, he owned the market and profited from the poor education, ill health, and powerlessness of countless rural African communities.

An image popped in: the dance, drumming thumping of the natives, mocking him with their flailing moves. He stuck his fingers in his ears and shook his head rapidly side to side.

"Shut up! Shut up! Shut the fuck up!"

He reached into his pocket and turned his keys. Over and over, he repeated the maneuver. He pacedsix steps forward, six back until his mind quieted.

Then he went into his cold chamber room to visit his dolls. The penetrating chill of his deep freezer invigorated him, and he forgot about all six fingers pointing at him.

One by one, he peered into their blank, adoring eyes. He caressed their icy skin. He traced their fingers down to the tips and held on for dear life.

He ignored the stench of decaying flesh and smiled.

Passion filled his man-sword as his excitement rose to meet his vigor. *So much better*. He set his keys aside and got down to business. If only he had a Queen to rule them with, then everything would be okay.

Soon, so soon. We will have her.

.   .   .

Three days. Zero hours. Thirty-six minutes.

EIGHTEEN

Give Your Heart a Break

JOLENE WENT to check on Elliot. Before she reached the curtain and peered in, the feeling of love surged through her body. She watched the slow rhythmic rising of his chest while a tender tingle filled her own. A space of peace rushed in and cracked her breastbone wide open.

Her fingers felt lighter. The air smelled cleaner. The carpet glowed with innocent perfection as the walls glimmered with clean and pure delight.

Then she looked back at the phone. Its outline, dirty and dark, filled her with dread. She shuddered.

She glanced back at Elliot. Tender, soft, lovely.

Then the phone. Evil, slimy, rank.

Who was she kidding? She deserved this payback for her sins, her impurity, her failure, and her open knees. The price she would gladly pay time and time again to keep her bastard.

She nodded her head and smiled. She could do this for him. That much she knew was true. For all eternity, if forced, she would stand in the heart of Purgatory for one more glance of her Elliot. She scoffed at the devil for his useless attempts to thwart her love for the blond-haired beauty she held so dear.

Elliot Grace Barton. Sure the middle name was a bit feminine, but so what? He was grace; he was pure love. The name fit him perfectly as far as she was concerned.

"Elliot Grace, I love you. Forever and always. Always and forever." She kissed her fingers and touched his cheek–the cheek she loved more than anything else.

She sighed and returned to the slimy phone that filled his bottle. The phone that padded his diapers. The phone that washed his sheets. The same phone that forced her to speak lie after lie about herself in exchange for her baby, her Elliot Grace, her bastard.

Then she nodded once more in acceptance of her punishment.

She was ready and willing to accept it.

The mouse scampered back down the heater pipe to feel closer to the warmth which filled quadraplex unit C where the light-haired baby lived. The cockroach stood up and stretched his antennae, trying to get closer to them. Something made him want to come out from hiding from underneath the couch and peer out despite the danger of being squashed by the clever lady.

The trees leaned in too, hoping for a moment more of the smell of love that oozed from the room where Elliot Grace Barton slept. The heavens gazed with unfaltering devotion for the unblemished child. The wind outside whistled a lullaby of pleasure for the delight of being present outside his window.

Yet the snake in the basement slept peacefully and full-bellied, oblivious to the creatures upstairs; he had caught a tasty mouse for dinner and couldn't have cared less.

NINETEEN

Part of Your World

ELISE SLIPPED EASILY into her lucid dream-like state. In the background, one of her favorite Dimitri songs played peacefully. Her forehead tingled slightly. She felt a light but oddly cool pressure sweep over her right arm. This was no normal dream. Things were too slow. Too normal. Too clear.

Lucid. I'm lucid.

She looked down at her hands and examined the creases and folds. The interconnecting complexity of the multi-directional lines prompted introspection despite her altered state of connection.

How intertwined are we? Are we just like the lines on my hands?

"For You, For Me" played on in her mind.

Are we all interwoven in some divinely beautiful dance? How much does my lifeline depend on everyone else's?

Another draft of air that smelled like mint.

Or do we just cross each other, oblivious and unaffected? Where do I begin and end? Am I really three times your love?

A waft of rose petals.

If the others weren't here, would I be? Are we all fractions of one being...pretending to be separate? Or are we really distinct and uniquely finite entities? How far have we come from our original state of eternal love?

The smell of ocean spray.

She suddenly realized she was no longer awake.

Dimitri, baby. Here we are. Lucid.

Even in her vision-state, she reached up to check her pulse. Ninety-four.

That's okay. My dark-skinned Latin lover, get me through this.

She looked up from her hands and surveyed her surroundings. The packed snow beneath her feet covered the tops of her snow boots like she had been standing here for years.

And then she realized she had. Five years exactly.

The problem is not to find the answer.

Jill stared at the face of the three-story house while Elise observed from within her sleep-like state.

What do I really know to be true?

An infusion of hot chocolate and marshmallows.

She felt in the middle of and outside of her dream all at the same time like some glorious mushroom-tripped hippie experience from her Widespread Panic-loving days.

Jill died here. Elise survived and moved on. Or did she?

A wolf howled in the distance, declaring its song of support. A butterfly landed on her nose, stopping to rest its wings. The tail of an alligator slipped into the icy water of a pond not too far away. A yellow-headed blackbird squawked and flew away.

What? This is Colorado, not Florida.

The problem is to face it.

The scent of a dwindling fire. The sound of embers crackling and giving way to the smoke of its final surrender.

She noticed the warmth of her thick jacket and sank into its padding.

It was the ski jacket her mother gave her when she still did things like snow ski. *Oh the irony.* She stepped back and laughed so hard that she almost woke herself up. The monster of darkness killed the strong-hearted Jill; Elise, the weak pig-hearted goddess, survived. *Interesting.*

She glanced back at the house.

Can I, the vulnerable me, face you?

For a moment, she expected a tongue to roll out of its foul-breathed orifice and lick her. She expected the upstairs curtains to blink in disgust. Dust clouded her vision.

A whiff of bleach burned her nostrils. Not unlike the hospital, though, a scent of something more rancid brewed underneath the bacteria-free scent of Clorox. *Bleach-covered death.*

Elise knew about lucid dreams and understood their power as a portal to out of body travel. From here, she could go anywhere she wanted to, unencumbered by her body. She could control everything if she willed it so. And everything here meant something critically important.

If only she could dissect out the symbolic clues.

She didn't move.

She looked across the street, scanning for a Lexus SUV. Nothing.

She located the mailbox and looked for a number to identify the house. Nothing. A street sign, a license plate, anything to identify her surroundings. Nothing.

She trembled, terribly cold despite the warm jacket. Mucous-covered vomitus burned her throat. She checked her pulse. Ninety-one.

No, Jill. We don't have time for fear. Keep moving.

The alligator surfaced again and winked at her.

"Truth or dare, eh?"

She trudged up the three stairs to the front of the house and looked at the number over the door. Six.

It wasn't a normal house address. It was something like a shadow over the door. It whispered darkness. It branded the house.

A thought popped in: *portal of darkness. Six kings of the underworld.*

She heard a cry from too far away to localize it. "Help me, Jill. Help us, Elise!"

She scanned, trying to locate the voice. Then she squinted down the snow-covered hill. The burning rays of the sun were just below the horizon. The sun would be up soon.

She mumbled, "Remember, it's darkest just before dawn. Remember, Elise, Jill, both of us."

She willed to follow the scream.

Then she looked at her hands again. They were clean and warm like they had just came out of the bath. The smell of fresh soap filled her nostrils. Baby soap.

Immediately, she was somewhere new but slightly familiar. She looked at the walls of the room in which she stood. Numerous colonial style photos of wigged men. *Statesmen, Presidents, something official?*

She heard the scampering of a mouse in the heater vent and the quick crunchy movement of a cockroach under the couch. Far away, she sensed the slow slithering of a full-bellied snake.

She smelled rank, old bed sheets covered just barely by the scent of lavender baby wash. The phone rang and rang. The tone was harsh and discordant, and she covered her ears to stop the sound from getting in to hurt her anymore.

"Stop it! Stop ringing! Stop!" She reached for the cord to pull it out of the wall. "Fucking stop. You are killing me."

But then something pulled her away from her hate. A soft desire to hold onto hope rushed in. Her chest cracked open, and her heart beat good and strong and lovingly.

She looked at her forty-three staple tracks. Gone.

She stumbled back, shocked by the lack of her scar, and tripped on a Fisher-Price toy music player. The green handle flipped up, and the lights twinkled orange and green and red. A song played "You Are My Sunshine." The toy's plastic purple feet marched back and forth and then in a circle. "The Itsy Bitsy Spider. " "Must wash the spider out."

Flash! The toy broke into three pieces and went silent. "No, no. No!"

She checked her pulse and then her chest. Normal. No scar. *Where did the scar go? Am I still a Firling?*

"No, baby. You never were," a distant but familiar voice replied.

She stumbled back in the doorway of a small apartment. Not her own. The smell of baby powder invaded her nose. She gagged while it filled her mouth. She spit it out to no avail. "Down comes the rain. Am I the rain?"

She checked her heart rate. *Too high.*

"Oh no, my pig-goddess heart. Help! Help!" she screamed.

"But you don't have one, baby. You never did," the voice said.

The phone rang, and she coughed as the baby powder filled her mouth, poured out of her ears, and obscured her vision with talcum fear. She clapped to clear the powder. Or was it dust?

She fanned away the cloud and scratched at her eyes to clear them. The reflection in the mirror was not her own. A woman, tall with blond, straight, dry hair stared back at her, no scars on her bone-thin chest.

Oh my God. Am I her?

"Yes," the same voice said.

She's the one he's going to kill. It's not me. It's her. Her eyes, so blue.

She tried to scream but couldn't. Baby powder filled the room.

"Who are you? I mean, who am I?"

Then she remembered the baby.

What baby?

Her baby. The lady's baby.

His name?

"Elliot," the voice answered.

Desperate to find him, Elise screamed the name over and over. "Elliot! Elliot, my baby. I'm coming to save you, Elliot. Oh my God. Elliot. Breathe, Elliot, breathe!"

The phone shrieked again. Its harsh, bell-like tinkling dug into her brain. The sound, so unbearable, made her recoil. She must stop it.

She staggered back and screamed again. This time, the powder was gone. The apartment was her own.

Her desperation increased. "Elliot, where are you? Elliot, answer me!"

She grabbed the phone to throw it across the room.

"Hello," a man said on the other end. "Hello? Hello? Is anybody there? This is Officer Blackwater. You said you knew Jill...Jill Vickery. You said it was urgent. I'm calling you back Ma'am."

Elise gagged, her throat so dry. She took a sip of water and rubbed her eyes. *Dry. So dry. Like powder.*

Again, the man said, "Ma'am, are you okay? You were screaming for someone named Elliot? Are you okay? Is Elliot okay? Should I call nine?"

"No. Don't hang up." She shook her head and took another sip. "Please." Then she remembered where she was. She looked around her apartment and sighed.

I'm back. I'm back in my body.

She put her foot on the floor to stop the spinners and said, "Can you hold please, Officer? But don't hang up."

"Yes, of course. Are you sure you are okay?"

She reached for her journal.

Clue three—alligator, photos of men? hair-blond, baby-Elliot, number-six, phone-hate, powder-dry.

Her hands shook violently. The letters were all jumbled in her head. But finally, they made sense again, and the letters formed on the paper.

I feel drunk, but I'm not. I'm out of sync with my body. Come on, Elise. Get it back together; you can do this. You must do this. You must face this.

"Officer Blackwater, you are not going to believe what I'm about to say. But I...I mean...we need your help. It's a matter of life and death. Jill's death. My life. And a stranger—her life too."

. . .

Two days. Twenty hours. Forty-seven minutes.

TWENTY

Gold Dust Woman

SILENCE.

"Officer?" Elise asked. The lack of sound burned her face, seared her skin. Nothing but a deep breath.

"Officer Blackwater?"

"Here. I'm listening. Go," he finally answered.

"Can I come down there or you want to meet me?"

"Excuse me?"

"I'll meet you half-way?"

"For what, exactly?" the man asked.

"You are the officer who worked Jill Vickery's case five years ago, right?"

"Yeah. Who's asking?"

"I can't really say. But"

"Then I'm not sure how I'm supposed to help you, Ma'am. Listen, it's late. It's Friday night. Why don't you get some sleep, and I will call you back on Monday."

"No!" She cut him off. "She... I... I mean we don't have any time to waste."

She swallowed, and a sickening weight settled in her stomach. Fingers up. Ninety-eight.

"Okay then," he said. "You better have something big, or I'm hanging up and putting *Law and Order* back on."

She laugheda little too hard. Eighty-eight. "You watch that crap? But you're a cop."

"I know, but I can't help myself. It's really good." He laughed, too, but not as hard.

Elise had one chance to get this guy to help her. Ninety-two. "If I told you something I couldn't possibly know, would you meet me half-way between there and here?"

"That depends. Both on what you know and where *here* is."

"Fair enough," Elise said. "Like I said, I think I can help you find Jill Vickery's kidnapper."

"And like I said, I'm all ears."

81

"Okay, here goes. She didn't die. In fact, she's alive and well. Except for that useless pig-valve heart of hers."

Silence.

"I suspect I have your attention now, Officer Blackwater, so I'll keep going unless you stop me. She escaped from her captor and his three-story house in a Lexus SUV to Strawberry Lake Reservation that night they found her on that boat."

"How can you possibly know that?"

Silence.

"Answer me," the man said.

She gathered her courage. Ninety-six. She dropped her fingers and shook out her arms.

"Wait. What do you mean three-story house? Who are you? How do you know about his house? The car?"

Gulp. Fingers to the wrist. One hundred and four.

"Well? Still all ears here."

"Because I'm the one who drove it away from that godforsaken place."

Silence. When her words sunk in, he dropped his drink. "Lady, I just broke my only wine glass. Keep going."

"Did you hear me? Didn't you hear what I just said?"

She stifled her muffled cries and sat down cross legged on the floor. One hundred and ten.

"Jill?"

"You mean Elise." Gulp. Back on hands and knees.

"They don't tell us the new name. In fact, they don't tell us anything once they assimilate you into the system. Where are you? My caller ID says Denver. How the hell did you end up back in Colorado?"

"ERAS," she said, crawling slowly back to her bed.

"What does that mean?"

Fingers softly to her neck once at the edge of her bed. Ninety.

"I'm on my way. What the hell is ERAS? And where am I going, Jill? I mean"

"Residency match system. I'll explain it later. Just hurry. The clock is ticking. Here's my address: five hundred forty-seven Chaperito Street. I'm about three blocks from Saint Lutheran's Hospital. You know the area?"

"Yes. Sure. I'm about two hours away, but you already know that, don't you." He looked around the room for his keys.

"Hurry, Officer Blackwater. Hurry. I could start that way. I'm off work tomorrow."

"Nope. That could mean my badge. Not to mention your life."

"They said I wasn't allowed to go back home."

"Jill, I mean Elise, don't open the door for anyone until I get there. Don't worry. This line is secure. And obviously, he doesn't know where you are or you would already be..."

"Dead. Again. Yea, I know," she finished his sentence. Hands down to her side. No need to check. She already knew the rate. Seventy-six.

He grabbed the keys and a couple of boxes as he closed the door.

"Hurry, please."

"Since your escape, Jill, there have been at least five girls that have gone missing.

We… Well, at least I think it's him. But we can't catch a break with any of the cases. We can't prove the girls were actually taken. Just that they went missing. He hasn't slipped up once. Well, since you got away, anyhow." He locked the door.

"What? I had no idea." Ninety.

"Why should you? Remember, you're dead and buried six feet under the ground in a coffin in Glenwood Springs. I'm walking to the car now."

"Good point, really. I've been busy." She remembered a few dreams over the past several years. Dreams about a three-story house. "They weren't dreams," she whispered. Ninety-nine.

"What? In the car. Backing up now."

"Never mind. Just get here." She set the phone down and screamed. She reached the toilet just in time to throw up. She lay down on the cold, tiled floor and sobbed while his news set in. *The problem isn't to find the answer.*

That asshole was still at it. *The problem is to face it.*

How many girls had he killed? How many women had that evil house consumed? One hundred and twenty. One hundred and fifty.

Despite her misery, her protective instincts kicked in, and she attempted to lower her pulse. Ocean waves, Dimitri babynothing helped. She was just too pissed off.

She had one trick left in her bag.

She rubbed her carotid arteries to engage the autonomic reflex system. At one hundred and fifty-eight, her pulse was dangerously high. This rate would kill her in less than thirty minutes if left unchecked.

"Are you still there?"

"Yes." She gagged. "See you soon. Thank you for answering my call, Officer."

"No, Elise. Thank you."

"Hold on." She put the phone down again and breathed slowly in and out while she rubbed. She knew this maneuver would bottom out her heart rate, but that was surely better than no heart rate at all.

One hundred and eight. Better, baby. Remember, you survived this already. You're the only one...though. The only one. That chick and her baby are counting on you. If you can't do this...they die. And who knows how many more women.

She raised the phone back up to her ear. "Okay, I'm ready. Just get here. I'll be waiting up. Hope you like TV dinners, minus HBO. That's all I have."

Dial tone only. The cop had already hung up.

Sixty. That's better, baby. Yeah, yeah, I know it feels shitty, but shit is better than eating golden dust in a coffin.

She tried to stand but couldn't from the dizziness. In ten minutes, though, she would feel fine. And then…

Face it.

Two days. Twenty hours. Thirty-six minutes.

TWENTY-ONE

Peaceful Easy Feeling

MARCUS KINCAID LAY in his bed and stared at the ceiling. He laughed a little to himself, not quite sure why. Excitement? Anxiety? Even he didn't know.

The urge to go back downstairs surfaced. But he mustn't get lost in his passion; he knew that.

He picked his nose and flung the firm yet partially moist glob on the wall. The idea of his maid cleaning it pleased him. He felt better, easier and lighter. The urge to go down again almost passed. Almost.

He grabbed the rock on the bedside table and palmed it. Without looking, he twirled it–six times to the right, six times to the left.

The buzzing in his ears was definitely louder now. Soon, he suspected it would overtake his ability to think so clearly. He looked at his clock for reassurance.

Tomorrow at this time, he would have her heredownstairs in his chamber.

Then, all that was left to do was throw a party to drown out the buzzing voicesa lovely little wedding celebration that only he was privy to before he took her as his bride.

If she passed the first night, she would get a chance to live. At least a little longer, that was. If not, she would join the others in the freezer. Broken pieces of useless dolls.

Well, almost useless. He still had some uses for them.

Finally, the surges of his desire pulled too strongly. Like full tide, the waves of his passion washed over him.

He jumped up and went into the bathroom. He splashed on some cologne. Then he put some spearmint paste under his nose like they did on *Law and Order,* his favorite program.

Slowly, with mounting anticipation, he descended into the heart of his chamber.

He counted the stairs as he went.

"Six plus six. That makes twelve." He whispered, "That's twice as good as six."

At the keypad, he entered in his codesix, six, six.

"Six for me, six for her, six for mother."

He inserted his keys and rotated them–six times forward and then six times back. Just to be sure, he repeated the motions.

The deadbolt disengaged while he pulled back its rod from the space that sealed the opening to his kingdom.

I am the key that opens you, my doll-lock.

A clownish grin overtook his lips.

Invigorated, he went down and did what made him feel the most powerful to the frozen beauties, the same beauties who waited anxiously for their Queen.

He could almost taste Jolene's royalty in his mouth. He would do his work tonight in honor of her soon-to-be arrival.

He would show the other dolls how she would do better than they had. How she would keep her mouth shut, holding in her love and respect for his awe-inspiring manhood.

Her silent approval would be proof of his royalty, too.

He turned the handle to the icy chamber six times to the right and then six times to the left before he opened the refrigerator door.

The gush of rank frost-covered air oozed out of the small space and into the main basement area.

But all he smelled was the pure, refreshing scent of spearmint. Just like on his favorite show.

He chose the doll for tonight and positioned her perfectly for his show of grand power.

The others observed with glossed-over eyes focused intently on his graceful thrusting ballet.

In his final throws of ecstasy, he announced, "Jolene, I'm coming for you, my beauty. I'm coming for you."

Underneath the buzzing in his ears, he was certain they were clapping.

TWENTY-TWO

Send in the Clowns

WHEN KINCAID HAD TAKEN the stairs down, so did Doctor Wendi Patterson, the night shift intern at Saint Lutheran's Hospital of Grace.

She descended the twelve steps to locate the all-night staff-only cafeteria, hoping to get a fresh cup of coffee to wake up her sleepy neurons. She still didn't have a clue about what she was supposed to be doing, but so far, she knew what she had done.

She knew exactly whom she had almost killed with her ignorance.

"I'm a clown," she muttered and sat down for a brief moment of rest. Her legs ached from carrying the weight of her worry. Her hands, though, had stopped shaking hours ago; they could only quiver for so long.

She took her first sip of liquid energyblack, fire-hot, and straight up, without a hint of the sugary indulgence of flavored non-dairy creamer. She puckered up her lips at the bitter taste of overcooked beans and shrugged. *If this is fresh coffee, then I'm Betty Boop.*

"What is non-dairy creamer anyway?" she asked the cashier, who quickly went back to the business of filing her nails and chewing her bubble gum. *Pop.*

What the hell could creamer possibly be made from that requires no refrigeration? And why would an intelligent person ever drink it?

Boop-oop-a-doop. Let it go, Betty.

For a moment, she stopped her mind from wandering to terrifying topics that were still more benign than the business of saving...and sometimes killing, patients. Topics like cleavage-peeking cartoons.

But then it got the better of her.

She thought about petroleum-product-covered chicken nuggets made of mashed up cartilage and chicken by-products that clueless moms fed their innocent and unsuspecting children in the back seat on road trips. *Where's that little white dog of ours, Betty? What's his name? Bimbo. That's it.*

She gagged at the idea of packaged dried beef products on convenience store shelves that had been there for God only knew how long before they were opened and enjoyed by people who could never read the names of, much less understand the risks of, chemicals contained in that fleshy stick of dried meat by-product. *Nitrates. Ugh. Bet Bimbo wouldn't even eat it.*

"Bimbo. What kind of name is Bimbo?" she asked the lady at the register.

The cashier raised an eyebrow at the odd question but didn't bother to reply. Her nails couldn't afford the interruption. *Pop.*

Wendi looked at the spotless floor and wondered the long-term consequences of annihilating every still-killable bacterium on planet Earth as the rates of pediatric asthma and allergic illness reached epidemic rates.

She ticked her eyes back and forth like a cuckoo clock and laughed. *Boop-oop-a-doop.*

Then she frowned. She tossed her empty cup in the garbage. *Where's the freaking recycle, Bazooka lady?*

She thought about the massive numbers of children diagnosed with autistic-like syndromes after taking vaccines for illnesses not seen in this country for decades; the rocketing rates of unexplained premature ovarian failure in young women after taking HPV vaccines; the cloud-colored stripes across the sky that she noticed yesterday morning, which couldn't possibly be explained by common airplane traffic.

She shook her head and muttered, "The list is endless in this three-ring circus."

Then she poured herself another thick cup of black goo while trying to invert her knee and simultaneously toss her head back and flutter her eyes.

"Nope. No Betty here."

She took another bitter sip.

"Nope. Not fresh."

Still no response from the attendant besides gum smacking and popping.

What exactly is soy lethicin?

She decided she could survive without the liquid energy after all, coffee creamer substitute or not, and threw it promptly away in the non-recycle bin.

In a world filled with danger, surely the women of Denver County would not survive her as well. What was she thinking when she decided on this specialty? Two patients, mother and baby, that she could simultaneously fail with one fell swoop of her mistakes. All of a sudden, politician sounded like the perfect career for her. After all, she had always been the queen of this or that committee for everything from drug-use prevention to extracurricular activities.

Not even I can kill a debate opponent by messing up my speech, right? Damn, law school sounds exciting.

A tear welled up in her eye that she quickly wiped away. She wasn't sure what was worse, exhaustion or the mounting fear of going back upstairs and screwing up. Again.

"Boop-oop-a-doop," she whispered.

There was no time to cry. Flash! She was back on L&D one hour ago.

The delivery of the cocaine-snorting rich chick in Room One had gone well, initially at least. Baby delivered fine just like her textbook said it would.

But the placenta got stuck. Wendi couldn't get it out. By the time her third year resident got there, she had pulled off the flimsy little cord, and blood had spattered everywhere.

It splashed in her eyes. It coated the floor. It stained the walls red and painted her failure crimson.

Red, red, red. Proof of my incompetence.

The third year laughed at her and said, "Rookie mistake for the rookie intern. Better luck next time."

The rest of the team took the lady back to the OR to get the placenta out under anesthesia. And of course, the case went fine. Fine...after two units of blood and a lot of four-letter words directed at the stupid fucking intern, anyway.

She may have been the stupid intern, but she was way too tired for any fucking. Her joke made her laugh, and that gave her the courage to trudge the remaining stairs back up to the second floor where women and their babies depended on her to have better luck next time.

Hopefully she would.

As Wendi went back up to serve the ladies, Jolene took a call to serve the men. Then she said the things that were required to please the client in exchange for a super-sized box of name-brand diapers for a sensitive-skinned baby who drank organic milk.

As the client spilled his priceless pearl sins all over the floor, the towel, the whatever, she suppressed a gag because $5.99 a minute wasn't nearly enough money to listen to him enjoy it while she begged for another dose, another drop, another whatever.

Clenching her jaw and holding her stomach, she affirmed how much she enjoyed his body, his power, his control over her, his large and painful penis, his whatever. With revolting vigor, she convinced him that her worthless body ached for just one more moment of his touch.

She moved her hand from her stomach to her mouth. *Speak no evil.*

Her mother's three-monkey statue mocked her. One monkey had his hands over his ears. One had his fingers in his ears. The third monkey was shaking his finger violently at her. *No, no, no! Jolene, shame on you.*

She looked away. "If only it was that easy," she said to the cockroach that scampered across the floor. She wondered when it would get easier. How long it would take to get used to this.

She already knew the answer. Never.

She hid the phone in a drawer and gagged again.

Besides, she had enough diapers for the week now. The other scum could talk with someone else now. Tonight, she had swallowed all the slime balls she could possibly stomach.

The scent of baby powder drew her to the bed, and she grinned. Then she pulled back the covers and crawled into bed with Elliot. She placed her arm under his glorious buttercup locks.

Within seconds, tonight's sleep fell hard and fast on her.

In her dream, she chased Elliot.

Once she caught him, she twirled him in the air as she sang him his special song while he cooed.

"I love Elliot. I love Elliot. Yes, I do. I love you. I love Elliot very much. I love Elliot...v-e-r-y much. Yes, I do. I love you."

He giggled as he ran from her to his daddy, who waited with open arms. They hugged, and a moan of pleasure escaped Jolene's lips. A serene expression replaced her furrowed brow, exposing her pale but lovely features.

Jimmy turned to her and said, "I love you. I miss you, Jolene. Where did you go? Why can't I find you? Why did you leave me? Did you think I was a clown? Could you love me?"

Briefly, she awoke with muddled confusion, looked around the room, and quickly fell back asleep.

"Jimmy," she whispered. "I'm right here."

Then she snored.

After Officer Blackwater hung up the phone, Elise stewed in silent reflection. The seriousness of the situation was indisputable. She had gone from no connection to her prior life to calling the officer who had worked Jill's case those five, long-forgotten years ago.

She tried to remember him but couldn't. Couldn't even remember his first name. Really, should that surprise her so much? She had forgotten about being kidnapped for almost two months, escaping, and then almost dying in the hospital.

I mean died, don't I?

Jill died. Maddie, the mangled kitten, died too. Only Elise survived.

Slowly, she traced the scar down her chest again.

Then she lay down...just for a minute.

Flash-flash-flash! She stood in the center of a tunnel of light.

She looked down at the creases of her hands.

I'm dreaming. Shit. I fell asleep. Wake up. Pull yourself back to awake.

All of a sudden, her body was flush with the ceiling. She could smell the fresh paint.

What? What the hell?

She rolled over, mid-air, and looked down at her body sleeping on the couch. Her neck, contorted to one side, hung there. *Ouch, that's going to hurt.*

She swirled around the room, connected only by a fine and shimmering silver cord to the body below.

"Now I'm a Firling flying like the other fairies," she said and chuckled.

She flew upward faster than speed could measure, right through the ceiling. A peaceful song played in the background. It sounded more beautiful than anything she had ever heard.

Suddenly, she stopped in front of an old London-style telephone booth. Without hesitating, she knew what to do and stepped in, picked up the receiver, and held it to her ear. A buzzing came through. Then a crackling sound just like an old LP record player.

A voice on the other end spoke. "We are all here," it said. "We are waiting for you to find us."

She panicked. Her heart pounded. Ninety-nine.

"What? How can I have a heart out of my body?"

"Hush, you are only a heart pretending to have a body. Your heart is real. The body is just an illusion," it demanded as several overlapping sounding voices melted together. "Silence is the key. Face him. Be impeccable with your word. Be impeccable with your intention. Place all your focus on your true heart. Your body means nothing. Only your honorable heart will survive. That was always the agreement."

The line went dead. Her pulse pounded harder but not faster in affirmation. "Yes, that was the agreement."

A wolf howled.

The phone rang again. This time the voice said, "Elise, it's Blackwater. I'm here. Let me in."

She lifted her neck up slowly from its sideways position. The heaviness of her physical form shocked her. When she stood, the room seemed brighter than usual. Tiny silvery sparkles filled the air.

She checked her heart rate. *One hundred and two. Fine.*

Still rubbing her sore neck, she opened the door and caught her breath. "Officer Levi Blackwater." The words just oozed out.

Guess I do remember. Her original notes returned to her. *Not blue jeans.*

He smiled but only with his bright eyes.

She stepped back and muttered, "Um, blue. Scrubs are blue. So I'm wearing blue. But I spilled some burrito."

His cheeks joined his eyes in the smile.

She bit her lip and, unable to resist, smiled with her eyes to match his. Surely she had said enough stupid words about burrito stains. One hundred.

The long black-haired and bronzed skinned man stepped inside the room and cleared his throat. He traced his finger across the brown stain on her pocket, and finally his lips joined the cheeks and eyes.

Elise just held onto her chewed up lip and wouldn't let it go. Ninety.

"You should really ask for some I.D., Elise," he said while searching for a place to set down an old cardboard box.

On the top, the box was marked "Jill Vickery" in black marker.

"Right there is fine," she said and let her lip go. One hundred and five.

With a thud, the box dropped to the floor.

Two days. Eighteen hours. One minute

.

TWENTY-THREE

If I Knew Then

ELISE FELT PULLED to yet terrified of the box all at the same time. Unable to look at it any longer, she looked back at Officer Blackwater instead. *Better.*

Her eyes involuntarily followed the strong curve of his broad shoulders down to his hands. *Much better. Those hands.*

"Coffee, water, or expired milk?" she offered, pulling her eyes back to his chiseled face while she gestured toward the kitchen.

"No, thank you," he replied.

"Okay then," she said as she offered her hand. *My hand.*

"Officer Blackwater. Call me Black or Blackwater as you prefer. The officer stuff is ridiculous under the circumstances really."

"Okay then," she said. "Elise. I go by Elise now even in my own mind."

"Well, I'm all ears. Like I said before." He grinned and mimicked a howl."

She laughed nervously. "Weird, but okay." She remembered the burrito comment earlier. *Maybe not so weird.*

"Tell me what I came here to hear, Elise."

"Okay, but I'm afraid my information comes from an unusual source."

"Yes, go ahead. Mind if I turn the TV off?"

"No, but…"

When he bent down to work the machine's control, she noticed the scar on the backside of his neck. Deep. Serious. Probably from a knife. Probably almost killed him.

He didn't miss a beat.

"Gun and knife club, Elise. Not Jill. Courtesy of a wigged out drug dealer, I'm afraid. You were saying."

So weird. Burritos, howling, vision. All weird.

"Saying… I was saying…"

All of a sudden, the absurdity of the situation dawned on her. She was about to tell another human being that she had visions and that her visions were telling her that her kidnapper was about to strike again. The same kidnapper she had been unable to remember anything about...until now, all of a sudden.

I'm a freaking nut job. Yep, psych ward here we come. Bye-bye, medical degree.

She had no proof, absolutely none, other than her spiritual ravings that some blond, skinny chick and a baby named Elliot were in mortal danger from some guy whose face she couldn't even remember.

For a moment, she considered taking it all back.

"I was just kidding. Want to get a drink instead?" The invitation sounded pathetic even in her mind. *But...those hands touching mine. Please.*

Face the problem. Be impeccable. I agreed to be impeccable.

Shit. What if she was right? What if she never said a word and some helpless lady died because of her weakness, her inability to face her own past, the same past she had already survived.

She didn't have much of an excuse to stand on, and she knew it.

Fuck. I'm really going to have to do this. Do they have CD players in psych hospitals?

She took a long hard swallow and started pacing. *I'll miss my music for sure.*

He stared at her without blinking, his eyebrow raised.

"Um," she started, "I think what I have to say might sound a little weird." *I'll miss this pathetic apartment too, I think.*

"Like burrito weird?"

She giggled, still looking at the floor, unable to meet his gaze.

"Okay. I'm good at weird," he said.

"Maybe not this weird."

"Okay. Over a beer, perhaps?"

"Yea, that's probably a good idea." She slapped her thigh and laughed. "Or maybe a shot instead?"

"Only if it's a burrito shot." He winked and offered a thumbs up.

"Tequila it is." She wanted to but didn't wink back. *Those hands.*

They trudged down her back stairs, past the stumbling boozers, to the liquor store one street over. They left with a six-pack of beer and a bottle of tequila in silence.

Finally, when he couldn't take it anymore, he said, "Changing Woman has worn a heavy white skirt this winter, huh?"

"Who? Skirt? What?" Elise said, suddenly aware of her unflattering scrubs.

"Mother Earth. It's been a heavy winter this year."

"Oh, I understand now. Sorry. What tribe are you?" She turned to face him and locked eyes.

"Navajo. My mother was born in a hogan," he said.

Elise assumed he probably meant a traditional Navajo home of mud and brick. She nodded. "Go on. Please."

"It has been many moons since I was home, but I can still see my mother's wrinkled face scowling at me about some thing or another when I close my eyes." He laughed and gave Elise his best furrowed brow.

. . .

94

This time, she couldn't resist. "Like this?"

"Perfect. You look just like her. Except the hair, the face, the beautiful face." He touched her lips faintly, right where the scars were that no one else knew about. But he knew. He was there.

Elise coughed. "How did you end up so far from your home and your mother's disapproving glares?"

He started to answer but stopped himself.

"That's okay. I have my fair share of secrets too. Later. But I'm guessing it has something to do with this scar."

He nodded so slightly that anyone else would have missed it.

She couldn't resist touching his neck.

He never pulled back. Nodded again. Less subtly.

More silence.

She rubbed her nose and kicked the snow nervously.

"Yes and No. That's a very long story. Perhaps another day. Let's talk about you. More importantly, how did you, of all the people on this lovely planet, end up back in Colorado after…?"

"Well…"

"No, you go on. Please."

Elise went on to explain ERAS, the electronic computer system that assigns medical students to residencies, not unlike a really expensive computer-dating scheme. She joked about how she always picked the wrong guy even without a computer's help.

They both laughed, and she dropped her hands to her side. The right one accidently touched his.

He still didn't pull back.

"Oh, I bet the Feds were pissed." Blackwater laughed so hard he snorted, and he grabbed her hand intentionally. "You back here after everything they did to get you out."

She touched his neck again with the other hand.

"I know, right? But maybe there was another reason I ended up here. Blackwater, what do you think about destiny?"

"Like I said, I'm Navajo, so I believe every thing, every animal, every tragedy serves a purpose."

"Okay. Now you go on. Please." She squeezed his hand.

He squeezed it even tighter. "It is no accident I am here or that you are there. That cockroach is a message. That tree is whispering in your ear. A mouse has meaning. A snake another. A cat. A bird. The wind is trying to get your attention. When we speak, we say more than words. When we touch, more than our skin connects."

Authority oozed from his voice.

She blinked to see him more clearly. *These hands touching my hands. These eyes seeing me.*

Deeply, she gazed into his dark, black eyes, taking note of the smooth, age-less appearance of his honey-glazed skin. So deeply, in fact, she saw herself in their reflection.

She nodded and took one large, strength-gathering gulp of saliva.

"Then you are exactly who I need to help me, to see me through this. Who she needs. Who baby Elliot needs. Help me, Blackwater. Help us all."

Two days. Seventeen hours. Twenty-two minutes.

TWENTY-FOUR

Look What You've Done

WENDI WAS PRETTY SURE her night couldn't get worse. But then it did.

The Spanish-speaking patient continued to pass large blood clots four hours out from her repeat C-section. Despite multiple attempts on the behalf of the chief resident, she still refused blood. If the bleeding didn't stop soon, without a transfusion, her heart would go into failure. Then her kidneys. Then her lungs. At least that was what Wendi's Intern Survival Guide claimed.

"*All bleeding eventually stops*," went the famous saying.

Well, Wendi wasn't laughing. Not one little bit. She couldn't actually imagine anything less funny right now. Except maybe the dog she didn't have, refusing to eat petroleum coated nuggets and drink non-dairy creamer.

Boop-oop-a-doop.

The lack of political correctness in the hospital shocked her. The doctors made fun of the patients. The patients made sexual advances on the staff. The nurses slept with the doctors. And most of these assholes smoked cigarettes on the roof of the parking garage before, after, or during shift.

Boop-oop-a-doop. Might as well look down my shirt.

Last weekend, she had lunch at a local cafe next to a group of night shift nurses that were drinking cocktails before work. Before.

Worst of all, Gabe Carstein, the emergency medicine third-year resident she *used* to have a crush on, asked her if she wanted to do a line with him and his chief resident.

What was I thinking when I signed on for this job? Law school please.

Health reform didn't have a clue how big the problem really was, she realized. The Federal Healthcare Task Force didn't know the first thing. Deceit. Burnout. Lying. Cheating. Revenge.

God only knew how many errors killed patients while doctors screwed nurses in the call rooms. Or how many communication barriers resulted from disgruntled staff taking inadequate patient histories based on preconceived judgments that had nothing to do with information being lost in translation.

Look at the rich chick she had delivered earlier.

If she had missed none of her prenatal appointments, no one would have dared think to drug screen her. Yet, line after line, she snorted away every good chance she ever had to be a mother.

Perhaps she and Gabe should hang out Saturday night too?

Disgusting failure of a mother.

"Bitch," she muttered.

Then it hit her. She was no different while she stood so tall and proud in judgment of that never-to-see-her-child-again mother. Who said that financial abundance inferred morality? Who said the druggie's life was any easier than the disheveled but well-intending sex worker who fell into the wrong group of friends at the age of fourteen?

And who, exactly, knew this baby wouldn't find a better life in the hands of an adoptive mother forever grateful to be so blessed with a child she could have otherwise never graced with her unconditional love.

Wendi's head swam with ideas about how to repair the broken system of healthcare from a ground-up approach. She hummed over the idea of psychological support training that started for medical students and continued through residency. She imagined retreats in the woods where attendings and other senior personnel explored approaches for acclimating new doctors to the stress of having people's lives in their hands. She envisioned support groups for nursing staff and post-traumatic outcome counseling. She thought of ways patients could take their own histories and really choose a physician with a well-suited bedside manner and personality for them. Physician wellness programs. Mentoring programs. After residency follow up courses for free. Culture sensitivity training. Free business education and billing orientation. Leadership skill instruction.

The listendless.

Perhaps soothing music would better embrace a healing environment in health care facilities? Even hanging the power of positive affirmation-inviting art on every wall. She scanned the walls, eyes wide with the possibility of...

What if...?

Her mood quickly went from discouraged to hopeful as she processed all the change she was uniquely positioned to help implement. The good she could do was unending. *Maybe I did the right thing by not going to law school?*

The overhead alarm sounded. "Code Blue in"

Wendi didn't have to wait to hear the room number. She knew where she was headed and started running.

As she stood to leave the Board Room, the main Labor and Delivery room doors flew open with the onslaught of potentially drunk or high hospital crew members called the C.A.R.T, or Cardiac Acute Response Team. The death-party was made up of critical members from all the appropriate disciplinary teams, including the same Doctor Carstein who *used* to tickle her fancy so sweetly.

Damn. These guys only come when things are bad.

And that meant someone was about to die. The same someone, she knew, who had already refused the blood.

Instantly, she imagined the cute, little, chubby infant growing up without a mother in a life made of loss and tears. The same tears that flowed down the hall from her now-widowed spouse. The one who knew nothing about raising two small children. Not yet anyway. Soon he would though. Too soon.

"Why God? Is this really your will?"

While she choked on emotion, she gathered herself. This was why they called her MD, Medical Doctor. Because she would go into situations like this head held high. The letters were a title of honor; she got that now. She would do what others simply couldn't. She would hold the hand of a newly-made widow as she relayed the terrible news to him. She would sign the Certificate of Death and fill in the blanks for why and how. That was the meaning of MD.

But why this woman, God, and not the one next door?

Why that father? Why that baby? Why that two-year-old sister who would never see her mother again? Why wouldn't the woman take the blood? Why didn't her husband make her?

Too many whys to swallow. She shook her head and tried to see what else it might mean but couldn't. She just couldn't.

Had the family even understood the seriousness of the situation when it was explained to them in some language they couldn't speak? The blood would have easily saved her, saved him, saved them all from this unnecessary tragedy.

She clenched her fists and groaned.

But after she questioned her right to feel so angry over this and focused on how she might serve the family instead, she took a few deep breaths to calm down. Then she walked slowly to the room. Running was already pointless.

A subtle gush of cool air escaped when she stepped into the room. *The woman's soul moving onto the next journey, probably.*

The physical body of the twenty-six-year-old woman was all that remained on the blood-soaked bed.

Still shaking her head and holding back the catch in her throat, Wendi witnessed the suffering of the exchange this man had just madewife for daughter. *All I can do is be present for this problem. Finding the answer isn't the problem.*

Still, she wondered...why? *Facing this was the problem.*

Wendi would come back later to speak with him and help him face the un-faceable. For now, only her silent prayers could serve him.

"God, grant him peace," she whispered. "May his angels…"

He sobbed so loudly that he never even noticed her presence. But something had. A subtle light in the corner flickered, and Wendi knew the man was already being held by something far more powerful than she.

She closed the door, which echoed just like a coffin lid.

As she walked back to her station in the Labor and Delivery Board Room, the code alarm sounded once more. This time, though, it came from the room that contained the nurse from Pueblo. The one where both patients, another mother and her baby, were about to die.

TWENTY-FIVE

Where Your Road Leads

THE SWEET-FACED NURSE with severe respiratory distress from influenza-related pneumonia desaturated again. She was already on a high-pressure ventilator. There wasn't much more the team could possibly do. The maximal dose of anti-viral and anti-inflammation medications had already been given without any improvement in her status.

Now, it was simply up to God.

As Wendi, powerless to really do anything, rushed to answer the code call, she thought about that. *Up to God.*

Why do we turn to God last in a medical crisis?

If God really existed, then he was the very driving force of intelligence that created the body to begin with. If anyone could "put it back together", surely it was *He*.

There was still one thing she could do for this lady. She closed her eyes and prayed while five other MDs swirled round the room doing nothing at all.

After the others were all long gone, she remained, eyes still closed.

She prayed for the woman's lungs to heal. She prayed for the woman's immune system to fight off the attack of the flu virus. She prayed for the doctors to do all the right things. She prayed for the unborn fetus to get the chance to grow to a ripe old age. She prayed that one day she would tell this story and finish proudly with a happy ending about how everything just magically turned around at the last moment. She prayed for peace in the minds of the family members. She asked for a miracle.

In fact, she claimed it; she owned it. She called it into being.

And then she prayed for herself.

She prayed to find her purpose. She prayed to be seen and given the task she came here to do. She prayed to serve. She prayed to know, to understand why, and to see the gift in all this tragedy. She prayed to reconnect with a higher source and her most authentic self. She prayed to find inner peace and share it with others not as lucky as herself.

When she finally placed her hands on the chest of the dying woman, she offered up whatever healing love she had to give. She felt an urge to send out her own energy as she reached up to touch the woman's expressionless face.

So she did it.

She envisioned a soft pink light come swirling out of her heart and lungs and move onto the woman's. She imagined the pink light traveling into the smallest parts of the woman's drowning lungs and then come back out again.

At first, the pink light was quickly replaced with a smoky grey color. But slowly, little by little, the pink color stayed for longer. She kept doing this until the light stayed put. And then with one last wave, she surrounded the woman in a pulsating cocoon.

She stepped into the hall, closed the door, and walked away.

By the time she reached the end of the hall, she heard the incessant beeping of the woman's oxygen monitor stop. The saturations were up from eighty-two percent to eighty-eight percentenough to support brain function and possibly maintain cardiac function.

And as Wendi turned the corner, so did the woman, from dead to only possibly dying.

The intern whispered, "Up to God"and kept on walking.

TWENTY-SIX

I Surrender

BLACKWATER SAID NOTHING, but his eyes lifted hers tenderly and held her gaze.

Elise, slowly at first and then more urgently, overflowed. She didn't have time to sort out what to share first, so she just let loose.

Starting with the story about her grandmother's fire, she explained how throughout her whole life, she had found herself awake in her dreams on occasion. Even been able to travel at will to places she didn't even know. Had seen her own body from outside herself, especially when really tired or just upon waking.

She hinted that perhaps there was more to say but stopped, drained from sharing so much so quickly.

Still, Blackwater said nothing.

"I warned you." She cracked open the beer and lifted it to her lips, but his hand stopped her.

"No. Don't," he said. "Tell me the rest before you have one sip. It will cloud you, and I will not hear what you are not saying as clearly."

"What?" She scrunched her nose.

"It will block my connection to your truth beneath the truth." He tapped her nose gently.

She put the lager away and began again.

Without specific details, she explained that she was having what she would call visions about her kidnapper. That she had clues. Clues that suggested…

"I believe you," he said.

"And?"

"I see you." His lips parted and exposed his perfect teeth.

"And what else?"

"What else is there?" His breath, minty and fresh, surprised her. She wanted to breathe it in deeper to her core.

She puffed out her cheeks, trying to find the words that would help her forget about his breath. "I'm not sure that's good enough, mister." *Good enough.*

"I'm trying to help you, Jill. I mean, Elise."

"Then help me, Officer."

"Blackwater, please."

"Just help me. And the little boy. This time, a little boy is involved. Say or don't say what you want to, but help me. This time, he's going to kill a little boy."

More silence. No words. Only mint.

"Damn you, cop. Speak. I've spilled my guts, and now I feel like a freaking idiot." She slammed her hand on the table.

His pupils dilated.

She scrunched her nose again and shook her head quickly.

He touched her nose again and smiled warmly. "I see you."

"Then help me."

After several more minutes of reflection, he said, "Elise, you have the gift of a Spirit Walker, although you fight yourself from within, I think."

"You think?"

He grinned. "I will help you find your way. And hopefully, you will find the answers you are looking for."

She sensed truth in his words but was still embarrassed by her vulnerability.

"I think the problem isn't finding the answer." Checked her pulse. Ninety. She picked up the beer and lifted it to her flawless lips.

He swiped it from her hand and poured it and the other five down the cracked porcelain sink. "The problem is facing it," he said.

" Yes. I guess that's that then, Mister Wisdom."

He sat down and placed one arm around her shoulder while he pet her nose with the other.

She pushed his hand away. "Stop that."

He laughed softly. "Never. Do you have any idea how long we...I mean, you actually have?"

"Yes." She locked eyes with him, and without breaking the intensity, she added, "Until Monday night. Then she dies. And I guess the boy, too." Her gaze turned to the floor, and she shuddered.

"Elliot," she whispered. "The boy's name is Elliot."

Two days. Sixteen hours. One minute.

TWENTY-SEVEN

I Wasn't Expecting That

"WELL, THEN WE BETTER GET STARTED," Blackwater said.

"Okay, but there's something I haven't told you yet."

"Okay. Like I keep saying…I'm all ears." He coughed, but it almost sounded like it covered a subtle growl to her.

The sharp beauty in his gunmetal grey eyes shocked her. She caught her breath and resisted the urge to reach over to him and trace the scar on his neck with her finger.

Are you a Firling too, Blackwater? Who are you? And why do you affect me like this?

She suppressed a moan and grunted with a cough to cover it up. Her cheeks turned red, and a bead of sweat gathered on her forehead. "Is it hot in here?"

"No." He smiled.

Quickly, she reached up and palpated her carotid. One hundred and twenty. *Your heart, Elise. Remember your pig-goddess heart.*

She massaged the right side to slow her rate. One hundred and twelve. *Better, little lady. Slow it down.*

She walked to her player and turned on the Dimitri disk already inside. "Would you totally freak out if I played some music to help me relax?"

He tilted his head but said nothing.

She held the CD case in her fingers and smiled, familiar comfort already kicking in. She traced the mark in the corner, almost an eight, followed by what looked like a seven and wondered what it meant. 87.

After the first track kicked in, he replied, "No. But you're odd, little lady."

"When I get nervous and my heart rate gets too high, it places me at risk for failure. This pig-heart is less than perfect."

His right eyebrow creased, and he laughed. "Am I making you nervous, Elise?"

"Well...maybe just a little."

"Is that good?"

"I don't know. Yet." She walked back over to him.

"I think it is safe," he said, placing his silky-smooth palm on her cheek, "to believe that I am the least of your worries. Do not fear me of all things. I've been trying to avenge Jill's death for five years. Why would I hurt her now? I don't want to hurt you at all. In fact..."

"Yes?"

He never finished his sentence. He stroked her cheek instead.

She felt heat linger where he had touched her face. It melted her skin and burrowed into the deepest part of her and zinged through her center. She turned away and looked the other direction, unable to tolerate the strength of it, the pull of it, the fire it suggested.

She bit her lip again. "Exactly why did you pour out those beers?"

He grabbed her wrist and turned her back to face him.

Her center pulsed and moistened.

"To hear you better."

God, those hands. Hopefully he can't hear my pounding heart or the thoughts I'm thinking about those hands of his.

She sighed but not loud enough to cover up the word "hand" as it escaped, and she covered her mouth, trying to pull it back in.

He said nothing, but his eyes twinkled while he pursed his lips shut too.

To distract herself from the other stupid words threatening to fall out her clumsy mouth, she said, "Tell me about the others."

"The others?"

He touched her cheek again.

"The other women you think he has taken. Tell me their names. I need to hear their names to stay focused, I think. I need to know I'm not crazy."

"If you think it will help." Now he bit his lip.

"I do. So that I can..."

"Can what?"

"Stop that."

"Stop what?"

"Your lip," she said and scrunched her nose.

"Only if you stop that. The nose thing. It distracts me too much."

"Deal. I need to find the courage to remember what he did to Jill. What he did to me. Your lip isn't helping me stay focused either."

"Good." He laughed. "But that's a bad deal. But okay. For you."

"Thank you." She straightened her nose.

"What do you mean…remember?" He freed his lip.

"That's how I help her and the little boy. By remembering the terrible things"

"Oh, I didn't realize you didn't"

"Remember? Nope. Nothing. That's what my visions are about. They are flashes of my memory. Of how he... Of what..."

"Elise, I am so…"

She couldn't finish her sentence. She didn't want him to finish his. "Hush. Don't say it."

He had seen the photos of her face. The holes in her lips. The marks on her thighs.

Her breasts. She didn't need to finish. In fact, he knew exactly what the creep had done to her.

He touched her cheek once more and smiled, still surprised at how well she had healed up. The plastic surgeon had nailed her repair.

Blackwater opened his file box on the coffee table and brought out six manila folders.

"This is Beverly Jones from Colorado Springs. She was visiting her best friend from high school in Denver three years ago. She never came back home. Her car was found abandoned in a grocery store parking lot, unlocked with a full tank of gas and a map on the passenger seat. She was only twenty-one."

He replaced the picture in the file.

"Go on," Elise said.

"This is Lisa Davidson from Aurora. She was twenty-three. Like Beverly, her car was found not too far from a grocery store where her credit card was charged the last day she was ever seen. That was over two years ago."

As he put the second folder back, he looked her in the eyes and tilted his head to the side.

"More. Make me look at more," she said and put her fingers to her neck.

"And this is...was Terry Robertson, age twenty-four. Pretty much the same details. Last seen leaving for the grocery store. Her car was never found. Four years ago."

She turned the song up and swayed side to side.

He shook his head. His nostrils flared. "Keep going?"

"Hell yes. Go." She twirled in a circle to the music, both hands to her neck.

"And Delynne Pickers from Steamboat Springs. She is...was the most recent one. She went out to get margarita mix for a holiday party and never came back home. Her car was wiped clean. Gone without a trace."

"Damn."

"Mariah Wilson. Same story. Different grocery store but similar story."

"There's one more. Still go on? Are you sure?"

Elise turned round and faced him, knowing all too well who was last.

"And this is Jill's folder. You know her story, your story. It was five years ago, almost exactly, when she went missing."

"Five years... So long, so short. A lifetime really."

"You don't have to look at the pictures."

"Actually, I do." She bit her lip now, and he placed his hand over her lips.

She took a deep breath but didn't reach up to her neck. Somehow she didn't need to with his fingers on her mouth like that. *Those hands holding me.*

"Why don't we just put a pin in that for now? Until we talk about what happened the day he took you. Tell me everything."

"I'd love to say I remember, but I don't. Not yet, at least."

"It must be a pattern. Every year around this time, he takes another girl. As far as we know, you were the first. And like you, they are all young, fair skinned, and beautiful."

Beautiful? You think I'm... She swallowed hard.

"Beautiful." The word dripped off his lip and lingered there like rain tempting the desert.

She shook her head to clear the pull to that word. *Beautiful. He's beautiful.*

"No. You're beautiful," he said like he had heard her thoughts.

"The visions must be true then."

"Yes."

And if she wasn't totally nuts, she just spoke to every one of these dead women on the phone in her latest vision.

"Help me," she whispered and staggered back slightly.

Suddenly, she remembered stopping at the grocery store to get a litter tray for her newly adopted kitty, Maddie the mangled.

"You mean Jill the mangled," she whispered and dropped onto the couch as the weight of it settled in.

That kitten had been the death of Jill. Of her.

Two days. Fifteen hours. Zero minutes.

TWENTY-EIGHT

Dark Side

KINCAID LAY COMFORTABLY in his bed, resting safely in the certainty of his plan. Under his pillow, he coveted several of Jolene's previously discarded items.

While he slept, he softly fingered his new prize possessions. Each one, sacred to him, symbolized her love for him. He knew that without a doubt.

She loved him; she waited for him. God only knew how many years she had waited for his glorious gift of silence. He planned to offer her what he had always been denied. That had been his agreement to the Kings.

His lips curled up as he imagined her gratitude, even in his slumber.

In the morning, he would bring his Queen home.

Jolene opened her eyes and gasped. The feeling that she was being watched shook her. Her heart pounded so loudly that she could hear it in her ears. She placed her right hand over her chest and felt her bounding heart through her skin.

She quickly yet tenderly lifted up Elliot's head and returned it to their king-sized pillow. Then she tucked the blankets safely all around him.

Efficiently, she checked every door and window. The locks were all engaged perfectly in place. She peered past the three deadbolts positioned to protect the entry door and out the peephole. Nervously, she looked up and down the small space that connected all four of the units in her building.

No one, nothing lurked in the hallway.

She wiped her sweaty palms on her nightgown.

Once more, she checked on the baby before making a quick trip to the bathroom to reapply deodorant before returning to bed.

Once safely back in bed, she pulled the blankets up to cover her chilly shoulders. She snuggled into Elliot and inhaled the scent of his perfection.

Ah, my favorite smell in the whole wide world.

She tried to fall back asleep, but she couldn't. Something in the air smelled wrong. Something in the back of her mouth tasted rotten. The sweat coated her inside and out. A hollow worry turned her stomach.

She decided she must be nervous about leaving Elliot at that church tomorrow. Well, later this morning, anyway. It was already tomorrow.

The mouse scampered down the heater pipe, searching for the only other mouse he had ever known, his brother. As he arrived at Jolene's unit, he stopped to watch for a moment. The way she held that baby moved him. If only someone had ever loved him like that. He didn't even know his mother. Had she ever embraced him so tenderly?

He didn't bother wasting time scrambling about for a few scraps of food in here; he knew better. This unit was always spotless, never a morsel to spare. If he wanted this lady's leftovers, it was out back in the dump for him.

He wiped his paws to clean himself. Then he took one last longing look at the baby, so perfectly cradled in his mother's arms, before he scurried back up the vent.

The heat would come back on again soon, and then he would be stuck here all morning wishing someone loved him like that. And he'd better find his brother fast. The sun was almost up.

The cockroach silently watched the whole exchange from the corner of the windowsill. He agreed. This unit was no good. Way too clean for him.

Besides, something very nasty was headed this way. He felt it with those creepy antennae of his. He could come back then, maybe. Besides, he planned to visit the basement where he could get a better look at the snake. He had a feeling he knew where mouse's brother was.

Downstairs, the satisfied snake slept soundly. Perfectly still in the basement, he slumbered. Full-bellied and warm next to the radiator pipes, he couldn't be bothered with anything at all. Why should he? This had never been his problem to begin with.

As for mouse's brother, he had run out of struggles at the bottom of the snake's gut. His worries, this lifetime…in this world at least, were officially over.

TWENTY-NINE

Back to December

WHEN WOULD Wendi's shitty night ever end? She sat down and wiped her forehead.

The only good news seemed to be that the lady on the ventilator had oxygen saturations steady at ninety percent now. Her impending death already felt like a memory thousands of years old.

"Move on," life shouted. *"She will be fine,"* it declared. *"It was always up to God."*

The newly widowed father of two from down the hall had to be removed by security. He kept shouting that his wife was fine. He demanded to see her body and touch her hand again so he could show us all. He consented for the blood now. In fact, he demanded the blood and said he already signed the forms. If only they would check the forms.

The two-year-old daughter was safely in the hands of a social worker that would address the family's long-term needs in the morning after the translation line was up and they could start talking to extended family members. The newborn was safely wrapped in a blanket in the nursery, oblivious to the trauma her entry into this world had called forth.

The wealthy cocaine freak never even bothered to sign out AMA, against medical advice, after being informed again that she would never hold her own son. No one knew for sure if grief or addiction motivated her to walk out while supposedly taking a smoke break downstairs.

But worst of all, Gabe Carstein, the used to be cute resident from the ER, kept calling her.

"You okay, babe?" he said. "It's hard to watch your first patient die. I know. Mine died last December. I go back all the time. I'm here if you need me. If you want me to be. I'm sorry, babe."

She glared at the bathroom mirror.

"What? While you slip out back, you lousy hypocrite, and snort lines, walking around proudly wearing your name tag that screams MD for Malingering Dick-head."

Her anger swallowed her whole. She wanted to shout at him, shake him, and ask him what the hell he was thinking by putting others, and especially himself, in such jeopardy.

She told the mirror in place of him, "Don't you call me babe."

She imagined pulling him aside and slapping him senseless. *What was he thinking? What if he had a heart attack? A stroke? A ruptured brain aneurysm? While he did one of his lines?*

But then her judgment slapped her once more. Her anger was nothing more than disguised disappointment. So badly, she had needed him to be different, to remain untainted by the bleach-covered scent of death and dying in this abusive place. His line became a symbolic cross, nailing him to a rotten, wooden T.

And she was the one who had strung him up for all to see with her scornful eyes of contempt.

Perhaps forgiveness offered them both a better option?

She picked up the phone and dialed him.

"Doctor Patterson here. I need Doctor Carstein, your resident on call tonight."

"Yea, we know who he is. He keeps asking if you have called. Hang on a minute. He's in scrubbing some old dude's butt ulcer."

Wendi listened to the soothing music on the phone. Dimitri maybe? It encouraged her patience. It cooled her fire.

"Hey, Wendi. I was hoping you would call. How are you, babe, after that lady died and all? You know, you did all the right things."

"Shut up," she said. "Stick the nice guy shit up your ass for a minute."

"Okay, but I"

"Seriously, Gabe, do you want a chance with me? Because if you do, listen and listen good."

"Okay," he replied, shocked by the bare honesty in her voice.

He took a breath of the air, which smelled cleaner.

"I'm a good girl. I'm not pretending. That's who I really am. I don't drink heavily. I don't smoke. I don't do drugs. I tell the truth. I am honest to a fault, almost."

"Keep going," he said. "You have my attention."

"I don't put up with lying, drugging, cheating, stealing, or any other childish games. If you want me, then the only way you will get me is by being yourself. The self you hide when no one else is looking. The self you don't want anyone to find out about. The self you have spent your whole life trying not to be. If you can handle that, then you can come over to my place after we get off shift. After I go to church and pray that this place never makes me forget who I really am. You know where I live. The back door will be open, and I will meet you, the real you, there. Or don't bother remembering my number anymore. Got it?"

The phone went silent, followed by a dial tone. His bottom jaw dropped.

The overhead call cried out, "Delivery in Room Six. Doctor for delivery to Room Six."

Wendi stood to answer. Without realizing it, she traced the letters that followed her name on her nametag, MD, Medical Doctor.

Yeah, but still My Damn self.

THIRTY

The Song Remembers When

BLACKWATER LOOKED AT HIS WATCH. "It's four thirty a.m. We are running out of time. Look, Elise. Look, see, and remember."

"Yes." She swallowed hard and cleared her throat.

He opened Jill Vickery's folder.

One by one, she held the photos. The first was taken at the marina. Jill's...her...eyes were shut, and she looked so pale and lifeless. Her mangled hair surprised her. But her lips, they were the most startling thing of all.

She reached up and touched her lips to check.

He touched them too, and her shoulders dropped softly.

Is that really me? Is this really me?

"Look, you incredible woman. If you are going to suffer this, at least make it count for something. What do you see?"

"I'm wearing my favorite old T-shirt."

"More."

"I forgot about that damn shirt. It was my favorite for like...forever. Where is it?"

"Evidence, of course. More. Keep going," he replied.

"And my hair. It's all matted. With what? What is that in my hair?"

He sighed. "Some kind of industrially modified glue. We were never able to trace it, but we think it came from Africa. It is commonly used by indigenous people there for making textiles and crafts."

"Oh my God. Look at my legs, my feet. So...black. Why are they so black?"

"Also some industrial product. It's a dye that seems to come naturally from the trees in the rain forests."

"My lips? Why would he do that to me? To us?"

"We are not sure exactly. I was hoping you would remember."

She shook her head.

113

"We think…" He wanted to tell her that the police thought it was some part of the maniac's fetish but didn't finish before she spoke again.

"In one of my visions, my feet hurt…so, so badly. It felt like it was wedged or pierced somehow. Like my toenail was ripping off. But my lips?"

"Check your toe. Feel the subtle scar? You didn't imagine that. See."

He flipped to the next photo, which showed her destroyed feet. A wave of nausea crested, and she ran to the bathroom, swallowing as fast as she could to keep the secretions from coming. As her vomitus splattered the wall, a pressure grabbed the back of her neck.

Blackwater swept her hair up and held it high on her head.

She wiped the stink from her mouth, and she dared a glance at his beautiful face. Then at her own lips in the mirror.

He bit his and smiled more with his eyes than his other facial features.

"Stop that. You promised." She traced the fleshy outline of her mouth again. Then she traced his.

His eyes beamed, and his mouth followed suit.

Unable to feel so hopeful and so broken at the same time, she looked away.

She could hear her heart beating. *"Swish, swish, swish."*

She went to the kitchen and poured herself a glass of water to wash the taste of stomach acid from her mouth. Ninety-five.

Keep it together, girl. Remember your heart. You survived this already. It's okay.

She traced her lips once more. Just in case.

She turned to Blackwater with tears in her eyes and said, "He nailed my feet to something, didn't he?"

"That's what we think. We can't be absolutely certain, though. You could have injured yourself while escaping. We just don't know. I'm sorry, Jill, um…Elise, that you have to go through this. If I could do it for you, I would."

"I believe you," she said and scrunched her nose. "Paybacks are hell. I really do believe you. Why did he do that to my mouth?"

"We have absolutely no idea. Well, almost no idea." There was no point in telling her.

"Spill it."

"It serves no one. Not yet."

"Another pin in it then?" She surprised herself by genuinely smiling.

"Yep. Lay with me now. I will keep you safe as you walk with Spirit. I will witness what happens, and I will write it down for you, for us, for her and that little boy."

"For Elliot."

She nodded and wiped the tears away. *Yes. Those hands can keep me safe.*

Silently, she took his hand and followed him to the bedroom ten steps away. And then she lay down and closed her eyes to welcome the very two things she had fought off for so many years nowthe truth of her past and the arms of a man.

Two days. Fourteen hours. Thirty-three minutes.

THIRTY-ONE

Feels Like Tonight

FLASH, flash, flash! The swirling tunnel appeared before her. She went in. A spinning sensation throbbed all around her. She felt the undulating pulse of magnetic energy that swirled everywhere.

She looked at her hands to ground herself.

These are my hands; I'm here. The I that cannot die. I am here.

She felt the heat of the emerald grid of Mother Earth underneath her feet.

"Thank you, Mother, for grounding me."

Then she risked glancing back over her shoulder. The silvery, shimmery cord traced perfectly back to her body held so safely in his embrace.

Blackwater tenderly caressed her forehead in a wave-like pattern and softly touched her hair.

Why the fuck am I going this way when I could stay with him, safe in his strong arms...feeling that touch.

"Go now, Elise," he whispered. "I will be here when you return."

Shit. Here goes nothing but badness.

She turned to face the tunnel again. The brilliance of flashing light surprised her every single time, still after all these years of traveling where others couldn't or dared not. It was like a year's worth of lightning wasted itself all in one little space. She looked back at her feet now; they were black again from the rain forest dye.

Her will called forth to show her more.

A house came into view.

Instantly, she remembered...or experienced. Who knew? But she was there, back again. The scent of bleach and rotten flesh swept over her. Waves of nausea threatened, but she shoved them back down again.

Her tongue rubbed up against some kind of cloth. Saliva dripped from the corners of her mouth. Then she gagged on the cloth handkerchief inside it.

Unable to move her arms, she couldn't reach up to free her mouth or check her hair.

She tried to move her legs, but only her left side would respond. Her right foot was stuck on something.

The room, swallowed in blackness, offered no sight. She demanded to see, to understand, to know what was happening. A faint whisper of green-tinged light filled the room. She looked down once more and saw that her right great toe was nailed to some type of platform. Some kind of stand.

Flash, flash, flash!

She opened her eyes to the pressure of an elephant on her chest. *So heavy, so heavy, so heavy. What's so heavy on my chest? My heart, my heart. It's breaking. My heart.*

For a moment, the pressure let up and then came down again even harder than before. Her eyes were covered with something so she couldn't see much.

But she knew it was daylight by the hint of light coming in from the edges of her mask. Below her waist was a numbness, a disconnect...as if she had lost the ability to feel her lower body. The pressure came back once more. Then up again. Then down.

And then she realized why she couldn't sense below her waist. She had chosen not to.

Good girl, Elise. There's no reason to feel this.

"See me now," a harsh voice shouted.

She trembled. It was him, her captor. *Terrible.*

"See me now, you bitch. See me now."

As the monster pulled off her blindfold, the flashing resumed.

Flash, flash, flash!

And she was back in her own body in present time, still held safely in those strong, ageless arms.

She turned to Blackwater and looked at him. *Beautiful.* For the first time in years, she looked deeply into another person's eyes. She dared him to see her, the real her. To prove she was no fake. After all, she was the real deal.

She pulled him tightly to her and breathed in the scent of him. Musky. Spicy. Delicious. She touched the silky smoothness of his hair and rubbed it on her cheek. "So beautiful." Her tongue tripped on the syllables, but somehow they got out anyway.

"So beautiful." He did not pull back from her touch. But just bit his lip instead and grinned to invite the intensity of her approval. His affection and passion oozed out and soaked her.

He had wanted her, wanted to save her. For years probably, he had dreamed of holding her safe in his arms instead of seeing her mutilated by that creep in the photos. The photos in the box. The box he opened way to often wishing the pictures were of someone else, anyone other than her.

Unable to say something so ridiculous with his mouth, he used his body instead. The pressure from his arms increased slightly encouraging her to sink into the center of him.

But instead of more pressure on her chest, she noticed a lighter opening, a joining, an ecstatic union with his energy. Despite the hardness of the force on her breasts, she felt easy and comfortable.

The more he pressed, the more her heart opened.

Now it was his turn to smell her. Lavender. Floral. A hint of Chanel No. 5 still trying to tempt him from under this morning's soap on her skin. "So damn beautiful," he said one more time.

She narrowed her eyes and tilted her head to see him more clearly.

He reached down and touched her fingers one by one. "Your hands," he whispered.

She tickled his chin and drew his eyes back up to hers. "I see you instead of him. Instead of that..."

"My God. Your eyes."

She touched his and then her own lips and smiled. "Your lips."

"Now your lips."

"Yes, please."

"Oh yes, please." He traced his fingers down her forty-three staple tracks. Now at her waist, he drew out the same figure he had followed on her forehead. As he did this, her desire for him reached the point of no return.

"Your body." The light left his eyes and reflected off hers and bounced around the room despite the darkness.

"Your body now. Yes, please." She nodded.

"I see you. Oh God, I see your beauty."

Forty-three ways to entice me.

Now wanting him so badly, she moaned with anticipation.

"But I also want to see these lovely toes. May I?"

She groaned, and her fluids increased.

Like he could tell, he took a deep breath of her scent and licked his lips.

To torture her, he stopped at her midsection before he moved down to her toes where he slowly kissed them lovingly one by one.

When she thought she would explode with desire, he whispered her name. "Elise, my love. My little Elise. Love me now, please."

Forty-three ways to beg you...take me now.

She pulled his shoulders back up to her chest and brought the fullness of his weight onto her body. She felt the firmness of his masculinity and wanted it, needed to claim it, needed to satisfy it, needed to serve it, needed it to serve her.

This time, he looked even more deeply into her eyes. "Are you sure?"

"I've never been more sure. Yes. Please. Love me now."

And then he kissed her. Sweetly, his tongue ran along her lips and over the edges of her teeth. He tasted like the fruit from her personal garden.

Then he offered his mouth fully to her as she opened her mouth even wider to his caress, to his taste, to his flavor.

Forty-three flavors of perfection. Delicious man. Oh you taste like...

She let out a groan of delight.

He giggled.

"Help me remember what my body feels like," she said. "I don't want to remember him, but I do want to remember this."

Forty-three ways to feel you. You inside me. Me inside you.

"Yes. Please," he said. "Don't close your eyes. See me. See us."

Forty-three ways to know you completely. From inside myself.

And so she did. Never once did she look away. Never once did she back down from the fullness of their connection. Never once did she hide inside her own mind as he opened her insides and joined her in the warmest, wettest place within the goodness of her.

Forty-three ways to see his love, feel our love. From inside myself.

"My body," he moaned.

"Now my body." She met his moan, squeezed her buttocks to prove she meant it, and took his fullness even deeper within her. So deep.

"Oh, baby. You feel so good." He moaned as his hair fell across her face.

"You feel so good, so right." She held him down and wouldn't let go.

"Yes. Right there. Please. Right there."

"Right there."

He smiled and let her have all of him. Right there. He felt her muscles spasm before her cries echoed the motion of his service to her pleasure. The same pleasure that pleased him beyond his ability to describe it.

He couldn't hold on any longer. Why should he?

And unable to resist, he surrendered his essence to flow into her core and allowed his passion to escape with hers down her leg and onto his.

Forty-three ways to feel ecstasy with you. As you.

"My body," he said.

"Now my body." She sighed, but not with a trace of sadness, only total relief. "Oh…"

She trembled and instantly burrowed into the center of the sheets with him in the bed covered by the proof of their precious rivers of intimacy.

Then her flashing vision tunnel resumed. She should reach up and check her pulse, she knew. But for once, she didn't care if her pig-goddess heart killed her and just smiled instead of worried.

For the first time in as long as she could remember, she acknowledged yet denied the flashes trying to pull her into another realm and stayed in his strong arms instead.

"My body," she whispered and was gone in peaceful slumber and surrender.

"No mine," he said and fell asleep, too.

Two days. Ten hours. One minute.

THIRTY-TWO

Wrecking Ball

"FORTY-THREE WAYS TO screw up by fucking a cop," she almost muttered. Thankfully, her mouth kept it mostly in until she had closed the bathroom door.

What the hell was I thinking? Where's my eternal love now, Dimitri? Is it you? Is it him?

She stared at her perfect lips in the mirror while they mumbled, "Fuck me. Fuck you."

She had to be sure they felt as normal as they looked. She reached up. Traced the top. Traced the bottom. Then she wiped away his kisses.

What the hell was I thinking?

She glanced at him from the doorway.

I was thinking about him. Look at him. Lovely. Those hands in my hands. His body in mine, as mine. Delicious. God he's so beautiful.

She considered licking her lips to see if she could still taste him. Then she decided against it. Decided she would much rather taste the real thing, not the memory.

That hair. The smell of itargon oil, musk, cinnamon, pure bliss.

The smoothness of Blackwater's skin evened out her fear. The shimmer of his hair gleamed through her darkness.

That face. That face pressed to my face. A mirror of my face.

The peace in his expression calmed the angry ocean of her emotions.

Perhaps he is my eternal love, not you my imaginary Latin lover. He's real. You're not. Is any of this real? Am I already dead? God, I hope so.

She walked back to the bed, fingers down to the side, utterly unconcerned with her pulse.

Without opening his eyes, he softly squeezed her hand, and she let him. She lay down, rolled on her right side, and buried her face in the manly scent of his armpit. The almost sweaty smell of his musky aroma, mixed with wood and eucalyptus and topped off with the lightness of exotic oils, blew through her core. Blew her away. Blew her home.

Swam her right back down a river named desire.

Her pelvic muscles flexed, her body already wanting to hold onto him and his manhood once more. Taking a deep breath, she moaned softly.

He smelled thick and balmy yet surprisingly clean. His eyes were smiling even in his pretend sleep state. She knew it; she was right.

She squeezed her buttocks together tightly even though it hurt a bit and imagined him already back inside. And right there, right where she was too sore to mention, she yearned and wished to be even more sore than she knew was possible. The friction of his fullness stretching her to the limit, the drops of his love washing her clean while it pushed her further outside her comfort zone and down the rapids of that river she had forgotten how to ride. *Yes. Please.*

In contrast, she smelled the hot, sticky, salty scent of his fluids on her sheets. Tainted with a waft of metal and sugar, the smell of spilled fluids threatened to transport her back to the place she knew so well a dark curtain of shame that had imprisoned her way too long, shackled by guilt and fear. A hurt that only offered more hurt the more attention she gave it and more proof that she would never be good enough for anything more than the suffering she so deserved.

"No," she whispered. "Please, no." *Can't I just love you?*

He stroked her finger lightly, drawing her back to him and away from the past and all its lies and injury. "Yes. I'm sorry. Forgive me."

She chose not to delve into her painful past...and smelled his innocence instead. She smiled and forgot all about the suffering. "Thank you."

In an instant, she fell back asleep wrapped in his arms.

Flash, flash....flash, flash, flash!

The tunnel of lightening wonder appeared. She fell through the bed onto the floor underneath. Yet there her body was, still snuggled in his embrace on the bed.

I'm out of my body again.

She gazed back at the tunnel, which called her name.

"Jill. Enter now, Jill."

In the corner, she spied the golden eyes of a benevolent wolf, which, surprisingly, evoked no fear in her. He tilted his head, looking intensely back at her. His kind honesty oozed out of his fur while he howled. Obviously, the call was on her behalf.

It beckoned she go. It pushed her onward. It claimed a guardianship of her intention.

She accepted its support without question.

She stepped in, stepped through the tunnel.

Flash!

Paralysis.

Her head wouldn't, couldn't move. She felt evil surging through hateful fingers squeezing, probably bruising her arm. *The kidnapper.*

"No. Please. You bastard!"

The digits pinched her harder and harder, but still she didn't make a sound; she refused to acknowledge his grip on her.

"You cannot hurt me. Not now. I escaped your grip. This isn't real. Jill is already dead, not me."

He lifted her up and locked her in place with some kind of external pressure, some kind of locking device. She felt the belt notch. The metal arms anchor pressure across her midsection.

She kept her eyes closed and pretended to sleep. Eventually, he stopped pinching, unable to get a rise out of her, and walked away. *Thank God.*

Her nostrils burned. Some type of harsh chemical nearby. The fumes familiar, like from her art class back in high school. *Oh my God.*

The glue. The fucking glue. He's about to...

As soon as she remembered, the hot liquid ran down her scalp, and she went even deeper inside to keep from reacting. Still blindfolded, she clamped her eyes more tightly closed. He would not get the best of her.

Silence is my friend. I will not betray myself. I will speak no evil–another one of my agreements.

Flash, flash...flash, flash, flash!

She looked down at her feet supported by a billowing cloud-like whiteness as if they were part of the clouds. Somehow, her presence made the cloud solid.

Instantly, the telephone booth appeared.

She went in and lifted the receiver to her ear.

"The honorable one you know so well. You will stand honorably up for her on her honorable behalf. And then you will hear her honorable truth. In return, she will honor your heart. You will try to save her, but she will save you. It is the only way to honor them all."

The line went dead. *Buzz...*

Flash!

Eucalyptus. Mint. Exotic oil. Scents too lovely to be anything, anyone other than him. She smiled despite the memory of the device, the glue, the phone.

"Wake up, sleepy head," Blackwater said, kissing her softly on the nose. "The clock is ticking."

"Did I say anything in my sleep?"

"Something about the phone. A butterfly? You called me honorable. Said you would find a way to save me. You marked a shape over and over on your arm with your fingernail. Pinched it, actually. "

They examined her arm more closely. A scratch with red but clear edges. The number six.

She gasped. *Six, six, six.*

"What the devil is that?" she asked and laughed as best she could. It was a flat, empty laugh.

"I have no idea, but something tells me you...I mean we will find out very soon. Too soon."

Two days. Seven hours. Seventeen minutes.

THIRTY-THREE

Unchained Melody

WENDI STEPPED through the front door of Old Saints Mary's Cathedral Church slowly and felt instantly revived. Then she marched right up to the first pew and sat down. From her pocket, she retrieved her rosary and took a long, hard look at the chain that could do so much.

She marveled at the glimmer of light erupting from the clear crystal stone in the center. A silver cross underneath offered a classically handsome and fine supportive finish. The beaded arms of the cross around the silver inner cross felt cool and smooth to her touch. She felt even better than revived. Peaceful even. High, almost. Caressing it up and down, she entered a blissful place of surrender to its meaning, its power, its cross beneath its cross. It was beautiful. Mesmerizing. Undeniable. Consuming. Honoring. Addictive, almost.

The image of her drug-addicted patient popped in. Could this be how the mother felt on drugs? Why she traded her baby for a dose of white-powder-induced state of bliss?

"God, are you still mine?" she asked. "Am I still yours?"

She glanced at the statue of Mother Mary. She couldn't break her gaze despite an intense desire to further inspect her rosary, the source of so much comfort for her. She thought about all the nights it saved her, comforted her, and pulled her through so much pain. Even…through the memory of the accusations of what her father had done.

Like the woman's drug habit had comforted her.

"God, am I any different than that woman?"

Daddy, what happened all those years ago? Did you murder that woman? Was she your mistress? Did you ever love us?

She sighed and then placed the necklace back in her pocket. She faced the Divine Mother who stood so serene and confident, arms open wide while offering love to anyone willing to accept her grace. The crown of stars over Mary's head shone with the brightness of purity, of innocence, of service from love rather than sacrifice. Her blue, flowing garment fell lovingly over her shoulders.

To Wendi, the image offered a feeling that if spoken would say, *"I will wrap you in my love. I will keep you safe and warm, my child. Protect you from what they said about your family."*

Wendi's gaze rested on the floor in front of the statue, which seemed to peer deep into the heart of the Earth with tender and intimate support. The bouquet of white and yellow flowers at the base suggested hope and a promise to see a better way.

Yes, Mary. Show me the truth.

She sighed again, louder this time.

Show me how to hold them in your loving embrace. Help me be a mother to the mothers. Help me do better. Be better.

"Honor. Yes. That's the word I feel—honor," Wendi whispered.

As she stood from the pew, her tired knees quivered. The same knees that would probably be marked with two fresh bruises tomorrow.

"Fill me with your grace, Mother. How do I go on like this?"

The urge to kneel in prayer despite her heavy legs, burning arms, and weary eyes would not be denied until she fulfilled it. Stumbling, she marched to the Virgin's feet and rubbed her knees to prepare them.

She could feel the rosary in her pocket: the curve of the fine beads, the quality of the heavy cross, the strong and valuable materials of the luxury chain.

Wendi kneeled down next to another woman, her knees smacking the cold stone floor. Normally, she might have flinched from the pain, but today, she was too tired to react.

The woman next to Wendi had long, platinum hair pulled back loosely with a head-band—the lace fine and complex but discolored and tattered at the edges. The hairpiece could have been ten or one hundred years old. The frail woman's clothes were soft and light but obviously too large for her petite frame. And she clutched the photo of a small child with lovely golden locks that God Himself couldn't have pried from the tight grip of her right hand. Her eyes, bloodshot, skittered back and forth from the precious photo to Mary's face.

Oblivious to Wendi's arrival, the woman continued her prayer out loud.

"Mother Mary, Mother Mary, I know you. I know I do. Help me see you in myself. Help me be a mother worthy of her son. Help me find my way out of a life of sin. Help me make a better way for my little one. My baby. My love. My everything."

Wendi gasped. Even though her eyes were almost closed, she saw the boy's image clearly in her mind's eye.

"My bastard." The woman shuddered, completely giving into her sobs.

Totally forgetting her fatigue, Wendi placed her arm over the other woman's shoulder. She brought the woman's devastated eyes lovingly into her embrace and patted the woman's back tenderly as she looked at the photo. The image was exactly the same as the one she had seen with her inner vision.

"Sh, sh, shhhh… It's okay. It's okay," Wendi said as the woman surrendered to the fullness of her sadness, her disappointment, her failures, her pleas, her prayers, her urgent requests for a better life, a better way.

Unable to repress the urge, Wendi said, "She's here with you. I know it. I feel it deep inside."

The blond-haired woman looked at Wendi with a hint of hope in her eyes so terribly wounded by years of fear and doubt but shook her head.

"It's okay, dear. Mother will guide you."

"But how will we get through this?" The woman trembled like a mouse trapped without shelter in a storm. "How will I make it all okay? How will I ever be good enough for him?"

Wendi cried with her as a familiar melody entered her mind and lyrics flowed to match the tune in perfect harmony. *Elliot, I love you. Yes, I do. I love you.*

Parked down the street, the Range Rover hummed, almost silently, genuinely pleased by its own efficiency and warmth. The gas tank celebrated its overflowing liquid gold that swished ever so slightly from side to side.

The master inside sat patiently watching one unit of the quadraplex in particular. He hit the seat-warming button and smiled while the heat flooded his thighs. He fingered his keys hanging from the ignition. Six times to the right, followed by six times the left, he twirled them.

The SUV was pleased. It knew that soon the master was going to go in and take her.

I had a vision. A perfect vision of light
People on a stage. Loving hearts ablaze.
And what they danced was a love's parade.
And through a wall of pain, a message came.
For you, for me.

"For You, For Me" by Dimitri Arion

THIRTY-FOUR

Let Me Love You

ELISE DARED NOT LOOK Blackwater in the eyes. Yet she dared not look away, either.

She stood to dress, but he turned her round to face him instead.

"What?" She sighed, narrowed her eyes, and pushed the air out hard.

"Oh no, my sweet Elise. Not for a minute. You look at me. You see me. You let me see you. Don't even think about going back inside that prison you've been living in. You are out now, and if you want to save that woman, this is where you need to stay. Presenthere in the now."

"But"

"But nothing. I have no shame in my joining with you, so don't you try to cover up our connection with fear. I will not have it."

"Look at me then," she said.

"Yes." He narrowed his eyes firmly to match hers. "Please."

She dropped her robe and exposed her naked self.

He gasped. He tried to drag his reaction back, but it was already out. The scars. So many scars. "Baby. Oh God."

"Look at my mutilated body. Look at my ruined chest. My scars. The slices up and down my fucking legs. The wounds that will never heal like my lips did. Look at what he did to me. You fucking look at me then, Blackwater. Yes please?" She rolled her eyes and clicked her tongue harshly.

He shook his head.

"No please. My joke of a body in full daylight. Look at it then."

She opened the drapes wide and stood in the full sun.

He pulled his hair back behind his ear and tried to keep her gaze.

"What do you see? Who do you see? Look at what he did to Jill, and look at all that's left of me!"

She stumbled back, catching the edge of the curtain with her hand.

"Get it out, Elise. Get it out." He drew the curtains back closed and stepped forward to embrace her. "I do not need the sun to see you clearly. I only need my heart to feel you clearly."

"Damn your bullshit talk, Blackwater. Don't speak to me like I'm some made-up character in a book." She yanked the curtain down from the rod. As it fell to the floor, she crumbled to the ground with it.

He sat down next to her and remained silent but attentive.

She heaved from the intensity of her emotions. The sobs came forth in great throbbing waves of pain. Like the oceans, her waves crashed on the beach of his support. She threw her hate at him. She pounced him with her disappointment. She hurled her fury.

Yet he faltered not.

She swung years of solitude at him. She tossed him all her unworthiness. She covered him in all her failures, in all her broken promises.

Still, he faltered not.

"No matter what you show me, all I see is the beauty in you." He bit his lip and tried to lock eyes with her and added, "Nope. No bullshit. No book."

She screamed again, pounding her fists against his broad, hairless chest.

"Fuck this life, cop!"

"The raw strength of your power, of your broken soul looks perfect to me. I see wounds that are finally ready to heal." He squinted. "Nope. No bullshit."

"And fuck your flawless skin!"

He touched his neck and said, "And when you see yourself through my eyes, you will know how perfect you are, how perfect you have always been."

"Whatever. Don't distract me from this disaster that defines all that's left of this goddamn nightmare."

"Everything other than your perfection is an illusion. Actually, it's delusion. And it has never been just some story. You are so much more than a story."

She returned his gaze and held it this time.

He lifted her up in his arms, and wrapped her in the soft robe tenderly.

She rolled her eyes but smiled just barely with the corner of her mouth.

Very intentionally dragging his teeth to his lips, knowing it would drive her crazy, he said, "When you cannot stand, I will be your feet."

She caught her breath and blinked her eyes, refusing to cry.

"When you cannot see from the tears in your eyes, I will be your sight."

She clasped her hands behind her back and shook her head violently as the tears coursed down her cheeks. Her makeup slid down with them.

"When you cannot feel, I will remind you the beauty of your passion."

He wiped her eyes and cleared the sloppy black streaks. Then he gently laid her back down on the bed and gave her an Eskimo kiss. "Please do that thing with your nose. Please."

"You mean…yes, please."

"Yes. Please," he said, drawing out the words and letting his hair fall in her face while he nibbled on his lower lip temptingly.

"Beautiful still," she said and took in a full breath of his scent.

"When you are wound too tightly to remember yourself, I will unravel you, all the beautiful and complicated layers of you," he whispered, pulling back her robe again to expose her vulnerable body.

"I'm so ug"

"Perfect. Beautiful. Mine. Dance with me, baby."

The warmth gathered between her legs, and her inner soreness disappeared under a desire too undeniable to name.

"Yes..."

"Please," he finished for her.

He caressed her scars. Every single one, finishing with her forty-three staple tracks, loving them back to wholeness.

The sweetness in his touch filled every defect in her skin, and she moaned while he healed her wounds with his attention to them.

She covered her mouth and sobbed silently.

"When you are lost for words, my Elise, I will help you...*for you, for me.*"

She laughed lightly and looked back up into his eyes. "You know...I've got a thing for another man. I feel I have to be honest and tell you about my affair. My endless love with Dimitri."

"I love Dimitri too, you know. I used to have one of his CDs, but I lost it. Sort of. Sort of gave it away. But that was a long time ago. But I don't mind. You are enough woman for both of us. I can share you, I think, and never get jealous."

"Share you..." She smirked. "Hmmm..."

"Share me, Elise."

"Only if you keep biting that lip like that."

"Now that's a deal I'll take," he said as he traced his warm and muscular hands up and down both of her legs, lingering wantonly at the place where her essence gathered to meet him. Softly, he opened the space of her most tender layers and traced the inner edges of the door to her inner heaven in a slow, deliberate circular motion.

"Say it, my love."

"Yes. Yes."

"I'll say the rest for you. Please." He giggled low but soft and deliciously.

"God you are so beautiful," he said and tested the edge of her waters with the tip of his finger. One at first and then a second...so, so warm and welcoming, so ready to quench his fire. Unable to delay their union, he lowered himself into her. His hands in hers, his eyes locked on her, his hips made a gentle motion that rotated hers and exposed her full passion to him. With one gentle thrust, his firmness opened her folds in all the right places.

"Right..."

"There," she finished for him. She fully opened her throbbing thighs and lifted her right knee up and draped her leg across his back, offering up every petal of the flower of her core willingly to him. So willingly. So willingly.

"Who doesn't love Dimitri?" she asked, still laughing as he pressed down and made short, quick circles that milked her inner cocktail. Her drink increased to show him how much she liked the way his body danced with hers.

Back and forth they waltzed. Slow then fast. Soft then hard. Firm then gently. Deep then light. Seven times one way for every one in contrast.

She rolled him over and sat up so that he could see her clearly in the sunlight coming through the open window. "My turn dancing on you."

"Yes. Please."

She giggled and pushed the full weight of her body down before rocking forward and back. Faster and faster she made the motion until even she couldn't tell you which way was up and which was down. Several times, she paused to stop the movement, knowing all too well where it was taking them.

Finally, she was unable to stop herself and kept going where there was no option but ultimate release.

"Oh, nice. That's so nice, Elise," he said and groaned trying to deny the obvious. "Too nice. Too nice. So fucking nice…oh."

She arched her back in approval for his explosion and moaned to call it forth. "Give me all of you," she whispered. "Yes. Please. Yes. Please."

"Yes. Please," he affirmed. And as he reached the peak of his love for her, filling every hole she had ever suffered with his purest intentions, she inhaled the floral aroma of his hair and opened her eyes once more to see him clearly.

Immediately, his pleasure with their union consumed his face and spread like a wildfire to hers while his spasms of joy gathered and set him free.

Her tears had dried while the rest of her oozed so much pleasure at pleasing her man. And yet again, she never looked away as the heat of that same contagious pleasure surged through her root in fulminant pulsating waves of bliss to match his.

"So beautiful," she said and laid her glistening breasts down onto his firm and muscular front, completely unaware of her own staple tracks, never once reaching up to check her heart rate. And a surprising thought that gave her immeasurable relief swirled through her mind and drizzled down her chest with all her perspiration. *My chest.*

"My chest," she whispered, unable to hold the thought without sharing it.

"Yours," he said and meant it.

What pig-goddess heart? She didn't have one. Hers was perfect now.

Gently, he traced a line down his flawless skin with her finger just like he had done down hers earlier and smiled with both his eyes and lips.

"All yours."

Two days. Four hours. Twenty minutes.

THIRTY-FIVE

Never Again

JOLENE LEFT the other woman's embrace and returned to the nursery for one last look. She knew she had to be brave for her son, so she fought back her tears and put on her best happy face.

Elliot waved back at her through the open window of the nursery from the strong arms of the nun who held him so perfectly in her arms.

"Let's go color, Elliot," she said. "Mommy be back soon. Come play with Sister Maude. I like to color. Want to help me make a picture for Mommy?"

The nun turned the little boy away from his mother's gaze.

"Love you, Elliot. Forever and always. Always and forever," Jolene said, blowing him a kiss.

Then she shuddered.

She couldn't escape the thought that she might never see him again. They had never been more than twenty feet apart, and the separation tore a great rift in her heart. Part of her gasped for air, unable to catch her breath as if she were drowning.

"He will be fine, Mommy. The faster you go, the better he does. So don't worry about him. He's just fine," Sister Maude jovially mouthed through the window.

Maude had a gregarious yet calming nature that made it easy to see why the little ones loved her so much.

She added, "I'm the Nursery Director, so don't worry. I've done this about a million times, Mommy. Okay?"

"Yes, Sister," Jolene replied. "It's not him we should worry about, right?"

As Jolene stepped away, she overheard Elliot laughing.

"Me too," Sister Maude said. "Red's my favorite color, my sweet big boy."

Jolene felt better now for sure. But the emptiness gnawed. The thought wouldn't go away.

Never see him again. Say goodbye.

She shook her head and wiggled her shoulders, unwilling to give into such an absurd fear.

Never see him again.

She blew him one last kiss and sang their song. Their special song.

She felt better. Much better.

Head up. Get it together. We've got a hair appointment today.

She walked past a Range Rover, starting to feel lighter and less empty.

"We actually have a hair appointment today," she said again. This time out loud, feeling even better.

Never once did she look up. Why should she? She was just walking the two blocks back to her apartment.

Kincaid watched with amazement. How could his luck be any better than this? No more little baby in the way. He wouldn't have to snap that stupid little neck after all. His doll was alone and utterly vulnerable.

Surely this was his chance.

He stepped out of the SUV and softly closed the door. He wiped the excited sweat from his palms on his pant legs, which covered his large, muscular thighs.

Then he fluffed his dark, wavy hair to ensure an attractive appearance. He put a small but potent mint in his mouth to smell his freshest. And then he grabbed the Ether bottle and put it in his back pocket.

The blond woman, utterly lost in her song, never even saw him coming.

"Ma'am?" he said.

"Um, yes?" the woman said as he blocked her way to the stairs up to her unit.

"Do you know where a lady named Jolene lives?" Kincaid smiled genuinely.

"Who's asking?" she said, trying to decide whether or not to be nervous. Besides, she was in a hurry. She had a hair appointment, and the clock was ticking.

The image of Elliot popped in. *Never again.*

"Well, Ma'am," he said, flashing his perfectly white teeth, "I've got some really good news for her. If you could show me which apartment she lives in, that would be great news for us all."

"What kind of good news?" she asked, certain that such white teeth confirmed the man's sincerity and her safety.

"Well, I don't see why I can't tell you. You look pretty nice to me. Can you keep a secret?" he said, looking at the ground and bending forward slightly.

"Yes. I'm good with secrets, actually."

"She's won some money. And lucky me, I get to deliver the check."

"What? She won some money? Really?"

"But it has to be in person to be official and all. My report gives me the building number, but I don't know which apartment she lives in, you see," he added.

"How much money?"

"Well, you didn't hear it from me, Ma'am, but it's a lot of money. I suspect she'll be moving out of here if you know what I mean."

"Oh," she said as the idea of money for Elliot flooded her mind. *Never poor again.*

The things she could do with it got the better of her. Besides, what kind of crazy men have such perfect teeth?

"So help one of the good guys out here," he said. "Which unit is it?"

"It's me, actually. I mean, I'm her. Jolene."

"Well, it's your lucky day then, doll. Let me show you what you have won."

"Okay," she said, following him up the stairs.

Never once did she seem to notice that he knew which apartment they were heading to.

As Jolene slipped out of consciousness, Sister Maude chased the adorable Elliot around the pews.

She waved at Wendi as she left the confession booth. Wendi, totally unaware of what was happening, thought about the blond-haired woman from earlierthe same blond-haired woman who now lay unconscious, bound and blindfolded, in the back of a Range Rover which happily headed back home to Steamboat Springs.

She, too, walked the two blocks back to her unit, utterly lost in the distraction of her reality. Her thoughts led to more like-minded thoughts that swirled and swirled faster and faster in her cognitive mind. These same thoughts took her out of present time and imprisoned her deeply into the madness of her past failures. Her father's failures.

THIRTY-SIX

Rise
_____

THE WEIGHT of the world sat on Jolene's eyelids.

She felt paralyzed within her own body. She struggled to maintain consciousness. She couldn't figure out what the hell was wrong.

Why won't my eyelids open? Where am I? Why can't I rise?

She tried to move her hand but couldn't. Her brain must have lost the signal. She attempted again to no avail. Her body failed her. It would not respond.

Where am I? What is happening?

Then she remembered when she had felt this way before: in the middle of the night, after a very, very bad dream, right after she had run away from home.

Over the next six months, after the nightmares had started, she went crazy. She would toss and turn in bed at night, trying and trying not to fall asleep all at the same time.

In her terrible dreams, a tall, dark man chased her through the forest. Like some lousy B-rated horror flick, she kept tripping on something underfoot. Slowly he followed, certain that his gradual but steady pace would outmatch her panic-driven attempts at escape.

Always, without fail, she ended up in the same place: in front of a three-story madhouse determined to eat her alive. Panting, she narrowly escaped the monster's grip, hoping to find refuge in a house almost as terrifying as her attacker.

Once inside the house, she screamed out for help, only to find the house echoed and amplified her fear with its sick and twister laughter. Now the house became her assailant bent on keeping her imprisoned inside for all eternity. Room after room, she searched furiously and fruitlessly for a way out...any way out.

Trapped in a horror movie, tripping on acid in her own mind, she couldn't find her way out.

After what felt like an eternity, she would manage to find a narrow and twisted pathway through a painfully small and menacing route fraught with death and destruction.

And just when she lost all hope of escape, a glimmer of the dark night's sky teased her. Once finally outside, after barely surviving a million pitfalls, she emerged unscathed. Yet he chased her again. Always the same manprobably a demondark with his head bent down, looking from his ominously grey jacket. Never did he make a sound, but always was he behind...and perpetually gaining on her.

The memory of her recurring nightmare flittered terrible images through her mind. Her throat tightened, and her breathing became short and gasping. Yet still she couldn't move her limbs.

Like in the dream now, she willed herself awake. She demanded her body move and rise up. She refused to be denied. She would awaken from this paralyzing dream, this horror game of hallucinations, goddamn it. She clawed to consciousness, awareness, and safety bit by painful bit.

A pressure on her hands, bindings probably, made her feel like something was holding her down, preventing her from waking.

Her body slept on, but her reeling mind flailed perfectly awake.

She tried to screamnothing!

Where was I last? Where was I when this happened?

Then she remembered the nice looking man with the check. The perfectly white teeth. His shy smile. His nervous gate. His glancing side to side.

She had let him in her apartment.

No. Actually, he had led her to her apartment. The same apartment he supposedly didn't know the location of.

Oh my God. Did I? Could I have? Did he? Oh my God...

Elliot's face popped in. Their song played.

I love Elliot. Yes, I do.

For a second, she held onto a sliver of hope. She felt a little better. Terrible, but better. Then she remembered the man reaching into his pocket and pulling out a bottle of...something.

He had called her name just when he reached around and grabbed her neck. But he didn't say Jolene. He had called her...Jill.

She was certain he had said, *"Jill, my doll. I've finally found you. You must have missed me."*

"I'm Jolene, remember?" she had replied.

And the last thing he had said was, "Not anymore."

Oh my God! What is he going to do to me?

Then she returned to a prior thought. Her baby. Elliot, her beautiful bastard.

"Elliot!" she screamed out in her tortured and floundering mind.

"Elliot! Elliot!"

Although her mouth betrayed her and no sound came out, she sang a song over and over again.

"I love Elliot. I love Elliot. Yes, I do. I love you. I love Elliot very much. I love Elliot v-e-r-y much. Yes, I do. I love you."

Her only prayer asked for his safety, his peace.

Never once did she ask for anything else during the two-and-a-half-hour drive over the unconcerned, bitterly cold Colorado road to Steamboat Springs.

THIRTY-SEVEN

Don't Say a Word

KINCAID SMILED WHILE HE DROVE. The radio played his favorite songs. All the other assholes on the road stayed out of his way. As he sped toward his den, the intensity of his pleasure mounted to full throttle.

He turned the butt-warmers in his Rover up to high heat. The sensation washed over his buttocks and groin, and his blood surged to his organ of dominion. Full with hot pulsating passion, his sword reminded him of his power, his control, his inevitable demonstration of potency, his hammer of authority.

"Look at me now. See me, Jill. See my power," he shouted, dancing to the rhythm of his favorite song. "I've got you back, my doll. You must have missed me."

While the eighties alternative band sang the provocative lyrics, Kincaid's power thoughts took over his mind. He reveled in his strength, in his God-like ability to dress up and manipulate his doll. He thought of the outfits he would dress her in, the positions he would make her hold. Their glorious reunion.

Ah.

He couldn't resist singing along. The words called him out into the darkness. The song finished, and he giggled, high-pitched and prolonged.

If only she kept her useless mouth shut, he could let her live.

"In fact, don't say a fucking word." He beamed, still dancing in his seat.

One peep and clearly she deserved to die just like all five of the other useless bitches in the basement. *Well...kept in pieces.*

He moaned.

Pieces of dolls, all in pieces.

As if they could be happy there without him. He was their glue. He put them back together.

He turned out the shape of a circle on his strong thigh. Three times to the right. Three times to the left.

Six is better. Six circles for my sixth doll, my sixth Jill.

Then he turned the circles againsix times to the right, six times to the left. *I love the number six. Six Kings.*

As he drove, he noticed the license plates in front of and beside him. The sevens teased him. *You are in the perfect place.* The sixes taunted him. *Don't forget about the nurturing mother. The devil. The Kings, my favorite.*

He laughed at the stupidity of so many humans, clueless that the plates were always talking to themurging them, guiding them. Such a shame that only he could read the signs since he didn't need any guidance.

He knew exactly what to do. He laughed again. High-pitched. Prolonged.

Now he turned his power thoughts to the party planned for him and his bride. The one in his trunk. How delicious the idea of knowing he was the only one who knew what the party was really for.

He envisioned all the stupid puppets dancing up and down to the loud music, oblivious to the source of their celebration. All the while, they thought they were invited over to his mansion for their pleasure. But really, it was always and only for him. His great display of joy intended only for his silent pleasure as his oblivious guests partied for a reason of which they were totally unaware.

When they all left, saturated in booze, drugs, and their own ugliness, the glorious silence of their absence would fill the house, fill his soul, and quiet his mind as he descended into his chamber of power to take his bride.

◎

Elise sat up straight and turned to Blackwater, terror in her eyes. "He has her. I am sure of it."

The radio came on and starting playing an old song. One from her old junior high school grunge days. That famous alternative band, probably.

Two days. Two hours. Twenty-two minutes.

THIRTY-EIGHT

Live to Tell

"HOW CAN YOU BE SURE?" Blackwater asked.

"I just know; it's like he's singing out my name. It's like I can hear him talking to me. I feel constricted like my hands are tied behind my back, but they are not. I feel a band across my neck as if he is cutting my throat. Obviously, he has her. I'm telling you. He has...Jill. He has me...again. Damn it, say something!"

She looked at her hands intensely, trying to get...and yet not get a response out of him.

She wanted to crawl under the floor. She wanted to hide under her discount store rug.

Is living in a cheap room, cheaply decorated by a dime-a-dozen rug, really living? Really, is it? Maybe I'd be better off dead. Maybe I am already dead, and this is one big posthumous hallucination.

The dry skin of her hands screamed neglect.

Her cuticles complained abandonment. Her fingernails, ragged and ridged with lines of malnourishment, shouted betrayal.

Are these hands buried in a grave in Glenwood Springs?

For a moment, her mind tried to distract her from the elephant in the room by focusing on all her faults. And what could a useless, powerless shmuck like her do about a serial kidnapper?

A serial killer. A serial mutilator. A life destroyer. An identity thief. A pig-hearted goddess maker. A forty-three staple piercer. A helpless torn-eared kitten taker. A rapist. An innocence robber. A soul sucker. A freak of nature. A devil. A king of horror.

Really, who the hell did she think she was compared to this kind of a monster? How was little old Jill...Elise supposed to save the world from an asshole of this magnitude?

Blackwater took her hands and looked at them, too.

"Nope. Still here. Not bullshit. Perfect. Not some story in some book. And very powerful. Your size does not fool me. That scar on your chest does not pull any wool over my eyes, either. I see you, even now as you try to hide from me and from this."

"Why me?" she said, the words empty and flat.

"Why not?"

Stunned by his response, she groaned. "What the hell is that supposed to mean? Are you trying to say that somehow I deserve this? That I caused this? That I did this?"

"Yes and no. Yes you did. And no, you did not."

"What? What the hell does that mean?"

"Are you the weaver of the tapestry of life?" he asked. "Who are you to think you might grasp the meaning of this kind of a situation?"

"What? Speak English for God's sake."

"Yes. Exactly. For God's sake. When we come into our life, there is always a greater force than we could ever imagine directing the course of our experience.

That intelligence sees this experience with a grand knowledge as the ultimate voyager from the place of understanding the entirety of this puzzle of life and how each piece in it connects to the next.

That intelligence understands the ripple effect of every action, thought, or feeling caused by each puzzle piece moving within the puzzle."

Sigh.

"Accept it. Accept your assignment."

"Okay. What if I can accept that? What the hell does that have to do with me and why I have to find some insane freak and stop him from killing some blond bimbo I don't even know?"

"Because you can."

"Screw you, cop."

"And because you do know her. She is whoever she is, yet she is also you. Her name is Jill as far as you are concerned. And that is who you are saving Jill. Not to mention the little boy that you don't have yet. You are saving him as well."

Silence.

"You only see your piece of the puzzle, your thread of the tapestry. If and only if you play your part can all the other pieces fit, can all the interweaving threads form their portion of the weave. Without your piece, all the others are meaningless."

"Whatever, Mister Gun Strapped to Your Belt."

"Perhaps you cannot choose what piece of the puzzle or what color thread you are handed. Truthfully, your only real choice is whether or not you will play it out and weave it through. Will you make your fate your destiny or your downfall?"

She paced. A thought returned. *Finding the answer isn't the problem.*

"Decide, Elise, because the world is waiting on you to create its majestic piece of art. And never doubt for a moment anyone else could play it or weave it better than you."

The problem is facing it.

She shook her head to clear the thought. To refuse the advice.

"Piss off, Mister Flawless Chest. I don't need this crap."

But on some level, she did…or it wouldn't be happening.

What if I faced this? Then what?

Blackwater sighed, sat down, and rubbed his neck. His scar.

"The fact that you have it to hold is the proof that you were meant to. And now it's not only my chest. It is now your chest. Don't you see? See how your piece and my piece are interconnected?"

She sensed the truth in his words just as her anger surfaced and demanded she set it free.

He smiled, raised his left eyebrow, and rubbed his neck again.

"Got you," he teased and drew his teeth down to his lip.

"Don't you dare."

"Truth or dare, you mean," he said and put his toes over hers.

"My foot?" she scrunched her nose. She raised her foot quickly, but he stepped back before she smashed his.

"But also mine. Do you see?"

"No!" She stomped the floor instead and shook her head. Fast, faster, side-to-side. She stomped again. Harder. When the wooden plank split in two, she laughed. "Okay, maybe yes…a little."

Blackwater stepped forward and stomped with her.

Then he leaned over and kissed her. Hard. "Yes. Please," he added, laughing more with his eyes than his mouth.

She surrendered to his intensity and kissed him back. Harder.

Her passion moved through her in place of covering and suffocating her. It cleansed her instead of annihilating her. It claimed her with honor instead of destroying her. She felt her center heat up and pulsate.

Like a wave of intensity, the fullness of her emotionsrage, fear, loss, sadness, anger, hate, and lovewashed through her as his probing tongue reached the center of her heart.

He was right.

Everywhere deep down inside, she had always known it.

Face it. Face him.

She refused to crawl back inside her little chest, her little scar, her little life, her empty bed.

Face myself.

Jill would not be denied. Not this time. And the boy, too. He called her out like a prince from the darkness as well.

"I'm coming, Jill," she whispered. "I'm coming to get you back. I'm coming to save you, save us...save me, save him, save us all."

She took a large gulp of water and sat back down on the couch. "I'm hungry. Let's get some food."

"No way," he replied. "No way. Not now of all times."

"What do you mean?"

"Haven't you noticed your connection to your visions is greatest while you are sleeping, usually right before you wake?"

"That's true. But I've never thought about it."

"It's because the impurities in your food are not getting in the way. We are fasting, and we are going to stay that way as long as our bodies can stand it. Don't worry; I'm here with you. We will do it together. I will show you how."

"What if I get weak?"

"Then I will hold you up."

"Okay. Whatever it takes. I'm ready. Let's do this. I got a puzzle to finish."

He laughed and raised his eyebrow again.

She bit her lip and said, "Truth or dare."

"Both. Both," he said and scrunched his nose.

"By the way, I always hated finishing puzzles. And that was even before I knew one would try to kill me one day."

He glanced at his watch. "Look at the time. It's running out."

Two days. Zero Hours. Ten minutes.

THIRTY-NINE

Thinking Out Loud

BLACKWATER CLOSED his eyes and lay down beside her. His erection betrayed his desire to love her physically again. But there wasn't time for that.

"Just go with this, okay?" he said.

Nod.

"Imagine your feet sinking down into the Earth, deep within Changing Woman at her core. Ask her to ground you, to keep you strong and centered."

"Okay."

"You will feel a tingling in your feet...perhaps even to your knees. Imagine lines of emerald green coming up from the Earth and now moving onto your legs. Okay. Now imagine peering deep into the Earth and anchoring your feet amongst the rocks and stones."

"Yes. I am standing on pink crystals."

"Now, add a bright light from above coming down and into your mind."

"Got it."

"Breathe very quickly in and out thirty times."

"Seriously?"

"As death. Yes."

"Please."

"Please," he said, all sensuality missing from his voice. "Now offer up your gratitude for three precious memories...all of them until you are them, are in them."

Her forehead smoothed over, and all the muscles in her neck relaxed while a smile lifted her mouth up. She heard her pulse in her ears. Sixty-two.

"Perfect, Elise. Now ask to be a perfect channel for the wisdom of God. Ask to be a clear channel for the light. Nod your head, and I will know to continue."

"Flashing. I'm already flashing," she said. "My forehead, tingling."

"Good. You are doing very well. If you can't hear my voice, that is okay. Know I

147

am here. The whole time, I am here. Your heart will hear me even if your ears are deaf to me."

Nod.

"Now, imagine six rays of light coming out the back of your mind. Give thanks to each of them. Feel the change in the room. Feel the support from each ray of light as they gather speed and intensity and join back up with the original light that came down from above."

Nod.

"You are so beautiful. Your soul so clean and clear. Lovely."

Her smile spread.

"Now, very slowly, breathe in through your nose and out your mouth thirty more times. In comes the light from something that stands behind our sun. It is almost like you are connecting your belly button to the sun that is the source for the sun. Can you feel the warmth in your abdomen?"

Nod.

"I may lose you now. Go with it. Just go. Follow the wave. Follow the vibration. Do not be afraid. I will call you back if you are in danger."

Elise pointed to her heart.

"Yes, I will keep an eye on your heart rate. If it gets too high, I will call you back to your body."

Nod.

And then she was gone.

A swirling door of possibility opened above her head. The door looked old and ancient...like the wooden door from a long-forgotten castle. The royal blue paint cracked at the edges. It swirled to the right, and for a moment, she just watched it twirl. From the cracks beneath and behind the door, a golden light came forth, the same golden light she saw coming like a light string from her belly button to a ball of blinding light a thousand lifetimes away.

"How do you step through a spinning door?"

"Spin with it," Blackwater offered.

As she started to rotate clockwise in perfect timing with the doorway, a group of fourteen lights encircled her. Behind these lights, a large group of white-hooded things came into her awareness. Beings, guides, probably.

A pink pulsation filled her line of sight.

The color of your heart.

It was time to walk through the door.

She did. Fearlessly.

She entered a magical garden of tropical looking plants and animals that were unknown yet familiar to her. Vines trailing from above tickled her arms and legs. Birds flew overhead, calling forth a song she had always known. Its tune, so delicious, penetrated her skin, and an orgasmic bliss pulsated through her entire being. It was like a Dimitri tune. Almost, not exactly. Maybe even more harmonious.

She remembered the song. Every note.

Here she sensed a version of love so big and clear that she had ever known was possible. The love felt like the soft, perfect warmness of fluffy pancakes, like the gentle wings of a butterfly, like the forgotten strength of her mother's arms, like the smell of rain cooling the hot afternoon pavement, like Dimitri singing for her ears only…the whole night through.

She looked down at her flawless body. No forty-three staple track scars. She gazed at her perfect hands. No wrinkles or lines of malnutrition.

A band of wolves howled, so she looked to the far edge of her field of vision. The largest of them, a gorgeous beast with dark, black eyes, stepped forward and bowed.

She bowed in return and kept walking.

Once she approached a large cliff, she stopped. Down below, she saw the roof of a tri-level house. Parked out back, a large white SUV rested on freshly made tracks in the snow.

A smell of something awful wafted up. Bleach? Followed by something rancid.

She had arrived at her destination.

She was just about to jump down when the large, black-eyed wolf pounced her from the forest's edge. He knocked her over unscathed but kept running.

She turned around to follow his path.

Flash, flash, flash!

She looked down at her feet. The shoes were not her own. She felt nervous on the inside. Excited, probably.

A man led her up the stairs of an apartment building. Hers, perhaps, even though she had never been here before. A similar-looking apartment, but not this one. She trailed and then closed the door behind herself.

But I have been here before.

She smelled soiled feces in the garbage bin, and then it hit her.

Diaper.

I'm in the victim's apartment. Pay attention, Elise. Find the freaking clue.

She heard the familiar slow and deep voice. His voice. The monster.

How many times had she heard that same terrible voice in her nightmares? How many times had she felt his breath steaming down her neck while she desperately tried to run away?

If she turned around, she would see his long, dark coat, his slow confident gait always gaining on her as she tried furiously to get away. All the while, she kept falling down, her foot caught by a stone or twig like in every predictable horror flick.

She tried to move her body away from him but couldn't. Her damn legs wouldn't go. They weren't responding to her commands.

Because they aren't my legs. They are the victim's, and this has already happened. I'm her. She's me. I can't change it. Slow down your heart, your broken and weak pig-goddess heart. Help me, Dimitri; help me now. For you, for me. Take me dancing a thousand miles away from here.

All of a sudden, she was standing in a closet, looking at clothes that weren't hers. He was behind her, but there was nothing she could do to defend herself.

"Defend the woman. Only you can help her now," a subtle thought in a voice not her own echoed through her awareness.

She reached into the closet for something. A jacket. A hanger. Anything. But her arms never moved. Frozen. Trapped in a nightmare.

But as the clothes swayed to the side, even though she hadn't moved them, she noticed a picture on the back wall—an old poster that was half-destroyed. She clawed hopelessly for the curled, discolored green edges of the parchment just as she felt his hand slam tight against her mouth.

Her body felt heavy, weak, and empty just as she crashed into the floor.

Flash, flash, flash!

She stood at the edge of the cliff again.

She tried to regain her balance. To remember the apartment. Recall the clues.

The picture. The poster in the closet. What was it? Damn it, Elise. What was it? Remember!

A song played. Like "Eternal Love" almost, but not quite.

Is it Dimitri? Tell me it's Dimitri. Help me, Blackwater. Help me, Dimitri.

Convulsions set in. She stared at the house between spasms. If her lips moved, she would have screamed. Somehow, though, she knew she had no lips.

What is that? Music. Who's he playing it for? Me. Yes, yes, yes, he is. I'm sure of it. But it's so loud. It hurts my ears. It's too loud. Turn it off!

The music softened immediately.

The house swayed side to side gracefully. It beckoned her, tempted her to dance with a soft melody. Like Dimitri would.

It wanted her. Would most likely stop at nothing to have her.

She couldn't tear her attention away from the house despite her jerking body. A tar-colored liquid seeped from the edges of its walls, and a black, dark funnel formed above its roof.

It was sucking her back in. It demanded she respond. It needed her, and in its own sick way, it loved her. It offered eternal desire. Never would it tire of the obligate obsession to own her.

The wisps of dark clouds were close and getting closer, bringing a sultry scent with them. Musk with a thick spiciness. A drumbeat tempted her to dance.

Is this what I want? To be forever loved, needed, desired?

Her legs fasciculated. Her arms flailed back and forth. Her head jerked. Her mouth foamed.

She tried to stop the movement but couldn't.

The wolves howled.

She was going to jump. Damn it, she wanted to be loved. She needed to be needed. If she completed something, perhaps it would complete her. Was that so wrong?

A pressure filled her chest. A tugging, band-like sensation surrounded her abdomen. *"Jump,"* it called. *"Come home to us forever,"* it begged. *"Stay, stay with us always,"* it argued. *"We have five others, so you will never be lonely. You will never feel neglect. You will be the Queen of the dolls, eternal royalty as our most prized possession."*

Dimitri's voice floated in. "My love!" it declared.

She looked briefly away.

A moan, so dark and deep, exploded from within the house. Its roof levitated, and a swirling army of bees, flies, and locusts swarmed toward her.

Dimitri's voice cried out. "For you, for me."

His melodic voice begged her back. "Choose us, choose this song instead. Not this. Not this place. Not like this. You don't want this, Jill. This isn't love; it's death."

"But I'm not Jill. I'm Elise. I'm Elise. I survived this already. I'm not dead. I'm not dead. Jill's dead. Not me! I'm Elise," she screamed.

Flash, flash, flash...flash, flash!

She awoke in Blackwater's arms, still jerking.

"What the hell? Where am I?" she demanded.

"It's okay. It's okay. You're back. Drink this water now. And eat this chocolate, too. Eat it now. Hold me. Hold you. Hold us."

She checked her pulse. One hundred and ten.

"The CD please. Play "My Love". It's number" she started.

He fast-forwarded to the right song before she finished her words.

One hundred and two.

She smiled. "That was freaking weird."

"You can say that again."

"How I'm reaching out for you," they sang together.

Ninety-six.

He did a mock dance, twirled to the right, and bowed.

Eighty-four.

"Thank you. I was scared," Elise professed.

"Me too." He leaned down to kiss her. Soft. Tender. Sweet. Slow.

She opened to his embrace. She accepted his tenderness. She allowed his unconditional allowance. She surrendered to his intensity.

She blinked her eyes to see him, clear her vision. A faint pink outline surrounded him and then quickly faded as a wolf howled off in the distance.

One day. Twenty-two hours. Thirteen minutes.

Elise took a quick bath and felt tons better. Blackwater was still dancing to the CD.

He laughed nervously when she returned.

"What the hell happened?" Elise demanded.

"I was just dancing. Like I said, I have this thing for Dimitri too."

"Not that, you goose. Earlier."

"Oh, duh. I'm not exactly sure to be honest," he admitted. "I tried to take you to All-Knowing Mind so that you could see what you needed to. But then something happened. Your eyes started moving rapidly back and forth, and I knew that something else was penetrating the field."

"You can say that again, for fuck's sake," she replied. "Hold me. Just hold me. Tell me I'm okay. Tell me that somehow this will all work out."

"Yes, but I think we have to be honest here. This is bigger than I suspected. You need more help than I know how to give you. I'm starting to worry that he knows you are alive. And that somehow..."

"Somehow, what?"

"That he is hunting you down from inside your mind. Shit...maybe we should stop this. Maybe we let the woman die. Maybe we start thinking about you and stop worrying about everybody else."

"What the hell, traitor? What about the tapestry? What about my important piece in the puzzle of life? What about I'm strong enough or I wouldn't have it to play?"

"I know I said that, but now...now I'm scared. I'm scared for you. And that makes me scared for me. And call me Levi. My first name is Levi. Call me Levi, damn it."

"Levi." She said the word, his name dripping off her tongue like honey. She said it again, softer, in a whisper. "Levi."

He pulled her close to him. When he kissed her, he traced the scar on her chest without realizing what he was doing.

But she missed it not. Not a bit.

She felt the terror mounting, too. She was in trouble. Big trouble.

One day. Twenty hours. Seventeen minutes.

FORTY

Hard to Say I'm Sorry

WENDI MARCHED up the flights of stairs on the backside of her quadraplex. Like all the other similarly shaped houses for rent on her block, it had four units: two up and two down. Hers was made of dark brown stone and brick that suggested strength and durability.

She loved the house. Even a quarter of its strength was enough for her.

Her back door was unlocked, slightly open. A rose hung loosely.

"Gabe," she whispered.

When she stepped into the hallway, the unmistakable smell of freshly baked cookies reminded her of family. For a brief moment, her mind returned to the sad woman with the long, pale hair pulled back in a headband from the church.

"Who are you, lady? Why are you so broken?"

She stared intensely at the tulip and bunny rabbit covered carpet that served as a threshold upon which she washed her cheap, dirty dishes. She wondered who made it and why they had chosen rabbits instead of birds for the spring design. Why did the bunnies need ribbons on their necks? Why pink tulips instead of yellow or purple ones?

She returned to her higher mind and stepped out of the distortion of her cognitive mind.

Empathy for the woman rushed back in.

"Why so wounded, so devastated? What could you have possibly done that would make you think God would be unable to forgive you? Don't you know he always forgives you? Always loves you?"

She imagined the woman's grip. The photo. The boy.

"Just like you looking at the photo of your baby...would you not always forgive his beautiful face? Would you ever deny your son love or your acceptance? Why would you think God would feel differently about you than you feel for your own child? Aren't you a child of God? Who told you that was how it worked? That somehow your Father could ever stop loving you even if you acted from an unimaginable place of suffering?

Don't you know that God sees your weaknesses as a call for love, as a call for God's perfect embrace, not a reason to deny you the same love you so obviously need? Your faults are an obvious place that he can remind you of his love more perfectly, rather than an excuse to desert you, to abandon you in your time of greatest need."

Who knows how long she stood there frozen in her sadness and reflection for this nameless stranger.

Gabe watched her from across the room.

She heard his breathing, not.

She saw his expressions, not.

She noticed his movements, not a one.

She was not really there. She was still present for the woman and the child in her photo.

In contrast, he witnessed everything she did.

He noticed every line that formed around her mouth, curved down in pain. Every muscle tensed in worry. Every subtle smile as Wendi pondered the all-accepting love of a parent for a child.

When she finally noticed him, they both said nothing. Neither avoided the other's gaze. Neither was willing to break it. Neither moved.

And then they did.

He swept her into his arms as her tears began to fall. The tears showered down for the truth in her. The drops splattered for the truth in him. For the honesty present and the honest presence between them. For the bare acceptance of their connection as humans in a world so filled with pain that its inherent beauty was so miserably lost. All of it offered over in exchange for but an illusion, a distorted delusion of truth.

"I'm so sorry," he said.

She cried for their truths. She grieved for the recently delivered mother who would never see her baby because of the drugs she traded for real love. She mourned for the father who lost his wife in exchange for a child. She cried for the sister who traded her mother for her new little brother. She spilled for the wounded and infected lungs of the nurse with pneumonia. She shuddered for the buttercup-blond-haired boy in the picture that the woman clenched so tightly. She ruptured for Mother Mary who lost her beloved son some two thousand years ago. She wailed for that same beloved son whose only dying request was that his assailants be forgiven because they did not know what they were doing. And then she cried for herself and the loss of her own innocence in a world that had all but forgotten itself. And last but not least, she cried for her father and her devastated mother.

"So, so sorry," he said again.

She blubbered for every "I love you" she withheld from her mother after she renounced her father as a liar, as a cheat, as a murderer. She mourned for the loss of her father who she never really knew. She spewed for the strangers down the street who walked aimlessly from one trash bin to the next looking for something worth holding onto.

She cried for Gabe and all the expensive lines of uselessness he had snorted up his nose.

And the tears washed her dirtiness clean.

They spilled over Gabe's disgraces and purified him, too, as he tenderly carried her down the hall to the bedroom. Bodies exposed, they let all the layers of deceit and dishonesty fall to the floor with their clothing. And then he joined her body in the perfect union of the perfect expression of physical love and acceptance as he made love to her for the very first time.

"But for this, I'm not sorry," he said.

And there was no place where she ended and he began as their love exposed itself for both of them to see its glory. Eyes red from the downpour, they were both fully and purely present for it all.

As she fell asleep encircled in his embrace, his body still joined with hers, her final waking thought returned to the woman with the long platinum hair.

"Who are you? Who is Elliot?"

Then her mind drifted off into the oblivion of sleep.

When Wendi woke up, she was alone in her bed. She followed the sound of the television into the living room. Gabe sat naked on the couch, eyes still swollen from crying.

She sat down next to him.

He sniffed and wiped his eyes dry.

"Wendi, when I was three years old, my twin baby brother died." He stared at the floor, unable to meet her gaze.

"I'm sorry. I didn't"

"I never even got to know him. To be honest, I don't really know what happened. It was something to do with his blood chemistries."

"I'm sorry," she said again.

"Part of me, and probably the best part of me, must have died with him. Ever since, it has felt like I will never be complete again."

"I'm so sorry, Gabe."

"And then I spent the next twenty years trying to save him. Trying to kill myself instead. Trying to be him. Trying to not be him. Trying to forget him. Trying to remember him. Trying to stop the emptiness, the pain, the loneliness, the battle of trying to figure out who the hell I am. Who he could have been if I were the one who died instead."

She handed him a Kleenex, but he stared blankly at it, clueless what its purpose might be.

"I mean...why him? We were identical. Why wasn't it me?"

"I don't know, Gabe."

"When I got into medical school, I knew...I just knew that I would find the answer to my suffering somehow."

"I hear you," she said.

"What a stupid joke. How pathetic am I? I believed that if I was a doctor, I would have all the answers. Answers for little Joey. Answers for me. For Mom. For Dad. But nothing changed. Nothing. I was still just the same useless, half-dead me with the letters MD on my nametag. The same half of a pair of twins, unable to ever be enough. Enough for the both of us. Enough to make either of my devastated parents forget.

Enough to make them want me instead of the son they lost. But the only difference was my mountain of debt."

"Oh, Gabe, I'm so"

"Stop. I don't want sorry. Really, what the hell did sympathy ever do for anybody? I want the pain. I want to feel real again. I've been numb, so goddamn numb, for so many years that the pain actually feels good. It feels pure and honest. It feels raw but valuable. It feels like me. It finally feels...I don't know...authentic."

"Go on. I'm listening."

"I know. I know. And you see me. You actually see Gabe, not the other brother who didn't fucking die. How long have I been standing there hiding while secretly dying for someone to just see me? To notice me through all the crap. The charades. The bullshit?"

"Me too. I know exactly what you mean."

"Well, I see you. I see the sweetness in your eyes that barely covers your sadness for all the suffering in others. I see the strength in your arms that keeps you from collapsing from the devastation of all the pain in the world. I see you keep getting up over and over again just trying to make a difference in a world constantly slamming you back down, oblivious to your love. I see how honest you are even when...it will hurt you, because that matters more to you than the useless game we've all been playing. The game of...look at me...look how brave and strong I am while I hide behind a mask pretending to be something I'm not."

"Yes. Get it out."

His chest heaved, and he rubbed his eyes again.

"Well, I'm done with that, Wendi. I want to be real, to be me, to just be me. After all, that's all I've ever really owned. Me. The truth of me. But now, sometimes I wonder if I even know who I am anymore. Maybe Joey survived. Maybe I'm the asshole who died. Maybe we are all already dead and this is hell!"

He laid his head in her lap. Then came shaking and short jerking movements of his back as twenty years of sadness poured out of him and spilled onto her, her thighs, the floor, and out through the cracks under the door, down the stairs, and out into the street of Washington Park.

One quadraplex down the icy street, a cricket joined in a mourning song as a drop of moisture trickled past him. A mouse scampered woefully back up the heater pipe, startled from the dole atmosphere while he looked for a warmer place to nest that night. A riveting sadness filled his empty heart. The air reverberated and echoed his grief off every dirty, white wall. The mouse still couldn't find his brother and felt more alone than he knew was possible.

In contrast, a snake in the basement slithered across some half-folded laundry, unaffected by the blue mood of the others. He still couldn't have cared less. And he had never been sorry. Why would he?

FORTY-ONE

Make You Feel My Love

THE TIRES SCREECHED, and Jolene's body rolled over as the car suddenly stopped. She tried to prepare for the impact by flexing her muscles. Nothing. No response. As the grating noise of a horn honked furiously nearby, she returned to her thoughts of Elliot. The last memory of him laughing in the nun's arms. She played out a new and improved version.

She blew him a kiss and rushed back to take him in her arms once more.

She tried to move her legs. Move anything. Nothing.

If she could have screamed, she would have.

"Let me go back in time, baby. I won't leave you. I won't be so stupid. I promise, baby. I won't talk to the terrible man. I'll never leave you again. Ever. Never."

The lovely scent of baby powder coated him in the memory.

"Let me smell you, my perfect baby. Elliot, please let me smell you one more time. Please, my baby. I love you so much. Please, baby, reach for Mommy."

She caressed his soft, perfectly formed hands. She twirled him around in a grand display of joy and tickled him as he laughed his sweet, adorable laugh.

"See? No man, baby. Just you. Just me. Just us. Forever. I promise, Elliot. I'll never screw up again."

She sang him their special song as he stroked her cheek with those same perfect little hands. She stroked his cheek back the cheek she loved more than anything else in the world. She knew that much was true.

"*L-yut want hot baba, Mommy*," he said.

She ached to fulfill his every good desire.

"Anything you want, baby. Anything. Forever."

"*Mommy? Where go bye-bye, Mommy? Elliot no see Mommy.*"

The horn honked again, and she rolled back over. Her head smacked the side of the car, but she couldn't adjust it. Screw her throbbing head. She returned to her thoughts.

"What if I never see you again, my sweet baby?"

"No, Mommy."

It wasn't just possible. It was probable…she'd never see her baby again.

Her thoughts remained perfectly clear.

"What if my body never works again? What if I'm forever trapped like this, unable to get away, unable to find my way back to you, my baby, my everything, my perfect little bastard? Will you think I left you on purpose? Will you never know how much I loved you? Will you even remember my face, my name, my touch? What I wouldn't give to have every second back I ever spent on that terrible phone. I could have spent them with you instead. If I had just gone back to my mother's house, this never would have happened. I could have watched you grow up…instead of this. Oh, Elliot, I ruined everything. Why can't I do anything right? If I hadn't talked to that man and let him in the house… How could I be so stupid, so useless, so awful? Forgive me, baby. Forgive me, baby. Forgive me for what I've done. I love you, baby. Forever and always. Always and forever."

Her heart shattered with the thought of her baby missing his mother.

Yet she ignored the throb in her skull.

The pain of separation from Elliot wounded her more than anything a murderer could do to her now. She would feel his torture, not.

She was already deada shell of nothingness stripped by the terrible absence of the promise of the only thing that had ever mattered to her, the only thing that she ever had: her bastard.

FORTY-TWO

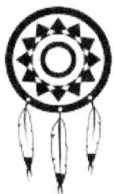

Stand by Me

SISTER MAUDE LOOKED at her watch again. Then she paced around the pew.

The low-pitched church bell rang, and she jumped.

Where was Elliot's mother? Something felt terribly amiss. The light-haired mother of this lovely child seemed to be the least likely mother of all the children to return last. The mother obviously adored her baby. Who wouldn't? He had been an absolute angel.

Usually Cindi, the single mother of four rowdy and difficult to control heathens, was the last to pick up her four rotten little offspring. Actually, Maude couldn't blame her. If she were Cindi, she would show up first and pick them up last as well.

The thought made her laugh now that the four devils were gone. At least until next Saturday, that was.

Instantly, her thoughts returned to Jolene, Elliot's mother.

Maude stopped pacing, her legs too tired to keep marching, and sat down on one of the deep mahogany pews. After a brief reprieve, she tried to stand once more, but the weight of her worry made it hard for her to stand back up. Her shoulders sank into a thousand what ifs...

She looked at her watch again, glaring at the little hand.

Eight hours. Thirty minutes. Too late. She had put in a long day.

The hauntingly deep and solemn church bell startled her again, confirming simultaneously that it was well past closing time. The Mother's Day out event had ended over two hours ago.

Maude didn't know what do to. She looked for a procedure, a protocol, a guideline. Nothing.

Should she take the boy home with her or wait a little longer? She prayed for guidance. She prayed that she might act in accordance with the highest good.

She dialed the number on the sign-in sheet once more. Still no answer at Jolene's house.

Thankfully, the little boy was safely asleep in the nursery crib.

Had the mother abandoned the boy and left a false number? Was her name even really Jolene. Maude couldn't be sure, could she? The address was local, so perhaps she should just call the police.

But then she remembered Wendi Patterson, the sweet doctor-in-training who kneeled at Mother Mary's feet earlier. She had put her arm around the blond woman. Did she know Jolene? Perhaps the boy would be safe with her?

"Yes, yes...I will call that Wendi, and she will help, I'm sure," Maude muttered.

The cold smoothness of the church floor surprised her as she opened the drafty office door. A gust of cold Denver air caressed her forehead as she leaned into the Rolodex. The hard marble slab table declared its indifference to Sister Maude's problem. It could not be bothered with such futile concerns like that of a mother and her child.

But instead of fury, the icy marble surface infused Maude's fingers with a zing of firmness, giving her the resolve to finally make the call for help.

Unlike the grey and white swirling shining surface, she did care. And she would call. Wendi would help, she was sure.

Wendi answered on the first ring.

"Wendi? Ms. Wendi Patterson...I mean Doctor Patterson, is that you?"

"Yes. Who's calling?"

"Wendi, it's Sister Maude, and I need your help. I really need your help."

Wendi hung up the phone and frowned.

Now why in the world would she have been able to help that nun? She stepped into the steaming shower still wondering why.

So odd.

She didn't know that woman with the long, lifeless hair in the headband from the Jane Doe she and her anatomy tank partners had dissected in anatomy class as first year medical students.

As if humans should ever be...dissected.

Steam filled the shower, and Wendi wrote a name on the foggy shower door: Mrs. Wilson. She traced a heart around the letters.

Wendi flashed back to Anatomy Lab. Back to Mrs. Wilson's last stand.

The poor woman, eyes yellowed from jaundice, had died from a fatal case of a rare liver disease called Wilson's disease. Her intestines stained a vivid, Christmas tree green. They had almost called the corpse Mrs. Clause but had decided against it because Emily Boots, one of the tank-mates, had a thing for Santa. In fact, she hummed Christmas songs during the more difficult sessions.

Wendi's thoughts swirled with the soapy water down the shower drain. Unable to resist, she hummed "Rudolph the Red Nosed Reindeer."

Wasn't dissecting...something reserved for the insentient creatures without feelings of any kind...like worms and frogs? Perhaps cockroaches, snakes, and mice? Like reindeer, even?

What freak of nature medical school administrator had decided that every medical student needed to coat their skin, their hair, their soul, their consciousness in the

160

formaldehyde that preserved a human body...destined to be chopped into a thousand pieces?

Wendi reached up and touched her nose. It felt shiny.

For what value, exactly, was all the chopping?

She thought of the games the other kids hadn't let her play. She sighed, full of empathy for poor old Rudolph.

What supposed knowledge did dissecting a human body birth? What was the exchange for, really?

Did they do this deed with the devil of anatomy for some elusive understanding that could possibly be derived...always and only from such behaviors as chopping, cutting, excising, and dissecting another glorious human that had been so giving of themselves in the name of science.

She cleared the steam, the fog, hoping to see Santa. To hear him say, "Ho."

The stink of Mrs. Wilson's oily sarcophagus still saturated her skin. There was no bearded man bearing gifts in a magic bag.

She scrubbed her body harder, but still felt dirty. She longed for snow, pure white snow, to clean her.

More soap went down the drain.

Why had they forced her...to dissect? She had offered to sign a waiver, but it was the chopping blade for Mrs. Wilson or expulsion for the might-never-become Doctor Wendi Patterson.

More soap down the drain.

Where's your sled, Santa? Won't that nose guide you here?

What was the real reason beneath the reason for dissecting the human being? The real purpose? The real service rendered but such debase and inhumane acts in the name of knowing, learning, and pretending to care?

Was it ever really about learning? Or was it, she wondered, more likely about extracting every last drop of humanity she as a doctor-person felt for another non-doctor-person? Surely this world could not turn round if doctors actually saw their patients as humans instead of subjects that fit in the same category as insects, worms, rodents, reindeers, and pigs that needed to be opened, explored, and dissected.

She drew a frowning face next to the heart.

She had thrown her coat, scrubs, and gloves from Anatomy class in a bin and burned them after she passed the final exam.

But did she pass, really?

She drew tear marks coming from the face.

Didn't the whole ordeal still slime her from the inside? Hadn't it placed an impenetrable barrier between her and the other humans that she would call...patient. A wall that she would never overcome, never climb.

Never...had she, the doctor, recovered from incising the ligaments of Mrs. Wilson's hands that once had lovingly held her babies.

Never...had she survived sawing Mrs. Wilson's lower jaw in half with a handsaw to view it better in sagittal section.

She wiped the face off the door and sat on the shower floor. She started the song in her mind again. From the beginning.

Santa, where are you?

Part of her had died from a fatal disease alongside Mrs. Wilson in that stink-filled pit of oily numbness: the anatomy tankthe coffin for them all.

She scrubbed her elbows again, this time so hard that they bled, and then she lay down on the cold, hard tile. Unable to stand the disgusting memory any longer, her thoughts took her back to the blond-haired woman in church. The one whose God had forsaken her.

Wendi thought about God. Thought about Santa.

They looked like the same guy to her.

She stopped humming about red reindeer noses and started saying Hail Marys instead. Mary brought her back to the church. To the woman. So sad, destroyed.

What an odd tattoo the blond-haired, nameless, and slightly prettier-than-average woman wore on her right forearm. It looked like a pencil drawn version of a deformed butterfly?

She looked back at her shower door, expecting the name and the heart to have returned. Nothing. The door was clear, except for some smudges.

What did the design mean, and why had the woman chosen to mark her body permanently with such a basic yet flawed drawing when she must have had the choice of it amongst a thousand other more perfectly formed butterflies at the tattoo parlor? Perhaps the woman did it herself with ink and a needle?

Wendi put pressure on her elbow, and the bleeding stopped.

She stood up and drew a name again. Elliot. Then circled it with a heart. A smiling face. No tears. Some balloons.

The sharp contrast of the hot moist and cold dry air in her bathroom formed a layer of condensation, which obscured her own image in the mirror.

Am I really even here at all?

Gabe's voice trailed from the kitchen. He sang along to a popular song on the radio.

Wendi wrote a name on the mirror next. Wendi. She drew a heart around it. No balloons.

The female singer's robust and melancholy voice sounded too old, too penetrating for the body that contained it. It demanded to be let free, to escape the confines of such a normal looking larynx as it wailed its songs of gut-wrenching heartbreak.

Wendi lost herself in the voice.

Frowning face next to the heart.

Did the songwriter come into this life so broken, so devastated by love, or had she somehow manifested that along the way? And if so, why? What was the purpose, the benefit of such terrible pain? Was the suffering itself the reason? Was the journey through the torture actually the destination? And what gave people like her such proclivity for suffering so terribly in the name of love? Did love want them to suffer so? To then, what? Be worthy of it finally after lifetimes and lifetimes of miserably losing it, grasping at it, gasping for it with a final screaming breath of agony?

She thought not.

She envisioned a new kind of love. One without limits. One defined by a lack of limits, actually. Eternal love.

Gabe cheerfully popped his head in the bathroom.

Quickly, she wiped the image from the mirror.

He glanced at the shower.

"Who is Elliot? Should I be jealous?"

"Nothing. Nobody. Never mind. No."

She shook her head. Heard the memory of Maude's voice asking about the woman. Thought about the musical artist Dimitri Arion. About "Eternal Love", one of his most famous songs.

"You ready for the best homemade pizza this side of Chicago, baby? Hope you're hungry."

"Starving actually," she honestly replied.

But not for food. For a new kind of love. Eternal love.

She looked at her naked reflection. Too heavy. Too fat. Breasts sagging. Blemished forehead. Boring hairnot curly, not straight. Boring colornot blond, not brown. Dishwater blond.

Boop-oop-a-doop. I am no sex symbol. I am a dishwater goddess. And I am starving.

She was starving for love, for unconditional acceptance, for connection, for uncompromising allowance, for answers to the millions of questions that plagued her, eternally searching for the peace of stillness in a doomed-to-idealism mind. For answers about her father. About what he supposedly did. Hopefully about what he didn't do. Could she have the genes of a murderer?

"Well hallelujah then, girl. I'm your man." Gabe chuckled, his enthusiasm coating her like honey.

"Yes, hallelujah," she said, forcing a smile, trying to buzz like a bee.

"Boop-oop-a-doop. But am I your girl? Or are you just another huge mistake I have made in a never-ending string of failures?"

She smiled bigger, forced it harder, and hoped, for once, that she meant it.

Or at least could fool herself.

FORTY-THREE

Already Gone

JOLENE MOVED HER RIGHT ARM. Barely.

It's wearing off the drugs...the poison...whatever. It's wearing off.

Slowly and with great effort, she lifted her right arm the tiniest bit. Still bound behind her back and tied to her other arm, it moved so slightly.

Thank God.

Her eyelids, still heavy like iron curtains over her eyeballs, didn't budge. She could wait...as long as it took...as long as it needed. Her patient confidence saturated her...on a sub-anatomic level.

Hope.

Her mind flashed to the outline of her right forearm marking. The slightly imperfect butterfly-like outline fluttered.

Hope, take flight.

How many people had asked her about that bizarre little tattoo job? Ten? Twenty? Who knew?

How many times had she lied about being drunk and the tattoo guy screwing it up as she ran out the parlor door, too terrified to let him fix it properly?

One person knew the truththe real reason behind its imperfectly made design, drawn perfectly to her perfect description: Jessie.

He had said his name was Jessie. But who knew?

He might have really been named Dylan, Andrew, Rich, Tim, or even a Bickford. He could have been named anything, trapped just like her in a world filled with billions of nameless assholes.

Flash! She was one year back in the past, taking Jessie's call.

The phone call felt different, lighter, easier when it rang.

The caller claimed that he didn't need the usual services. He required only that she talk to him...like he was just an old friend. Perhaps they might pretend they had known each other for years. Some kind of soulmates, perhaps?

She agreed immediately. Fine by her. She could use a soulmate.

He divulged his past. He confided his greatest fears. His greatest weakness. His eternal suffering.

In exchange, he asked for one promise. No lies.

He would know if she lied. He always knew. He was an empath.

That was his gift, his double-edged sword. He heard the thoughts behind what someone disguised in their deceitful and obscuring words of conversation.

She agreed. No lies.

"What is your greatest fear?" he asked.

She hesitated, afraid to answer him truthfully. Then she decided, what the hell. What did she have to lose?

"Never to know what it feels like to be good enough for somebody else," Jolene confessed.

"Good," he said.

"How's that good, Jessie?"

"Yes, that's really my name. I know you are wondering."

"Okay. I believe you. I knew a Jessie once. Sweet boy with kind eyes."

"Yes. Kind eyes. I can almost see them. Now they are glassy."

"Me too. See them, I mean."

Sigh.

"I am afraid no one will ever love me," she said again.

"Good. Good because you are one step ahead of the rest of the idiots on this planet. Most people have no idea what they are afraid of. They feel the stink of it. They taste the slime that coats them but remain clueless as to why. For me, it's never having the courage to go outside again."

"What do you mean? Don't you go outside every day?"

"No."

"What? Seriously?"

"Not for eight years now. I'm too afraid. I don't go outside. But I want to. So badly that it makes me sick."

She heard him clear his throat and then wipe his mouth.

"Oh," she said, lost for more appropriate words.

"Yep. It's a real bummer. There was this fire when I was a teenager. Big tragedy. Anyway, now I'm too afraid to do the one thing I want to do the most. I'm terrified of open spaces."

The story sounded familiar. Had she read about it in the paper, perhaps?

"What do you think will happen?" she asked.

"Can't say exactly. Just mortified. Can't control it. I start shaking, and then I go back inside. It's too hard to face it."

"There's a word for that right? Agora...abora...a"

"Agoraphobia. Yes. There's a word for a million and one fears. Mine is just one of them. So I stay in. I can get anything online, so I don't really have to go out to live."

"Wow. I never..."

"I know." He laughed. "You take walking out the front door totally for granted. For some people, it's a big deal."

She laughed back. Genuinely.

"I miss the stars, so I hired a painter to paint my ceiling like the night's sky. So here I stay, trapped and tortured by my fears, wrapped in the beauty of the night's sky."

"Wow. I'm so sorry. I guess I don't really know what to say. Have you sought professional help?"

He laughed again. "Yes. How about you?"

"I'm serious."

"Me too. As for a shrink…I can't drive to my appointment. And they don't do that kind of crap online."

She exploded at the absurdity of it all. "Bummer. That's awful."

"I know, right?"

Now they were both laughing so hard they couldn't stop. He snorted, and they laughed even harder. Then she snorted, and they roared again.

When he finally stopped, he asked, "If you could do anything differently, what would it be?"

She thought about it for one-millionth of a second.

"I would tell Jimmy about our baby. I would have asked him to run away with me instead of running away by myself. And he would know Elliot. And Elliot would know him."

She flashed back to present moment.

And I wouldn't be here…frozen and trapped in my own body while my poor baby is all alone thinking that somehow I could have ever left him on purpose.

Back to the memory, she returned.

"Jimmy had this birthmark, Jessie. It kind of looked like a butterfly on his right arm. And he hated it. He was so embarrassed by it. Whenever he talked, he shoved his hands in his pockets so no one would see it. No one knew about it but his mother and me. So I tattooed one just like it on my arm, too. So even if I was dead the next time he saw me, he would know that I never forgot him and his mark. The mark I loved on that arm of his I loved so much."

"That's beautiful."

"No. It's not. It's pathetic."

"I don't think so."

"Hey, I've got an idea, mister."

"Okay. What's that?"

"Why don't you open the door and look outside while you talk to me? I'm here the whole time. And I'm not going anywhere."

He gasped. Could he face it? Face his problem with her help?

"I'm staying right here 'cause you're paying me too much to hang up."

"But"

"Just do it. I know you can. I believe in you even though you don't."

"I don't know, Lisa."

"My name's not Lisa. It's Jolene."

"I know." In exchange for her honesty, he agreed to step outside.

And she stepped inside.

Inside her love for Jimmy. Inside her loss of it. Inside her greatest fear, too.

She flashed back to the present…where she was living it out, imprisoned by a monster that planned to kill her.

Her left hand moved. Soon, her eyelids would open, and she would see how much trouble she was in. For now, she kept them tightly closed, still hoping for a way to find

A way back to Elliot.

A way for Jessie to step outside again.

A way back to Jimmy.

A way back home to a world where maybe, maybe...one day she could be good enough to deserve the happiness of even a dirty life spent telling lies on the phone.

Deep in her gut, Jolene already knew better, though. A madman had kidnapped her. And she was going to die. *Elliot, my baby. I love you!*

FORTY-FOUR

Almost There

ELISE STARED AT BLACKWATER.

She shook her head and checked her pulse. One hundred.

She grabbed his hand and tried to forget about his suggestion that they back down now.

"I'm tired. You're tired. Maybe we just go to bed…Levi."

"Levi. It sounds nice when you say my name."

He held her, and she let him. Eighty-two.

They swayed side to side even though the CD player was off. Sixty-nine.

"Maybe this is all some big mistake and life will just be normal tomorrow. I will go to morning report in a few hours. Some poor intern will get her ass chewed out for something no one ever told her about. Then I can laugh and just pretend all this never happened."

But Elise already knew better.

This was happening. And in less than two days, a woman and her son named Elliot were going to die the same horrible death in the same horrible place that had mutilated Jill, a one-eared kitten, and a girl's small-town dreams.

He pulled her tighter. "Say my name again."

"Levi." Even her eyes smiled out the two syllables.

He stroked her cheek and kissed her on the nosethe nose he loved more than all the others. Lightly. Sweetly.

"Yes. Please," she said and then laughed. "The nose, not the rest. I'm too sore."

He bit his lip, and she laughed.

"Funny," she said, but quickly, her smile slid down her face, and she swallowed hard.

"No. Not funny. Shit, Elise, I don't want to lose you. I'm afraid. Did you hear that? This freaking police detective is scared. Terrified, actually."

169

She gave him an Eskimo kiss and held onto a new smile as firmly as she knew how under the circumstances.

He pulled her in tight again. "I lost you once five years ago. I don't know if I will survive if I lose you again...now that I finally have you back. I've looked at your picture so many times. Every time I thought if I could just save Jill...get her back, help her remember, then somehow it would all be okay. Maybe I'm a fool, but I feel like I've known you forever. I feel like you are part of me."

"Oh, now all the my chest stuff makes sense."

"Yes. Please." He raised his eyebrows up and down quickly twice and pretend nibbled on his lip. "Ouch," he said, the word coming out muffled sounded more like a howl than an "ouch".

The image of a howling wolf popped into her mind the same wolf that for so many years had stalked the edges of her dreams. Watching, waiting, protecting.

Her eyes widened.

Levi was the wolf. He always had been.

She squeezed him back, and it felt good and strong and right. Their eyes met, and she softly stroked his cheekthe cheek she was pretty sure she would love more than all the others for the rest of her life.

He offered a throaty moan, almost howled, and then smiled with his eyes.

"But how can you lose me? It's all in my mind, right? So what? So what if I go into that foul-breathed three-story house in my dream or vision? So what if I travel as a Spirit Walker, as you put it? How can he possibly hurt me if I'm physically here with you? How? So why should I, I mean we, be afraid?"

He wouldn't look her in the eyes.

"What? What are you not telling me?" she demanded.

Her voice quivered. Her eyes shifted down, trying to gather his.

Ninety-five. One hundred and two.

He finally looked up.

"Listen and listen good, okay? Two things could happen. The first is that he might figure out you are still alive. And then nothing, not even the best disguise in the Witness Protection Program, will keep you safe from his insanity."

"Why does he care about me so much? He's killed others...at least you think. More than just Jill."

"Because you got away. You got away from him. What do you think that does to a madman? I think every one of the others has been a stand-in for you, for Jill. He's still trying to kill you...by killing them."

"What? You have to be kidding me. But I..."

Once his words sank in, her heart raced, her stomach tightened, and her knees shook. One hundred and twenty.

He checked her pulse. He stepped toward the CD player and turned it on.

"Help me, Dimitri. Help me," she whispered.

The song began. She hummed along.

My love? Are you reaching out for me? Do you sometimes meet me in your dreams? One hundred and eight.

The subtle drumming. Ninety-four.

The soft tune. The sad yet hopeful melody. Her hips swayed gently side to side. *Do you know my eyes? Do you love my smile?*

What if Blackwater was right?

Then she remembered her vision from inside the next intended victim. He had called her Jill. Blackwater was spot on.

The song played louder. *Yes, I'll tell you where to seek my heart. I'll help you find your way, Dimitri.*

"And then… " Blackwater grabbed her shoulders. Held her gaze.

I wonder, too, Dimitri. Keep singing. Keep singing.

Her fingers stayed on her neck. One hundred and four.

"Freaking spit it out. Then what?" Elise said.

"When you travel in the spirit realm, there's a chance, although it's a small one, of not making it back to your body."

"What?" One hundred and ten.

"If he knew you were watching and he knew just what to do, he could sever your ethereal cord. And you would be lost...lost in a ghost world unable to rejoin your body."

"What the hell are you saying?" One hundred and thirty.

He met her eyes, and she knew he was telling her the truth.

She sat down, put her head between her knees, and started breathing deeply and slowly.

He sighed deeply and almost choked on the air. "That you would be dead, but not dead. Undead. In a useless shell of a body that no longer housed your traveling spirit. You, but not you. Flesh and bones filled with nothing."

"Are you actually serious?"

She shuddered and swallowed hard. She wished she didn't know. She wished she could go back to ten minutes ago.

"Take it back. Fucking take it back. Tell me you are kidding!" she screamed.

Silence.

He dropped to his knees and breathed in time with her.

She shook his shoulders. Hard. Then harder once more.

He finally responded. "I'm as serious as death."

"Make it go away. Take it back." One hundred and fifty.

"I can't."

"Then kiss me so I will forget you said it. Either take it back or take me. But take something, Levi. Take it now."

He laid her down on the bed and rubbed her carotids to slow her heart rate back down. One hundred and twenty. Ninety. Seventy-two. Fifty. Forty. Too low.

She rolled over, grabbed the trashcan, and almost spewed like a drunken college girl, but thankfully, it passed. Checked again. Sixty-six. Better.

He wiped the saliva from the corners of her mouth and started kissing her lips. Her neck. Her breasts. Her thighs. Every single scar. Her lips again. Her navel. Her hip arches. He paused by her pelvis and looked up to ask permission.

"I said take it." She slyly smiled.

"Yes. Please. So beautiful. You smell delicious." Then he kissed her inner foldsworking her core, nibbling lightly but wanting so badly to taste her very essence.

She moaned and opened her legs fully to allow his kisses to reach deep within her most sacred place.

In delight, she caressed his head, his neck, his shoulders to encourage him to keep going. Hard. Deep. Harder still. The urgency was so palpable around them that the room pulsed with an intention of pure unadulterated need. Want. More need. Desperate need. Yearning for intertwined and intimate connection.

He probed and pressed her pleasure button with his palm as his lips found hers again. He reached within her, pushing his fingers farther inside her warm petals, holding on, stroking her garden for dear life. Her rains welcomed him with obvious reciprocation of his need to fill her.

She arched with approval, gasped, and then grunted softly as her juices increased and dripped down his hand.

Flicking her tongue under her bottom lip, she held in all of the words. Her declaration of love. She wouldn't say it first. But goddamn she knew it was true.

Unable to tolerate her own silence, she offered one word she knew he could hear without recoiling in emotional fear from her affection. "Yes."

"Please," he grunted with her and kept petting her flower.

"Love me, please," she said with quick, gasping breaths.

To prove she meant it, she grabbed his throbbing manhood with her full hand firmly, pressed in, pulled up…returning his need, his passion, his hot insatiable love. She tore her lips from his and moved to his groin. Licking the edge of his smooth and tempting head, tantalizing the center of his tip lightly and provocatively while periodically visiting the base of his shaft with a quick moving tongue, she said it again. "Yes. Love me, please."

He moaned in approval, and she took him as deep as she could inside her mouth, mimicking the pattern that had satisfied her so much the last time they made loveseven to one.

Perfection–seven. Wishes granted–one. The meaning of the two numbers in numerology so effectively paralleled in our love making. The thought passed too deeply in her subconscious mind for her to even realize she had it. She was thinking about something, no someone, else.

Seven deep motions down to one superficial up.

Seven sucking movements to one light breath of minty air.

Firm pressure on his tenders underneath the shaft seven times and then letting go of them for the count of one, hoping it would draw out his strongest force of pleasure.

"So good," he said seven times.

She came up delighted that she could motivate his need to release with her. "So good. You are like candy to me," she said once.

"I want you to…"

"Me too, baby. Oh, baby."

"I want…"

"All of you. Love me now. Inside me. Love me now."

"All of us. Love us now. Inside you. Inside me."

Finally unable to hold back any longer, she positioned his manhood at the edge of her warm, dripping opening. Then she thrust down upon him intently.

When she groaned with his entry, he howled in perfect reply.

"Yes. I do love you. Love us. I always have. From both the inside and out."

One day. Eighteen hours. Eleven minutes.

FORTY-FIVE

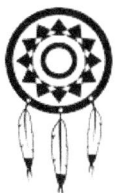

Separate Ways

ELISE SLID DEEP DOWN in the steaming, hot bubbles as Dimitri's voice tried to keep her out. He sang. She soaked. His serenade fell on covered ears. Only one word filled her mind once more. This time, it was…no.

She sank under the soothing water, and her faith, her courage, her strength, her ambition to be…something more…drowned with her.

"For you, for me," the lyrics moaned.

Elise moaned with them.

"That's the best it can be," she promised the maker of the music, her curly-haired Latino lover in a world of thieves. She sighed.

"I had a vision once, too, my love. And it was brilliant as well."

She imagined him dancing, moving so perfectly to the rhythm. Unable to resist, she reached out for his imaginary fingers.

"Yes. Show me. Please show me."

The song played on. Her throat tightened. Tears threatened.

As the tempo increased, she started slapping the water.

"Damn it, Elise. Get your shit together," she demanded.

Her thoughts bobbed up and down with the bubbles, gathering speed.

What is the difference anyway...between you, between me? What if I don't do it for you, for me? Will anyone else find the courage? Will they?

She started singing, unable to resist.

"It's time we stand together. Oh yes! And wake up to what we are. We are light, brighter than a star!"

The water stopped moving along with her thoughts.

Silence.

The next song cut in.

"My love!" the CD called. "My love!" it declared.

The usual song played, but she heard the chorus differently. *"Will you answer the phone, Elise? For her, for Jill, for you, for Maddie the mangled kitten, for the other five girls on the other end of the line, for God only knows how many other innocent women in the grocery store?"*

She gasped. Now she was having auditory and visual hallucinations.

"My love! How I'm reaching out for you." The CD commanded she reply.

Her terrified confusion battled with her clarity of purpose. The soap bubbles popped in her ears. The swish-swish-swishing murmur of her pig-goddess heart beat to the rhythm of the song.

It pulled her forward.

Her mind, witness to her personality, anchored her in stillness.

Who must be placed first? This woman? These five other victims? The unknown victims of some unimaginable tomorrow? Or herself, her sanity, and Levi's affection?

"And what about Jill?" her heart asked. *"Who will save her if you won't?"*

"Knock, knock," Blackwater said through the door. "Your hot chocolate is ready. Can I come in?"

"Sure, sure," Elise said.

But she was anything but sure. She shook the bubbles from her hands. Blew the hallucinations from her ears.

She wanted to be alone. And she didn't.

She wanted to run away. And she didn't.

She wanted to scream.

And she wanted to cry.

He leaned in and smiled.

Then he kissed her arm, starting at the shoulder and trailing to her fingers.

She wanted to pull back. And she didn't.

She wanted to make love to him again. And she didn't.

She wanted to tell him to get out of her private life. And she didn't.

Silence.

He traced the length of her chest scar and softly cupped the curvature of her breast under the fuzzy bubbles of her bathwater.

"Elise"

"Don't start. Just leave it. Just leave it a little longer. Okay?"

"I know this is hard, baby."

"Please, Levi, don't call me baby. It makes me feel devalued somehow."

"K. How about sugar lips, then?"

"Ugh."

"Love of my life?"

"Ugh...er..."

"I'm just kidding."

"Good. How about Elise?"

"Fair enough. Listen, I expected that you might feel conflicted. How could you not have intimacy issues after what happened to you."

"I don't have..."

He raised his eyebrows and smirked.

She made a small pinching motion. "Okay, just a little bit." She laughed.

"How about we decide to not push that right now."

"Okay, deal. Thank you. Let's go to bed."

He smirked again.

"To sleep, I mean," she said emphatically.

He grinned. "Sure, if that's what you really want to do. Sleep is so boring."

"And then we can see how things look...how I feel about things. We both have work in a few hours, and that, I think in a weird and crazy way, is a really good thing."

"I'm still up for not sleeping, too. Just in case you change your mind. Just so you know."

She shook her head. "Men only think about one thing."

"Yep. Now you know my only secret."

He involuntarily traced his neck scar. She pretended not to notice.

"Get out of here... after you hand me my robe and my hot chocolate."

After her bath, she lay down next to him. And even though she felt her center heat up, begging for his attention, she kept it to herself.

His snoring helped her deny it.

She looked at his neck. Almost touched it. Denied that, too.

"Maybe," she whispered, "I will wake up someone else. Someone without visions. Someone who hadn't already purchased a tombstone. Somebody like everyone else."

She giggled. "But I still want you."

He rolled on his side, and the snoring stopped.

But the second she closed her eyes, the flashes started up. First, she spun in a clockwise direction while she approached the ancient blue star-gate above her head. Behind it, a bright white light shone from a thousand suns away. The warmth oozed through the ancient ocean-colored door with cracked paint around the edges.

Blue. Why is it always blue?

The flashes intensified.

Out of curiosity, she froze the flash in her mind and objectively observed. In the center, a bright spider-shaped luminosity stretched forth its inviting tentacles of brilliance. The purity of the white was unearthly, more penetrating than any white she knew in her waking reality. At the tips of the light-fingers shooting out from the center were tentacles of silver intensityeach as hot, strong, and powerful as a bolt of lightning in a summer electrical storm.

Thunder clapped, and the pulsating light returned to normal speed.

"Thank you for showing yourself to me. You are beautiful."

When she turned around, she heard a meow in the back seat of her Toyota Corolla. She fingered her Minnie Mouse-in-a-red-polka-dot-dress keychain.

Unable to resist the temptation, she twirled the keyssix times forward and then six times backward to slow her unusually anxious mind.

Shit. He's about to take me. Oh my God. He's about to take me.

"Twirl, twirl the keys faster," she bellowed. She chuckled, high-pitched and prolonged. "Maybe that will stop him, stop the voices."

What voices?

With the strength of a metal vice, a large, muscular hand grasped her right shoulder from behind. The other hand twirled several rungs of her curly hair tightly around a fingersix times forward and then six times back.

"I have you now, Jill. You're all mine...again," the voice whispered.

Her head jerked back painfully against the headrest. She tried to turn around and face him but couldn't. He held her too tightly.

She reached up with her free hand to touch her chest, hoping he wouldn't notice the movement.

Please, no staple marks. Please. Elise, make sure there are no staple marks on your chest!

But there were.

Forty-three rows of two little holes each that would never heal, to be exact.

She grabbed the Minnie keys from the ignition and with a force she had never known possible, turned around to face him with the weapon.

He ripped her hair.

"I'll gouge out your fucking eyes, you creep!" she screamed.

But he wasn't there.

The only thing in the back seat was a meowing kitten with one missing ear, staring back at her. The kitten tilted her head to the right and meowed again.

Elise woke up choking in an empty bed.

Thump, thump, thump, her heart slammed. One hundred and thirty-four.

She slowed it down like the biofeedback expert she was.

One hundred and two. Eighty-eight. Seventy.

Next to her on the bedside table, a note read:

Think we have a lead in the case. Call came in last night. Call me later if you can. You were finally resting, so I didn't dare wake you.

See you soon,

-LB

The letters looked familiar. *LB.*

Next to the note, her gold and silver butterfly necklace sparkled in the morning light coming ever so faintly through the curtains.

Quickly, she snatched it up and put it on.

"Fly me away from here, butterfly. Let me ride your perfect wings to anyplace but this. I'm not a caterpillar anymore; I'm a butterfly. Tell me I'm a butterfly," she begged.

"He knows I'm alive. I know he does. God help me, Levi. God help us all."

One day. Fourteen hours. Fourteen minutes.

FORTY-SIX

Give Me One Reason

WENDI PREPARED MENTALLY for morning report. The curtains shifted, and she jumped. She dropped her coffee mug and drowned the cute, little bunnies on her rug.

She shook it off, unsure why she felt so nervous.

The phone rang. Her senior resident, probably.

What do you want? It's five-freaking a.m.

She checked the caller ID and gagged. She considered cleaning the rug first but answered the phone instead.

"Yep, Chief. Wendi here."

"Wendi, I hope you are well rested this morning."

"Why is that, Jack?"

"You mean Doctor Paulson, Wendi."

"Okay. For what Doctor Paulson?"

"For Doctor Buhl's grilling, of course."

"Excuse me? What?"

"About the dead lady, duh. Why are interns always so freaking stupid? I had high hopes for you. Thought maybe you were smarter than the rest...with such high scores on your Step One and Two Boards and all."

"Excuse me? What did you say? I must have misunderstood you. Did you just call me stupid?"

"Whatever."

She suppressed the acid accumulating in her throat.

"Go on then," she said, mocking a beauty pageant smile. She fluttered her eyelashes and tried to mask her disgust with a sweet high-pitched chuckle.

Tried, but failed. The charade was pretty lame.

Her chief continued. "You know, the lady that bit the dust while we were on call the other night. It is a sentinel event, you know."

"A what?" she asked, still shocked that another doctor had called her a stupid intern. Not to mention his tone devoid of humanity.

She felt a boop-oop-a-doop coming on.

"A sentinel event. Duh, Wendi. You are clueless, aren't you?"

"Excuse me?"

Her smile grew in an attempt to cover her clenched teeth. She fluttered her eyes again, but it wasn't working.

"Don't you pay attention in morning report? The term 'sentinel' describes an event in the hospital or other healthcare facility that could have resulted in the direct or indirect morbidity or mortality of a patient."

"So? I know that."

"You know...M&M conference, duh?"

"I'm still trying to understand how that involves me."

"The event initiates a process called an RCA: Root Cause Analysis."

"And?"

She held her fingers over her lips to hold in the boop-oop-a-doop.

"The RCA explores every facet of the events leading up to and during the same pain-in-the-ass event."

She twirled her hips and flipped up her foot.

"Okay, but what does that have to do with me? I never met her until after she had already died."

"You were there, Wendi. Duh."

"Still confused how that matters, Ja...Doctor Paulson."

Shimmy. Shake. *Still not working.* Her jaw clicked from the pressure of her death-bite.

"And if you were there, little intern, you were at fault. Obviously."

"What?"

"It's just the facts of intern life. So get ready to get your ass chewed."

"But I'm"

"And"he laughed"don't take it personally if you get hung out to dry. That's the way it works, Patterson. Diarrhea flows downstream just like water. As the intern who was on call that night, you are by definition...downstream."

"But I"

"I know, but that doesn't really matter. It's just the way it works. We've all been there."

The line went dead.

Just the way it works?

She shouted at the phone, "Well that is...stupid! Unlike me!"

She stomped her foot and shook her fists. Her TMJ kicked in, and she couldn't open her mouth. She reached up to adjust her jaw, forgetting all about sexy posturing.

"Ouch!" she hollered.

She cracked her knuckles and rubbed her neck.

She pointed her finger at her reflection while her jaw stuck again. Then she pressed on her cheeks to release it once more.

"How am I supposed to learn when all I do is spend time trying to...not screw up...not get blamed...not draw attention...not whatever. Screw this!"

She walked to the door, throwing her white coat over her shoulder.

"I'm not playing your game anymore, Doctor Jack Paulson. I mean, Jack-ass!"

She wiped the spit from her lips and stomped again as she locked the back door with her Betty Boop-in-a-red-polka-dot-dress key chain.

"Thought you would always save me. But not this time, eh, Betty? Boobs aren't everything. You do know that, don't you?"

The whole quarter-mile walk to her car, she squealed. She kicked the snow. She screamed. She jumped on the curb.

"What about the Hippocratic Oath? What about the practice of medicine? What about my learning? My future patients? My future career? When has any of this ever honored me? Honored my choice as a healer? Honored what I chose to do in this world?"

Her anger swirled faster and faster as the pieces clicked in place. Then she shifted her jaw again.

"Damn it. Ouch."

The medical educational system was so broken. At the core all the way to the deepest structure of her training, the whole stinking system was screwed up. Surviving the system obscured the possibility of learning from it. Each level up punished the level beneath it.

But why?

Because the previously emotionally sodomized doctors now had the chance to return the favor.

Well screw you and the butt-fuck without a reach-around, Jack-ass.

"Doctor Paulson, I mean." She spit and opened the car door.

As she clicked her belt in place, she added, "I have no intention of accepting blame for something I never did. Will I help? Yes, of course...but not by standing quietly to the side and taking the shit that flows downstream because that's my little intern...ly duty. The whole system reminds me of slavery, of injustice against women, of injustice against gays and lesbians."

She found her platform and stood on it. Slippery diarrhea-covered steps or not.

She looked in the rearview mirror and told herself once more where she stood. She straightened her back as she realized her stance was smack dab on top of righteousness and reasonableness. As usual.

For her, there was simply no other place to stand. She refused to live in a world made with anything less than integrity. She planned to make a difference with her honorability, just like Gabe said, no matter what the cost.

"Boop-oop-a-doop, Doctor Paulson. You can kiss my diarrhea-covered ass."

She twirled Betty's dress, and the engine roared.

As the car sped off, the tired little mouse scampered away. He had been up all night still searching for his brother. After finally giving up, he had tried to return the usual way into the building, but the snake was still there, sleeping like the devil he was. The other way in the building, which belonged to the blond-haired woman, had been too rank after that man in the Range Rover had leftthe smell of him so strong and terrible just like a portala portal of darkness for one of the six dark kings.

Brother mouse knew about portals. He had no intentions of ever falling through another one again. The last time had ended so poorly.

He looked at his little paws and flinched. Where were his goblin claws now? The precious gold? And his brother. Where was his brother now?

FORTY-SEVEN

Billy Jean

JOLENE REGAINED CONSCIOUSNESS BRIEFLY. She felt the pressure of someone's hand on her left foot. The grip was sweaty yet firm with sandpaper roughness on the surprisingly muscular fingertips. It had to be his.

His breathing sounded gasping and heavy. Either he was thrilled, worn out, or both. She didn't know which scared her more.

Don't ask, her mind warned. *Don't explore it, Jolene.* Her thoughts begged her to leave it be.

She smelled something salty and metallic near her nose and then felt a sticky liquid drip from the tip of it onto her lower lip. She let it hang there like the phone, dirty but unnoticed, unacknowledged, unexplored.

She sensed that her eyes would open if she tried. She decided not to.

She flashed back to one of the few memories of her father.

"Baby, baby, wake up," he said as they pulled into the driveway. He opened the back door, but still she played possum.

Pick me up, Daddy. I love it when you carry me, she wished. And then he did. She sighed and relaxed into the comfort of him.

The strength in his arms told her he would always protect her. The warmth of his chest told her he would always keep her warm at night. The tenderness in his touch as he softly rubbed her back told her he would always be there for her. It was a lie.

That was the last time he held her like that. He left the next morning in an eighteen-wheeler headed for the west coast after a screaming knife fight with her mother. She hadn't seen him since.

She felt piercing pain in her right toe, followed by a loud smacking sound as the sticky, thick drip slid down her chin.

For a moment, she wondered why the memory of her father would hurt so much. And in her toe, of all places. Her heart? Sure, that made sense. But her toe?

She didn't move or scream, still reflecting on the painful loss of her father. Was he dead? Was he still alive? Who knew? Only God knew; it was His little secret.

Then she realized it wasn't the memory that hurt.

A hammer shattered her right great toe in a thousand pieces. Smashed her dreams into a thousand nightmares.

Elliot! Elliot! Elliot!

She would have tried to move, tried to scream, tried to get away...but she couldn't figure out what she feared most: dying or surviving this and going back to her wasted life, her broken life so full of paina life where Elliot deserved so much more than she had to offer.

Elliot! Elliot! Elliot! My poor baby! Maybe that kid is not my son. I never deserved him.

Maybe his life would be better without her. Really, what did she possibly have to offer him? An efficiency apartment full of lies and pain. A dirty wall that held a phone that rang out in the middle of the night to reveal her sins. A life that excluded fathers and grandparents.

What kind of life was that for a baby as perfect as Elliot?

The church would find him a proper home; of that, she was sure. With his adorable buttery locks and sweet, tender disposition, an adoption agency would surely snatch him up in a second. He'd find himself in the loving arms of a loving mother with a loving husband and loving grandparents, all holding designer bottles she could never have afforded. *The kid shouldn't be my son.*

She couldn't hope to compete with a life like that.

A life full of love. A life of possibility never offered to her. A life of stuffed teddy bears and birthday parties. A life of popsicles and homemade chocolate chip cookies. A life full of swimming pools and camping trips. A life of designer clothes and fashionable shoes. A life of amusement park vacations.

A life far better than sex calls in the middle of the night could ever have hoped to provide at $5.99 a minute.

She allowed a single tear to fall.

She didn't deserve Elliot; she never had. She saw that now.

Elliot, I tried to love you right. I wanted to be so much more. I really did, my baby.

This was the perfect punishment for her unspeakable crimes.

Succumb to his torture, her inner critic assured her. *You deserve this*, it argued. *You worthless joke of a lousy, stupid mother. You should be thankful that he ever loved you*, the traitor in her own mind continued. *So stupid, so pathetic*, it argued against her better self. *It's laughable even. Elliot's better off without you. Hopefully he will never remember your name, your touch, your disgrace, your worthlessness. Who did you think you were trying to hold onto something so perfect, so gorgeous, so flawless? You...get over yourself. Lie down and die like a good girl now. Maybe God will forgive you on the other side. But I doubt He could be bothered to waste his time. He never loved you either. How could he? Look at you.*

As the last thought seared through her consciousness, she replayed years of her mother's hateful judgments. They sounded exactly the same. But these were her words. These were her own thoughts in her own inner voice. So they must be true. *The kid is not my son.*

Not a sound, she made. Not a peep, she uttered as he nailed her to his platform of dominion. Not a movement, she made as he tied her hair back and glued her head in place.

She accepted her fate and argued not.

Why should she?

She was a useless piece of shit. Always had been. Always would be.

To be honest, she saw the finality of her predicament as a gift while she lost consciousness again. But this time, it was not from physical pain but from the helpless, hopeless submission of her shattered will that was too afraid to attempt escape.

FORTY-EIGHT

Wheel in the Sky

ELISE CRUMPLED the note up and threw it in the bin. Then she French twisted her hair. She nodded approvingly at her reflection. *Serious yet attractive. Nice.*

One of her curly strands escaped the claw prison of her clip and bounced joyfully back into position.

Ah Lola, there you are.

She crossed her arms, making the shape of an X. Then she stepped back and said, "Get 'em, Tig. Take down the Holy Dark!"

She laughed remembering reading that scene like it was yesterday. Book One. Where the sidekick Tiger claws at the bad guy, Lola's evil uncle, and leaves a magical scar on the Holy Dark's chest that would burn for all eternity.

She trailed her finger down her own scar. Even under her scrubs, it felt hot. All laughter gone, she spit her toothpaste in the sink and replaced the curly traitor back where it belonged.

"I'm not a Firling," she said. "I'm just a doctor." She thought about adding some Star Trek comment but decided not to. Even to her, that joke had gotten old.

The toothpaste slimed the cracked, moldy bathroom sink. For a minute, she imagined riding the scum and paste through the pipes to the sewer plant but remembered the toilet water would be there too and changed her mind.

"It all ends up in a big stinky pile of shit-coated nastiness," she announced to Dimitri. She knew his lyrics were trying to melodically reorient her thoughts to a better place, but she wasn't playing that game either.

"Lola and Dimitri, you can both stick it."

As Dimitri sang about love, she rolled her eyes. But when the song came to her favorite part, she swayed a little. He hit the high note perfectly. Maybe the game wasn't such a bad one.

She let her hair fall back down her shoulders. Then she threw the hair clip in the trash. She envisioned Dimitri, her muse, grabbing her hips from behind, moving them sensuously back and forth, to and fro.

Better. This feels better.

Her butterfly necklace twinkled, and the memory of her granny surfaced.

"I love you, Granny, even though I never knew you."

She put on her coat and grinned, remembering her chaffed thighs. *Blackwater, keep turning my body like the wheels in the sky again, baby.*

He was gone, but the scent of him lingered on...and in her. She felt her center heat up and pulsate at the thought. She refused to wash him off. Stink or no, he was coming with her.

She traced her scar and counted the staple tracks.

Forty-three. Like she didn't already know the number.

But then she moved her hand to the left and felt the vibration of her heart instead. *Blackwater.*

Her eyes closed. *Yes, Blackwater. Yes.*

Softly yet protectively, a wolf howled from a corner in her mind. And in that moment, she decided. She refused to fear him any longer. Instead, she would covet the remains of him still inside. Even if it never happened again.

And what if he broke her already wounded heart? So what. At least she had felt the thrusting pressure of his connection deep within the place she had hidden for so longthe joyful place that some monster had taken from her in exchange for not remembering.

Screw that. I refuse to not remember you, Levi. I will not shut you and a better, newer me out ever again.

She was out and staying put. She traced her fingers round her eyes like a mask was there, and then she pulled the pretend layer off and tossed that bullshit in the trash. She mimicked her gorgeous cop. "Nope. No bullshit. No story. I am so much fucking more than a character in a book some bitch is writing."

Even if she failed miserably. Even if this nameless stranger and the boy died. Even if she died trying to save them. Even if she never felt the oscillating waves of one-second-spaced throws of ecstasy coursing through her pelvis again.

She was out and staying put. Mask off for good.

But as her clock dinged, she remembered the time.

She reached down, left the imaginary mask there, grabbed her hair clip from the trashcan, and rushed to her car. The sooner she got there, the sooner she was done, and the sooner she could settle this score for good.

She grabbed Levi's note, too, smoothed it out, and stuck it in her back pocket. Then she locked the back door with her Minnie Mouse keychain.

One day. Thirteen hours. Eleven minutes.

FORTY-NINE

Little Lion Man

WENDI SAT on the front row of morning report, turned to face the audience. She was ready for the diarrhea party. Forty pairs of eyes glared back.

Three letters, written in large, angular capitals, claimed the Board of Shame: RCA.

"Root cause analysis," she muttered.

Or was it really ruthless careless assholes? Or righteous callous addicts?

She rolled her foot around, pretending that her dirty sneakers were a fine pair of red Jimmy Choo's.

She stared at the "MD" trailing everyone's name on his or her hospital badges. *Medical doctors, maniacal dick-heads, menacing doubters, or better yet...all three?*

She wanted to shimmy her shoulders but decided against it. She put her hand on the table. That way, when the boop-oop-a-doop threatened, she might have enough time to shove it back in.

Doctor Buhl marched proudly to the front and began her lesson of submission. Wendi cleared her throat.

The Buhl paced. "As even the most oblivious amongst you already know, two nights ago, our unit of excellence suffered an outcome not worthy of this institution of greatness. At Saint Lutheran's Hospital of Grace, people don't die."

She marched the aisles and settled in front of Wendi.

"But"Doctor Buhl snorted"unfortunately for these residents, someone did. We are here to find answers for why that happened and then find a way to make it never happen again."

Wendi reached up and covered her mouth.

Unfortunate for whom? Us? Are you fucking serious?

Her dirty sneakers dug into her platform of truth. She straightened her back and coughed.

The other residents bent closer down to the table. They avoided eye contact and fiddled with objects like strings in pockets and fuzz balls trapped in their socks.

But not Wendi. She looked straight ahead and narrowed her gaze, hoping to find a sliver of value in the process.

"Sign the attendance sheet," Doctor Buhl commanded. "It is a legal document that binds you to confidentially regarding the events reviewed during this process of discovery. That way, you and the lawyers can't use it against each other, or the hospital, or me for a matter of fact."

Each pair of glaring eyes signed the sheet, giving their rights away and declaring themselves officially part of the charade.

Wendi raised her hand.

"Yes, Intern Patterson. You have a question?"

"Actually, I do, Doctor Buhl. Where are the nurses and the lab techs, the translators and the CART team? Shouldn't they have a voice in this process?"

"Oh, sweet, simple little intern always worried about everyone else. This is about us, the medical doctors, the captains of the ship, the determiners of life and death, the rulers of the hospital. This is our process. The others will be interviewed later. After the facts, from our perspective, have been uncovered."

"I see," Wendi said. She recalled that facts have rather little to do with perspective and everything to do with truth.

In a flash, she discerned the absurdity of the process fraught with deceit from the beginning.

As Doctor Buhl collected the sign-in sheets, she started with her admonishments even before the chief had presented the case for those in the room unaware of the patient and her unfortunate outcome.

Shaking her right index finger at them, Doctor Buhl viciously declared every pathetic mistake made that night.

Wendi, hand over her mouth, raised her other hand again.

"As the intern in a process like this, I suggest you keep your questions, comments, whatever to yourself. And bite your lip until directly asked a question about your actions that night, Doctor Patterson. Do you hear me?"

"Yes, Doctor Buhl, I hear you," Wendi said.

"Good. Getting brighter by the minute, dear."

"But I'm not listening. I'm afraid I can't do that. Keep my mouth shut, that is. There are a few of your facts that I will not agree to by my quiet non-responsiveness."

Gasp!

"Shit. Here we go," another intern grumbled under his breath from the back of the room.

Jack Paulson, her chief, kicked Wendi under the table. He shot an arrow made of stink eye at her forehead. *"Shut the hell up, little intern."*

But still she raised one hand. The one over her mouth dropped to her hip.

The boop-oop-a-doop was almost out, and she couldn't have cared less. She twirled her red heels and shimmied her shoulders.

"Well, that will be a problem for you then, I suspect," Doctor Buhl replied, redder in the face than Wendi's imaginary shoes.

"That depends," Wendi said, "on how you define the word problem. Because from my perspective, the opposite is a much bigger problem."

"I'm warning you, Doctor Patterson."

"Warning me?" Wendi said, fluffing her imaginary skirt. "That you will what? Put me in timeout. I don't think so."

Gasp.

I am an adult, same as you. And besides, that piece of paper I just signed," she said, pointing to the form in Doctor Buhl's hands, "says that my responses are truthful to the best of my ability to recall them."

"Doctor Patterson, I"

"You what, Doctor Buhl. You will fire me? You will strip me of the honor of sucking up to my chiefs and kissing your hairy ass?"

Wendi stood up and twirled. She laughed and said, "I just love this dress, don't you? Funny how it brings out the big lioness inside me."

"You have been warned. One more word of disrespect and you can hand over your badge."

"Here," Wendi said and threw her laminated image across the room and into the garbage bin. "Look at that. Three points. I should have played hoops."

The letters "MD" drowned amongst half-eaten food.

"MD"Wendi giggled"for my damn self. MD for my honest declaration and mute deserternot. You can have my badge, Doctor Buhl, and shove it."

Gasp.

Wendi twinkled her eyes like Betty would have. "And thank you for bringing up disrespect because that is my point exactly. You and your disrespect for the truth. Disrespect for the whole hospital team, other than yourself, of course. Disrespect for this family and their, not our, unfortunate outcome is an outrage!"

Doctor Buhl reached down and grabbed Wendi's badge, cracked it in two, and tossed it back in the trash.

She pointed to the back door.

"You, Intern Patterson, are officially dismissed of your duties. You can turn your lock and key into the main office by five p.m. After that, you will be considered tres-passing…little ex-intern."

"I don't think so. And make no mistakeI will have nothing more to do with this disgrace, this disrespect, as you call it, Doctor Buhl. And I will seek out my and that patient's rights to the full extent of the law."

Once Wendi reached the back door, she looked around the room. Seventy-eight eyes were glued firmly to the floor, unable to meet her gaze. Two glanced up. Elise Phillips.

Wendi saw herself from outside her own body and smiled. She almost roared but felt the gesture was too obscene or obvious. Subtle convincing had always worked best for her.

Elise held her gaze and dug in. She smiled and nodded.

The little ex-intern said, "Will none of you stand up against this disgrace, this tragedy, this process so unworthy of this patient and her family? Will none of you stand up, declare yourself doctor, and help heal this poor family by seeking the truth, not pointing your fingers to wash the shit downhill to someone lower on this joke of a totem pole. This pretense that you call medical justice? Will none of you break your eyes from the engaging and wondrous carpet of this room to look back at me, Doctor

Patterson, the one who held the father's hand as utter devastation washed across his unbelieving eyes?"

She pointed to her chief. "Jack, surely you have something to say about the translators and how our system, down without a back-up, failed her?"

He stuck his hands down into his pockets.

"Doctor Richards," Wendi said, shaking her head, "as Director of the Blood Bank, do you have nothing to say about how we could improve access to substitute blood products for patients that refuse real blood for religious reasons until we can be sure they understand the consequences of their uninformed decisions?"

She paced back and forth. Then became still once more.

"Will none of you stand up for truth if, God forbid, it means you might have to admit you made a mistake? That somehow you could have done better? That somehow you will learn from this unfortunate outcome? This outcome that has widowed a spouse and made two babies motherless in a world only concerned about hiding behind a process built on self-protecting lies."

A great and terrible hush settled over the room as even the callous Doctor Buhl looked intently at her own wrinkled hands.

"Well, I will not stand in this closet of ass-saving lies any longer. I will not step aside and accept my itty-bitty intern-ly duty of taking the blame for the fact that we let this woman die. I will rise and make the system better if you will let me, but I won't lie about my role or complete lack thereof in it, damn it. And damn you for thinking I should."

Her voice quivered. Her words fell like bricks in the river, splashing their faces with shit-stained guilt.

One of the other interns nodded furtively. Elise Phillips.

Elise knew something about standing up and helping someone else despite her own impending demise. Actually, she knew quite a bit about facing fears to stand on a pedestal for someone else's benefit.

A single tear traced Elise's cheek. Her kidnapper's next victim's face flashed in her mind's eye. A name popped in: Elliot.

Was this dead patient any different than the next victim? Was this family any different than her own that mourned the loss of their Jill, now six feet under the ice cold ground of the Glenwood Springs tundra in a hollow grave?

Wendi twirled round once more.

"When will the madness end if you don't end it now?" Wendi demanded, meeting Elise's empathetic glance.

"Never," Elise honestly answered. "Never. You are right. I see that."

"And what about the rest of you? What if it was your mother, your daughter, your best friend? Would you stand up then and overcome your cowardice?"

Silence.

"Do better. Be better, damn it. Be a doctor for God's sake, or go home shaking in your boots. You don't deserve the MD at the end of your name as you quiver behind the door of this disrespecting process."

Forty heads, minus one, swam with dizziness from her justified disapproval.

Wendi flipped her curly mane and grasped the door confidently.

No one moved.

She said, "I will not hide my greatness from you by tolerating your lies. I will not obscure the value of this woman by playing this game of worthlessness any longer. You were right, Doctor Buhl; this outcome is not worthy of this great institution. Are you?"

Doctor Buhl turned around to cool her cheeks. She knew Wendi was right, too, but she had played the game of blame so-and-so too long to know any other way back to righteousness.

As the door slammed behind Wendi, so did this dead woman's chance for medical justice. Never would the process uncover the real system flaws that resulted in the death. Never would they learn from their mistakes of arrogance and distraction. But instead, they traded the one chance they had to do better, to be better: a beast of an honorable woman, Wendi Patterson, MD.

Elise grabbed her tray and rushed out to console her friend. But Wendi was gone, catapulted from this platform of honor, bound straight for another.

Elise hollered Wendi's name once more. The echo of a memory reverberated off the walls.

"*You will honor the honorable one,*" said the five voices on the other end of the line from her vision.

The obviousness of it smacked her in the face.

Wendi Patterson!

Wendi was the answer to the riddle of this puzzle of death and disaster. Wendi was the only one who could help her save the nameless woman with the stringy, pale hair and a little boy.

"Elliot!" Elise cried and started running

As her stethoscope hit the floor, her feet hit the pavement outside the multi-story lipstick shaped building of greatness.

Without realizing it, Elise fingered the winged outline of her butterfly necklace. She trampled countless flowers to catch up with the last good chance she had left.

Oh how she ran!

She ran for what was left of her. She raced for Jill trapped in an empty grave of lies. She rushed for the nameless woman with the straight, pale hair doomed to die a terrible death of mutilation. She sprinted for a baby's chance to grow up in a world made better by his mother's love. She scurried for the eternal peace of five intertwined voices calling on a make-believe phone in a vision. She jogged for forty-three staple track scars that finally begged to heal their seeping edges made of pain. She darted for Maddie, the mangled kitten with one good ear. She marathoned for all the kidnapper's future victims who shopped carelessly in the grocery store, unaware of the evil that stalked them. She hurried to burn down a three-story house of terror obsessed with its wicked desire to consume her. She scuttled for Blackwater and the chance to feel his throbbing, passionate connection to ecstasy again. And she loped furiously faster and faster across the asphalt for her pig-goddess heart that finally beat strong enough to love him back.

"Levi!" she screamed. Breathless, she screamed again.

FIFTY

Take a Bow

"WHAT THE HELL do you mean you stormed out of morning report?" Gabe shouted.

Wendi clipped her seatbelt into place. She threw the cell phone on the passenger seat and trembled. After her shuddering ceased, she wiped her mascara-stained face and picked it back up and put it in her lap. Then she drove out of the resident garage for the last time this lifetime.

She placed the phone on speaker and sighed.

"You heard meout. Out the back door. That horrible monster. I hate her. I really do."

"You don't mean that, Wendi. You don't hate anybody."

"Except that Buhl. She's a ruthless, heartless bitch."

The heaviness of her actions sat like an elephant on her chest. Should she turn back? Get on her knees and beg?

"Go back. Go back now."

She could hear his expression over the phone.

"Nope," she said, trying not to imagine the begging squint of his eyes.

Pause.

"Suck up your pride," he said slowly and calmly, "and get your position back."

Pause.

She heard a drumming in the background. Gabe tapping his leg, probably. She glared at the phone.

He continued. "You can't do this and still become an OB, babe. You know what I'm saying is true."

"Still nope. Sorry."

"She has you by the horns."

"Yep."

She sniffed and wiped her nose.

"If you quit, you will never get another residency spot. All those years, wasted for some lady you don't even know. Think about it, babe. Is some undocumented field worker really worth throwing away four years of college, four years of med school, and a spot at Saint Lutheran's?"

"Please don't call me babe. It makes me feel like an infant."

"Really, babe. I mean, Wendi. You're smarter than this. I know you are. Use your head."

"What is it with people calling me stupid today?"

"Well..."

"I'm going to let that one go."

"Please, honey. Please go back."

"I can't. I won't do that. I won't take a fucking bow now."

"Are you freaking kidding me?"

She heard the anger rise in his throat. He swallowed. She, on the other hand, was done swallowing snot. She rolled down the window and, despite the gathering rain, spit on the ground.

The sky responded by spitting back.

She wiped her forehead and laughed.

She could almost hear her mother's Cajun accent. *"Big ol' fat rain. Yep. Fat rain is only found in the Deep South like proper chicken fried steak."*

The drumming turned into snapping. Snap. Snap. "Babe, snap out of it."

I'm still on the phone with Gabe.

She looked around half expecting to see the mossy tree lined roads from home. She cleared her throat.

"It doesn't matter who the woman was. It's the principle of the thing," Wendi replied, even though she doubted her own reserve.

She spit out of the window again, opened her mouth, and licked the rain.

Could she really trade everything she knew about medicine to stand on a soapbox called principle? Did this issue matter enough to trade all those sleepless nights drinking half-burned coffee at Denny's?

She looked back at the phone. Gabe's pleas oozed out and spilled down her thighs.

"Baby. Listen to what you are saying. This is ridiculous. Go back. Go back while you still can and crawl, crawl like a helpless baby. Kiss her feet. Lick her hairy ass. Do...whatever it takes to take it all back."

She stuck her tongue out. Then she rolled up the window.

She wiped her face dry and smiled as she threw her phone in the back seat. Gabe's ravings really didn't help her stay upright on that soapbox one little bit.

She stuck her fingers in her ears and screamed. The automatic windshield wipers clicked on, and she felt better immediately. She dropped her hands and smiled again. Rhythmically, the wipers throbbed to the beat of her bleeding and proud heart. In perfect timing, they cleared away her remaining dribbles of doubt.

Bowing down on her knees was not a position she was capable of holding. She rolled her tongue back up and closed her mouth tightly. She would lick no ass today.

Or ever, for that matter. *Every life is a stage. Every life plays its part.*

Lost in that thought, she rolled past the garage and out into the cross-section that would take her away from one path and put her on another. On a new stage. With a new life. She barely noticed the people walking past so caught up in a way of life forever closed to her. But maybe that was not so bad,

"Stop. Law school next?" she said, teasing a stop sign that she rolled through almost hitting a person flailing her arms back and forth.

"Shit, Elise." Wendi would know that springy brown hair anywhere. "Dude. Sorry. Wow," Wendi said, slamming on her brakes.

Elise banged her fist on the hood of the car and stuck out her tongue. "I know you haven't been drinking because this is not Snake Pit, and we only drink together on dollar night at Snake Pit, man."

"True. I'm a lousy date." Wendi laughed.

"Yes, you are. Stop trying to run me over already, and let me in."

They both smiled, and Elise climbed in the car. The CD cover had been right; Elise knew how to save a life. Wendi was going to help her. As the girls drove off, glued together by their intensity, Elise's pager went off.

Beep, beep, beep. Pause. *Beep, beep, beep.*

Two messages.

The first message read, "You are taking the intern call tonight, Doctor Phillips. Report to L&D stat."

The other read, "We think we have found her. We have a Jane Doe that matches her description. - Levi."

"Goddamn it, and no, I am sure as fucking shit not taking call. I am already on call, you assholes," she said, unsure which message had pissed her off more. She buried her head in her hands and screamed.

"What?" Wendi asked as she raised her right shoulder and frowned.

Elise read the second message again. Nothing about the baby., The cops must be wrong. Besides…her time wasn't up yet. She was sure of it.

"Hold on. I'll explain. Long story, my sweet friend."

"K," Wendi replied, ticking her head to the timing of the blades. She felt better immediately. The consistency of the wipers seemed to settle her even more.

"Some days, I think I might be going crazy. Sorry. Explaining stat. Promise," Elise said.

"I feel the same way. About cray-cray." Wendi laughed.

"I suspected as much. I need your help."

"Mine? Seriously? Then you are utter-fucked. Seriously."

"Yep. That sums it up. About as serious as pissing off the Buhl?"

They laughed so hard they both snorted. Elise put her curved fingers on her temples and swiped her right foot twice. Then she snorted again.

"Did you really tell Doctor Buhl that she had a hairy ass, or did I imagine that part?"

"Yep. Cray-cray like good old Randle Patrick McMurphy." Wendi made her eyes as wide as possible and laughed like Jack Nicholson in *One Flew Over the Cuckoo's Nest*.

"Awesome. You are my kind of girl. You were amazing pissing off Nurse Ratched by the way. Want to do something else amazing?"

"Like take a boat hostage and drink in the psych ward. Wait, shit, this isn't that story. By the way, I so love that you knew who I was talking about. Awesome sauce."

Elise scrunched her nose. "The book is so much better…"

"Duh, always is. But I'd love to be in a movie, too."

"If this was a book, we would kick the movie's ass," Elise said and laughed.

"Well, I have nowhere else to be since I'm not on call anymore." Another snort. "So I guess I'm all yours. Let's break out of this prison hole or…try some really good drugs."

"I was hoping you would say that. So are they. All five of them."

"They?"

"Yes. They. Six actually. Seven if you count Jill."

"Jill? Who the heck is Jill?"

When the red light turned green, Elise tossed her pager into the back seat next to the phone, and they headed for Washington Park.

One day. Seven hours. Seven minutes.

FIFTY-ONE

Unsteady

BLACKWATER CHECKED HIS SPEED AGAIN: eighty-two in a sixty. *Better watch it.*

In his unmarked police car, even he got pulled over on occasion. Of course, it always ended in a handshake and an I-know-so-and-so chat, but he didn't have time for crap like chatting right now. He had a mystery to solve. He had a heart to save. Two actually.

The call had come in thirty minutes ago, and he had left exactly thirteen minutes later. The hot spilled coffee dropped in delight still ran down his leg. He kept reminding himself that it was bad news for the victim and her family. He felt thrilled, but terrible. Excited, but mortified.

Apparently...last night, a blond-haired mom, baby on her right hip, went into the grocery store in the less-than-budding town of Kremmling, Coloradopopulation once 1,812, now 1,810, at about 8:00 p.m.

She was last seen trying to keep the baby from falling out of the buggy while she loaded her groceries. Her car, found deserted at the mouth of the Blue River a few miles south of town, contained the usual items to be expected.

Just like all the others.

A full tank of gas and keys dangling from the ignition. The door, left open, still dinged pleasantly when the fisherman discovered it about six hours after she was last seen. Twenty feet from her car, the local trash bin contained a torn blanket with black stains at the edge. Some blood splatters trailed away from the bin. It didn't look good.

The forensics team from Denver was on their way, and the scene was "shut tight as a virgin's knees" according to the local sheriff.

Blackwater flashed back to the phone call.

"Yep, you betcha. They're getting out the nets as we speak," the Glenwood Springs Chief of Police reassured Blackwater.

"Damn that asshole," he had replied while he strapped his guns and all his hope to his belt strap.

It must be her. It must be.

Happy but not, he sped toward the devastated little town as fast as four wheels would take him. He spoke to his reflection in the rearview, checking periodically for flashing lights behind him.

"People in little towns like this don't just disappear, doomed to be molested and mutilated. Maybe they will find her in the river? Maybe they will not? Which is better? Which is worse? Better for us, not for them."

Screw it.

He punched the gas.

He looked at his phoneone bar. Unlike the commercial. He needed a new carrier. He tried to laugh but couldn't. It felt too wrong.

The lady had been somebody's baby.

He slowed down to pull over and telephone Elise again. He had called several times already without success.

What the hell are you doing?

He dialed the pager number and waited.

Tapping his leg uncontrollably, he tried the radio to soothe himself. Some old country song about losing everything.

"Screw that. Call back, Elise."

After five more minutes, he pulled back onto the road, still unsure what to do next. The radio was off. He would have put on his favorite CD, but he had given it away. He smiled knowing he had done the right thing five years ago.

He had so many questions. Would Elise be furious that she had failed to save the woman? Would she be relieved it was finally over, at least for this year? Would the police finally find the clues they needed to nail this son of a bitch? Or would they find themselves clueless again? Would they even recover the bodies?

"Jill, I am trying to save you," he whispered. He dialed the cell number again and sighed. "Answer the phone, Jill. Return my page. Something. Anything, Jill. Um, Elise, I mean."

The fear in his voice shocked him. His fingers shook. A heaviness settled in his stomach. Unable to stop himself, he reached up and checked his pulse.

Elise, my love. One hundred and twenty. No good.

He tried to remember one of Dimitri's songs. The lyrics rushed in and saved him.

"And I want to show you, baby. I'll be true."

Without realizing it, he checked his pulse again. Ninety-five.

"I long to see the sun set in your eyes."

He felt better. Eighty.

"Because I wonder where you've gone, and I wonder what I've done. Are you somewhere reaching out? Can you feel me reach for you?"

So much better. Seventy-two.

"Elise, I love you, damn it. Let me start a life of loving you."

He pressed his foot all the way down on the gas pedal.

If this lady and poor little baby turned out to be the one Elise searched for desperately in her vision dreams, then the madness might finally stop. And he wouldn't have to face the possibility of the unthinkable.

"I lost you all those years ago. Tell me I can keep you for good this time," he cried, still staring at his one bar of signal, useless cell phone.

"My love! How I'm reaching out for you."

She will get my page and let it go. No more visits to his house, to his torture chamber, to her past. No more three-story houses.

"Please, Elise, let me save you and Jill both."

He hoped she would. But even then, he knew better.

A pack of wolves in the back of his mind howled.

She was still in terrible danger, but he dismissed the gnawing sensation in his gut while he put all his eggs in that basket of hope on his belt strap. A strap heavy from the un-dismissible weight of his gun. The same basket of hope that was about to destroy another family's life forever. The same basket of hope that meant the kidnapper was still on the loose and would hunt down another Jill a year from now.

But a year is a long time, right?

"In a year, I can get her away from all this insanity. I can keep her safe. I can save her. I can. Or will I just lose her for good?

He slammed the pedal once more. One hundred and twenty.

Elise dialed Blackwater's number again as they drove the ten-minute ride to Wendi's apartment.

"Damn it, Levi. Answer the freaking phone." Elise steamed. Voicemail for the second time. "It's me…again. Why aren't you answering? Call me back when you can."

Wendi cut in. "Who's Levi? And, girl, you better go back. I'm in big crap, but this is not your battle. And I'm not going to have your career hanging on my head, too."

"Yea, yea, I know," Elise said, totally unconcerned about what would happen if she didn't go back to get her ass chewed out by Doctor Buhl for doing nothing but going home on her supposed day off. Actually, as far as she was concerned, Doctor Buhl was lucky that she had showed up for morning report at all.

"What page, Doctor Buhl?" Elise joked, touching her face, mimicking her inability to believe, eyes wide in surprise that she had been paged to return for call.

Elise picked up a magazine from the floorboard and read the cover.

"Doctor Billy Thompson, MD, super star shrink turned cop. People magazine. Nice job, Doctor."

"I know him, you know." Wendi shook her head.

"No way. Seriously?"

"Yes. Taught most people everything they know about a barbaric but scarily effective technique called ECT. It's shock therapy. He used to be famous for it. Some place in San Francisco."

"Weird."

"Yep. He's shockingly cute, don't you think?" Wendi chuckled and batted her eyelashes.

"Nice. You are so funny. Not my type, but yea. Nice boots."

"Always wears boots. We went to the same medical school in Dallas."

"Cool. Is he single?"

"Yes and no."

"What?"

"Always in love with this classmate of his. Only they were both too stupid to know it. Tragic really."

"That sucks."

"Maybe one day? Who knows? Anyway...enough about him. What are we doing here driving away from a snorting bull like we own this place. I hear a song playing. Is that the theme from Wonder Woman?"

Elise chuckled, crossing her wrists across her chest.

Wendi laughed. "Thanks, but I don't think it works without the bracelets." She smiled and even laughed again. "I needed that. You are pretty funny too and a little too good at improv, lady. I better remember that when you are trying to convince me of something important in the future."

"You are right, you know?" Elise said, her surprise wiped from her sincere and intense expression.

"Yea, but that doesn't mean I did the right thing about it. Not for that poor woman and her family. Or for my career." She frowned but tried to cover it up by laughing at her own outrageous actions.

Elise nodded. "Well, you got me. Right here."

"I'll take that as a major compliment. Way more important than some idiot at Snake Pit telling me how cute I am," Wendi said and sighed deeply.

"Right here." Elise pointed to her pig-goddess heart. She intended to stop there but couldn't. The truth within demanded she set it free. "Have I ever told you who I really am?"

Elise chuckled at her own ridiculous question. Of course she hadn't. She had never told anyone. Except Blackwater, who already knew.

"Well, you had me at hello. But what is that supposed to mean?" Wendi asked and smiled genuinely.

"Lady, you are the bravest and most stupidly, ridiculously, irrefutably honest person I know. So I'm not going to lie to you, of all people, anymore. You're my best friend here. Did you know that? How pathetic am I? Try not to judge me too harshly for this, okay?"

"Okay, chicka. I feel the same way about you just so you know. I don't go to the Pit for the ugly boys and cheap gin. And I'm all ears. What do I have to lose for listening to my BFF anyway?"

They both giggled nervously and touched hands.

Elise smiled.

"And I'm the last person who will ever judge you."

"My name is not Elise. It's Jill. Jill Vickerey. She shivered as a cold, electric chill coursed through her at the mention of the name. One she hadn't claimed in years.

"You've got my attention," Wendi said as she pulled the car over and stopped at the side of the road.

"Five years ago, a maniac stole me. He robbed me of my life, my name, my heart, my kitten named Maddie, and my one good chance for a normal life."

"Go on. It's okay. I'm safe. You can tell me." Wendi warmly reached over and held Elise's hand while maintaining eye contact.

"And he did...unspeakable things to me. And now, I remember it all. Well, most of it anyway, after spending five years of doing anything and everything I could to forget. To pretend it never happened to me. Or anyone else. I almost died. My heart failed from the trauma. So to cover it up, they essentially killed me. Killed Jill, that is. This version of me named Elise woke up in the recovery room with a new heart, a new identity. Secretly, I was supposed to start a new life free of the psychological pain of being molested and destroyed by a maniac because I was given a new name."

"Holy shit. Did it work?"

"Nope. Not one bit."

"Oh my God. I had no idea."

"Why would you? Why should you? But here I am, this shell of a person still trying to escape Jill's, I mean...my terrible past."

Wendi shook her head. "Oh my God."

"Keep driving. It's okay. But I don't want to be alone, and I don't think you should either. Can I come home with you? And can we just cry about this until we are done with all the blubbering and moaning over our shitty little lives?"

"You bet, girl. And we will watch sappy movies and eat ice cream too, okay?"

Wendy smiled and changed the channel, trying to find a happier song.

"Stop. That's Dimitri. He's my hero."

"I won't tell if you don't."

"He's done it again. Kidnapped another woman," Elise admitted.

"Are you serious?"

"As death."

"Fuck."

"Utterly fucked. And only I can stop him. Help me be strong. Help me be enough. Help me keep him from doing this to some other innocent girl. I'm so scared. I feel so alone and fragile in a world filled with bad guys. Real bad guys. Not the kind that die at the end of the two-hour movie. Not the kind that Alex Cross kills on the last page of a James Patterson novel. But the kind that never gets caught and keeps killing real people. People like me. People like Jill."

Wendi swallowed.

"People just like you. People that make Nurse Ratched look nice."

"You're not alone in this. Not anymore. You got this crazy lady on your team of mad saviors of all the shitty little lives. I will help you feel safe and secure if I can. In any way I can."

A red cardinal flew past their window as they entered the outskirts of Washington Park.

Wendi shrugged it off as just another unexplainable oddity.

Elise did not. She knew better. She always had.

She fingered the butterfly necklace and tried to relax. It had felt so good to tell the truth. To own it. To no longer stand in the corner cowering from a past she was unwilling to remember any longer.

Elise straightened her back and tapped her forehead to ramp up the process, her connection. She checked her pulse. One hundred and two.

As Dimitri crooned, her thoughts swirled, and her forehead tingled. She placed her hand on the door to steady herself and keep the spinning at bay.

If the monster was gone and dead, would I still be Elise? Or would I take back my name, my life, my small-town innocence and smack him and his three-story house of terror across the face with the truth of me?

She grinned from the idea of ripping her shirt off and exposing her forty-three staple track scars of deceit to the whole wide world.

Screw you, asshole.

Without noticing, she took the clip out of her hair and let her springy curls fall across the smooth porcelain skin of her square shoulders. Then she briefly touched her necklace once more.

"I love that necklace," Wendi said, unlocking the back door.

"Me too."

"I used to have one just like it."

The bolt disengaged with a heavy thump.

"Really?"

"Yep. When I was a little girl. I wish I knew where it was so we could be twins."

They both laughed and touched hands again. Then they hugged, both afraid the other would let go first.

And in that moment, Elise realized they were twins, both firmly standing on crumpling soapboxes of courage and righteousness, hoping they were brave enough to be butterflies in a caterpillar-filled world of endless cocoons.

Elise let go first. She placed Wendi's arms across her chest in an X. Then she did the same.

"Lynda Carter." Wendi beamed.

"The real Wonder Woman, Wendi Patterson," Elise confirmed.

One day. Five hours. Fifty-five minutes.

FIFTY-TWO

When a Man Loves a Woman

KINCAID LAY IN HIS BED, eyes open, refusing to blink, desperate to see how long he could tolerate the pain. He played this game most mornings. He usually performed better upon waking than just before sleeping. But today was no ordinary day. It was an Anniversary. Today's results mattered more than usual.

He smiled. He squinted. He shook his head back and forth to prove he could do it. Then he laughed.

He caressed the soft sheets. Then he thrashed about some more, tightening his forehead.

The burning intensity felt so good and so bad. The contrast of the pain in his eyeballs to the soft, fuzzy, warm bedding underneath him augmented the experience. Pleased that comfort could co-exist so beautifully amongst suffering, he giggled again. The feelings were, after all, only nanoseconds apart.

"Or millionths of a millimeter on a razor blade apart," he cooed. He clicked his tongue in anticipation of watching it play out.

Back to my eyeballs. Focus.

He clenched his abdominal muscles to suppress another chuckle trying desperately to escape his pursed lips. Then he pretended to hold back a scream.

How long would he last if tortured?

How long had his mother lasted?

"Not very long." He beamed, unable to contain his laughter any longer.

He blinked involuntarily.

His laughter stopped immediately.

"I've lasted longer," he criticized, disappointed in his ocular reserve.

To distract his inner critic, he examined the firm confidence of his muscular extremities and the throbbing beauty of his organ of power. If it were possible, out of adoring respect, he would have fucked himself right there.

Instead, he probed his bellybutton and flicked the sour smelling lint on the spotless floor.

His phone vibrated.

Another text from Robert, his Vice President, probably.

Now more than three hours late for his monthly board meeting on the sixth floor of Mandinka Industries in downtown Denver, people must be asking Robert questions.

"You poor bastard. I know you hate people asking you questions that you can't possibly answer," Kincaid said to the phone. Still, he didn't answer it.

Later, when he could be bothered to text back, he would blame it on something: Verizon's cell service, perhaps; the distraction that had made him miss the call; his calendar function that had screwed up. Whatever. The litany of potential excuses was truly endless.

Besides, Robert could approve the minutes of another shit-filled discussion without his Superior's assistance. Kincaid imagined feces spewed all over the dung-covered statistics and gagged. He rose and went to the bathroom to wash his hands.

Kincaid wondered why none of his adoring idiot Inferiors ever wised up to the fact that he always missed work on the same day each year. So clueless. They were just too stupid to notice. And if they did, he had the perfect cover-up: the Anniversary of his mother's disappearance.

"Mother Darling, I miss you so," he declared to the mirror. Then he washed his hands. Six pumps of soap. Six rubs to the right. Six to the left. He flushed the toilet six times and stepped out, careful not to touch the door handle.

Mother Darling had left for the grocery store that morning seven years ago. She never came back from her last trip down aisle six, telling him to shut up for the last time.

Six is such a perfect number for a King. But seven might be even better.

"Really, it's just not the same without you around, Mother Darling. Where oh where did you go?"

He flashed back to the funeral. The flowers he had chosen were perfect. White. Clean. Totally silent. All six arrangements in a circle around her grave. They didn't make black bouquets, so he had chosen white.

He should have killed that nag years before he did.

Seven years ago tonight. The best night of my life.

The number seven teased him now.

His passion for numerology flooded in. The perfection of numbers enthralled his convoluted mind.

How the others jackasses on this planet always failed to notice the harmonic patterns all around them shocked him still. And shocking him, of all people, was pretty hard to do.

Three hundred and sixty-five days, he thought, remembering the last celebration.

His mind descended onto the harmonics of it.

The square root of three hundred and sixty-five is nineteen. Nineteen times pi is sixty. Sixty degrees forms the angle of an equilateral triangle. A threesome of pain. Pain in three directions for my Mother Darling. Mother plus me makes two; three times two makes six. Six Kings form a Womb, like Mother. The gestation of a human in the

Womb lasts two hundred and sixty days. Two hundred and sixty times pi is the same number as the symbolic value for Life.

"And in one nanosecond with a millionth of a millimeter of a scalpel, I can strip it all away. Death is so much cleaner."

White becomes black. Or better yet, red. Light becomes darkness. Six becomes seven. Son becomes Father. Mother dies for the King.

He inhaled the crisp Steamboat Springs air and held it as long as he could. He toyed with the idea of masturbating but quickly tossed it aside for the promise of a visit to the basement.

He firmly flicked his rock-hard sword of throbbing power seven times with his pointer finger to stiffen it up further. Eyes closed, he moaned with anticipation.

"Jill, I'm hard for you. I'm coming to get you."

Then he laughed at his clever pun while he took the stairs down. While he stepped down six stairs, his fingers caressed the perfectly white wall, which was about to be stained with red streaks. Then he took the next six stairs down. At the bottom of the stairs, he glanced back up the blank wall. So clean. So undemanding. He decided that he didn't need a clock to contaminate his view of his bloody streaks after all.

Besides, he already had his bride. Why should he give a flying crap what time it was?

Twenty-two hours. Sixteen minutes. Sixteen seconds.

FIFTY-THREE

Lego House

BRIEFLY, Jolene's awareness returned after the door shut behind the maniac who held her captive. She heard the bolt lock and unlocksix thuds. Then six more.

She moved her eyes from side to side trying to see. The wrapping that blotted out every hint of light blinded her. Total darkness.

I deserve this. This is all my fault.

She tried to move her feet but couldn't. Pain seared through her toes, forcing her to stop. The device, gripped around her waist, encased her mid-section in such a way that wiggling even the slightest amount was impossible. The pressure on her back confirmed her earlier suspicion. She was frozen in the lithotomy position.

I was never good enough for you, Elliot. I am so sorry. You deserve so much more than I could ever be, baby. I know that much is true.

Flat on her back, she lay trapped in a frog-leg stance exposing her most vulnerable center.

I loved you so much. I hope you know that. But…I also hope you forget me and how much I failed you.

The heavy metal and leather straps around her feet took her back to the first visit to the gynecologist.

"Put your feet in the stirrups," the old and soon-to-retire gynecologist told her. He coughed but didn't cover his mouth.

I am not a horse, but this is a stable, Jolene thought as they corralled her through the Pap smear gravy train at the Health Department Clinic.

She was there for irregular periods. The front staff treated her like a sexually trans-mitted disease waiting to be diagnosed. Chlamydia or herpes most likely. HIV possibly.

"I already told you, Doctor," she whispered, too nervous to speak any louder. "I am not sexually active."

The doctor laughed. The metal instrument clanged.

Why does it look exactly like a gun?

For a minute, she considered cracking a joke about...just lying there. Or guns. But after glancing at the doctor's otherwise blank eyes, she decided not to. Somehow humor didn't seem to be his strong suit.

He coughed again and wiped his nose on his sleeve.

As the cold, metal, gun-shaped device tore her hymen, she screamed.

"You weren't lying," the doctor said. "Well, I'll be damned." He laughed again.

The blood, along with her innocence, trickled down her leg.

She flashed back to present.

I never lie, you creep. But that wasn't really true, was it? *Except on the phone. I lie...on the phone, only.*

Instantly, the image of the statue from her mother's fireplace mantle filled her disordered and wandering mind to warn her that she was still lying. *"See no evil, speak no evil, hear no evil,"* the statue chastised. *"What do you really know is true? Speak the truth. Stop lying to yourself. Stop the evil. You made an agreement. Have you forgotten so easily?"*

"That's a weird thing for a monkey statue to say," was Jolene's silent response before she slipped back into unconsciousness, still swirling in her lower mind's self-hate.

This is all my fault. The perfect punishment for the perfect crime. If only I had been something worth something, I could have kept my baby. My love. My everything. My bastard. May you find something better than me, Elliot.

But totally deaf in her oblivion, she was done hearing evil.

Completely blind in her tunnel of pain, she was done seeing evil.

If only she could speak no evil thoughts, the trifecta would be complete.

The lesson announced its untimely arrival while Jolene started to die.

If only...

Soundlessly, the footsteps of the monster next to her fell, one after the next, as he silently marched to the tune of her eulogy. She couldn't hear it, though, as she re-entered her oblivion of eternal damnation.

She heard him not. She saw him not. She fought him not.

Twenty hours. Twenty-one minutes. Nineteen seconds.

FIFTY-FOUR

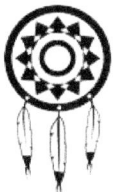

One More Try

BLACKWATER PARKED his car but refused to get out. The longer he waited, the longer he'd stave off having to look at the victims. The mess of them.

Eyes frozen in blankness. Like Jill's the day they found her.

He stomped the half-melted snow and clenched his fists.

Jill…Elise, where are you? Why haven't you answered me? It could have been you. It still could be you.

Perhaps he had time to drive away before the other detective recognized his unmarked car.

Death. The final sentence. The final agreement for us all.

According to Blackwater's superior, the cruel nets had snagged their painful prize one hour prior…on this otherwise lovely, frosty morning on the banks of Kremmling, Colorado's Blue Riverthe mother-child pair's final resting place.

Death is so cruel. So final.

The sun shone proudly in the clear sky, trying to beat down the few remaining flurries, deceitfully declaring it was just another normal day.

But it wasn't. *How could this be a normal day?*

He glared at the sun. If he could have stomped it, instead of the snow again, he would have.

He worked up the nerve to walk toward the orange banners. Two onlooking members of Joe T. Public glared back like somehow this was his fault. His doing. His wish. *Orange equals death.*

He swallowed hard but kept walking.

Run away. While you still can. Run from the orange.

As he approached, the divers pulled the frozen toddler's body out of the turbulent, frigid waters and placed his body on the shiny, metal gurney. Next to his frozen mother. *Eyes frozen in blankness.*

Like Jill on the boat.

Perhaps he still had time to drive away.

Jill, where are you?

Blue lips. A ruined face. Swollen neck. Blank eyes. All confirmed the obvious diagnosis. Death. A million stolen chances. A billion lost possibilities.

He shuddered.

Seeing the dead women sucked. Seeing the dead baby sucked worse.

"Goddamn," Blackwater cursed. He kicked the snow for the third time.

"Well, that settles it, then," the sheriff announced in his nasal backwoods accent. The rest of the work, he assured Headquarters via radio, might as well get done at the morgue.

"Coffee first, eh? Blackwater, right?"

They shook hands.

The sheriff popped a fresh piece of pink sugar-free gum in his mouth and started smacking. "She's all yours if you want her. Shame. Looks like she was kind of pretty. Other than that tattoo on her arm. I hate tats. Makes me think of Nam."

Silence.

Blackwater remembered something. *Butterfly tattoo.*

The sheriff kept smacking. He pressed his finger over his right nostril and blew out the other. Kicking snow on top of the resultant slime, he added, "After the joe, I'll go see the family, and then some cutting by Dr. Death and his little tape recorder," he said. Gum still popping, he climbed in his cruiser, clicked his seatbelt in place, and drove away.

FIFTY-FIVE

Love Song

BELLY FULL OF chocolate chip ice cream, Elise slept like a baby. Wendi pulled the soft blanket up and tucked it under her friend's flaccid feet dangling off the pull out couch.

Elise's rapid eye movements flickered back and forth.

Wendi wondered how it was possible for Elise to twitch like that. It usually took hours of rest to reach such a deep dream state—unless the person's mind had been starved of slumber.

Why are you so sleep deprived? Bad dreams, like me?

Wendi thought about the sleepless nights she lay in bed shaking, terrified she would have the same terrible dream—the one with the dark man.

Some nights, even watching Disney movies to distract her before bed failed to work. Other times, it did just fine. If cartoon characters, kindergarten plots, and musical mantras meant no more terrible dreams, she would watch them every night for the rest of her life.

The memory of her recurring nightmare consumed her.

In her dreams, a lanky, smoky-grey man chased her through the woods. Like some lousy B-rated horror film, she kept tripping on something underfoot. Slowly he trailed, certain that his steady pace would outmatch her terror-driven attempts to evade him.

Without exception, she ended up in the same place: in front of a three-story madhouse determined to own her. Gasping, she narrowly escaped her perpetrator's menacing grasp, hoping to find refuge in a house almost as terrifying as him.

Once inside the house, she hollered frantically for help, only to find the house laughing. Now the house became the vicious attacker bent on keeping her trapped forever. Room after room, she searched furiously and fruitlessly for a way out...any way out.

Somehow, she always managed to find a narrow and twisted pathway through a tiny and terrifying route ridden with more danger as her only route of escape. And just when she lost all hope of escape, a glimmer of the dark night's sky emerged. After finally exiting the house of terror, after barely surviving a million threats, she got out unscathed. Yet he...the dark monster, hunted her once more. Always the same man-possibly even a portal of darkness-with his head bent down, looking from his ominously grey jacket.

Never did he say anything other than, "*You fool. You're already dead.*"

But always was he behind her, taunting, teasing, and gaining on her.

Wendi shook her head to clear the image, the idea, the fear the dream invoked. She replaced it with her favorite Swahili phrase, "Hakuna matata."

She swayed along to the comfort gathering force in her mind and smiled, feeling better by the minute. *I am so...not dead. No worries for the living.*

Wendi picked up the beeping phone to check the message. *Gabe, probably.*

"Yep," she muttered. For the fifth time since they had made it home. She turned the phone off. The landline, too. Just in case.

"Don't you know me better?" she asked the blank phone screen.

She tried to relax but couldn't. She was just too alive for that.

"Done. It's done. Maybe we are, too. No worries for me, thank you."

She sighed, returning momentarily to the peaceful memory of lying in his arms, to her surges of sympathy for the story about his twin, to the sex.

Then she recalled the stories about the white powder up his nose, too. His disapproving tone over the phone. Him calling her stupid.

She should have seen it coming sooner.

"No worries...baby. Either you can see this my way or not, Gabe," she told her overweight tabby cat while shaking her finger.

The cat mewed.

"Or you can't. That simple."

She petted the feline traitor while she launched into her speech.

"But I am what I am. Just like Betty Boop. So it is what it is. And you can't change me anymore than I can change a cat into a dog."

The cat yawned and sat down in Wendi's lap. Clearly the thought of becoming a dog bored the Egyptian goddess.

"Or these flat breasts into sumptuous melons."

The cat leapt up and left the room, obviously not impressed by her master's suboptimal feminine features.

Wendi laughed just before Elise screamed.

"No. No. Don't. Let me go. You can't make me!" Elise begged. Thrashed. Screamed again.

Wendi stared, not sure what to do.

"I won't do it. I won't go down those fucking stairs. Not again. You almost killed me once, but never again. I don't care what you say. I can't hear you!"

Elise sat up, opened her eyes, and screamed again.

Wendi rushed over and grabbed her. "Stop, honey. It's me. It's Wendi. You're okay."

Uncertain where the pencil had come from, Wendi tried to pry the wooden spear out of Elise's clenched hand.

"What? Where I am? Where is he? The dark king!"

"Put the pencil down. You're safe."

Still shaking, Elise embraced her friend. Then she remembered her pig-goddess heart. Elise checked her pulse. She reached up and palpated. One hundred and twenty.

Too fast, Elise. Slow it down. Slow it down.

"Dimitri, I need you," she whispered.

Elise turned to face Wendi, still trying to slow her breath.

"Do you have a Dimitri Arion CD?" One hundred and twelve.

"That's a stupid question coming from such a smart girl," Wendi said, raising her eyebrows in an exaggerated way.

Silence. Confusion.

One hundred and ten. Ninety-eight. Eight-six.

"Does a bear shit in the woods?" Wendi asked in her best put-on hick accent? It sounded genuine. Too genuine.

Elise smiled, her pulse down out of the fatal zone.

Seventy-three.

"Well, put my man on then. He's kind of my hero. And if I ever needed a hero, it's right about now," Elise said.

"Sure."

The soothing rhythm immediately produced its intended effect. Swaying back and forth, both girls sang the infectious lyrics.

"My love! How I'm reaching out for you."

For a moment, they both felt great.

But then the phone rang. Wendi stood up. Too fast. She stumbled back in disbelief. The phone wasn't plugged in.

And five mumbled voices echoed through the room.

Eight hours. Twenty-two minutes. Twelve seconds.

FIFTY-SIX

Come to Mama

WENDI WOKE to a cool rag plastered to her clammy face. Elise was above her, mumbling words with closed eyes. Was she praying? Chanting? Channeling?

"And so it is," Elise concluded.

"What the ever-living crap was that?" Wendi demanded. "Please tell me I'm hallucinating. Because anything else...I'm not sure I can handle."

"I'm sorry."

"Sorry what? Sorry I'm cray-cray. Or sorry that something I can never explain just happened?"

Silence.

"We both heard it, right?" Wendi asked, more as a hopeful statement than a question. "Wow. Maybe I really am committed in a psych ward like good old Randle."

Elise nodded.

Wendi covered her eyes and shivered. "Tell me Nurse R. is not around the corner. Please. I do not want to be shocked. Not by her. Not by Billy Thompson either."

"I agree. Screw them both." Elise chuckled trying to lighten the mood.

"Both? What does that mean?" Wendi asked, squinting but still shivering. She grabbed a nearby blanket and wrapped it tightly across her chest.

"I'm sorry about both?"

"Billy and that bitch of a nurse."

"No. Both like you can never explain what just happened and like you are a freaking nut job if you help me."

"Oh." Wendi took a deep breath, turned her head to the side, and frowned.

"But mostly the former. The...can't explain...part. Sorry," Elise said again, turning away to avoid eye contact. She stuck her hands in her pockets and took three deep breaths of her own.

"You want to fill me in here? 'Cause my mind is reeling." Wendi pulled her blanket even tighter.

"I'm not your everyday kind of gal. Sometimes things happen around me that normal people have a hard time dealing with."

"Like?"

"Like…the computer explodes. The stereo freezes up and then changes channels. Thunder claps, minus a storm. The faucet starts dripping even though no one touched it. The lights flicker. Things like that." Elise tucked a loose ringlet behind her right ear and laughed nervously.

"And what else, Fire Starter? Do you known Steven King because…"

"Like the TV turns itself on and"

"The unplugged phone rings? Fucking weird ass shit like that?"

"Yep. Like that," Elise replied. She took her hands out of her pockets and checked her pulse. Eighty-eight.

"For how long have you had these kinds of…experiences?" Wendi asked, both curious and terrified to learn the answer.

"Honestly?"

"No. Lie to me, darling. Dude…yea, honestly." Her words covered her seething fear but only just barely.

"Since forever. Long as I can remember. Then one day," Elise said, touching her butterfly necklace, "my granny made me realize I was different."

"You can say that again."

"My mom, of course, has never accepted the way I am, so I learned at a young age to hide it from other people. In fact, sometimes I hide it so well I convince myself that I am actually normal and that..."

"That what?"

"That maybe I could live a normal life?"

"Oh, my sweet friend, that feels so heavy. Damn. That's terrible. I'm sorry."

The room felt dark. Clouds hung in the small room like butter clinging to the bottom of the cake pan on the half-dirty stove in the small kitchen.

"Heavy? Whatever..."

Wendi chuckled nervously.

Elise paced.

"It is what it is, and I have to face who I am. I've seen this coming for a while now. Like…five years, to be exact."

"Five years?"

"That's when he took me. Almost killed me, actually."

"Oh." Wendi swallowed. She tried not to let Elise see the trembling in her hands.

"So it's time to get over my baby shit and face this. Even if it terrifies me."

Elise stared at the floor, afraid to look up and meet Wendi's gaze and the possibility of another face-smacking dose of judgment. Her lip quivered slightly, and she tried her best to repress it by biting on it. It only made her miss Blackwater. "Yep. Bullshit. Wishing this was a story."

"Excuse me?"

"Inside joke."

"Okay." Wendi stood up, dropped the blanket, and walked over to Elise. Her hands no longer trembled. She had already decided. She was up for crazy. If she could take down the Buhl, she could face this, too. Wendi placed her arms around Elise who was obviously trying her best not to cry now. "How about an inside hug?"

"Yes. Please. Thank you, my friend."

"Well, it was just the Snake Pit dancing at first, but now I see we are so much more than dollar drink night pals." She twirled her foot and gave Elise her best Betty Boop eyes. "Why and what, pray tell, are you, a goddess of psychic badassery, terrified of, exactly?"

"Honestly?"

"Covered this. Lie to me…" Wendi shimmied, and Elise laughed.

"Well, since I just might die, I think I'll spill the real deal."

"Now you're talking. Go." Wendi twirled in her imaginary red Choos.

"That no one will ever understand me or love me for the way I am, ever. But right now, right this second, I'm afraid of him."

"Him?"

"That bastard who did this to me." Elise pointed to her chest.

Wendi touched the place tenderly and smiled.

"He's coming to get me. The phone call was a warning, Wendi. He knows I'm alive, and he's still trying to kill me."

Wendi stopped twirling. "What do we do? How can I help?"

"Honestly?"

"Yea, baby. Man, you are a slow learner. How did you pass the board exam?"

Elise blew air out her nostrils hard. Ninety-six.

"Go on. Please."

One hundred and fifteen. "I think I have to kill the crazy mother fucker before he kills me, again. And before he kills that woman. And her little boy. And every fragment of hope that I ever had of a normal life." One hundred and twenty.

Dimitri Arion sang softly from the speakers. The top of the CD player remained open. The CD hadn't moved. "My love! How I'm reaching out for you."

They should have screamed. They should have run. Instead, Elise said, "The problem isn't finding the answer." Seventy-four.

Wendi knew, although she couldn't explain how, that the proper response was, "No. The problem has always been and will always be facing it."

Too shocked to do anything else, they sang along to the lyrics filling the room, both trying to sound braver than they felt. When the chorus ended, they both laughed. Really, what other response could they offer?

Elise walked over and closed the top of the player. Sixty-three.

Wendi cut in first. "Okay, I'm not really into killing anybody, but it sounds like this freak monster could use a lethal dose of municipally acquired electricity. Screw shocking me. Let's shock him. Maybe I am Nurse Ratched."

"That's my girl."

"So I'm in. Unless there's a gun involved. I hate guns. Actually, they are the only things I've ever hated."

Elise laughed briefly. "Then help me go to sleep, go into my connection and leave my physical body so that I can find him and his wicked three-story house of torture and bleach-covered death."

"Bleach? Death? Sounds like a flipping hospital to me. How 'bout I just get the phone directory?" Wendi teased, and they were both surprised by their explosive giggling. They fell back on the couches like Peppa and George Pig, legs twitching in the air over the absurdity of the situation.

After the roar, Wendi asked, "You can do that? Leave your body, I mean. 'Cause that is freaking cool."

"Crazy cool. Yes."

"Totally." Wendi shimmied again. She was getting excited for real now.

"Yea, I know. It's amazing. I can teach you if you want."

"That sounds great. But after the psycho is behind bars. Justice first. And when he's frying, I'll try flying."

Again they laughed, both surprised how positive they felt about a life-threatening, against-all-odds kind of mission impossible.

Wendi's newfound sense of humor thrilled her. She had never been this funny before. She stole a glance in the mirror, fluffed her imaginary red skirt, and twirled round for one last good spin.

Elise chimed in. "You are just like her."

"Who?"

"Boop-oop-a-doop. Betty, you nut job."

"I love her."

"I know. Like I love"

Before she said his name, the CD player changed songs mid verse, and Dimitri sang another of his best tunes. This time, Wendi danced like she meant it, and Elise joined in. Then they each got a big glass of water and headed to the bedroom.

FIFTY-SEVEN

Goodbye My Lover

BLACKWATER LOOKED AWAY, still stomping the snow. The crew zipped the bag and the young boy's hopes of a long, happy life...up, up, up with the stink of it all.

As the others yapped, sharing small talk, he walked back to his car to travel the twelve miles to the local police station. Then he, detective Johnson, and the two bodies would travel to their small morgue for inspection. In the meantime, the surviving family would have been informed of the unthinkable. Hopefully, they would find answers. Answers about why. Answers about whom. Answers about how.

He tried Elise again. Still no answer.

No answers here. No answers for you. No answers for me. He was drowning in… no answers.

His pain settled on Elise and all her painful, possibly unnecessary explorations. Had they forced her memory for nothing? Had she remembered all of the torture for a black bag of baby bones and swollen faces?

Nothing...but perhaps another chance for more suffering a year from now.

Why does he do this every year at the same time?

Still no answers.

As the question rang through his mind, chills ran up and down his arms. Zing, zip, sizzle, the chills flooded.

A thought popped in: *ask.*

"Why do you do this every year? Who are you really trying to kill? Who have you already killed? And what does Jill have to do with this? Why did you pick her? Why? And why the grocery store? What happened to you in the grocery store?"

He watched all the unanswered questions crumble to the ground like the flakes of a tossed aside pastry puff...butter still sticking to the cake pan that birthed it.

Still he pushed.

Another thought. *Ask and you shall receive.*

"Where are you doing this? In your three-story house? What do you do to them there? And why? Who are you trying to punish? Why won't you leave my baby alone?"

He pounded his steering wheel, each question enraging him more forcibly than the last. By now, he was speaking so loudly he lost himself in his own mad world of queries.

Again Detective Johnson tapped on the window, but Blackwater ignored the rapping, oblivious to anything but his inquiries.

"Damn it. Who are you? What do you do with their cars? And why did you make it so easy for us to find this one? Not a traceall the other girls gone without a trace. No bodies, no clues, no cars. But this one so easy? It makes no sense."

Finally, he noticed the pounding fist slamming on his front windshield. He rolled down the window. His cheeks flashed red.

"You okay in there, Blackwater?" the detective asked.

"Um, yeah," he answered.

His cheeks burned.

The other cop laughed nervously.

"But I was a little distracted just now. Sorry. I was talking to the kidnapper. It's kind of my technique."

"Oh, okay. Whatever works for you folks over there in Glenwood Springs. Anyways, you got a phone call."

"But nobody knows"

"Well, they asked for you by name."

He put his ear to the receiver and asked anxiously, "Elise, is that you. Are you okay?"

"No, I'm not, Levi. It's Jill. Save me."

Beep. The line went dead.

Eight hours. Nine minutes. Nine seconds.

Jolene startled awake. Groggy, but awake. She tried to roll over but couldn't. The straps held her too tightly.

The thump, thump, thump of the music upstairs reverberated through her. Its movement taunted her with its sickening beats of repetitive mind-numbing thumping. It declared her imprisonment inescapable. It laughed at her and the nothingness of a chance she had left. It terrorized her with its rhythm of certain death, so soon to follow. And, most horribly, it reminded her of her separation from the one good thing she had ever known, ever held in a world of evil, hate, and suffering: Elliot.

My precious baby.

Instead of connecting to its pain, though, she chose comfort. With every ounce of life she had left, she dug into that lyrical tenderness, knowing even it threatened to desert her now in these last few hours.

She recited a song over and over; its words were the only things that mattered to her anymore.

"I love Elliot. I love Elliot. Yes, I do. I love you. I love Elliot very much. I love Elliot v-e-r-y much. Yes, I do. I love you."

She sang for him, her bastard, her baby, her everything.

She sang it again. The only words she had ever known were totally true.

Eight hours. Four minutes. Two seconds.

FIFTY-EIGHT

Piece by Piece

"SO TELL ME WHAT TO DO," Wendi said as Elise lay down.

"Basically, piece by piece…you just don't let me die."

"Seriously?" She narrowed her eyes and shook her head slightly.

Elise grinned and nodded, minus any uncertainty.

Wendi blinked three times. "You're totally kidding, right?"

"Nope. No bullshit. Serious as Nana's advice in an Alex Cross novel. A heart attack even."

"Okay, Ms. Suicide. Then tell me exactly how to do that."

"Well, first," Elise said locking eyes and washing all doubt from Wendi's face, "you play my baby love Dimitri."

"Shocker. Think he's here with us?"

"Probably. Maybe he loves me as much as I love him."

"Boop-oop-a-doop." Wendi chuckled.

"He keeps me calm. You keep checking my heart rate. If it goes over one hundred and twenty, wake me up as gently but quickly as you can."

"K."

"If I start thrashing or shaking, wake me up, too. Have some hot chocolate ready for me to drink after I'm done."

"Can do."

"This is the most important thing of all. You must write down anything I say because it might not really be me, this Elise body here, saying it. Got it?"

"No. Actually. But okay. Will do anyway. Can I say a prayer?" Wendi asked, pulling out her beautiful rosary and rolling it between her fingers.

"Duh, that's a great idea," Elise said, bewildered it had never occurred to her before. "You are so smart, my friend."

"Thanks."

"Wendi, I know it sounds nuts, but the same voices that called me earlier… They know you. They told me that you...the honorable one, would be the one who would help me."

"WTF?"

Elise nodded.

"Honorable. I've been thinking about law school. So…"

Elise chuckled. "So if anything I do or say sends you a thought or an idea that feels...I don't know...important or special or strong or whatever, then you do it. It might be the only thing that saves her, this desperate woman and her little boy."

"What do you mean a little boy?"

"She has a little boy named Elliot. His life is in our hands, too."

Wendi's jaw crashed open, and she stammered. "I...I" Wendi turned around to regain her composure as the dots connected and the pieces of the puzzle clicked into place. "I… But"

"What? What? You what?"

"I know her. I knew her." The words caught on her tongue and wriggled to get out but couldn't. She flicked her own cheek and shook her head quickly. "Shit. I've seen her. The lady. The victim. I met her at the church down the street."

Elise clenched her teeth and caught her breath. "That isn't poss"

"Damn. I don't know, but…"

Elise slammed her fist down on the bedside table. "You could have…"

Wendi started pacing. "I had no idea. How could I?"

"I'm sorry. I just… Explain. But what? Who is she? How? Why? When? Please tell me. For God's sake, explain."

"The other day after my call from hell when the lady died. In my arms… I held her in my arms. Oh, Elise. I could have saved her. If I had known. But I didn't, and I just let her walk away. She has pale, long, stringy hair..."

Elise took a deep breath and said, "Pulled back in an old, tattered lace hairband?"

"What? How did you know?"

"I've seen her, too. At least her reflection in the mirror, anyway."

"Oh my God."

"I've stepped on one of Elliot's toysthis fake CD player thing with purple feetand smelled his diapers, too. He's real. And so is she. Help me. Help me save them...and Elise. I'm saving her as well. Me, that is," Elise said as her courage peaked.

"Okay. Okay," was all that Wendi could think to say as her mind reeled from the pressure of the task at hand.

The image of the woman holding the picture of her little boy, eyes weeping at Mother Mary's feet, shoved her to the front of a stage. A hero's stage.

"Dear Father, Dear Mother Mary," Wendi began.

Elise grabbed her hand so tightly that the rosary beads dug into both of their palms. And together, they spoke the Lord's Prayer over and over until they were sure they had been heard.

"We only have seven hours left," Elise announced.

From across the room, the TV clicked on and then off again. The number 444 flashed across the screen and then went blank.

"The angels are with us," Elise said. "The fours are a message."

Then she settled into the pillow.

The number 777 flashed on the screen next.

"Don't tell me. That means we are exactly where we need to be," Wendi added.

"Yep. Exactly."

Possibly for the last time in this life, Elise closed her eyes to face her greatest fears, to champion her most important cause, to pay back a mother of a monster, and to try one last time to get her own life back by saving someone else's.

FIFTY-NINE

This One's for the Girls

IN DELIGHTFUL ANTICIPATION, Kincaid danced.

To the bumping music, he drummed his fingers back and forth like a video game pretend rock star. Side to side, he rolled his head triumphantly as if he were the source of her serenade.

Mine, not hers, he reminded himself.

In an instant, he flashed back to the night of his first kill seven years ago. They had just returned from the grocery store. Mother Darling had slapped him in aisle six after telling him to hush. He hadn't said a word, but the crazy bitch had slapped him again for effect. In front of the stranger, no less. Then she smiled for the last time.

She said that next time it would be worse.

He chose to disagree. He planned to tell her so.

The same kind of music played sweetly for him in the back of his mind.

"Turn that crap down. You call that music? It's awful. Just like you."

The voices got the better of him.

She lasted about ten seconds without screaming. But then she only gurgled, and he smiled for her.

Guess telling her would have to wait.

"For you, for me." Wendi mocked the song lyrics, digging into her cleverness. "I think, this is nuts. You say, have hot chocolate ready."

She wanted to laugh but just sighed.

"How the hell did you talk me into this?" she asked the peacefully resting body of Elise Phillips.

Elise looked like she was simply asleep. Wendi knew better; she was not.

Elise's chest rose slowly to a deep rhythm that overpowered the room. In...one, two,

229

three. Held...one, two, three. Then out...one, two, three. It was almost like a waltz—a powerful one.

The cycle repeated time and time again.

Wendi noticed she inhaled in perfect timing with Elise's waltz. At first...her attention to the symmetry disrupted it, but then it furthered the synchronicity.

Out of the corner of her eye, she observed the slightest flickering. It was subtle movement encapsulated in stillness. She assumed they were not alone.

She considered fear but decided against it.

Bravely, she whispered, "I see you."

In the far corner of her mind in her own voice, the thought came through. *"Yes, you do. You and your fiery lion heart."*

"I have seen you before, haven't I?" she replied, again so softly it was barely audible.

"Of course."

Wendi thought, *"I don't even need the words, do I?"*

"No, of course not."

"I will not fear you," Wendi said as she sank her teeth into her mounting courage.

"No, you won't. If you fear this, then you will not hear it."

Wendi nodded, certain this was the ultimate truth.

"This voice comes from love. God's fiery lion heart. You cannot listen to fear and love at the same time. No one ever can. It is always a choice in every moment—fear or love."

Nod.

"Same with sight. You can only see fear or love, not both."

Final nod.

"Last, but certainly not least, you can only speak one or the other. Never both...to yourself or others."

"Yes," Wendi whispered.

"Choose wisely, little one. No one can choose for you."

Wendi closed her eyes, and flashes of light consumed her awareness. Chills coursed through her. Simultaneously, her hand slipped off Elise's pulse and lifeline.

She suspected where she was headed. She was wrong.

As the flashes cleared, she found herself standing at the threshold of her own closet.

Six hours. Ten minutes. Fifteen seconds.

SIXTY

I'm Alive

FLASHING BRILLIANCE SURROUNDED THEM. Both of them. Elise looked at Wendi and smiled. She would have tried to explain the glorious streaks of swirling light if she could have, but words were useless.

Elise frowned. *"Why?"* she mouthed. Why was Wendi there of all possible places?

The high winds swirled around them with such great force that other sounds failed to penetrate the field. Elise shook her head. Tried again. Her lips were still, but her thoughts rang clear in Wendi's mind. *"I'm impressed."*

"Why?" Wendi titled her head and squinted.

"I guess you don't need me to show you after all the frying. You are already flying." Elise smiled and shook her finger playfully at Wendi.

"I thought so."

"First time?"

"Maybe, but I don't think so," Wendi replied.

"I always knew I liked you, soul sister. We are the same, I see. So, Fire Starter twin of mine, what do you see?"

"A closet. You?"

"Yep. The same. Why are we here? Do you know?"

"Oh, I was really hoping you had an answer for that one," Wendi thought. Her lips turned up in a smile. It would have been a perfect flirting glance for Betty Boop.

"Nope. No idea. So I'm waiting."

"For what?"

"The clue, of course."

"Oh. I see," Wendi answered, still clueless.

"If you are here... and I am here...then who is there?" Elise asked. She pointed through a swirling blue door back to the bedroom where the bodies of two women lay motionless, obviously asleep.

"Fuck. I'm sorry. Your breathing was so..."

231

"Rhythmic, yes. Works every time."

"Too well." Wendi shrugged but kept staring at the closet.

"Well enough."

"I'd say so."

Elise shrugged. *"When I lay down today, I knew there was a damn good chance I would never get up again. So c'ést la vie, eh? But you know what I will miss most if I don't make it back?"* She solemnly inspected the cord connecting her to her body in another universe.

"Besides Dimitri, you mean?" Wendi thought, trying desperately to disguise her fear, her guilt, her confusion.

"Hot chocolate in the cold Colorado morning, sitting all wrapped in your jamas and a big wool blanket on the front porch."

"Yes. Go on."

"Blowing my misty breath, getting ready for the next big swig, hoping this sip won't burn like the last, hoping my tongue will recover. I used to do that every morning before school. I haven't done it in years. If I get back"

"You mean, when you get back, right?"

"Wendi, that monster knows I'm alive and trying to find him. I can feel it. He wants, no needs, me dead. He's been killing me every year for the past five years. And I am going to stop him even if that means I die trying. Do you understand what I'm saying? And if you are as connected as I think you must be after seeing you...like this, then you know I'm telling the truth. Feel the prickles in your skin. They know it, too. So I hold no illusions from myself. Not anymore. Not this little Fire Starter."

"I don't know what to say."

"Then don't. Never say anything less...than what you know is true."

Nod.

"Just listen and watch and see. Because if I don't make it back, it will be up to you to make sure this mother fucker gets the chair."

The song in the background changed.

Dimitri sang the first words of a new song. They both joined in the chorus.

"You have me the whole night through." Wendi swayed in perfect time with the melody but never took her eyes off of the closet.

Kincaid traveled down the twelve stairs to prepare his beauty for tonight's offering. Her positioning was perfect. Pleased with his work, he performed the last few crucial steps.

As the needles and hooks dug into the doll's pale and perfectly smooth skin, his saliva gathered in the back corners of his mouth. He swallowed. Swallowed again, stroking his precious beastly manhood as he went about his work. Mind filled with power thoughts, he felt stronger than he had in years. Certain she was the one, his Queen that would finally quiet the voices.

"Jill," he whispered in ecstasy, "you look lovely."

Six hours. Six minutes. Six seconds.

SIXTY-ONE

All We'd Ever Need

AS THE HOOKS pierced her skin, Jolene went even deeper within herself. She returned to a conversation from two years ago in her memory.

"What do you see, Jessie?" Jolene asked.

Nervously, the caller answered back. "An open door."

"Beyond that, silly."

"I know what you mean. Baby steps, please." He laughed.

They both giggled at his silliness.

"Stop it. You're killing me," the woman begged.

"Never. Your turn."

He was just on the phone, but she felt his eyes could see her from inside her own mind. "In the mirror you mean?"

"Duh. Yea."

"Blond hair. Okay lips. Okay eyes. Okay figure. Not too bad. Like a four on a scale from one to ten."

"By the way, from my side of things, you sound, no, you feel like at least an eight, but you know that's not what I meant. Go deeper than that superficial bullshit story. I want to hear the real deal."

"You first," she teased.

"Fair enough."

She could hear him tapping something even over the phone.

"There is a light above the door that just barely accents the outline of the porch. Like twenty moths swirl in the light…in a circle like a never-ending dance."

"Yes. Keep going."

"They are trying to hang onto what they keep looking for but can't grasp it, searching endlessly for an answer that eludes them. It's almost like they have the answer but can't figure out how to face the right direction to catch it. Constantly eluded by it even though they are looking right at it, they still keep on searching, searching until they get up enough courage to fly directly into the light and let the light catch them instead."

"Then what happens?"

"Stunned as they smack right into the hot plastic's indifference, they fall back clueless and then circle again."

"I know how that feels. I have the answer but just can't face it."

Jolene grinned. He heard it through the phone. "Yes, that's a problem."

The tapping ceased.

"Maybe it's the only problem," the stranger answered as if he had known her forever.

"Yes. Or maybe not. Who knows?"

"Now you go." He started tapping again.

"Like the moths, I, too, am searching," Jolene said.

"Yep. Feel that."

"Trying to find something. Something worth holding onto. But unlike the moths, I don't even know what I'm trying to find. Crazy, but I think the moths are even closer than I am. At least they know what they are trying to find even if they don't know to grab it."

"Perfect."

"I just keep banging my head against the cold, uncaring world. But I'm tired of looping around again and again. There is no flutter left in my moth wings. And honestly, I'm not sure how many more times I have left in me, so unable to even sort out what I want from this cruel life."

"You do know what you want. I know you do. Keep asking questions, Jolene. You will find answers that way. I just know it."

"Well, I only know one thing and that is that I love my Elliot more than anything I have ever known before."

"Go with it. Circle that."

"More than I ever even knew was even possible. And I wish he knew Jimmy. And Jimmy knew him. That Jimmy still loved me even after all of this...this tragedy bullshit."

"Now you are getting somewhere. Follow that. Trail that feeling in your heart and see where it takes you, my friend who is worth so much more than five ninety-nine a minute."

"You mean six ninety-nine. It's after one a.m."

"There's no dollar amount high enough."

"Thanks," Jolene said.

Silence.

"Seriously," she emphasized.

The caller started tapping more loudly. "But I've got to go, my precious friend. The stars are calling my name. And this time, I think I'll answer them back. Maybe even face them. Ha! Even if it's just for a fraction of a second."

"Really? Oh, friend, I'm so proud of you. Just keep me on the phone as long as you need. When you step out the door, just hang up. I will know you did it—that you actually stepped outside."

When the tapping stopped and a few seconds later the line went dead, she saw it all in her mind's eye. She saw him go outside.

She simultaneously watched herself go deeper into what mattered most to her here in her torture chamber in present moment. Elliot. Jimmy. No, their love. No, not even them. Love itself.

She asked herself what she wanted from this life once more before there was no more life to ask it of. The answer, so obvious in retrospect, smacked her square across her face.

Smack! It hurt even in her mind.

Worse than her toe. The straps. The chains.

How could she have been so clueless all this time?

She knew exactly what she desired. She ached for the peace of acceptance and forgiveness. Of no boundaries. The amorphousness that was love. No borders. No box. No judgment. So simple, yet so inherently complex. So difficult, but so totally easy.

She tossed the four letters around. They seemed so small to her to mean so much. How could four characters be big enough to represent that kind of emotion? The kind that could only be defined by a total lack of definition.

Her oozing love for Elliot was her clue. It made so much sense from this loveless place that offered her only pain, death, and misery.

And perspective. Ironically, her imminent death offered that, too.

Just like the bottom of the last bottle of booze at rock bottom for a drunk, here she saw only two directions to move: sideways or up. Her ruined body had only so much sideways left.

When the sharp hooks dug into her legs, arms, and back to force her to hold her current position, she cut into her new awareness.

How could she give to Elliot what she had never known and, therefore, never owned in the first place? *You can't give what you don't have to offer. You have to own it first.*

Above all else, she wanted to not just be good enough but to be everything someone had ever hoped for. That someone…who she so desperately needed to be in order to feel complete and whole and perfect so that she had true love to offer her beautiful baby, her beloved bastard…was not Elliot not even Jimmy; it was her own most authentic self.

I've been looking for myself.

My own love. My own acceptance. My own forgiveness.

Not my mother's or father's or Jimmy's. Always, I've been looking for something that only I could gift myself.

As the weight of it crushed her chest open with the glorious awareness of the truth, she took it one step further.

And…that only I was powerful enough to withhold.

Before she went even deeper into the lesson life offered to her in this terrible place of pain, she lost herself to the swirling oblivion of death's doorstep from the bleeding, the knives, and the hooks that pricked deep underneath her skin as they simultaneously awakened her soul. The dehydration of her critical condition took its toll, and as her kidneys failed, her consciousness faded with them.

Upstairs, Kincaid thumped aimlessly to the music intended to serenade his withering bride. Little did he understand the resolution he had offered her through his torture.

"See me!" he screamed with his arms flailing out to the sides. Staring at his own reflection in the mirror, he imagined them to be beautiful fairy wings.

"Know my power now! This time I have you in my snares. You will finally see the greatness in me. The glory of me that you have been so oblivious to all these years, Jill. You bitch. You useless whore."

His eyes wandered down to his throbbing manhood. In advance, he congratulated himself on his victory. Victory over all her hateful words when he was just a little boy. Victory over the voices that entered his mind when he turned seven and had become a Portal of Darkness. A Black Portal. One of the Six.

Victory over the Dream Weaver, Sephubel, who had failed his assigned subject so many years ago from another realm, still suffering that same exact failure.

SIXTY-TWO

Closer

THE TWO GIRLS joined hands and energetic forces.

"Fire Starter number one and number two," Elise whispered. Wendi smirked. Elise shrugged. They both laughed briefly.

Behind them, the swirling blue door slammed shut in reply. This wasn't going to be easy. Elise frown-smiled.

"How do we get back?" Wendi asked, frown-smiling too.

After the dead bolt engaged, Elise answered, *"I have no idea. But if there is a way, we will find it."* The bolt clicked back and forth six times. Six more.

"Six. Always six," Elise commented.

On the other side of the door, the phone rang six times, followed by a longing wolf's cry. Blackwater, probably.

Elise stuck up her fingers to count the howls. Six.

She, asleep, her physical form trapped on the other side of the locked blue door, had no way to answer him. She also knew there was no way she could get his help unless something woke up her body or he ventured within the realm of the Spirit Walker as well. What were the odds?

He would have no idea how or why to do that.

So...they could wait, or they could find their own map back home.

"Let's find the clue and keep moving. Hold my hand. And no matter what, don't let go. Okay?" Elise told Wendi. She nodded twice to make sure Wendi understood. She gripped Wendi's hand and the rosary tightly. Then tighter still.

They both flinched from the pain of the beads and laughed at the absurdity of a deadly situation they knew no one would ever understand but them.

"Deal," Wendi replied.

"Good. What's the clue?"

"The number six maybe?" Wendi suggested.

Elise remembered the mark on her arm. Six. *This is your closet, right?"* she empathed.

"Yep. Looks the same to me."

Together, hand in hand, they stepped inside the structure as the edges warped and sucked them forward more forcibly. The wind gathered, and it became more and more difficult to hold on to one another's hand.

Elise opened Wendi's jewelry box. She placed a matching butterfly necklace around her friend's neck. Then she looked through all the drawers. Nothing. She pulled back the clothes and moved them from side to side.

"Anything out of place?" Elise asked.

"No. Nothing I can tell. Except the building stamp on the back wall. The edges look more faded. That is the only difference I can tell."

"The building stamp?"

She stepped in closely and touched its edges curling with age from the wear and tear from the dry, cold air of Denver.

"What is this? I've seen it before."

"Well, I just know that every building on our block has one. It was the label or stamp of the contractor who built most of these units in Washington Park some hundred years ago."

"Oh...I remember. I know where I saw this. I saw it in one of my visions. The same vision I saw her face. The victim. That means she lives on your block. She is your neighbor. That's why"

"Why she was at the church down the street."

"Damn it!" Elise stomped her feet. Slammed the door six times.

"That's why Sister Maude called me. She knew we were neighbors. I have to call Maude."

Elise shook her head and clenched her jaw, too angry to speak.

"Maude will know. She will know where we can find the girl. Maybe we can still save her and baby Elliot. If he hasn't taken her yet, we can still save them."

Simultaneously, they looked over their shoulders to the blue door. The same one still shut. Not just shut, locked.

They knew exactly what to do next yet had no way to go about doing it. Unless they could find another way out, that was. Another way back to their bodies on the other side of a locked blue door. But a closed portal was a useless portal.

Thunder clapped. Wendi jumped back and gasped.

A small roof erupted from the center of the spinning door. Once blue, the door darkened, turning brownalmost black. Then total lack of any color at all. Elise gasped and checked her pulse. Too high. One hundred.

The bolt clickedsix times forward, six times back. Somewhere in the distance, a clock ticked.

Elise traced her scar. Forty-three rows of punctures.

The door laughed in response while the roof evolved into a three-story house.

They dropped their hands and ran...as fast as they could.

"He knows we know!" Elise screamed. "Black portals lead to death. Only a king of darkness can use one!" She flashed to a scene where Lola Littleton in the fourth book had narrowly escaped a black portal through a window. Only Lola had real fairy wings to help her. Elise touched her necklace. It would have to do.

"The window!" Wendi yelled, pointing to the only way out and onto the roof of Wendi's building.

Just like in the book. The dream. The same dream. The only dream.

Five hours. Forty-three minutes. Sixteen seconds.

SIXTY-THREE

Can't Get You out of My Head

OVER THE THRESHOLD and onto the ledge, Elise bellowed, "Hold on!"

Wendi scrambled over the side of the roof, trying not to slip off the steep pitch. Her feet slipped on the cracking tiles. She was almost over the side.

"Bite me!" Wendi hollered, flailing her arms side to side, trying to hang on. Her fingernails narrowly grasped the weather vane. Her weight took it down. It bent, didn't break.

"Careful. He might if he can find a way through the window."

"Too much light out here for such a bastard made from the ultimate darkness, right?" Wendi asked, hoping she was spot on about light always penetrating the darkness and not the other way around.

"If this is Lola book four, then yes." Elise laughed. It was easier, truer, almost genuine. She twirled her hair and grinned when it popped back in place.

"Asshole. I'm not for dinner!" Wendi screamed and hung on for dear life.

"Brilliant fairy arms, Betty." Elise laughed again. Genuinely this time.

"Nice catch...if I do say so myself."

Wendi tried to forget about the thing on the other side of the window. Tried...but couldn't.

"Do that thing with your arms again." Elise reached down to grab her friend. "I have an idea."

Wendi scrambled back up to safety. Then she chuckled too. Genuinely. What else could she do? She circled her arms once more.

"What happens if the black door-slash-house monster gets out here and catches us?" Wendi asked, trying to sound braver than she felt. She circled her arms again for effect.

Elise returned the gesture.

Wendi already suspected the answer coming and couldn't pull her eyes from the window despite her arm movements.

"We die...like Lola's mother. Remember book three?" Elise said, minus any emotion.

"Great. That's what I figured."

Silence.

Elise bit her lower lip and squinted her right eye, deep in thought.

"Any ideas how we get off this roof and back in our bodies?" Wendi asked.

"Nope. No we. Just me this time."

"What? We are in this together..."

Elise chimed in. "Forgive me, Fire Starter two, if this doesn't work."

Elise stepped to the edge of the roof. No pulse check. Her hands were at her sides. Then she raised them up.

"No! Don't!"

It was too late. All doubt washed out Elise's eyes and slid down the side of the building. She obviously planned to follow it.

"The shock could kill you."

"Or wake me up. Who knows? Guess we're 'bout to find out, though."

"Then what?"

"I wake you and we find Jolene's place. Hope there's a clue there, I guess. Then call Blackwater. Get police help. Call the church. Maybe not in that order."

"Okay. I'm in. But your heart."

"You mean my pig-goddess heart? Well, I also have another heart now too. Maybe Blackwater's will pull mine through the shock of the fall. But just in case that really is just bullshit talk in some fucking story, you better be ready. If this works and I actually survive, I might not be all that okay for very long. You know CPR, right?"

"ACLS certified. Just last week."

"Good. Remember carotid massage for SVT and cardiac thump for V-fib."

"Why don't we have AEDs in houses these days?"

Grinning with a smile so wide her eyes sparkled, she winked. She kissed her necklace, which twinkled almost as beautifully as the power in her eyes.

Wendi kissed hers as well.

Elise traced her finger down her chest. "Forty-three reasons to kill you, you mother of an asshole."

"Forty-three? Isn't one enough?"

Elise opened her shirt and exposed her scars for Wendi to see. She put her arms back out, circled them, and giggled.

"Forty-three scars." Wendi gasped. "That asshole. He"

"He turned me into a Firling. Look how fucking amazing I am. Perfectly broken. Gorgeously mutilated. I am a lovely magical creature, aren't I?"

Wendi nodded.

"Just like Blackwater said. I am so beautiful."

"No bullshit. Utterly beautiful," Wendi mumbled, choking on the words.

"Hush. Not another peep from you. You're getting sappy on me. Don't have time for that crap when a monster's out to get us. Got it?"

"Then how about some lyrics? That'll do, Pig." Wendi stifled her cries.

"I love that movie. *Babe*."

"Yep, of course you do. A pig pretending to be a dog. Like you, a Firling pretending to be a victim. As if…"

Elise chuckled. "Dimitri is my first choice, of course." She winked again and circled her arms. "Get on with it then. I am sure you have a lovely voice."

"Sometimes you are wrong." Wendi sniffed and began. At first, the words caught in her throat, but they strengthened. She swayed as she sang.

"In love with you.

I'm certain now you're the one to never lose.

So I'm coming home."

Elise joined in as she flapped her arms in preparation.

"Just like you said was so.

And it's so clear to me now that I'm yours to have and hold."

They both knew the lines that came next. Ironically, it was when she would jump.

"So I'm on my way,

This time to stay."

Elise jumped. The following second lasted an eternity, which ended with a loud smack as her body collided with the pavement outside the building.

The whole universe froze, and time stood still.

"You are so brave," Wendi whispered, and the wheels of time re-engaged. She peered over the side of the house, feeling more than hopeful.

"Surely…"

Unfortunately, there was nothing new, except Elise's body was still there on the ground, her head turned abnormally far to the side.

It hadn't worked.

Four hours. Fourteen minutes. Fourteen seconds.

Jessie looked at the nametag on his hospital jacket. He still couldn't believe they had accepted him into nursing school. Jessie Reyes, Student of Nursing, it claimed.

He tapped his leg. Giving into the nervous twitch made him feel better immediately.

Jolene, the sex phone worker, kept popping into his mind today. He flashed back to the night they had talked. The night he had stepped outside for the first time in years. The night everything had changed. Her tattoo story had birthed his salvation from agoraphobia.

He stared up at the stars on his Washington Park apartment's ceiling. He hadn't had the courage to paint it over yet. Just in case. In case one day he wouldn't be brave enough to step outside anymore. In case one day he decided he probably wasn't a magical being anymore.

He looked in the mirror and smiled. Then he quoted his daily affirmations. He had stolen the section from his favorite series of books: Lola Littleton, book three, section on identifying magical creatures trapped in alternative realms.

He looked at the scar on his arm, the one he had inflicted after they hung up that night. The one that proved he was really a Firling. The one he hoped looked something like Jolene's tattoo. Her man's tattoo.

He began. "Magical beings bear a mark. Humans call them birthmarks or scars. They are not."

He rubbed the mark on his arm.

"Once a supposedly human creature realizes what they are, nothing can hurt them. There is no cause for fear. Ever. The mark is proof of immortality."

He looked out the door and trembled.

Then he remembered he was a Firling.

"No cause for fear. Ever," he repeated.

He sighed. Then he tapped some more.

"The magical being's appointed assignment will arrive once they wake up and accept the fact that they are not human. That they are infinite and simply having a finite experience as a human."

He looked at his badge and wondered when his task would arrive. He felt ready. He felt prepared.

"The assignment must be accepted. Once accepted, the entire realm's survival will become dependent on the being's successful mission because only one being can complete that part of the puzzle we are all completing together," he stated, quoting the appendix from the book from memory.

How many days had he done this? How many times had he sounded like a total idiot? He didn't care. His hands no longer shook. He stopped tapping. He glanced out the door again and smirked.

"I accept my assignment."

Then he got in his car and drove to work. First, he passed a woman who was screaming. He couldn't be sure, but he thought she had just hollered something from an old Betty Boop cartoon.

SIXTY-FOUR

Jump Then Fall

WENDI'S MIND REELED. What had happened? Elise's body was still on the ground. She tried to stay optimistic. Maybe it was just taking longer than she had expected. This dream state felt like it was outside of time. Maybe there was no such thing as time here. Perhaps she shouldn't worry so much.

But...

If Elise had woken up in the human world, wouldn't she have woken Wendi by now? Shouldn't something have changed?

Wendi listened carefully. Some drums, a soothing, sensual melody, played faintly in the background. It seemed to be getting louder.

She glanced back down. Elise's body appeared to be flickering in and out...to the rhythm of the drumbeat.

Then another sound came in. Chains rattling. Clicking. Mechanical sounds. She knew it was the monster. He was getting closer. Almost to the window, probably.

Her mind wandered momentarily to Gabe. If she had just listened to him...like a good girl, she wouldn't be in this mess. She should have minded her Ps and Qs and kissed Doctor Buhl's ass like he had suggested.

What was her integrity...her truth...her honorability compared to survival?

"Everything," a voice called out. Five intermingled voices, actually.

She shook her head up and down, not afraid of the voices in the slightest. They were beyond the concept of fear. Fear was a joke in their presence.

"I know you," Wendi said. A statementnot a question.

"Of course you do," the voices answered.

Wendi smiled. She felt peaceful considering the situation. Elise below, probably dying. An evil monster stalking her. Voices speaking to her.

The drumming beat intensified. She swayed along unable to resist the pull of it. Immediately, she understood. They were coming to claim Elise. They were playing *her* song. It had a Dimitri feel to it. He could have easily played it, written it just for this occasion.

Chills everywhere. Elise had been soothing herself all along. She was playing her own song. She just didn't know it. Wendi gasped thinking about all the times she had heard Elise give Dimitri credit for saving her heart.

Elise had never needed him. He was a stand in. A substitute. A version of herself. She had only needed herself.

"Only she could save herself. That's true, isn't it?"

In confirmation, the voices replied, *"The honorable one, do you accept your assignment? Is your heart ready?"*

Wendi briefly considered hesitating. But really there was no point, was there? Could one really deny their purpose? After all the toothpaste and soap washed down the drain, was there anything else left behind?

"Is that even an option?" she asked.

"No. Not really. But you can deceive yourself into thinking that it is."

"Just like no one else can really save me but me, *right?"*

"Good, little one. Very good."

"Yes. I accept."

Wendi adjusted her butterfly necklace. It kept getting caught on the small scar on the back of her neck. It was an old injury. One she hardly ever thought about.

"Jump, then fall," they commanded.

Wendi raised her arms and started flapped.

"I already have," she hollered, plummeting to the ground.

For a moment, she soared, floated, hung in midair. The wind lifted her up. At least, it seemed to Wendi. The sensation felt familiar. Like she had done it a million times before.

She sailed parallel to the street, expecting to experience the jolting collision any moment…like falling in a dream, perhaps.

Her arms refused to give in. Involuntarily, they pumped down hard trying to propel her back up from where she came. But it was to no avail. Her head smashed into the side of the building.

Instantly, she woke up back in her own apartment. Her head throbbed.

She sat up and tried to scream but couldn't.

Her pulse raced. She tried to stand.

She checked her carotid pulse. Rate easily over two hundred.

Too dizzy, she sat back down and heaved. She clenched her stomach, trying to suppress the sickness building in the back of her throat.

"Screw that. I am never jumping off a building again," she said to Elise.

Silence.

Wendi stumbled. She tried to reach her friend, still convinced everything was okay. They had escaped the monster. They had made it back home.

But Elise was on the other side of the room. The wrong side. Not where she had been sleeping.

The covers, ruffled. Pillows on the floor, scattered.

Elise had obviously woken back up and gotten out of bed.

Wendi was so dizzy. Spinning, spinning in circles of confusion. Her pulse pounded so hard her jaw rattled. Well over two hundred.

Why was Elise across the room? On the complete other side of it?

What had happened?

"Oh my God. Help us!" Wendi shrieked. Elise's leg was turned underneath her in an abnormal position.

Wendi palpated her own pulse again. One hundred and eighty.

Elise's pig-goddess heart! No!

Elise wasn't sleeping.

Wendi remembered the flickering image at the bottom of the building. The gold string, so faint.

Elise was dying. Dead already, probably.

Wendi ran to her side. She heaved twice more, this time no longer worried about getting sick on the floor.

Fingers pressed to Elise's neck.

Please. Please.

Nothing. No pulse.

Fingers pressed to Elise's wrist.

Nothing.

Hands on Elise's back.

"God, please. Please, not like this. We are so close!"

No rise. No movement.

In a fit of desperation, Wendi rolled the body over. The body limp, heavy, lifelessn-ever moved.

A song played, audible to Wendi even back in her body on the Earth-plane. It sounded like one that Dimitri might have written...but hadn't.

Four hours. Zero minutes. Zero seconds.

A song played for Jolene, too. One for her baby. One for her bastard. She sang it as best she could, fluttering back and forth between alive and dead.

"I love Elliot. Yes, I do. Yes, I do. I love you."

Swirling in her personal hell, she decided to add a new line. It seemed like the right thing to do as the skin of her thigh ripped from the sharp blade of a monster's knife.

"I know this much is true. I love you. Yes, I do."

She tried to think of anything else worth holding onto and discovered there was simply nothing left.

Her blood seeped down her ankle and dripped to the floor. Surprisingly little blood considering the extent of the laceration.

"I know this much is true. I love you. Yes, I do."

The things she knew were true she could count on one hand.

One finger, to be exact.

. . .

Three hours. Thirty-three minutes. Thirteen seconds.

SIXTY-FIVE

In love with you

I'm certain now you're the one to never lose.
So I'm coming home,
Just like you said was so.
And it's so clear to me now that I'm yours to have and hold.
So I'm on my way,
This time to stay.

"In Love with You" by Dimitri Arion

SIXTY-SIX

Baby, Can I Hold You Tonight?

THE UNTHINKABLE HAD HAPPENED. Elise...dead after so much suffering. After they had come so close.

Wendi's ACLS textbook flashed in her mind's eye. Could it be coincidence that she had just completed the course? Probably not. What were the odds that she had been the one intern to take the course before her ICU rotation?

She closed her eyes and turned to the page stored in her photographic memory. The protocol flashed in her mind.

Get AED. As if...

She thought about running into the main office. To the convenience store around the corner. Surely they'd have one there. She needed an Epinephrine injection.

Not enough time to leave.

Then she remembered what Elise had said earlier. Cardiac thump.

"My bee sting Epi pen," she hollered.

Wendi ran to the bathroom. Found the syringe under a box of old Kotex. Rushed back.

"You knew. You freaking savior trapped in a human body...you knew this would probably stop your heart."

Wendi screamed and slammed her fist on the table.

Then she injected the serum in Elise's thigh and threw the used device across the room. She glanced at her bookshelf.

One book drew all of her attention.

"Just like Lola Littleton. Book five. Damn you, Elise. Maybe this is just a story? Shit!"

She pulled back Elise's blouse to expose the unthinkable. Her mutilated body, one not worthy of this brave hero. So surreal.

Touching Elise's thick keratin scars made Wendi cringe. Not from disgust but from horror that some freak was capable of such madness.

"Forty-three reasons to come back, my sweet friend," Wendi declared as she raised her arms above her head.

She, Elise, the woman, the baby...only had one chance left.

Wendi was injured, too. It would take every ounce of power she had left. She thought about the stories of mothers who pick up cars off their children. Fathers who dive underwater longer than a human can supposedly survive.

Friends who bring back the dead.

She imagined her and Elise laughing about this whole ordeal...years in the future. Telling the story of how the meek and honorable Wendi had saved the un-savable Elise. Watching their children play hide-and-seek together.

She remembered the character Randle in *One Flew Over the Cuckoo's Nest* and how he had died so that so many others could live. "Damn all the literary symbolism. You will not become him. Fuck. I'm the crazy one...not you."

Then with the force of love embraced with the grace of the wings of an angel, she pounded.

"One, two, three times, my love," she wailed, thumping out the lyrics that consumed her mind.

Fingers to Elise's carotid.

Nothing.

Fingers to the wrist.

Nothing.

Pupils fixed and dilated.

She pounded again.

One. Two. Three times.

She begged, "Not like this. Not this way, damn it! I'll shock your heart as many times as it takes. I'll drill a hole in your fucking head if I have to. Wake up!"

Wendi considered pounding again for the fifth time. "Again," she said.

Then a sixth.

A seventh.

Too many times now. It had been at least ten minutes by this point. She sighed and dropped her fists and sat down.

"Brain dead is not worthy of you, my brilliant friend."

The song consumed her now.

"Go in peace, you beautiful woman."

She didn't know how to sing Elise's song, but she knew Dimitri's. She stood for one last dance to honor her friend before she called 911.

"So thankful for all the love that you've shown to me.

The dreams and visions of hours past,

Still fill my breaking heart.

And as the final raindrops fall on our last night,

There's one thing more I have to say.

You will always be one, two, three times, my love."

Yes you're..."

Wendi stopped, unable to finish. She held her pounding head and gave into her misery, her failure, her fate. She had obviously failed her assignment, and the puzzle was ruined.

She glanced at the Epi pen across the room and screamed with rage. The tragedy. The shock. All of it, so unfair.

And then she heard a sound.

Time stood still again. Perhaps it had been still the whole time?

At first, she thought she was hallucinating. But she was not.

Elise mumbled almost imperceptibly, "One, two, three times, my love."

Together, they finished the beautiful song. "And I'll always want you."

Wendi embraced her friend who said these last things before she lost consciousness again: "Gun. Jolene's. Two doors down. Top floor. Key under mat. Gun under bed. Bullets above stove. Go. Go now."

Three hours. Four minutes. Five seconds.

SIXTY-SEVEN

The Dance

WENDI SCRAMBLED despite her throbbing head. She trailed down the stairs with eyes closed to stave off the spinning. She put her hands on either side of her face to keep herself focused.

Like a horse. Blinders. Wear my blinders.

The thought, *horse,* dangled in her mind like a noose trying to hang her. Like a lover destined to leave her. Like a song on a broken record player.

Like the last page of a book missing, dooming the reader to the eternal madness of not knowing how the story ended. Like the last sputters of Mrs. Wilson's body surrendering to her last night in the anatomy tank's formaldehyde before they cremated her remains and shipped them to the family.

I love horses. I want to ride another horse. How long has it been?

A memory surfaced.

She had been five, maybe six at the most.

Wendi sniffed, wiped her eyes, rubbed her neck. The memory, so powerful, washed through her even though it was twenty years old.

Sneaking a peak at the foal. It should have been delivered by now.

The smell of freshly packed hay wafted into her brain. A metal smell, too. One that shouldn't be there. One that suggested something had gone terribly wrong.

Clanking and clinking. The sound of horseshoes hammered into perfect position, perhaps? Stable doors locking into position. People running to and fro. Shouldn't they all be in bed or celebrating the birth?

Wendi carefully tiptoed through the tack room, trying not to get caught out of bed at this hour; the moon had replaced the sun eons ago.

She should have been asleep and stayed in her bed. She tried not to step on nails or strewn about tools. She didn't want tetanus, did she? Something stung her neck. A loose nail or hook, probably. She touched the sore, wet spot and licked her finger.

Metal, like the smell in the air. Blood.

255

She felt the blood trickle down her back and shivered.

She heard her mother's scream before she heard the gunshot. At first, she thought she had been discovered. But the truth was so much worse. Blood everywhere. So much. Too much. Way too much.

Bailey, the mare, was bleeding to death after birthing the foalbreech and too large, the labor too long.

Bailey had been Wendi's horse.

Now she was just meat for the pigs and flies.

Wendi never rode that terrible pony. That one that had killed her Bailey.

Never rode another horse again, actually.

Could never look at a gun, either.

Like the one that murdered Bailey. Like the one in her hand. Like the one that killed her father in retribution for what he had done in a drunken fit.

She put the bullets in and cringed.

Holding a gununthinkable. Having to shoot it to take an innocent lifeun-survivable.

She put it in her back pocket and tried to ignore the heaviness that it forced upon her.

The knowledge of where this game they were playing might end up slathered her in guilt and shame.

Another thought trickled in. Hers, but not…at the same time.

"You accepted. You will play it out honorably."

She considered replying.

Instead, she spit on the ground and fluttered her imaginary skirt. She flashed her eyelashes and faked a smile. She would have said the words, but what was the point. She knew they heard her thoughts perfectly clear. *Boop-oop-a-doop.*

Two hours. Thirty-six minutes. Seventeen seconds.

SIXTY-EIGHT

New Kid in Town

WENDI OPENED her own apartment door, not sure what she was more afraid of: the gun in her back pocket or Elise dead on the floor.

Elise muttered, "Get the car, Betty. We've got a fuckface to kill."

"Yes, madam. Anything else?"

"Gun. Did you get it?"

"Yep. How did you know where it was?"

Elise shook her head. "No. Don't ask."

Wendi would have shown Elise the device, but that would have meant touching it again. She patted her back pocket and faked another smile.

"You're too good at that," Elise said.

"The faker-shmaker smile?"

Nod. "I call it a frown-smile."

"I know. I think I'll make a great lawyer, don't you?"

"Too good, actually."

"Elise, how did you know where the gun was? That she had a gun to begin with?"

Elise shook her head again. She looked at the clock and started crawling to the door, obviously too weak to stand. "We have exactly two and one-half hours to make a three-hour drive through the ice and snow. Help me get my wimpy ass in the car. I'll explain on the way."

Wendi faked a flimsy laugh to complement her fake smile. Elise offered her the same smile back.

"Forty-three reasons?" Wendi asked, trying to lighten the mood.

"No. Forty-six."

Elise pointed at her chest and sighed. She raised three fingers in the air.

"Me, her, and the baby?" Wendi answered.

Nod.

. . .

Two hours. Twenty-six minutes. Six seconds.

The smacking of the sheriff's gum was more than he could stand. One more freaking smack, click, or pop, and Blackwater was pretty sure he would totally lose his mind.

He started humming to distract himself. It was a new melody. One he couldn't exactly place. But he knew it like he knew every long, shiny lock on his head. He pulled back his hair and confined it with a ponytail holder he kept hidden in his pocket. He allowed the melody to continue in the furthest corner of his mind.

"Never thought I'd be standing here with a squaw cop wearing a pony."

Blackwater bit his lip like he was a walking stick of gum.

The sheriff chuckled. Then he belched and resumed his smack, crackle, blow, and pop routine before he took a sip of his black coffee. It sloshed like mud from the rim of his cup over his stained teeth and back down.

Backwash black gold. Disgusting.

"Got some good old Dunkin' holes and thick black joe in the back office. Not much for us to do here really."

Blackwater paced attempting to rein in his thoughts. He knew better than to judge another person, but some days, it was harder than others. *The thought of food...unthinkable. Coffee as well.*

"The family?" Blackwater asked, feeling an intense hate for anything that had to do with coffee beans or pastries.

"Trailer park trash. Not even out of bed yet."

"Maybe they work nights?"

"Doubt it. Who cares? They're human garbage. Poor white trash."

Blackwater considered responding, *"Like pale skinned squaws?"* Then he remembered the accusations he had just thought about the sheriff.

"Well, how long until we know time of death?"

"Does it matter?"

Blackwater thought of Elise. The clock in her dream. The timing of this murder was off. Why? Why did the killer do it sooner than the original vision? What changed the course? Altered the tapestry?

The woman should still have about two and one-half hours left to live. But here she was...purple-red on the bottom half, the liver mortis already settling in. They had found her in the water, but he could tell she had died lying down from the way the blood had settled. His knowledge of forensics was minimal, but every cop knew that meant she had been dead for at least three to six hours for the color change to have already set in like that. The rest of her swollen, oozing, already stinking like rot.

He quickly glanced at the other body bag. The one across the room. The boy. The same boy who would never go skiing. Never ride a bike. Never have a first day of school drop off. Never have another birthday cake wish go un-granted by his family's limited trailer-park budget.

Elliot. I'm sorry.

He wanted to run out and buy every toy in the local Target and pass them out like Santa at the trailer park community center.

I want to give you every single thing you ever asked for but never had. Even the ones you never knew to ask for. Every goddamn one of them. New Buzz Lightyear. Tonka Truck. No problem. You can count on me, Elliot.

"Fuck this job," Blackwater muttered, struggling to get his emotions under control. He didn't do kid crimes. That was left for the thick-skinned dead-eyed cops amongst them. The only ones calloused enough to survive this kind of madness.

He couldn't take it anymore. He headed to the back door, unable to look at the little black bag any longer. Even Target couldn't cover that up with wall stickers made in China.

Elise, I'm coming to find you instead.

"Send the family my con…con…dolences."

Silence except smack and pop.

"Damn. You are not like me. I can't… I'm leaving," Blackwater said, struggling to keep his words steady yet failing miserably.

Another pop. One more slobbery smack.

Blackwater grabbed his pager and stared at a message that wasn't there. "Got to take this one. Sorry."

"Right. Sure you do," the sheriff said while simultaneously resuming his popping. Under his breath, he mumbled, "Bullshit story."

Blackwater let it slide.

"Wimpy ass squaws should have drums not guns," the sheriff said as if Blackwater had already left the building.

"Elliot, I'm so sorry," Blackwater whispered and placed two fingers in the air as a final salute, not giving a crap about the asshole cop, his gum, or his flagrant prejudice.

"You mean Ephron," the sheriff said as Blackwater left the room. "Boy's name was Ephron."

"No?" He turned back around and faced the sheriff and locked eyes with him.

"Yes, actually." The cop wiped his nose.

"Are you sure?" Blackwater steadied himself against the wall and then started tapping his head against the cheap wood paneling, harder and harder with each thump.

"You are one weird injun. But I'm sure. You don't forget a weird name like that in these parts, boss."

As the significance set in, Blackwater started running. How much time had he wasted? Elise, the next victim, baby Elliot…all of them were still in terrible danger. Target and those creepy red balls out front would have to wait.

"The call came in about an hour ago. This is Jessie Reyes, right?" Melissa, the director of nursing students, asked.

"Yes. Seriously?" Jessie said, unable to catch his breath as his heart rate increased. Surprised at the undeniable urge to do so, he checked his pulse. Ninety-six.

The director could hear him tapping over the phone. "You okay? What's that sound?"

"Nothing." Checked again. *My divine assignment, probably.* Eighty-five.

He stared up at the ceiling and smiled. It was a fake one. But a fake smile was better than balling. At least until he finished the call and hung up.

The stars on his celling glowed even brighter than usual today. Surely that had to be a good sign. He believed in signs. He had to in order to make it through the day. The days outside of his apartment, that was.

He took a deep breath, trying to gather what courage he could. He started tapping once more. If the stars were shining, then he could do this. He reached down and traced the outline of the scar on his arm. A real one replaced the fake smile. He didn't feel like balling anymore. Not one little bit.

"Why me?" he asked, no longer tapping.

"I have no idea. Random, I guess?" the nursing director replied.

"Clinicals don't start for three weeks."

"Yeah, yeah, I know. I make the schedule. Remember?" the nurse affirmed.

He could hear her shifting her papers over the phone. Obviously she had already approved the appointment.

"Me, of all the possible students?"

"Yep."

"Yampa Valley?"

"Right-O."

"Today?"

"Now, actually. Preferably yesterday. It's a long story no one cares about."

"I do and"

"Just say yes." She sighed and cleared her throat. Now she was tapping something, her pencil on her desk, probably.

"I'm supposed to be at Denver General for all my rotations. That was a criterion for my acceptance."

"I know." More tapping. Faster. Harder. She cleared her throat again.

"My cats, Plompous and Pearl, who will feed them?"

"Bring 'em. Yampa Valley has a condo for nursing students. Stocked and animal friendly."

"But"

The pencil cracked. He heard it, but he felt it, too. "They expect you for the night shift. Seven p.m. Be there."

"But"

The line went dead.

Jessie traced his scar again, and then he packed his bags, gathered his cats, and put his favorite square of starry sky covered cloth in his pocket. He had a three-hour drive ahead of him through the ice and snow. Lucky him, he had just put his snow tires on.

SIXTY-NINE

Lonely Boys

ELISE CLIPPED her belt in position. She moved the magazine on the floor to the side. It flipped over, and the man on the cover stared back at her. Chills. She knew that meant something but was too exhausted to ask what.

"You said you know this guy," Elise half-whispered. Her throat cracked. Wendi offered her a bottle of water.

"Yes. Med school."

"His smile..."

"So genuine, I know."

Silence.

The heaviness in the car lifted a little.

Elise picked up the magazine, unable to resist. She breathed heavily, fatigued from such a minor maneuver as bending forward and sitting back up.

Without even noticing, Elise reached up and checked her pulse. Ninety and somewhat irregular. Mild congestive heart failure, probably.

She might not make it three hours without oxygen, a hospital, possibly a new pig-goddess heart. This heart's time was marked. "Tick-tock," she mumbled.

"Dimitri?" Wendi offered.

"Ye..." Unable to finish the word, she nodded.

The beautiful song started. They both felt better immediately. Elise closed her eyes and moved into the melody.

Wendi whispered, "He does cold cases now. Billy, I mean."

"You can't take your eyes off him. I can feel it. All the way over here...even with my eyes closed. Why?"

"Other than his adorable smile and innocent eyes, you mean? Yes. There's a reason. I've never told anybody."

"Well that will make two of us then. Go for it." A curl sprung in front of her right eye, but Elise was too tired to push it behind her ear.

"Where are we headed, by the way?" Wendi reached over and fixed the loose strand.

"Thank…you. Steamboat Springs. Floor it."

"Okay. Okay to both."

Sigh. Sigh. "Trust me. Please."

Wendi took the exit and punched the gas. Eighty.

Elise kept breathing in and out as deeply as she could.

"I know... I know that much is true. The trust part."

"Spill it."

"My dad." She pressed the pedal harder. Eight-five.

Nod.

Even the song paused for Wendi to answer. The engine surprisingly silent for such high revs.

"Death row. Executed for a crime I know he never committed. If Billy could solve the case, then..."

Silence.

"Then maybe…" Wendi's eyes glossed over at the possibility.

Elise opened her eyes, touched her butterfly necklace, and gave her best effort at forming a genuine smile.

"Then his name could be cleared, and I could take my real name back."

"You faker..." Elise coughed. "Twins."

"Yes. On the advice of the defense attorney. Said I would never make it in a world where anybody knew who my dad was."

Sigh. Breath. "Get it. How you feel..."

"Walking around with a name that isn't mine sucks." Wendi adjusted the mirror and noticed they were almost the only ones on the road. Too snowy today.

"Lying." Breath. "Every minute." Sigh. "Every day."

"Yep. Aren't you curious who I really am?"

"Nope." Smile. "Already know. Wendi. Friend. Fire Starter." Bigger smile. "One in a million. Soul sister."

"Gwendolyn Beckons. I am the only living daughter of the infamous Williams Beckons." Wendi sniffed and looked out the window. Her mother's image filled her mind. The guilt. The anger too big to repress.

Wendi slammed her fist on the armrest. Then she cracked the window. The cold air rushed in and invigorated them both.

"Who murdered..." Elise started. "I mean...chopped…" Sigh but softer. "To bits and then burned…" Deep breath and cough. Eyes back open. "Denise Swan?"

"Matriarch of the powerful tech gods of Silicon Valley."

Slower, almost normal breath. "In a fit of impassioned rage...over a love affair gone bad." Elise shook her head. "I remember."

"Supposedly."

"I never believed that story. Stupid. We were six? Or seven?" Checked her neck. Seventy-two.

"I was twelve. I'm quite a bit older than you," Wendi said.

"Didn't know. Never thought."

"Why would you?"

Elise closed her eyes once more and sank back into the seat. Her breath labored again from the effort of speaking. Even an inexperienced intern would notice.

"Your heart has failed you, Doctor Phillips."

"Con…concur." Cough. "Guess pig is about to be bacon." Elise snorted and tried to laugh. Instead, she coughed. She cleared the small amount of pink froth from her lips.

"It's bad."

"I know. I'm dying. Drive faster."

Wendi pressed her foot harder, trying to make the car go faster, but the pedal was already on the floor. She looked at the clock.

"How long do we have?"

"Don't ask. Cover clock. Don't look…k?"

Wendi punched Steamboat Springs into the navigation. At this rate, they would arrive way too late, and she was already twenty miles above the speed limit.

"You gave me an idea. Sigh. "Let's play a game," Elise suggested.

"Serious?"

"Yep. Alex Cross." Sputter. Sigh.

"Or a heart attack. Shit, Elise, this is really bad."

"No bullshit. Good story." Cough. "Lousy ending."

Wendi swallowed and applied a brave mask to her face. Elise wouldn't see her cry. "And the game is called..."

"I know this much is true." Elise smiled.

Wendi caught her breath. She flashed back to the day before her dad was executed. They were only allowed to see him under supervision…in case he went wild and killed them, too. *Ridiculous.*

"That's the last thing my dad said to me. He said as long as I could name the things I knew were true, that I would always be okay. Then he told me that when he took his dose of death the following day, he would still know three things: that he loved us more than anything else in the world; that one day, somehow this would be okay, would serve a higher purpose; and that he was innocent."

Elise took a deep breath and coughed up more froth.

"I did believe him too. At the time, anyway. Some days, doubt gets the better of me," Wendi said, blinking her eyes to clear the tears she was forcing back.

"Perfect. That's beautiful. K, me first." Elise said.

Nod.

"Anything's fair, right?" One hundred.

"In love and war, my friend. And this is war."

Nod. Ninety-six.

The guests were already dancing, infused with the oblivion of mind-altering drugs, lust, and brain-numbing music. One drop of liquid roofie per cocktail. One drophappy. Two dropsuninhibited. Three dropsdrowsiness. Four or more dropsperfect amnesia.

Marcus Kincaid grinned, delighted with his cleverness. No one would remember any details of the party. No one but him, that was.

He would remember every lovely little detail. Like every year before.

His phone vibrated. Robert, most likely.

"You're nothing but a shit face," Kincaid said, clicking the ringer off.

Robert and the fake Mandinkan imports could wait until tomorrow. Right now, the only thing that mattered was this party. This ceremony. This celebration. This Anniversary.

He glanced at the punch bowl and grinned. "Mother Darling, drink up."

If he could have patted his own back, he would have. He looked at the clock. He could almost hear it tick. He tapped his finger to the tune of a ticking second. The pain of waiting another hour was ripping him apart. He loved it. Loved the irony. Loved the torture. The anticipation. The mirror. The Womb.

Kincaid had already notified the local taxi transport. They would be here in just over one hour. When the last guest left, he would go down.

Down to his bride. Down to his Queen. Down to see if she had survived the sutures. Down to see how her lips looked, forever sealed in perfect silence.

The contrast of his surroundings delighted him like the fine blade of a scalpel. So close, but so far. Nano-millimeters even. So loud up here. So quiet down there.

He took a big sniff of bleach. Smelled like a nice clean kitchen. "Mother Darling, see what a good boy I have been?"

Nothing could have been further from the truth.

Clean. Silent. Ah!

Unable to suppress his expansion, he loosened his belt. He clipped and unclipped it six times before deciding on the final adjustment.

The song climaxed with one final spasm of thump, thump, thump to the classic techno beat. He counted it out, unable to resist. Six hard beats. Six softer. Then six beats even more intense in confirmation of the plan.

The perfect song for the perfect doll.

The perfect serenade for the perfect Anniversary.

The perfect dance for the perfect King.

One hour. Twenty minutes. Seventeen seconds.

SEVENTY

Talking to the Moon

THE GLIMMER of Wendi's necklace distracted her from the speed limit sign. She was now well over twenty-five miles above the limit. They were still due to arrive in the general vicinity about ninety minutes too late.

Elise sighed and gargled, trying to clear the fluids.

Wendi quickly remembered to…not think about the clock. Then she focused on the game, trying to forget about the time. The time that had already killed Jolene because they were not going to make it.

"Go. Your turn," Wendi said…not looking at the clock. She put the magazine on top of the instrument panel and nodded her head. Billy Thompson's face fluttered with the heater vent. He nodded, too.

Deep breath. Cough. "I know that if I die stopping this fuckface of a monster…that my excuse of a life was worth it." Cough. "That I lived a good life. I will walk up grinning at Peter."

"Awesome. Okay, let me think. Anything, right?"

"Right." Elise giggled and then spit out more froth.

"The best color is orange. Almost pink like your foam but more orange than that. Why, you don't ask? Because it looks great on me and never asks for anything back. It offers but never takes. I like that. I'm like that. I am orange."

"Cats…are better than dogs," Elise said and meowed to prove it. She thought about Lil' Tig and Lola. Then she thought about Maddie and wondered what ever happened to the poor cat.

"Totally. I know that sex can be both terrible and wonderful. Sometimes at the exact same time."

"Yes. Please." Elise closed her eyes and imagined him, her man.

Wendi smiled knowing she may never have the chance to get so real with someone again. That this was her last chance to confess her deepest beliefs.

Elise just moaned softly.

Wendi wiped her eyes once more. "That every child deserves a chance to know how amazing, how beautiful, special they truly are."

"Yes. Bam." Cough. "Every adult, too." Elise wiped mucous from her lip.

"That you are so brave. So big."

"Ditto."

"That every time I tried to define myself as not something, I ended up proving I was exactly that." Wendi thought about the house she grew up in. She thought about all the lies she had told by changing her name.

Elise smiled and then grimaced again.

"That trailer park girls don't play croquet well...just like my favorite author said in her gut-wrenching collection of inspirational personal essays." Wendi laughed imaging the letters written by the woman to her soulmate before she ever met him. At the end of the book, in her last letter, she described standing across from him at their wedding. The same wedding where she walked down the aisle to some James Blunt song instead of the traditional march. "Dude, that lady is weird, but I know this much is trueif anyone ever tells my story, I hope it's her. She's a sap pretending to be tough. Like me. Maybe she is me?"

Elise snorted. "Maybe I am you too? And I fucking hate croquet. Ugh." Elise tried to reach her neck, but her hand was just too heavy. "And I've never stepped foot in a trailer park. How the hell am I supposed to know which direction the damn ball goes? And the mallet–too heavy. Pathetic game."

"Totally."

"Rich people games suck." Cough. Wipe. Deep breath.

Wendi laughed a hollow, nervous laugh. She looked away from the pain crawling back up Elise's face, distorting it once more.

Elise sighed and shifted her position before she went again. "Oh...that the best thing about Levi is how good his hair smells. Damn." She groaned. "So feminine, so manly. Yum."

"TMI. TMI, girl." Wendi shushed her, yet secretly, she hoped both she and Elise would experience the comfort of a strong man again. One finally worth her beating heart. She thought of Gabe. How he couldn't see what really mattered in her. Her truth. Her authenticity. The five voices had been right. Nothing else mattered more than that.

Elise oozed, the thought of Blackwater flooding her womanly structures from the inside. She remembered his words about unraveling her when she was wound up too tightly.

Wendi paused the conversation knowing Elise was lost in loving thoughts.

"Unwind me, baby," Elise whispered, swimming in the image of loving her man once more. The one man she was willing to admit...had stolen her broken heart.

"TMI. Hello. I'm in the car too. Stop it. I can feel you getting all hot and bothered from over here, and it's making it hard to drive."

They both laughed again. Wendi reached across and wiped Elise's lips for her, never once pulling back in disgust but reaching forward...like a mother would to comfort her sick baby.

"That if I wasn't afraid, I would have lived my life so differently," Wendi confessed.

"Oh, that's good. Keep going, please. Follow that," Elise suggested.

"That in every situation, you only have to choose between two options: love and fear."

"Yes. Keep going."

"That every problem is the same problem: trying to teach us how to make that one so seemingly simple choice."

"Beautiful," Elise said.

"That I don't want to be afraid of who I am anymore."

"Yes. Why would you?"

"That I am perfect just the way I am."

"So true."

"That being anyone other than who I really am was never really a choice but an illusion of a choice," Wendi said.

"Lovely."

"That I chose love from this day forward."

"Me too."

"That love and hate are the same emotion, only separated by the scalpel made from the same blade of fear that cuts us each apart...day in and out."

"Perfect."

"And if I refuse to be afraid, that the only thing left is actually love."

"Bingo."

"Thank you. The game is amazing. You are amazing."

"That the only thing"Elise coughed"that is scarier than being amazing...is being ordinary."

"Yes."

"That the only thing more terrifying than telling Levi that I think I love him is never getting the chance to."

"He might not know?"

"Impossible!"

"Men are fucking thick. He probably thinks you want some other guy."

"No way." Cough. Wipe. Spit.

"Then do it. Tell him before he gives up on you."

"He'd never…"

"Then that is enough of a reason for anybody without a desperado heart. Girl, tell him."

"K." Cleared throat. "Promise."

"Me next."

Nod.

"That my biggest fear, other than schizophrenia, of course, is no one having anything interesting to say about me at my funeral."

"Nice. Not possible," Elise said, still trying to laugh instead of cough. But it was no use.

Spit. Wipe. "That the only thing worse than remembering what that asshole did to me was not remembering. The not-knowing is so much worse." Cough.

"Fair enough," Wendi said. She reached across and palpated Elise's neck. "It's getting worse."

"I know. We are close now."

"We will get there right on time, won't we?"

"Of course."

"Yes."

"Billy Thompson will solve your father's case. I'm sure of it," Elise said and grabbed Wendi's hand warmly.

The magazine cover nodded and slipped to the floor.

"That there's no one I'd rather die with than you. But if I get to pick, I say we both live. How's that?" Wendi thought of her horse, Bailey, and her father and nodded. "Let's live."

"That Betty Boop has nothing on you, girl." One hundred and ten.

"That you are just like Lola Littleton. You are a Firling if I have ever met one. That you are not a story, but if you were, Elise, you would be a best fucking seller."

"Awesome." One hundred and thirty.

Wendi pulled the gun out and stared at it. A million things flashed through her mind. She stared at the taxis going past, one after the next, too distracted to notice how weird it was for a school night.

"That I am a fighter. Always have been. And so...are you."

"That the house wants to eat me," Elise added. She thought of her dreams...always running away, crawling out of the attic. The same confined space. The same dream. One hundred and thirty-four. More foam.

"You are dying, Elise."

"Yep. Hurry." An idea popped in. *Go in the way I came out.*

"Fuck me."

Elise looked up and then closed her eyes once more. She groaned and foamed at the mouth. The worse it got, the more it seemed that she knew which way to guide Wendi to drive. One hundred and thirty-seven.

Wendi shook her head, but a tear escaped.

"Find a three-story house. At the end of one of the streets. We are very close now."

"How do you?"

"Don't ask." Elise grunted. She clenched her jaw, pain obviously distorting her pleasing features.

"Dark overhang. Windows like eyes. A red carpet, glistening, rolls out the front door like a serpent's tongue. The number six above door. Go." One hundred and forty.

"How long?" Wendi asked.

"Twenty minutes." Cough. Gag.

"Are you telling me that we just drove over two hundred miles in sixty minutes?"

"Yep." Cleared throat.

"How?"

"One day, if we survive, I'll tell you. Hand me the phone, and drive until I tell you to stop." Spit. "Sorry. So gross."

"No. Get it out."

"K. Thank you." Elise moaned and spit on the floor. One, two, three times.

"My love," Wendi joked, feeling nothing like joking. The flimsiness of her attempt at humor, pathetic at best.

Eyes still closed, hand over her heart, Elise texted Blackwater. Wendi scanned the surroundings.

At the same time, they both said, "Stop here."

From their position, the street was dark. He wouldn't see them coming...until it was too late.

The only question was...too late for whom?

Zero hours. Nineteen minutes. Nineteen seconds.

SEVENTY-ONE

Hallelujah

THE CLOCK TICKED. They only had a few minutes left.

They snuck around the back, Wendi holding Elise up, holding them both together.

They waited briefly, too nervous to proceed.

Nothing. No one.

A dog barked next doorsix times.

A wolf howled in the distance.

Wendi asked, "How long?"

Elise held up ten fingers and then spit out more pink foam before she put her hands back over her heart.

They made their way to the back steps, Elise on her hands and knees.

"There's no way you can climb down there. Look at you. Can hardly stand. It's like you're in heart failure or something, you wimp," Wendi teased.

No one laughed. It didn't seem right. Not here.

Wendi took the gun, loaded it, and put it in her back pocket. "Well, how did you know about the gun, the apartment?"

Elise spit. "While I was dead, the Five told me. They are with the blond-haired woman now. Jolene. They got us here in time through a time portal."

"And the baby? Elliot?"

"Don't know for sure. They didn't or couldn't say." Elise bent over and heaved–six times.

Wendi steadied her and helped her wipe her mouth.

"Key. Rock. By the back door. Turn it. Six times each way." Elise closed her eyes and dropped to her knees.

Wendi wiped her mouth one more time and then flicked her cheek. "Elise! Stay awake. There's just one more thing I know is true. That mother fucker will die before you do, damn it. That I will save you."

Elise smiled best she could. It would be her last smile at Wendi.

The effort took all she had, and Elise collapsed on the ground, heaving, coughing, convulsing.

Nine minutes. Wendi looked at her fingers. Nine held high.

In the distance, something clawed, trying to get out. A cat, perhaps?

"I'm going anyway," she whispered, trying not to look at Elise's jerking body. If the clock trick had taught her anything, it was that facts could be bent. She shook her head. No magazine to cover Elise. She shook her head again and swallowed.

Wendi climbed down the back stairs and fidgeted until she found the rock. The key fit, and she turned it–six times to the right, six times to the left.

Wendi was in. Behind a large freezer. A funny looking cat flew past. The striped beast knocked over a piece of wood.

She caught her breath. Covered her lips to stifle her scream.

Shit! He heard me. Heard me. Damn cat! Don't die now, Wendi. Not like this. Elise dead. Me dead. Jolene dead. Elliot.

How would she explain such a failure to Peter at the gates of heaven?

"Sorry I screwed up, and the cat knocked over the wood. I killed us all in one fell swoop. Sorry. Boop-oop-a-doop. Let it go, Betty."

She would have flipped up her imaginary skirt, but there wasn't room.

Focus. Focus. Or you're already dead.

She fingered the gun once her enemy, now her only friend. Could she use it? She wasn't sure.

She cowered, crouched behind the biggest freezer.

Legs shaking. Pulse racing.

Eight minutes.

She held up her fingers, counted them once more.

She waited for the knife in her neck. The bullet. The smack. The slap.

Nothing.

The humming appliance had masked the noise.

She could smell the stink from there. His stink. Bleach-covered death. Same as the hospital. Same as her nightmares.

The memory of her recurring nightmare consumed her, taking her away from the smell but right back to it.

In her dreams, a lanky, smoky-grey man chased her through the woods. Like some lousy movie, she kept tripping on something underfoot. Slowly he trailed, certain that his steady pace would outmatch her terror-driven attempts to evade him.

Without exception, she ended up in the same place: in front of a three-story madhouse determined to own her. Gasping, she narrowly escaped his menacing grasp, hoping to find refuge in a house almost as terrifying as the creep who chased her.

Once inside the house, a scent, so strong, burned her nose. Bleach-covered death. She hollered frantically for help, only to find the house laughing, the smell magnified. Now the house became the vicious attacker, bent on keeping her trapped forever. Room after room, she searched furiously and fruitlessly for a way out...any way out from that awful smell.

Somehow, she always managed to find a narrow and twisted pathway through a tiny and terrifying route fraught with more danger as her only route of escape. And just when she lost all hope of escape, a glimmer of the dark night's sky emerged.

After finally exiting the house of terror, after barely surviving a million threats, she got out unscathed. Yet he...the dark king, hunted her once more. Always the same manprobably from a portal of darknesswith his head bent down, looking from his ominously grey jacket.

Never did he say anything other than, *"You fool. You're already dead."*

Hospital is death. This life is death. We are already dead! I am already dead. This is hell. We made this hell and called it life.

The absurd thought gave her a certain measure of strength. If she was already dead, what could this monster really do to her...besides trap her eternally in this house?

Fuck you, asshole. Without fear, I am more dangerous than you. I am only love. Only light. Light beats darkness every time.

She risked a glance. More open from the side.

The woman chained, strapped in place, bleeding.

Not just some woman. Her name is Jolene. Elliot! Where is the baby?

The idea of the little boy gave her even more strength.

The contraption held her...Jolene, in an inhuman position. She must already be dead. Another waft of pure stink.

Seven minutes.

She looked at her fingers. Seven.

I'm dead. You're dead. We are already dead. Daddy, look out. I'm coming home. Fuck hell. I'm out of here.

Wendi stood, utterly fearless, and aimed at the monster.

She disengaged the safety and held the gun steady.

The thud of the metal shattered Kincaid's perfect silence.

He turned, cracked his neck. Looked up from his dark grey jacket.

It was he. The one from her dreams.

"Who the hell are you?" the creep demanded.

"Your worst nightmare, asshole."

"I doubt it," he replied and laughedsix times.

Six minutes.

She glanced at her hands. Six.

A thought popped in: *Six is for mother. Not king.*

"Let her go. Put down your knife!" Wendi demanded.

His blade was aimed right for the center of Jolene's womanness. He planned to slice her to pieces with his steel blade of demented love.

"Jill, I love you, my precious bride. My glorious doll. Make love to me."

Wendi swallowed, disgusted by all the times she had let someone do the exact same thing to her. Slice her to bits from the inside. Use a penis to dissect her like Mrs. Wilson.

The symbolism and irony were undeniable.

Five minutes.

She glanced at her fingers. Another thought*Five is for change.*

"This is my made up hell," she announced, "and you are about to meet your maker for a change."

Kincaid laughed again, thinking about a childhood memory. About Sephubel. About becoming a Portal of Darkness, a dark King of the Underworld.

A howl in the distance emerged. Five howls, to be exact.

The door clangedsix times forward, six times back.

Kincaid's blade pierced Jolene's pelvis. He pressed forward and giggled as the red stream spilled at his feet. He should finish it now, but why? The woman could wait a little longer. Why not make it a threesome? Like for Mother Darling.

Kincaid stepped forward toward the intruder. Wendi shot his foot.

He stepped again. She shot his leg.

He stumbled, closer by the second. She shot his chest.

A door in the distance fell to the floor. Three more bullets from far away.

A cat meowed. Five times.

Several people rushed. Too many sounds to understand. Coughing. Spitting. Howling.

Four minutes.

Another thought, *"Four is for the angels. We are with you, our little angel."*

As Kincaid's blade reached Wendi, she shot a fourth time. Her bullet missed his head; his blade did not miss hers.

The floor stained red with Wendi's blood, mingling in a perfect cacophony with Jolene's.

Three minutes.

One last thought. *"Three is for the ascended masters. You are now a master. You have completed your assignment. You will ascend."*

Blackwater, still half-carrying, half-dragging Elise, pulled out a gun and aimed. But something was wrong.

The weight on his hip shifted. He was light. Too light.

"Elise!" he screamed. A cat crossed his path. Tiger striped markings. A torn ear.

Elise had already grabbed Wendi's gun. The next moment lasted an eternity while the universe stood still.

Flash!

Elise returned to her nightmare. To the only nightmare. To the every nightmare.

How many times had she heard that same terrible voice in her dreams? How many times had she felt his breath steaming down her neck while she desperately tried to run away?

If she turned around, she would see his long, dark grey coat, his slow confident gait, always gaining on her as she tried furiously to get away. All the while, she kept falling down, her foot caught by a stone or twig like in every predictable horror film.

Until the last time...maybe six nights ago.

Right before he grabbed her hair from behind, she dug her heels in, spun around, and faced him. Eye to his eye-less pits, she spit at him, flapped her arms, and flew off. Instantly, he fell to the floor, thrashing and screaming in pain.

Flash! She was back in real-time.

Before Blackwater saw it, could do anything about it, he heard it: Elise spitting pink froth on the floor and a gun exploding.

Time stopped. The bullet moved slowly enough for them all to observe it cross the air, pierce Kincaid's skin, and blow the monster's cranium apart, much more effectively, much more efficiently than any anatomy class handsaw.

Kincaid staggered back, a hole spurting crimson from between his eye-less pits. His dark blood mingling in a perfect cacophony with Jolene and Wendi's.

Two minutes.

Another thought in Wendi's mind. *"Two is for faith. Must have faith."*

Elise collapsed on the floor next to Wendione hand on her heart, the other on Wendi's.

Wendi's dying words sputtered from her mouth. "In death, we all bleed the same red. Even that fuckface. Why did I have to die again to realize that I was already dead? He tried to tell me. I wouldn't listen. Was he trying to help us?"

"Listen to me now, my friend."

"Yes."

"I know this much is true. That I love you. That I always have. That I always will."

"Yes." Fainter.

"And that I will most certainly see you again."

"Yes." Barely there at all.

"Boop-oop-a-doop. Let it go, Betty. It's okay. I can hear them playing your song. Shall we dance one last time?"

"Boop-oop-a-doop."

"Yes."

"The song. Elise, it isn't Dimitri's song that you love."

"I know. It's mine. It always was."

"Forty-three reasons for one last dance then."

"No. Forty-eight, my sweet, sweet friend."

One. Surrender to a higher power.

There would be no more thoughts for Wendi. Her heart stopped exactly one minute later. Simultaneously, Elise's heart went into fulminant failure.

Blackwater howled. Too many times to count.

Kincaid sputtered. About six pints worth.

As the rest of the officers reached Blackwater, he screamed in agony. He reached down and caressed Elise's curly hair, choking on his final words as they dragged him away. "You were the one with the broken heart, but mine was the one that needed saving. Take mine. Yes. Please. Take mine instead."

It was the last time he would see her with a broken heart.

Zero hours. Zero minutes. Negative three seconds.

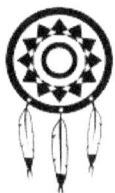

SEVENTY-TWO

Night Train

JOLENE SMILED EVEN though her lips wouldn't allow it. In fact, she didn't have lips, so she couldn't really smile. She smiled anyway.

Her heaven was lovely. She wondered how long she must have been dead for all her Livies to be here. Talking to her like this. She could smell them. Feel them. If she was still in a body, they were so close that she could have even touched them.

She heard a soft tinkling behind them like a train, a night train going somewhere that might bring them all safely home.

She could hear her mother's voice apologizing over and over. Admitting how selfish she had been. How she would do things differently if she could. How she could finally see what mattered. How she had missed her baby so much. How she wanted to be a proper grandmother. How she'd make everything right if only given another chance.

But then…

The best sound of all. In fact, the only sound that had ever really mattered to Jolene. Her one true thing. Elliothappy, laughing, cooing, playing with something that tinkered and buzzed. His voice, his glorious voice speaking, speaking the same word over and over. "Da Da."

She still couldn't figure out why…if she was in heaven…she still felt so stuck, unable to see, unable to move. But that was okay; she knew it would all work out eventually. She had learned her lesson after all. Speak no evil, only truth. Not to doubt, but to dig into the truth. The truth of what she knew, of who she was, and who loved her…even if she hadn't loved herself.

But even that didn't matter anymore. She loved herself now.

She had all the love she would ever need. She was chock full of love. So she could finally give it away. After all, she owned it now, and the only way to keep it was to give it away. To Elliot. To Jimmy. Maybe even her mother, one day.

Besides, the comforting sensation kept reminding her to hang on. A tingling where her arm would have been if the monster hadn't sliced her to bits. In fact, right where her tattoo would have been.

The one just like Jimmy's birthmark.

Like a flower of possibility, layer on top of layer of the wonderful pressure, formed in the perfect shape of an almost unrecognizable butterfly. Over and over.

The other five were here, too. A sixth voice had joined them...a few minutes ago. Maybe even a seventh? Encouraging Jolene. Helping her through. Through what, she wasn't quite sure. But it didn't matter. She'd make it through...whatever that meant.

Now she knew two things for sure. And that was lovely, wasn't it? Had made every little bit of her suffering worth it.

Elliot said the word again. "Da Da."

And she smiled once more. Even though she didn't have lips, she smiled way too big for her face.

Jimmy reached over and touched the mark on his beloved's arm again. Over and over. It was proof that she had loved him. Like he had loved her.

He knew that much was true.

He looked at the beautiful boy. The one that must be his. The eyes, the same as his, so clear. The gorgeous blond hair made so that he could love every single strand for every day he had left to love them.

He rolled his sleeves back to show his mark, too. The one the same as hers. Exactly the same.

Why hadn't he owned it sooner? Seen the beauty in it. Like a flower of possibility, layer on top of layer of the wonderful mark, formed in the perfect shape of an almost unrecognizable butterfly.

He would stay here in her ICU room as long as it took, tracing the mark, encouraging her, helping her through, helping her find her way back to him.

SEVENTY-THREE

Bonfire Heart

FOR A MOMENT, Jessie considered telling Jimmy the truth. That he had been the one who found the letter that his patient named Jolene had kept hidden in her back pocket. That he had made the mysterious call to New Mexico. But then he decided against it.

Besides, there was something even better than recognition: the truth of the one thing he knew to be true—that he had successfully completed his assignment.

Grinning, he thought back to the Lola Littleton section on magical beings trapped in alternate realms and wondered how many *people* quoted it each morning like he used to. He giggled, pondering how many Firlings might live amongst the clueless humans. Some of them aware of it like him now. Others still oblivious to the gift they had come here to be. *Whatever. Does it really matter?*

He had done well with his assignment. Clarity regarding his successful mission was acknowledgment enough for him. He traced his matching arm mark and gave thanks to serve a higher purpose.

Besides, he had another patient to think about. The short, curly-haired intern in training would be out of surgery soon with a brand new heart. A bonfire heart that beat like a fire would—good and strong. The one her best friend had given her to replace the dead pig's heart.

"What are the odds?" he whispered. A thought popped in: *Surprisingly good, considering, my friend.*

A perfect donor with the perfect blood type at the perfect moment. The only gift that could still come out of what had happened to the pair of them.

The four of them, actually. Two dead, both the other intern in training and the kidnapper. The remaining two, Jolene and Elise, might live. Might.

Jessie had heard a rumor that the surgeons had been ordered to play Dimitri Arion's Greatest Hits for the whole case by the Chief of Staff. Some crazy thing about how the longhaired cop had been so insistent about the music. How it was utterly critical for the woman's survival.

He heard two cops running down the hallplain clothed police flicking a CD back and forth. The longhaired one grabbed it and turned it over. He touched the corner. He said something about a mark. Did it have a mark? An L and a B in the bottom corner. One for Levi Blackwater. One for him.

The other cop replied that it had a number. 87.

"Flip it over! Read it upside down, you fool!" he bellowed, jumping up and clapping.

"I knew it!" the longhaired cop cried and dropped to his knees in prayer. As he wailed, he said, "You did that. Had me leave it for her. Thank you. Thank you so much."

Jessie rubbed the star-covered cloth in his scrub pocket and decided maybe the CD thing wasn't so crazy after all. He grabbed his stethoscope and put it over his shoulders. After considering tapping his thigh, he decided not to. It didn't feel right anymore. Didn't feel necessary.

He grabbed his assigned chart. Elise Phillips. OR Two.

The number two symbolized faith. It was certainly the best room for the case if there ever was one.

He heard the cardiac monitor beeping as he walked past and knew everything was going well.

The patient's rate beat regularly and strong like the flames of a bonfire. Elise Phillips would be fine. The other gal, Wendi Patterson, not so much, unfortunately. But at least one would be just fine. The other had been long gone for a while. Dead on arrival. Just like that creep, Mr. Kincaid.

When he turned the corner to reach the nurses station, Jessie smiled. The CD was already playing in the OR, and he loved the song that came on first. Unable to resist, he sang along to the sensual and engaging melody:

"My love!
How long I've searched for you inside my life…
And in my heart I've felt you too often to deny.
I sometimes meet you inside my dreams.
My love!
How I'm reaching out for you.
I've always known your eyes.
Always loved your smile.
You're all I've ever needed.
And my heart's forever yours."

He gave the other nursing students a high five and added, "I don't care who you are; you have to love Dimitri. He's just that good. My love. Yes, Dimitri. I'm reaching out for you, too."

The phone rang, and the secretary, after giving him a funny look, told Jessie to pick it up.

When the seven intermingled voices on the other end of the line asked him a question, he paused. He reached into his pocket and rubbed his cloth. He looked up at the ceiling and shrugged.

Smiling, he laughed and then said, "Yes, I accept. I'll always say yes."

The other student nurses, oblivious to Jessie's conversation, had already gone back to the business of reading their patient's charts.

As best they could, at least, in spite of the undeniably powerful music. The humming grew as the infectious lyrics spread from one person to the next:

"Tell me where to seek your heart,

For I cannot find my way.

Let me start a lifetime loving you."

SEVENTY-FOUR

Just Say Yes

TO THIS DAY, there rests a mysterious grave in a small town named Glenwood Springs, Colorado. The headstone has no name, no date. The only thing it says is, *"Know this much is true."*

A couple and their ratty looking cat visit about the same time each year to place flowers on the plot. The odd little patch stays green and dry no matter how terrible the winters get...as if it knows they are coming.

Each year, the couple plays a song on a portable CD player. The melody, sensual and engaging, makes them sway along. Even the feline dances about to the tune. And when they leave, they whisper something to the cat and a bird that lingers nearby in the tree. The woman traces her finger down her chest, points two of her fingers up to the sky, picks up the tiger-striped animal, and they walk back to their car.

.

Epilogue

ABOUT ONE MONTH after the initial text was discovered, two pages were found attached to the same headstone. It is included here for completion's sake:

If you are reading this, you have obviously found my second manuscript. Each of these volumes serves to tell a story within the greater story yet stands complete and meaningful, in and of itself. Each also, of course, leads naturally and unforgivingly to the next. We've covered this before. This shall be the last time.

I suspect you will quite easily find the way to the other texts now as your internal teacher has shown you the way.

This is the story that ended, or should I say, began all stories. I know. I can still feel you whispering under your breath. You have heard this story before. Yes, that is true. Of course you have. After all, you helped call it into being.

I better add that this manuscript is not intended for the faint of spirit. Thus, at any point along the way, I give you my full permission to close the book and simply put it away until you are ready to read the rest of it. Although, I don't think you will. You are too far in. That is because you seek the truth now. That is your new way. You are ready. We hoped you would be.

Awake. Eyes opened. Finally.

Sit here, my Livie. Marvel at what happened.

Our story unfolds, as usual, just at the crack of the glorious light of dawn in a large hospital. This time, in Denver, Colorado in the early twenty-first century.

Back when we didn't know very much about life, we knew about hate, fear, and struggle. We knew about darkness, horror, pain, and scarcity. We knew nothing of love, and we knew nothing of ourselves. We didn't understand the power of our hearts and the incredible value of understanding our personal truths. Of course, there were a few of us who did...to some extent, but not enough. Not enough until...

Well, there I go, already getting ahead of myself and our story. Your story.

Listen, my Livie. Listen with open ears and open eyes and, better yet, an open bonfire heart. Uncover the next layer of unfoldment…of your awakening. The search for personal truth.

Awake. Eyes opened. Finally. Journey home offered. Again.

Oh we have missed you so.

We need you at home. Find your way back soon.

We love you and always will.

…Know this much is true.

Nine months later, the next manuscript arrives.

Books in the Sinister Series

A Sinister Bouquet: Awakening
A Sinister Vision: Know This Much Is True

About the Author

A. Nicky Hjort is originally from the greater Dallas-Fort Worth area of Texas. She writes stories that cross multiple genre lines, from paranormal romance to Sci-Fi thrillers and back again. And in some subtle way, all of her manuscripts are connected, with their purpose to explore all facets of love and what it has to teach us. Her journey into writing began with her clinical background as a medical doctor when she wrote her first fictional short story about medicine. She hasn't stopped writing since.

Facebook author page: https://www.facebook.com/Author.A.N.Hjort
Twitter: @A_NickyHjort
Website: www.anickyhjortbooks.com
Blog: www.ANickyHjortBooks.com
Instagram: https://www.instagram.com/nickyhjort

Other Works by A. Nicky Hjort

A Sinister Bouquet: Awakening - Book 1: Devyn Mitchell has a choice… listen to the voice of her unborn baby – or die- again. After a near death experience, Doctor Devyn Mitchell finds herself not only mysteriously pregnant but able to communicate with her fetus. She has two choices: give in to total madness or surrender to her new reality, which just may be the only way she and her family will survive the obsessions of the Homeless Hunter's mind. A true paranormal romantic thriller, A Sinister Bouquet: Awakening, the first of the Sinister Series, will take you right to the edge of what you know to be possible and then drop you in a place so dark, so terrifying, that the only passageway out is through the blinding light of awakening. Wake up. Open your eyes. Finally. We've missed you so. (MA18+ for graphic sexual and violent content)

Where Tyndra Turns to Ardnyt – The Norn Novellas: In the center of a magical world there grows a beautiful and terrible chasm of climbing plants. On one side of the Ivy Wall we find the hell-of-Tyndra, on the other, the heaven-of-Ardnyt. But legend has it that in the middle…lives a preternatural beast that imprisons and tortures the children from both sides. When the war against time begins, Azza will have to cross over the Ivy Wall, something that has never been done before by a living being. But if she does make it through, she just might discover who she really is and how she became trapped in this alternate reality. A fairytale at heart, this is the first chapter in the epic saga of the youngest and most fickle of the four Norn Sisters. The same feisty immortal creature who must escape her inherent inner darkness to learn the meaning of love. A veritable palindrome from start to finish, the narrative of Where Tyndra Turns to Ardnyt journeys through duality to discover what shocking truths emerge when up becomes down, life becomes death, suffering becomes release, and the most unexpected endings become the most surprising beginnings. Welcome to a place where forwards and backwards are exactly the same direction. Here Where Tyndra Turns to Ardnyt.

The City: The Jane Harvest: Winning battles means Ink honors, prestige, and life itself. …Yet nobody understands what losing truly means. On another planet two hundred years in the future, twenty-one-year-old Isla Jane struggles helplessly to figure out who she is and what her world really means. Marked with a forbidden tattoo of the rising sun, she is a natural champion of humanity and a gifted warrior in Heats– lavish battles fought in the conjoined minds of the participants for the morbid amusement of the masses. Despite Isla's desire to fade into the background, she emerges as an obvious leader of her people when the senseless assassination of a youth forces her to face the truth. Her volatile world, disguised by its elaborate battles and constant mayhem, is a prison without bars and a coffin, the lid already half-closed, that they must escape. But when she vows to find a way to bring her people back home, Isla will have to deconstruct consciousness and the very nature of the space time continuum to unravel good from evil, truth from lies, and survival from true love. Welcome to the City–where it takes lives to save lives...

Also from the Lavish Publishing family

A New Life Series
Samantha Jacobey
https://www.lavishpublishing.com/authors/samantha-jacobey/

Bikers, rockers and the FBI clash in a dark, mature adult romantic thriller – Tori Farrell will go through hell to get her new life in a completed seven book series!

To what lengths would you go to break away from a life filled with pain and suffering?

Tori Farrell has lived a dangerous life. When you grow up with a Motorcycle Gang of Mercenaries and Drug Lords like the Dragons, a normal life is more like a fairytale. For years, she accepted her dark reality, a world consisting of drugs, sex, violence and murder. In the end, she learned the most valuable lesson: survival.

After years of being ruled by the Dragons, Tori uses her skills of seduction and assassination to free herself from the grasp of the people who vowed they would never let her go. Taken in by the FBI, she fears not everything is what it seems, and soon finds herself lost in a web of lies and deceit. She thought getting away from the Dragons would put her on a path to a new and better life, but now she must face the cold hard truth... there is always a price to be paid.